CIVIL

Civil Blood

MEREDITH STEPHURE

McArthur & Company
Toronto

Published in 2007 by
McArthur & Company
322 King St. West, Suite 402
Toronto, Ontario
M4V 1J2
www.mcarthur-co.com

Stephure, Meredith
Civil blood : a novel / Meredith Stephure.

ISBN 978-1-55278-670-3

I. Title.
PS8637.T483C48 2007 C813'.6 C2007-904168-X

Cover and text design by Tania Craan
Printed in Canada by Webcom

The publisher would like to acknowledge the financial support of the Government of Canada through the Book Publishing Industry Development Program, the Canada Council for the Arts, and the Ontario Arts Council for our publishing activities. We also acknowledge the Government of Ontario through the Ontario Media Development Corporation Ontario Book Initiative.

10 9 8 7 6 5 4 3 2 1

For J. W. S.

From ancient grudge break to new mutiny,
Where civil blood makes civil hands unclean.

—William Shakespeare, *Romeo and Juliet*

HISTORICAL NOTE

In seventeenth-century England, the religion of the monarch was an issue of life and death. Charles II had no legitimate children: his heir was his brother James, who, sometime during his long exile under Cromwell's rule, had turned to the Catholic faith. In the last years of Charles' reign, a furious battle raged to exclude James from the throne in favour of the Protestant daughters of his first marriage, Mary and Anne. James' enemies considered that his religion, his friendship with his cousin Louis of France, and his new marriage — to an Italian Catholic princess — would lead him to betray his country and the Church of England.

By this time a general return to the old faith in England was unthinkable. Too many families had profited from King Henry's seizure of church lands a century before. Monasteries and abbeys were now private manor-houses. Their rich farmlands, orchards, breweries, and libraries, their furnishings and tapestries and gold plate, had become personal property. That Rome hungered to retake these was an article of Protestant faith. That it wanted to drag England back into spiritual and political servitude was another. English Catholics were a despised and hunted handful whose disloyalty was taken for granted.

When James took the throne in 1685, the "Protestant party" was still plotting to replace him with his daughter Mary and her husband, William of Orange. Dutch William would keep England safely Protestant; he alone could unite England and Holland to fight the growing might and threat of France. And he had English royal blood: his mother had been James' sister.

King Louis, marching enormous armies into Flanders and Franche Comte, ravaging his way to the very doorstep of the Hague, had shown that he meant to overrun Europe. He had to be stopped; and in William's eyes no loyalty to James, no tie of either blood or marriage, was more compelling than this necessity. Louis wanted Europe; William needed England. In 1688 the crown seemed within his grasp, for James was an old man without legitimate sons.

But that summer the Queen gave birth to a healthy boy. The child, James Francis Edward, was immediately received into the Catholic faith. The Pope stood sponsor. The same week, seven bishops of the Church of England, including the Archbishop of Canterbury, were imprisoned in the Tower for refusing to read out in their dioceses the King's declaration of religious liberty for all. London rioted. The King was burned in effigy as a French-loving traitor. Nobles and churchmen wrote to Prince William, imploring him, in the name of God and the Protestant faith, to come and "rescue the nation."

On November 5, 1688, Dutch warships sailed unchallenged into English waters, and William brought his army ashore.

PART ONE

Charters Park, Oxfordshire
November 1688

1 THEY MET IN THE JUSTICE CHAMBER: Thomas de Chastelain, and two boys, aged five and nine, accused of poaching. It was a hanging offence. De Chastelain's secretary, Fulke, consulted his notebook. "The boys and their dog were found trespassing on Lord Burcote's grounds, my lord. The bailiff says they stole trout from the fish pond."

The Justice Chamber, pillared and marble-tiled, musty, ice cold, was designed to awe. The arched ceiling soared thirty feet into the air. There was a dais at one end. Chiselled in stone over the bronzed doors was the motto *Non desideriis hominum sed voluntate Dei*: not by the desires of men, but by the will of God. It was something de Chastelain strove to keep in mind when dealing with his fellow-sinners.

He looked down in silence at the two boys and their filthy dog, whose long fringed tail had left a sweep of mud across the polished marble floor. He had no time to spare for this; even now, the bugles were sounding the Stand to Horse. He was about to take a troop of horses, mustered under his own banner, to the royal army in Salisbury. He was also delivering supplies, for the King's field commanders were short of everything from flour to lead shot. The Dutch had caught them wholly unprepared. Every troop in the royal army had been mustered out of winter quarters, but the Secretary of War still needed volunteers.

Rain mixed with sleet beat against the uncurtained windows. There was no fire. A single candle guttered on the desk. Thomas thrust his gauntleted hands under his arms to keep them warm, and walked up and down as if he were once again in court, presenting evidence to the lord chief justice. His breath hung like a cloud on the frigid air.

"Theft," he said, "is a capital offence. Occasionally, at the judge's discretion, the sentence is commuted to transportation. That means working like slaves in the canebrakes for the rest of your lives. You work eighteen hours a day and are beaten if you dare to stop. You are chained to your cot. You eat what the dogs leave behind. You can be whipped, stoned, or starved, at your master's will. You might have your hands cut off, or your eyes put out with hot irons. That is the law, sirs, and I do not see that I should flout it simply because it is my own sons who are guilty. Do you?" He stopped in front of the boys. "Well? Do you have a reason I should not hand you over at once to the bailiffs, and see you hanged?"

Five-year-old James burst into tears. His older brother, Piers, looked as if he might be sick. They had been hauled in directly from the park, and stood goosefleshed in their sodden clothes, water pooling at their feet. James sobbed so hard that he choked on his own spit and started to cough. The dog, upset at the noise, moaned and howled.

"Lord Burcote's pond," said Thomas, when he could make himself heard. "I told you to not to go there. Would you walk, uninvited, into a man's house?"

"Lord Burcote told us we could look at the heron's nest by his land, sir," said Piers. "But he is from home, and the bailiff didn't believe us."

Thomas' frown deepened. The ribbon of marsh between his property and his neighbour's was a wild and desolate place, which the boys were forbidden to explore alone.

"What has Lord Burcote's permission to do with it? You

did not have mine! In any case, you were supposed to be at your lessons with Master Hammond. Trespass, disobedience, and theft: by my faith, boys, you promise well!"

"But, sir, we took nothing — "

James was still wailing. Thomas, putting a hand on the small, dishevelled head to silence him, saw a crust of dirt behind the boy's ear. Piers, too, was filthy, his fair hair in rough knots, his breeks fastened with a length of twine. Their mother would never have permitted such slovenliness. But Elizabeth was confined to bed, and Alys, the boys' nurse, had taken sick. It was Alys' niece Brigid who had been looking after the children, and Brigid — Irish-born, unlettered, implacably Catholic — was like a creature from the bog, all wild red hair and unravelling petticoats.

"The bailiff says that you stole trout from the pond, Piers. Do you say he is mistaken?"

"I say he's a damned liar."

Thomas gripped his shoulder. "Watch your tongue! And give me a truthful answer! What were you doing there?"

"Theo ran away. I think he was chasing a rabbit. And James — I *told* him not to come, sir — fell in the water, and I had to get him out. That's all."

"Neither of you took any fish?"

"No, sir. Only some old sticks we threw to the dog." Piers crossed himself and kissed his dirty thumb. "I swear it, my lord, before the blessed Virgin and the throne of St. Peter."

The Virgin and the Pope. Here was proof of Thomas' suspicion that Brigid had broken her word not to teach the boys Romish prayers. His voice hardened.

"A simple yes or no will suffice, Piers. But if you took nothing, what made the bailiff accuse you of theft?"

"I expect he was angry because Theo knocked him

down, sir." Piers examined the toes of his scuffed boots. "Knocked him down in the mud and then — " he paused, as if searching for the correct word.

"Pissed," said James, looking pleased to be of help. "Theo pissed on him while he was trying to get up. And it was a mighty one, too, sir, because he drank the cook's beer this morning."

The dog thumped his tail and slobbered foolishly. Thomas, knowing that at all costs he must not laugh, must not smile, avoided Fulke's eye.

"You must work to control him better, then. And I believe you, Piers, when you say you did not steal. Yet you did climb the fence by the marsh, and you did go on Lord Burcote's land, both of which are forbidden to you. Worse, you put your brother in danger."

He glanced down at James, whose face was beginning to turn blue. What manner of man was this bailiff, who had charged his sons with a crime they did not commit, and then had sent them home, in this weather, in an uncovered farm cart? But one fault did not excuse another. His obligation was clear.

"You must both ask pardon of Lord Burcote's household for this morning's disturbance. Then you, Piers, will compose a treatise on obedience. Two pages, in Latin and French. In addition, you will both spend an extra hour at prayer."

Piers looked as though he would have preferred the tortures of indentured servitude. But he kept silent, and sent his brother a scornful look when James flung his arms around their father's knee and sobbed gustily into his greatcoat. With difficulty, Thomas disentangled him.

"One more thing. There must be no japes of this kind while I am from home. I will not have your mother disturbed when she is unwell. You must help her by looking after your brother far better than this, Piers."

"Yes, my lord."

James sneezed. Thomas brought out a handkerchief to clean his face. The dog shook himself, spraying them all with muddy water. James wiped his nose, smearing his face from cheekbone to chin, and said, "Sir, if the new baby is a boy, will you and Mam still keep me? Piers said you would drown me in the river."

Thomas' blue eyes narrowed. "That was last week," Piers cried, "when he threw my new boots in the midden!"

"I did not! The dog took them!"

"Liar!"

"I am not! It was Theo!"

"Enough!"

It was as if God had shouted at them. Fulke unhooked his eyeglasses, and made a business of putting some papers into a satchel. The Stand to Horse rang out again from the courtyard. Thomas looked at his children and felt weariness, like a fever, in his chest and head. "*Silent enim leges inter arma,*" he said. "Do you know what that means, Piers? No? You have not been keeping up with your Cicero, then. 'Laws are dumb in time of war.' But I am determined it shall not be so. Not in my house. While I am gone you will both conduct yourselves as I expect. You will mind Master Hammond and your aunt Grace, when she arrives. You will say your prayers and ask God to forgive you. And you will swear, on your honour, to keep the peace between you."

"'Love ye one another,'" said James piously. "That's what Brigid tells us."

"Give me your hands," Thomas ordered. The boys knelt and he put their cold fists together. "This is how they took the oath of fealty in the old days. James, remember that you have a duty to show your brother the same respect that you show me. As for you, Piers, you have a duty to deserve it. Don't forget, either of you."

He let them think this over for a moment. Then he knelt down as well, and put his arms around them. James played with the bunch of ribbons tied at his shoulder. "Are you for the King now, sir?" he asked in a small voice. "You wear his colours."

"I have always been for the King, Jamie."

"But Mam says you would not sign his order putting the bishops in the Tower," said Piers. "Is that why you have not been at Court? But why do you fight for the King, sir, when he sent you away?"

"I sent myself away, my son. In any case, should that be the test of your loyalty — how well you are treated?"

James wound the ribbons around his dirty hand. "Will the King be happy to see you?"

Happy was possibly the last word Thomas would have chosen to describe his reunion with James Stuart. "I don't know," he said. "But he is my King and I gave him my word, just as you have given me yours now. Your word of honour is like a promise to God. Never break it. Never bargain with it. There is no price you can put upon your honour, and no way to redeem it once it is forfeit — "

The bitterness he heard in his voice brought him up short. He was saying too much. The boys stared him, baffled but trusting. Whatever he said to them, be it mad, fantastical, or an outright lie, they would believe it. He had a responsibility to be just.

He got to his feet, putting a hand on each boy's shoulder. "Go upstairs and change out of those wet clothes. You may watch us march from there. Tell Brigid to give you a hot drink and some food." He added, as Theo pawed his boots, "And take the dog with you!"

The door closed behind his children and the dog. He stood for a moment at the window, watching the rain sluice down. Out beyond the lawns and the park, the grounds ran to the river. In summer he would take his boat out and row in his shirt sleeves, with the sun upon his face. He would tie up under the green willows and eat his simple lunch of bread and cheese. And then, drowsy with the sun, he would put his hands under his head and sleep, his work forgotten in guilty pleasure. Often the boys came with him, and the dogs, and they made a day of it, returning grass-stained and muddy at dusk.

But the boat was in the shed now, and the placid river had become inhospitable, cold and swollen with rain. It seemed that even God had turned against the King. The east wind that had blown the Dutch ships across the sea now squalled out of the southwest, keeping the royal fleet helplessly bottled up in the Channel. The royal navy had failed, and the army was bleeding like a wound. Each day hundreds of men were deserting to William's camp in Exeter. This sprang not from any love of Dutch William, who was a foreigner and therefore suspect, but from an unalterable hatred of James' church. Men hated the Pope more than they feared either the Dutch or the Devil, and they would not fight for a King who walked around with beads and a rosary in his pocket, crossing himself as if he were an Irishman.

Three royal regiments had deserted to William — an exodus led, in part, by the King's own nephew. The elite cavalry entrusted with collecting intelligence had fled. Other nobles and courtiers, members of the king's personal household, had followed. The Secretary of State had run to Rotterdam. All this was bad enough, but for Thomas there had been worse news still.

Yesterday a letter had come from an old friend, Henry Finch, who for three years had been chaplain to Thomas' father-in-law, Lord St. Clare. Finch wrote that St. Clare, setting off to join the King, had ridden into Devon instead, and nearly succeeded in delivering his entire retinue into the hands of the enemy. But there had been a fracas when it became clear that his destination was the Dutch camp. "Lord St. Clare allowed me and some dozen others to leave," Finch wrote, "though at first I thought he would force us all to go with him. He took into Exeter a company of men-at-arms, with supplies of horses and gold, and offered a bounty to any of us who would follow."

Thomas, eating cold beef and bread at his desk while he looked through the post, had felt his insides begin to churn, as if he had found a mess of grubs in his meat. St. Clare: judge, privy councillor, former ambassador, lord lieutenant of two counties; impeccable blood, enormous wealth. And now he was William's new man. The loss of the cavalry was nothing, compared to this.

Thomas had burned Finch's letter and then, turning coward, had avoided his wife because she would see at once that he was keeping something from her. If only St. Clare had talked to him first — talked to him or written. But he had been away on the Continent these past few months, or so he had told Libby. Brooding over some imagined snub, he had refused to speak to Thomas before he left, only God knew why; St. Clare's tempers, like his drinking-bouts, were unpredictable and spectacular, but seldom long-lasting. Thomas had learned to wait them out. Soon St. Clare would be thumping him on the shoulder, calling him "dearest son," and pressing upon him some peace offering he did not want — a set of solid gold candlesticks, a cask of Portuguese wine, or, most memorably, a suit of armour that had once belonged to the Holy Roman Emperor. His roarings were mostly strut and swagger. Thomas had realized early in their acquaintance that his father-in-law relished controversy for its own sake, much as he enjoyed a good French brandy or a jar of strong tobacco.

But this was treason, and the price was death. He could not bring himself to tell Libby, who was ill and eight months pregnant, that her father was a criminal. The truth would become public soon enough. Inevitably there would be warrants sworn out for St. Clare's arrest, bailiffs descending on his house, privy councillors summoning his friends and household for questioning. Libby might be spared because of her condition, but her brother Leopold —

He all but groaned at the thought of Leopold, the troop's first casualty, who was lying upstairs with his leg encased in plaster. A fortnight ago he had been in Oxford on business and had come to Charters afterward, bringing his two young children. The visit was meant to be a short one. But then the King had called out the army, and Leo, in a fiery burst of resolution, had announced that he would join Thomas' company. It was the last thing Thomas had expected and the least welcome, for he knew that his lovable and kindly brother-in-law would be about as much practical use to him as Theo. Leopold was a respected scientist, a member of the Royal Society, a happy, peaceable man who carried beetles in his shirt pocket and could not bear to see anyone suffer. A houseful of noisy children and dinner guests, his wife, Abigail, presiding over a mountainous Sunday roast, a mechanical snuff box or Chinese water clock to build in his workshop...that was Leopold's idea of heaven. He loved to entertain his guests by taking apart their watches and putting them back together again, and enchanted the children by building thumb-sized machines: a working water wheel, a tiny clock, a matchstick windmill. He had constructed an ingenious device to kill the rats nesting in his kitchen, but was too kind-hearted to use it. Thomas could not imagine what he would do if he met Dutch soldiers. He would buy old Schomberg, William's Commander-in-Chief, a beer and a wedge of cheese, and talk about iceboats. But he was so intent on joining the army that Thomas had given in, reasoning that it was not his place to dissuade anyone from serving the King.

He had divided the troop, sending Leopold ahead with Sir John Lee, his old friend and fishing partner, who had charge of the baggage train. They had left Charters yesterday morning with a well-armed escort guarding the supplies. But shortly after their departure the skies had opened, unleashing the worst storm of the season. The sledge carrying the cannons had overturned, sinking to the bottom of a slough; the baggage wagons, mired immovably in axle-deep mud, had had to be abandoned. When Leopold was unhorsed and broke his leg, Lee called off the march and returned to Charters. Leo had been installed in one of the guest chambers, and his children, seven-year-old Samuel and five-year-old Beatrice, had thrown in their lot with Piers and James. Thomas thanked God that they had not been involved in the fish pond fiasco. He turned from the window.

"Fulke, where have you put this bailiff?"

"In the kitchen, sir."

"Do you know anything about him? Is he new?"

"He took up his place last week, sir." Fulke lowered his voice, as if Burcote, out of town, might overhear them. "I believe he is some kinsman of the family, sir, a cousin's nephew. He's what you might call simple."

"Perhaps he's not too simple to understand what the penalties are for libel and false accusation. Tell him that if he speaks to my children or goes anywhere near them again,

I'll piss on him myself. Well, words to that effect. And see to it that Theo gets an extra chop for his dinner."

There was a wry gleam in Fulke's eye. "Very good, my lord."

"You have the direction of the courier? My keys?"

"All here," said Fulke, and he patted he breast pocket of his vest.

"There is a hundred pounds in the cash box and I have put three hundred more with the goldsmith, in case you need to draw upon extra funds for the household. You must send to me at once if my wife should need me — the children — "

"You can depend upon me, sir."

"I know it and thank God, my friend."

A red patch flared on Fulke's dry old cheek. "My lord, all who have the honour to know you...your household, your friends...you have only to ask. There is no one who...." He checked, as if restraining himself from some indiscretion, and held up the candle to light Thomas out the door. "Godspeed you, sir. If I were not too old, I would go with you."

"I need you here," said Thomas. He crushed the secretary's warrant into his coat pocket, where it would keep company with scraps of paper, old keys, tidbits for the horses, coins for charity, and an ancient plug of tobacco. His pockets were the despair of his tailor. The Stand to Horse sounded again — hellish, insistent, out of tune. "Tell them I'll be out in ten minutes."

He whistled up his own dogs from the hall, a slavish trio who followed him everywhere: a wolfhound, a whippet, and a fat old spaniel named Lucy. They surged around him and accompanied him, in a flurry of wagging tails, up the great oak staircase to his wife's bedchamber.

2 THERE WAS SCAFFOLDING on the north side of the bell tower, where the masons had been at work. Decayed stones had broken loose from the parapet, crashing down the sheer wall face to the water below. But the weather had put a stop to the work. The scaffolding stood empty, black and glistening with rain. A heavy canvas sheet tacked across it cracked and bellied in the wind.

On a clear day there was an unobstructed view of the Downs and the Chilterns from the windswept roof. Oxford lay to the north, Dorchester to the southeast. In between, a sprinkling of tiny villages and hamlets hugged the river. Charteris St. Mary, the village that gave Charters its name, was no more than a few stone cottages and a patch of open field where people pastured their family cow or goat and collected free brushwood for their cook fires. The rich acres of Charters' forest, park, and home farm surged like a green ocean around the village, with St. Mary's church the landfall, its graceful spire rising a hundred feet into the air. Both the church and the castle had been old when the Plantagenets were kings.

But Charters was no grim medieval fortress. Encircled by water, shaded by willows, it resembled a small Leeds or Chenonceau, a place so lovely it might have been a jewel set in stone. Six hundred years had turned the walls to living earth: plants grew in the interstices of the stones and the decaying foundations were green with moss. Waterfowl — black swans, shelducks, mallards, geese — swam in placid, leaf-strewn streams and nested under the willows. On cold winter mornings, river mist and frost turned the landscape into a cathedral of silver.

Charters' quietude and grace, its crumbling peaceful charm, was like that of a castle dreaming under some spell of enchantment. Thomas' love for it ran so deep that he was half-ashamed. After the dirt and strife of London, nothing was sweeter than living here in seclusion. His undeserved exile had been more of a reward than a punishment. Looking after his lands and tenants, fishing with his boys, writing speeches on legal reform (with his dogs as critics in place of His Majesty's privy councillors), playing the music of Corelli and Dowland, entertaining friends, studying the stars through his precious telescope sent from Padua — all these civilized pursuits had been a welcome truce in the war of his public life. But his respite was over.

He suddenly remembered his father, sitting with his books and his dogs about him, saying, "I hope you never know what it is like to fight your own countrymen...to see your home desecrated and your lands destroyed, and know the names and faces of those who did it. Never forget that Cromwell took this place by treachery. Took it and would have burned it to the ground, had he not decided it would serve better as a barracks."

But he could not afford to think about that now. It was forty years ago, longer than his own lifetime, and all traces of the Roundheads' occupation had been purged. His father had even summoned a priest to purify the bedchamber where Cromwell had slept. And in the Great Hall, where the Roundheads had stabled their horses, a mural showed the restored king solemnly unrolling a three-foot long parchment that elevated Sir John de Chastelain to Baron "in reward for his untiring zeal and loyalty to His Majesty the King and to King Charles of Sacred Memory."

As a small boy Thomas had been convinced that "of Sacred Memory" was the King's surname.

He lifted the door latch of the bedchamber. Unlike his ancestors who had built this tower, he was a tall man, and had to duck under the stone lintel to enter the room. The dogs rushed ahead of him, jostling and barking, and he hushed them in case Libby were asleep.

But the bed was empty. The hangings were open and the coverlet flung back. The room was dark. Cold invaded his ribs. "Libby!" he called.

There was no answer and he called again, "Elizabeth!"

"I'm in the dressing room."

"Are you ill?"

"I'm fine." But this was followed a moment later by the sound of retching.

"Do you need help? Some water?"

"No. Thank you."

There was a certain careful patience in her voice that made him desist. He sat down at her writing table and rubbed a hand over his eyes as the muffled retching continued. He knew this kind of violent sickness should be long past. But it had continued through the weeks and months, and a fortnight ago she had run an unexplained fever. Dr. Spencer had ordered complete bedrest, but Libby was a poor patient, rebelling against confinement and refusing to drink the boiled chicory root prescribed for her. The burned-down candles on the escritoire, along with a flurry of papers, showed that she had been writing letters last night instead of sleeping.

The door to the dressing room opened and she emerged holding a basin in one hand. In her full-sleeved, high-waisted bedgown she might have been a young Florentine matron. There were pearls fastened into her ears and her hair, a dark rich spill of Botticelli curls, stood out from her face as if on wires. She was so pale that Thomas went at once, risking a rebuff, to help her to the bed. Her hair was damp at the edges, as if she had just washed her face, and he detected a smell of sickness not entirely disguised by peppermint leaf. There were shadows, deep as bruises, under her eyes.

"You didn't sleep, Libby."

"No. You?"

"No. We were clearing the road."

He realized suddenly that he had not washed or even scraped off his boots before coming up. He was unshaven, grimy, as rank and filthy as Theo. But it was not the least of Libby's graces that she did not mind.

He set the basin on the nightstand and looked to see there was fresh water in the bedside pitcher. Then he turned away to build up the fire and light the candelabrum. Out of deep shadow the room sprang to life — the new green velvet bed hangings, the lacquered screen with a white robe thrown over it, the crystal vase jammed with a bouquet of weeds from the children. Tall arched windows framed a view of the park. The last of the autumn roses floated in a bowl on the dressing table, next to Libby's silver combs and brushes.

A book lay open on the floor and Thomas picked it up. *The Divers Orations* of the Duchess of Newcastle. Libby made a small gesture of protest and then lay still, her slender ringed hands folded inside her shawl.

"Men would fain bury us in their houses or beds, as in a grave; the truth is we live like bats or owls, labour like beasts, and die like worms...melancholy for want of pleasures, helpless from want of power." In the margin Libby had written in her bold, upright hand, "We are barred from any useful work or public life,

and even though we bear children, unless we are saints or madwomen, our very names are lost to posterity."

Thomas set the book down, feeling unaccountably wounded. What had possessed Libby, the most loving and gracious of wives, to seize upon these odd ravings? The Duchess of Newcastle — "Mad Madge" — a woman famous for appearing half-naked in public, had been able to publish her opinions only because her besotted husband was a Duke. Her acrimonious essays on marriage and men had provoked howls of amusement and outrage from every quarter.

Libby was no Mad Madge — thank God. But she was not conventional either. Her upbringing at St. Clare's hands had been unusual, to say no more. As a small child she had shared tutors with her brother, read the same books, and accompanied her widowed father everywhere he went, from the Inns of Court and Whitehall to Fleet Street and the Marshalsea prison. In the course of a single day she had met both the Archbishop of Canterbury and a kinsman of Moll Cutpurse's, the notorious bawd and thief. She had smoked her father's pipe — once only, for it made her sick — and knew how to clean a pistol, shoe a horse, bespeak dinner at a chophouse, or buy tobacco. She frequently rode or walked unattended. Thomas, brought up to treat women with tender solicitude, found this independence alternately charming and appalling. He would allow no petticoat rule in his household, but he knew very well the difference between government *de jure* and government *de facto*.

Thinking of St. Clare had brought him into the room with them, a solid, almost visible presence. He kissed Libby's hand and rubbed her knuckles against his unshaven cheek. To tell her about her father now seemed monstrous, yet to keep silent was worse. Somehow he had to prepare his wife for what lay ahead.

"Libby, there's something you should know."

"I know already. I've seen them."

Thomas looked at her and she said, with that same hint of steely patience, "The children. I know they fell into the water. And I know that you kept them downstairs in a room without a fire, for fifteen minutes, while you talked about hanging them."

Indignation warmed her face and darkened her eyes. "Thomas, how could you? You know that James is sick with a cold."

In fact he had not known, but this would only condemn him further. He was not sorry, in any case, to be diverted from what he had been going to say. "Theft is a capital crime. I had to be sure they understood the consequences."

"What they understand is that their father was willing to send them to the hangman. James will have nightmares for a week. And as you will not see them again until Christmas — "

"I'll be home in a fortnight. This business will not take long."

"You said that when you went to Scotland with John Graham, and you were gone half a year."

It was unlike her to bring up past sins. Surely she knew that he had not stayed away willingly? But he supposed there were few wives who welcomed the influence of her husband's friends — especially when one of them was Scotland's most turbulent son, the much-loved and much-hated Major-General John Graham of Claverhouse, Viscount Dundee. Where John went, trouble soon followed. But this would be different.

"I'll be in Salisbury ten days," he said. "A fortnight at the most."

Her look of incredulity made him reckless. "You may

tell the kitchen to start preparing food for the christening. And we must have a godparent. Who shall sponsor this child? Have you considered?"

"I would like to ask Grace."

That silenced him. Grace was his favourite sister — his other sister, Louisa, had married and gone to Scotland while he was still in school — but her behaviour since her recent widowhood had set them at odds. Childless herself, she had founded a charity school in Clerkenwell, teaching orphans how to read and write. She was growing eccentric with age, wearing three shawls at once and forgetting to pin up her hair; like a pilgrim she trudged around the city with a rough-hewn staff in one hand and a basket in the other, from which she dispensed food and medicines to the sick and homeless. This was harmless enough, even laudable. Widows traditionally devoted themselves to good works. But they also traditionally devoted themselves to the memory of their husbands, and Grace had worn black only a few weeks before she began keeping company with a young man, Jacob Schuyler, who worked in the King's printing house. The printer, Henry Hill, was a devout and kindly man who had taken Jacob in when no one else would hire him, for the young man was a Quaker who had suffered in prison for his faith.

Schuyler was only twenty-eight, fourteen years Grace's junior, which alone was enough to make Thomas think his sister had run mad. On the occasion of their only meeting, Jacob had called Thomas "Friend" and refused to bow or remove his hat. All burning eyes and righteousness, he might have been a martyr sizzling on the gridiron instead of a suitor pleading his case. His parting words — "Friend Thomas, repent!" — had sealed his doom. Thomas had dismissed him out of hand and ordered Grace back to

Charters to help supervise the children. She had agreed without protest, but had twice delayed her departure. Had duty not intervened, Thomas would have returned to London to pry her from Schuyler's arms.

"Jacob is a good man," Libby said, "and he loves your sister."

It was disconcerting how often she responded to his thoughts instead of his words. "That doesn't mean he's fit to be her husband. You know what I think."

"But if the Bishop were to approve Grace, herself, as sponsor — "

There was small prospect of that, Thomas thought. His sister had been attending the Friends' meeting house instead of going to church, and the Bishop hated Quakers and Ranters almost as much as he loathed Papists and Presbyterians. It seemed safe enough to say, "Ask him."

Then, too late, he remembered that Libby had successfully challenged the Bishop once before. She had defended a crazed old woman who had stood up in her rags, Medusa-haired, to deliver a sermon in church — a crime for which the penalty was imprisonment or flogging. "Tell me again why it is, Your Grace, that the church forbids women to speak about God in public," Libby had said, "for I have never been clear on this point. I wish to be instructed." And the Bishop, flushed and self-important, immaculate in his robes, had given a lecture that somehow ended with an offer to escort both Libby and the old woman home in his own carriage. No doubt he had been picking lice out of his cap for weeks.

Libby touched her lips to his cheek. "My sweet Tom! Thank you."

He could not forbear picking up, as if it were some kind of soiled laundry, *The Divers Orations*. "I am not, then — let me see — a tyrant and devil, keeping you in a 'hell of subjection?'"

"You must read on further," Libby said. "You will be pleased that she contradicts herself entirely. Listen to this." She took the book from him. "'We have no reason to speak against men, who are our lovers and protectors; they admire our beauties and love our persons — '"

"I do love your person," Thomas said. "Ardently."

"Hush! It hurts when I laugh."

"Then you must be quiet," he said, and kissed her so hard that she had to push him away to catch her breath. The book fell to the floor again. She took his hand and placed it on her bedgown, so that he could feel the child kicking violently at her ribs. "See what you have done now."

He smiled into her eyes. *Always I will remember that first hour, when my eyes were blinded by your light...* That graceful line of Ronsard's was something he might have said to her, had he the gift of paying compliments. But his courtroom eloquence always deserted him when it came to his wife.

The child under his hand kicked again, this time with such vigour that Libby tensed with pain and the colour left her face. Labour like beasts, he thought suddenly. Die like worms.

He got up from the bed so abruptly that he disturbed the dogs, who had been dozing at his feet. On the pretext of mending the fire, which was already blazing like a torch, he went to the hearth and stirred the logs with one of the blackened irons. A small explosion of ash and cinders made him cough.

"Tom," Libby said. The tenderness in her voice was like a kiss upon a bruise. "I wrote that note to myself when I was thirteen. Will you hold it against me now? I would rather that you throw the book into the fire."

He was tempted to do so. He longed to ask her to whom she had been writing last night, why she had been reading Margaret Newcastle, if she were indeed unhappy. But he had no time for such a discussion and no heart for it either. He would not be a stage husband, overbearing and ridiculous. He set down the fire iron and came back to the bed. Libby took his hand.

"If this child is a girl, will you mind?"

"I shall give thanks, fasting."

"I would like to name her Katherine. And Cecily, for the second name."

Once more he could find nothing to say. The year after James was born they had had a daughter named Cicely, a tiny edition of Elizabeth, who had died before she was three. That name recalled a small cold hand tucked confidingly into his pocket, an urchin grin, sweet childish kisses. His lambkin he had called her, among a host of other fond and foolish pet names: sparrow, poppet, Madam Gooseberry. It had been over a year now and he still looked for her face at the family table and listened for her voice. Her favourite toy, a straw-stuffed doll named Bernadette, still presided over the nursery bed pillows.

"Libby, I don't know. I'll need to think about it."

"Don't think too long, my love."

The Stand to Horse rang out stridently from the courtyard. Libby flinched. But she spoke in a calm, sensible voice, as if she were a city wife sending her husband out to his business for a day. Thomas was grateful for her practicality. "There is clean linen in your pack, Thomas, and your own stirrup cup. I had a physic made up for you. You should take it morning and night, in a little hot wine, to keep sickness away. And there is a powder, if you suffer from one of your headaches or a wakeful night — "

"The doctor told you to rest, not make up medicines for me."

"For two weeks I have done nothing. And when Grace comes she won't allow me to put a foot out of bed."

"Thank God for that," said Thomas. "If this weather delays her beyond tomorrow, then you must send for someone from the village to help you. You need someone to look after the children besides Brigid."

Brigid. Brigid with her saints and angels and thumb-kissing. He had forgotten all about her until this moment, as he had forgotten about St. Clare. But he had run out of time. He could not imagine what effect his silence about St. Clare would have, whether he was protecting, or destroying, what mattered to him most. There was a bog under his feet where once there had been solid ground.

He took Libby's face between his hands and kissed her. "I love you," he said. "Remember that. God bless you, sweetheart, and keep you well."

"Wait, Thomas. Leopold asked me to give you this." Her face softened. She was seven years younger than her brother, but her attitude towards him was fondly maternal. "He ground the lenses himself."

It was a perspective glass, as cunningly wrought as if Galileo or Kepler had designed it. Thomas put it up to his eye. He would be able to see the ticks on a Dutchman's horse with this. Or the diamond in St. Clare's ear. He closed the glass and put it safely in his pocket. Right now he did not want to think about Leopold or Leopold's father.

"Tell him thank you. Even General Churchill won't have one this fine."

With a kind of grim extravagance that surprised even himself, for he was not given to sentimental gestures, he took one of Libby's roses from the bowl and fastened it in his buttonhole. It would not last five minutes in this weather. But the look of astonished pleasure on her face was worth it. God forgive him, he had never been like the other men who had wished to marry her, those lacy, perfumed cavaliers who asked to carry her fan or drink wine from her slipper and wrote sonnets comparing her to Dante's Beatrice. He was still humbly amazed that he had been her choice.

As he looked out the window on the way down the stairs, he saw that the rain had turned to snow.

3

SIR JOHN LEE WAS A CALM, kindly man with a face like a well-scrubbed elderly choirboy's. When he was fifteen he had joined Prince Rupert's cavalry in time to fight at Edgehill. He had spent nine years under arms and then had lived in exile with the royal court, sharing a pallet with rats and selling his shoes to buy bread. Afterward he had asked for no reward except the restoration of his own modest property. He was an old-style cavalier, courtly and dignified, bone-loyal to his church and his King, a man who in sixty years had never gone back on his word. Thomas had wanted him to command the troop but Lee had refused, saying he was much too old. The last time he had been on a battlefield was at Worcester, thirty-seven years ago.

Since then he had married, raised a family, and lost them all. His first wife had died of fever, his children of smallpox. His second marriage had ended with the death of his wife and her infant in childbed. There was no son to inherit the estate; when Lee died, the property would go to a cousin or nephew, Thomas could not remember which. He had volunteered, Thomas knew, as much from loneliness as from duty. His neighbours had become his family. James and Piers were the grandchildren he had lost and Libby was his beloved daughter. Even the dogs had adopted him.

Leopold's accident and the ruin of the baggage train had upset him deeply, although neither had been his fault. He had worked all night helping to clear debris from the road and he still wore same mud-stained clothes he had ridden out in, garments so old-fashioned that he might have been auditioning for a role in a play about the civil war. There was a lovelock plaited into his long white hair and he wore a small pointed beard, unfashionable now for a generation. Over his padded doublet he had fastened a tarnished cuirass buckled with worn leather straps. A broad lace collar, once starched and white but now sodden in the rain, bunched over his armour. He had on an ostrich-feathered cavalier's hat and a pair of embroidered gauntlets. By contrast, Thomas' stringy-haired chaplain, Martin Whitby, suited in black broadcloth and plain half-armour, could have been Oliver Cromwell himself.

They took off their hats as Martin offered a hasty one-line prayer — "Beware that thou forget not the Lord thy God, amen, march" — and then formed up, thirty of them, the aristocracy and wealth of the county: friends, neighbours, sons, nephews and cousins, all of whom had known each other from boyhood. Lee was the oldest of the company and Thomas' servant, seventeen-year-old Malachy, was the youngest. Command had fallen to Thomas, but there was scant formality about it. The troop had been so hastily scraped together that there had been no time for proper outfitting. They wore civilian clothes with ribbons knotted at the shoulders, colourful sashes, broad-brimmed feathered hats, and some, like Lee, had buckled on pieces of armour that had been unearthed from the dust of forty years' storage. They carried a motley assortment of arms raided from household collections and displays: sporting rifles, horse-pistols, fowling pieces, even ancient arquebuses manufactured in Henry VII's reign. In their knapsacks and pockets and saddlebags they had crammed as much of the salvaged baggage goods as they could carry. Thomas carried silver plate in his pack, and his pockets bulged with candles, flints, salt, and packets of tea.

He turned in the saddle to look upon his house. Three heads, two fair and one blazing red, showed at an upstairs window. Brigid and the boys. Three pairs of arms waved extravagantly. Then the casement opened and Brigid pushed her wild head into the rain. "God defend ye, sirs," she called out in her horrible Irish brogue. "God protect — " but the storm tore the rest of her words away, and she had to bang the window shut.

In the past hour the wind had risen to a gale, with an edge to it like a fresh blade. Their route cut through parkland to a crossroads marked by an arched stone bridge. Beyond this, a sea of mud led to the village, where a handful of thatch-roofed cottages had water rising to their doorsteps. The church of St. Mary, standing on a knoll overlooking the green, looked like a ship grounded on a reef. Beside it, the lych-gate opened into a deluged graveyard. The landscape was sodden, drowned, littered with debris from the storm. On the edge of the common the squatters' hovels, built of rubbish and sod, had collapsed into watery ruins. There was no living being in sight, not even a stray dog. The horses sank hock-deep into the mud and the Standard, a drenched rag flapping wildly around its varnished staff, fell into the ditch.

The wind drove a torrent of sleet mixed with snow into Thomas' face, down his back and into his eyes. His horse, Pilgrim, a sorrel with great soft eyes, gentle and patient as Job, stumbled and sweated through the muck. They travelled in the deep ruts left by the baggage train, whose wreckage was visible all along the route. Lee had laid down planks, but these had sunk uselessly under the weight of the loaded wagons. At the top of a steep embankment they saw where the sledge with the cannons, pulled by a team of draught horses, must have broken loose from its moorings and rumbled like a battering ram down the escarpment into the slough at the bottom. From time to time they had to dismount and clear fallen trees or other debris from the road. Somewhere along the way Thomas lost his gloves, and his horse cast a shoe. A postboy on foot could have travelled faster.

By the time they reached Harwell, the brief daylight had failed. Thomas shoved his frozen hands into his pockets and conferred with Lee, while a squall of snow whitened the air between them. He had already decided to stop: with luck the weather might be cold enough to freeze the mud and slush into something resembling a road, and they could resume their progress in the small hours of the morning. In the meantime, they invaded the Henry V public house for a mouthful of food and a few hours' rest.

The inn yard was another slough. The clump of sycamores sheltering the house shed wet leaves on the roof, and the ivy had died away to a miserable tangle of brown sticks. The house sign, half-eaten by weather and rot, swung on rusted chains, its painted presentment of Henry V unrecognizable except for the crown.

After a cold supper the men lay like the dead on the taproom floor and benches. The young bugler had his instrument under his chin. Lee had fallen asleep with his back to the wall, his hat askew over his forehead. His face was grey, the face of an old man who should not have spent the better part of two days and nights out in a storm. Thomas found a rough blanket and covered him up before unlatching the door and walking to the stables to visit Pilgrim.

It was full dark now and still snowing. There was no one on the road. The wind bit into his face. The "Protestant Wind," William's friends called it, arranged by God to blow on behalf of the invaders. But William's friends conveniently forgot, or did not acknowledge, that the army sent to liberate the Protestant Church was two-thirds Catholic, a raffish horde scraped from all the countries and faiths of Europe — men who would fight for anything if they were paid enough, and who cared nothing, one way or another, for England or England's church.

The familiar musty stable smells were somehow comforting. It was a compound of horse, leather, hay and dung, to which Thomas had been accustomed since he was old enough to walk. Pilgrim, brushed and fed, stood in the far left-hand stall. Thomas ran a hand over the velvet muzzle and for some time stood with his eyes closed, breathing in the horse-scented warmth. He was no longer thirty-two years old, soldier, husband and father, but a boy so in love with his first pony that he had slept in the straw to keep it company. Pilgrim nuzzled his cheek. Thomas, dreaming of home, shook himself awake and went out again into the cold.

In the taproom he pulled a chair up to a battered table in the corner and sat down with a cup of wine. Half the company was snoring. There was a pervasive smell of wet wool, tobacco, and mud. Thomas took out his cherrywood pipe and laid it on table, but did not light it. When Libby had taken sick he had made a desperate bargain with God: spare her and I will build an almshouse, feed the poor for a year, pray, fast, give up the vice of tobacco, have patience with Grace and her Quakers.

He tried to imagine his sister in a starched white apron and cap, keeping silence in the Friends' meeting house — Grace, who was once as lovely as her name, who used to have a wardrobe full of bright dresses, who loved to sing and dance! Any man who could effect such a change had to have some extraordinary attraction, and from the way Grace had hung upon Schuyler's neck, Thomas suspected what that might be. Apparently not all that flaming zeal was reserved for God. The thought almost curdled the wine in his mouth.

"Hold him! Hold that horse!" Lee muttered. He was talking in his sleep. Thomas put a hand on his shoulder, shaking him slightly, and after a moment Lee's snores resumed. Thomas felt a sudden enormous affection for him, for all of them, these friends and neighbours who had volunteered not from any expectation of glory, but a straightforward sense of duty.

Duty. How unfashionable a word, and one that, like loyalty, seemed to mean less every day. It seemed that everything now boiled down to money. Parliament had not supported King Charles' pro-French policies, and so he had dismissed it and turned to his cousin Louis for financing. French gold had bought English silence while Louis made himself the scourge of Europe. No doubt Louis had expected James to follow his brother's lead. But James, beginning his reign with the most loyal parliament ever assembled, had had no need of French subsidies. If only he had been sensible enough to keep friends with that parliament, his religion might now be seen as a personal matter instead of a national threat. And his friends, those few he had left, would not be struggling through the muck to meet a Dutch army.

Thomas pushed that thought aside and concentrated, instead, on their route. At least the weather played no favourites. This same storm that was keeping them from Salisbury would also confine the Dutch to their camp in Exeter. There would be no pitched battle until the weather blew itself out. Even then, after so much rain, the country around Salisbury would be a vast lake of churned mud, unfit for artillery or horses. He had not seen such foul conditions even in Scotland. Three years ago he had ridden circuit there with John Graham, who was responsible for military as well as civil justice in the southwest — no sinecure when the rebel Covenanters were up in arms, burning property and murdering government officials.

Graham had invited Thomas to see, first-hand, the administration of civil justice in Scotland, to meet the Commissioners and his particular friend Sir George MacKenzie, the respected Lord Advocate. It was meant to be a civilized tour of the country. But that summer the Covenanters had declared war on the King, and the whole of the southwest had gone up in rebellion like a sheet of flame. Armed with whatever weapons they could find — illegally imported Dutch guns, old-fashioned pikes and civil war muskets, rusty farm tools — the Covenanters had fought like madmen, refusing to surrender or say the four words that would spare them: God bless the King. In their eyes, the civil war had never ended. They recognized no sovereign except Jesus and no law except the Bible, at least those parts of it that were convenient to their cause. Their ministers assured them that the killing of a soldier, bishop, or any royal official was a holy act whose reward was instant salvation. The brutal murder of the Lord Primate of Scotland, in the presence of his daughter, had been hailed as a noble and pious deed.

Thomas, thinking it cowardly to go home as soon as troubled erupted, had stayed on, finding out what "circuit court" meant in the midst of a war. John Graham's moss-troopers had camped out in the open that summer, holding makeshift court in thatch-roofed bothies and dispensing summary justice to the rebels. The southwest was under martial law and John had been given the powers of judge, jury, and executioner, all in one. He was implacable in pursuit of the Covenanters, hard and unyielding in the exercise of his duty. This was Scottish justice at its most basic, the legacy of over a century of deep religious and political strife. From that summer stemmed his dark reputation as the persecutor of the godly. But he was equally rigorous with his own men. There would never be any question of insubordination, let alone desertion, in a regiment under John's command: he would shoot first and deal with the consequences later. In spite or possibly because of that, his hard-boiled troops revered him.

At this moment he was somewhere on the road with the Scottish cavalry. His senior colleague, General Douglas, a big, loud man with a head like a bushy black turnip, had command of the foot. Thomas remembered meeting Douglas in Edinburgh, remembered the bellowing Scots voice and the full black beard, the air of intolerable self-importance.

Suddenly he was too tired to eat. He rested his forehead on his fists, willing himself to sleep. But it was a long while before he fell into an uneasy doze, and then he dreamed, grotesquely, of Brigid. She was sitting cross-legged by his neighbour's fish pond, trailing a freckled ankle in the water. In her county Mayo voice she told Thomas, "There has never been an Irish Pope." Next to her the King, in full coronation panoply, stood drinking from a stirrup cup that John Graham had polished with a rag. "I have seen my lord St. Clare," said the King, "and he will be dead within a week. Let us drink to our friend George!" But when the King dashed the dregs to the ground, there was blood in the cup instead of wine. The drops spattered Thomas' face, and then became a gush, a torrent. He was drowning in blood.

He awoke with a start, his heart thudding like a kettle-drum in his chest, and found that in his sleep he had overturned his wine cup.

It was three in the morning. The bugler was sounding the Stand to Horse.

"It's still blowing hard," Lee reported. "But the snow has stopped." He looked into his friend's face. "Are you all right?"

Thomas nodded. But he felt unable to talk civilly to anyone, even Lee. He drank a cup of bitter black coffee and walked out, weary as death, into the torchlit courtyard. One or two stars pricked through the scudding cloud. The inn yard was full of horses and dogs. Men were talking, cursing, walking up and down to warm themselves in the cold. The inn door opened and banged shut again, releasing the smell of frying bacon. Someone must have roused the cook. An ostler clanked by, with a slop pail in each hand. Malachy, his sleepy face a blur in the dark, led up Pilgrim, and Thomas rummaged in his pocket for a chunk of carrot. His foolish dream so oppressed him that he could not shake off the effects. With his wolfhound, Magnus, running at his stirrup, he rode out of the inn yard to scout the road ahead. The cold air was like a sea mist upon his face.

Seeing the half-eaten head of King Henry on the house-sign had jogged his memory of the play. *You have conspired against our royal person, joined with an enemy proclaim'd...* Who knew better than St. Clare the cost of treason? To hang on the gallows until choked and livid but not dead; to have your bowels gouged from your body, then to be torn asunder by horses, and the pieces flung like offal into unconsecrated ground — what fresh title or fortune was worth the risk of such a death?

Beyond the circle of torchlight there was utter darkness. Perhaps his father-in-law was wakeful this night as well, walking around the Dutch camp, studying the same blowing cloud-wrack, the same pale stars. *Every subject's duty is the King's, but every subject's soul is his own....* What was going on in St. Clare's soul, that he had abandoned his children, his honour, and his country?

An intolerable sadness and anger knotted his chest. He patted Pilgrim's flank, urging him forward.

4

DR. RADCLIFFE HAD FINISHED BLEEDING the King. Temporarily, at least, the pain in James' head had ceased. But he did not expect the respite to last. For forty-eight hours he had been having nosebleeds so violent and disabling that he had been confined to bed. His nose felt broken, as if a mailed fist had smashed the cartilage.

The doctor bowed himself out. James sat by the fire in his dressing gown, nursing a cup of well-watered wine. On the other aside of the arras were his attendants, the nobles whose privilege it was to help him dress, pour scented water into his basin, and hand him his towel. He had turned them all out while he used the close-stool. The results would be collected for examination. But the truth was that Dr. Radcliffe had no remedy for the sickness that ailed his King.

The storm had blown itself out. There could be no further postponement of action. The army, if not the sovereign, was battle-ready; for two weeks his staff had been working twenty-four hours a day organizing the campaign. An endless flow of paper went out daily from General Churchill's desk to the Chequer Inn at Charing Cross, where each regiment kept a courier for the purpose of transmitting orders to regiments in the field. Lord Feversham was Commander-in-Chief, but Churchill was the brains and guts of the army command, a man upon whose leadership James placed an almost painful dependence. Each morning he had met with Churchill and his staff, trying to show he was master of the situation even though his nose bled and his head hurt.

Their plan was simple: take the army southwest with all speed and confine the Dutch to the peninsula. If Admiral Dartmouth could bring up the fleet in time and destroy the Prince's ships, the Dutch would be trapped between the sea and the royal army. But, at last report, the English fleet was still out in the Channel, battered and dispersed by the storm.

James had been told that Gilbert Burnet, the exiled English bishop who sailed with William, had commandeered the pulpit in Exeter cathedral to give thanks for their safe voyage. But he had preached to an empty house. The gentry had not attended. And when Burnet treasonously omitted the usual prayers for the health of the Prince of Wales, even the choir had fled.

But the Dutch still had an audience. In Exeter it was fair time, and despite the weather people travelled by cart or on foot to enjoy the sights. James' intelligence reported that when Prince William rode into the city at the head of his troops, it was regarded almost as part of the entertainment. The big Swedish and German soldiers in their furs and breastplates, the exotic feathered Africans, were as much of a novelty as the usual tumblers and fire-eaters. The invading army was like a raree show. To a gawping country audience, the Prince's agents had read out a paper that justified the landing of troops as an act of salvation. The phrases were noble: preservation of the Protestant faith, restoration of the rights and liberties of England, the recall of a free parliament, the protection of the Succession...

Copies of this document had been distributed. Most people, being unable to read, had used it to wrap their fairings. But one of the copies had found its way into James' hands. He learned that his son-in-law apparently believed that the Prince of Wales was an impostor, a commoner's brat smuggled into the palace by order of the Pope.

It was then the nosebleeds had started. But he had concealed this coincidence from the doctor, and thanked God, although not publicly, for the storm that prevented him from leaving London. But now there was no excuse. Dr. Radcliffe might wish to keep him in swaddling clothes, but the army would not accept nosebleeds as a reason for their King's continued absence.

He propped one foot on the hearth-fender and massaged his temples. His face in the shaving-mirror that morning had looked grey and weary, unrecognizably old. The fine blue eyes were shot with blood; the cropped fair hair under the wig had turned ashen. "The comeliest prince in Christendom," as someone once had named him, had become wrinkle and bone. His skin felt dry and hot to the touch. Yet he was colder than he had ever been in his life. The fire did nothing but blister his shins, while his back froze. Dr. Radcliffe put this down to the "sluggish humours common at Your Majesty's time of life."

But, at fifty-five, he was not yet ready for the infirmities and indignities of old age. He still rose at dawn, and spent hours in the saddle without discomfort. He could walk ten miles at a stretch, and his abstinence at the table had kept him slim as a boy, when half his contemporaries were sunk in mountains of gouty flesh. But gluttony had never been one of his besetting sins. Pride, yes, and concupiscence.... even now, in the aftermath of the vow he had taken (again) to be eternally faithful to his wife, he could not forbear thinking of other women. God pardon him, but he craved the solace of their company, and the comfort of their flesh, the way other men craved tobacco or wine. He regularly berated himself for being so undeserving of his wife's loyalty. But even with his regrettably lustful habits he was chastity itself, compared to his brother Charles.

Charles had teased him, of course, about his mistresses, and his subsequent guilt, telling everyone that the women he chose were so ugly that he did his penance by looking at them. Charles had always teased him. In their boyhood it had made him angry; now he felt it might be worth his hope of salvation to hear that lazy, mocking, affectionate voice just once more.

But Charles was dead, and he, James, must carry on, in the worst crisis of his life since the civil war.

It was forty-six years ago that he had hidden behind a hedge with Charles, and watched in horror as their father's standard went down in the mud at Edgehill. The dead bearer, Sir Edmund Verney, had grasped the royal standard so firmly that the Roundheads had had to cut off his hand in order to seize the flag. Charles, reluctantly obeying the King's orders, had escaped to safety in France, but James had been captured by parliament and held prisoner in London.

It still pleased him that he had managed to outwit his jailers. Dressed as a maid, he had escaped to Holland and found refuge with his favourite sister, Mary, whose son, William, was now encamped on his doorstep with an army. He seemed to have travelled full circle. Only now the enemy was not Cromwell, but his own flesh and blood. Even with both armies fully mobilized, and the Prince's paper in his hands, he could not believe that he was going to fight his nephew. For the first time he was grateful that his beloved sister was dead, for she could not have borne to see this.

Phrases from William's Declaration marched like a ghoulish army through his mind. Saviour of the Protestant faith! Guardian of the Succession! It was impossible that a man of William's coldly incisive intelligence could believe the preposterous stories about the Prince of Wales. It was an excuse, no more. William was using the spur of ancient hatreds to prod the ignorant and prejudiced into thinking that the Pope had interfered in the Succession. And those who affected to believe it, all those who had deserted, were guilty of more than simple political treason. Their misuse of religion was an offence to God Himself. And they called themselves patriots! What kind of patriot willingly plunged his country into civil war?

It was his determination to avoid this catastrophe that had finally given him the strength to act. He had signed orders putting every company and troop in England on active duty; he had called for volunteers and sent out the fleet; he had ordered four thousand soldiers down from Scotland under the command of General Douglas and John Graham of Claverhouse.

He mused on the reliability of the Scots. Forty years after the civil war, people were still telling him not to trust them. Scottish traitors had betrayed his father to Cromwell and forced his brother to forsake the noblest of their father's allies, Montrose, whom they then butchered.

"Trust no man," Charles said after that. And once he was crowned, Charles never spoke again of Scotland, or Montrose, or their father's murder. Instead he had made pleasure the only reason for living. The world was faithless, rotten, lascivious — why not be damned along with all the rest? Horses, women, dice; these were all that mattered, all that counted, after their father's head had rolled in the dirt, and Montrose had been hacked to pieces. There was no man without a price, and no faith that could not be broken.

But James had spent some time in Scotland — unwillingly, it was true — and he had made friends there whom he felt he could trust. He hung on to that thought the way a drowning man might grip a spar.

The gentlemen on the other side of the tapestry were growing restive. "Sir?" one of them asked respectfully. "Do you need assistance?"

"No."

This it was to be King, so confined by ceremony that he could not even use the close-stool in privacy. But then he had been ill. There was some justification for their anxiety. He had to show he was well enough to lead his army into battle, prove to his Court that he was still the King. Prove, as well, that his personal courage — which he had demonstrated often enough in battle, on the seas as Admiral, and even in the streets of London long ago, fighting the Great Fire — had not deserted him.

And what men among these courtiers were his genuine allies? To whom would he entrust his life, and, more precious still, the lives of his wife and son? He counted on his fingers. John Churchill. Thomas Bruce, the Earl of Ailesbury. John Graham. Lord Dartmouth, his beleaguered Admiral. John Drummond, the Earl of Melfort, his chief Scottish adviser.

Not many, among so great a throng. His faith was like a sword dividing him from his fellows. But he would not recant, not even to save his throne. He had always been steadfast in his loyalty to the Church.

In other areas he had given in. He had permitted his daughters to be raised as Protestants; he had resigned as Lord High Admiral rather than break the law that prohibited Catholics from holding public office. Both his children had married Protestant princes. But because he would sooner die than abjure his faith, he was accused, most unjustly, of putting Rome before England and conspiring with the French against his own country.

No one trusted him. Even the Church of England, that

unfailing prop of the monarchy, had defied him, as the universities and city corporations and his own Court had done — all turning against him because of their crazy fear of popery. Without these traditional supports, he stood alone. The army he had raised, on which he had spent so much devoted care and attention, had seemed his only staunch ally... until the desertion last week of three crack regiments.

Friends, courtiers, churchmen, the army; ironically, in trying to achieve religious good-fellowship, he had fought with everyone around him, Catholic or Protestant. People called him obstinate, self-willed, short-sighted, a tyrant. The worse his reputation grew, the more determined he became to prevail against his critics. He had dismissed from office anyone who disagreed with him. He had dissolved parliament. He had publicly rebuked King Louis and argued with the Pope. He had imprisoned the Archbishop of Canterbury in the Tower, disputing so bitterly over that with his council that he had banished its President, Thomas de Chastelain, from Court.

He had trusted Thomas and liked him enormously, even if he did not always understand what went on in that lawyer's brain of his. His loyalty, if not his tact, had never been in doubt. His background was irreproachable: staunchly Royalist father, charming French mother (James remembered her with particular fondness), a family solidly aligned with the Stuarts. But Thomas had been shipwrecked on the matter of the bishops.

"Sir?" It was Dr. Radcliffe again, from behind the arras. "With Your Majesty's permission, I should like to examine you."

James emerged from behind the tapestry, still holding his wine cup. Dr. Radcliffe respectfully led him to the bed, and he lay down amongst the green velvet hangings. Solemnly, silently, the physician took his pulse, examined his eyes, tongue and nose, and felt his abdomen. The doctor's breath smelled sour and he looked tired. But he had been in almost constant attendance on the King for two days.

James allowed him to anoint his temples with a mixture of egg white, rosewater, alabaster, and flax, which was supposed to staunch nosebleeds. The room stank of boiled herbs. He stared up at the carved and gilded bedposts, and into his mind rose the memory of a scene he had thought long forgotten — his younger daughter, Anne, placidly eating sweets, while her sister, Mary, wept hysterically after meeting her prospective bridegroom.

"I will not marry him!" she screamed. "I will not!"

James had been sympathetic, for William, short, plain, and asthmatic, was hardly the beau ideal of a prince. His qualities of intelligence and hard-headed determination were not those which would appeal to a romantic-minded young girl. Moreover, his private life was enigmatic; there was a persistent rumour that, God forbid, he admired masculine beauty more than feminine. Mary had locked herself in her room after meeting him, only emerging at the express command of her uncle King Charles, who told her that the marriage was a political necessity.

"He has eyes like a fish!" she answered wildly. "And I don't want to go to Holland! I would rather die!"

Anne had looked up with her blackbird's eyes and said calmly as she rummaged in her comfit box, "But you shall have fine new dresses, Mary, and jewels. I won't mind whom I marry, so long as he is not too old."

"You married! You'll be as fat as a Martinmas hog if you keep eating that way!"

And somehow the political discussions, the high talk of preserving the Protestant Succession, had dwindled into a schoolgirl fight between the princesses, with Mary yanking Anne's glossy ringlets and Anne shrieking in protest. James had taken them both on his knee, comforting and soothing them equally. Another comfit for Anne, his Roly-Poly, and a kiss for Mary.

In the end, Mary had learned to tolerate her husband and even, if her letters could be believed, to love him. But William remained as icy as ever in public, and after eleven years there was still no sign of an heir. While James unhesitatingly blamed this on his son-in-law, he did not want to inquire too closely into William's personal habits. The Prince was said to keep a mistress, one of Mary's own ladies-in-waiting, with whom he drank cocoa and talked politics, instead of going to bed — a thing so incomprehensible it was almost sinister.

Thank God that Anne, when she married, had remained comfortably at home. Her husband George, an amiable and unambitious young man, had come from his native Denmark to live with the royal family in St. James' palace. George might have few interests and no conversation at all, but at least he was not a monster of treachery. And he liked women, in the same uncomplicated fashion that he liked his horse and a hot dinner on the table.

"Sir, I beg you to lie still," said Dr. Radcliffe.

James closed his eyes. Lately, too frequently for his peace, he had been dreaming of his father. They had last seen one another at Hampton Court, the royal residence that became a prison. Father and son had talked in the presence of guards. That memory, so precious, occasionally terrified him by its lack of clarity. He ought to remember each word and did not. But then neither of them had imagined that the meeting would be their last on earth.

Now and then, walking through the magnificent gallery

of paintings his father had collected, he would pause in front of this one or that, remembering his father's pleasure in acquiring it. Painting, music, literature, architecture — all these gracious arts had flourished in a court more dignified and cultured than any England had yet seen. But his father had not been firm enough. For the sake of peace he had surrendered to his enemies, and it had all ended in a shambles of blood and terror. Together parliament and Cromwell had conspired to kill the most civilized King in Europe, and now the descendants of those murderers were gathering in Exeter.

Abruptly he sat up, jostling the doctor's arm. He could not afford to lie here any longer, while so great a press of business awaited him. He had ministers, councillors, courtiers, ambassadors, the Secretary of War and the Provost-Marshal General waiting to see him, all with their own particular fish to fry. He had an army to order and an invader to defeat.

He thrust his feet into brocade slippers. "We leave for Salisbury in an hour," he said. "Pack what you need."

"Sir, you cannot think of travel — " Dr. Radcliffe began, and then broke off, for James was already stumping past him out the door. He had ceased to be a patient; this was the King giving an order. "Send someone to find Churchill," he said. "I shall be with the Queen."

He put on a burst of speed to leave his courtiers behind and entered his wife's apartments alone and unannounced. Her ladies, prettily flustered, swept to the floor in deep reverences. But one brown-haired mademoiselle dared to smile at him. She kept her chin up and arched her back as she sank to her knees, spreading her lutestring skirts with one hand and her little painted fan with the other. The fashion of extreme décolleté in gowns made this salute irresistibly charming. James stared, smiled, and speculated.

Then, meeting his wife's eyes, he hastened to kiss her with more than his usual zeal.

Mary Beatrice was twenty-three years younger than he, and her air of serenity was deceptive. Her tranquil dark eyes, her pure, oval face and sweetly full-lipped mouth, all combined to leave an impression of exquisite repose. But, as James knew to his sorrow, an imperious Italian temper burned just beneath the surface. Mary Beatrice had been known to throw hairbrushes when she was angry, and she was not above shouting at her faithless husband in public. If he had thought, fifteen years ago, that he was marrying a lovely meek child, now he knew better. Mary Beatrice had made it clear what she thought of his infidelities.

But just now, as mother of the heir to the throne, she had no serious rival. Together they went to look at five-month-old James Francis Edward, who lay sleeping in his lace-shrouded cot. There was a bubble of saliva at the corner of his mouth and James put out a tender finger to wipe it away. This child, his only surviving son, was more precious to him than his own life. The baby had been grievously ill after his birth, and the doctors' diet of gruel and raisins had nearly killed him. But, put to the breast of a healthy wet nurse, he had begun to thrive. Now he was out of danger, except from the political enemies who talked of strangling him in his cradle. James knew this was a legitimate fear. Even allowing for exaggeration, there could be no doubt what would happen to the child should he fall into Dutch hands.

"He has a good colour. How does he feed?"

Mary Beatrice told him of her satisfaction with the wet nurse. They discussed their son's feeding, his bowels, and his teething. It was a source of infinite pleasure to them both, and to James held more significance than any report from

Exeter. He put his hand on his son's head, feeling the hair soft as down under his fingers. A gold crucifix on a pearl chain lay at the foot of the cradle. It had been blessed by the Pontiff himself, and in spite of present circumstances, James regarded it as a symbol of hope.

One day this child would rule over three kingdoms. He would be the servant of God, the protector of his country, Defender of the Faith. He would prise open the minds of his countrymen and let in the fresh, sweet air of reason and the love of God. Citizens of all faiths, if they professed loyalty to the king, would be safe from persecution; worship would be a thing apart from politics. James knew this was possible, for his friend, William Penn, had lighted the way.

Penn was a man who in earlier years had been fined, imprisoned, and socially damned for his Quaker beliefs, an outcast who had had to go to the New World to practice his faith. But his loyalty was a rock. There was no duplicity in him. James, with a soldier's directness, much preferred Penn's honesty to his courtiers' platitudes. It was Penn who had convinced him that freedom of worship would encourage, rather than threaten, the country's stability. But this was an idea so radical that few would accept it. Few believed, either, that he wanted to liberate anyone except the Catholics. But Penn had believed him.

He stooped to kiss the soft cheek of the future Defender of the Faith, remembering how Prince William, some thirty-eight years ago, had squalled in his arms.

5

THOMAS SADDLED PILGRIM AND RODE alone into the countryside around Wilton, three miles from Salisbury. It was dark, but no pickets challenged him. There had been so many desertions by now that General Feversham had stopped sending out scouts or posting sentries.

Rain was falling again, a cold, thin drizzle that would likely turn to sleet during the night. It was dark and almost eerily silent, with nothing to show that the main body of the army was camped nearby. William himself could have ridden, unmolested and unrecognized, through the deserted village streets. Thomas sat for a few minutes, looking at the lights pricking through the dusk. If the Dutch chose this moment to attack, they would plough through the King's demoralized army like Moses parting the Red Sea. He thought that Feversham should have sent out scouts. Under guard, if necessary. It was shameful that they lacked the most basic knowledge of the enemy — whether or not William himself were still in Exeter, or even what road his troops were using on their march east. The lack of information made any strategy impossible.

But Thomas remembered from their days on council together how cautious General Feversham was, how correct. Nothing in the Frenchman's experience had equipped him to deal with mutiny. In the King's absence he had not dared to take charge, and as a result, all discipline had failed. No watches, no pickets, no drills; insubordination and wholesale desertions were daily events. The royal army was a sieve instead of a shield. There was even talk that Feversham wanted to retreat. It would be easy to say that he was a coward or in Dutch pay, but Thomas thought the truth was that the situation was too much for him. If he had obedient soldiers and trustworthy officers, he would know what to do. But his soldiers refused to obey their officers without written orders, and his officers were abandoning their men in the field.

The lifeblood of the army was draining away and it remained to be seen if the King could staunch it. He had finally arrived in Salisbury with his entourage, and had ordered a review at Warminster for the following morning.

In the meantime there was nothing to see or hear except the rain. Thomas wheeled around and rode back to his quarters. The company had been broken up, billeted in and around Wilton, and he shared a garret in the Jolly Miller hostelry with Lee, while they awaited orders. The lodging was crammed from root cellar to attic with soldiers, some of them rough recruits who had been shipped over from Ireland for this emergency. But the Irish, knowing they were despised, kept to themselves.

There was nothing jolly about the Miller or its environs. The taproom was filled with scarred, stained benches and tables and there was no glass in the windows, only oiled paper. The shutters opened on a forecourt filled with rubbish. They were supposed to wash in the scullery and eat in the taproom, but Lee had brought his own kettle, which he hung over the grate in their room to make broth or stew. He might ride in the mud and sleep on bare floorboards without complaint, but he was fastidious as a young girl about his food. He had brought his own packet of China tea and used his own silver cup and spoon. Thomas said it reminded him of King Louis, travelling to war with his trunks of cutlery and his pastry chefs, and Lee grinned sheepishly. On their arrival in Salisbury he had come down with a severe cold, but he had refused to make any concession to illness. It was bad to see him with that grey look in his face; worse to hear him cough and hear the wet thickness in his chest.

He was nursing a dish of tea in the dark when Thomas returned. His jacket and his cloak were spread in front of the small fire and his boots steamed on the fender. Thomas lit a candle, and as the room flared into sudden light he saw why the old man had wanted to sit in the dark: the left side of his face was scraped and bruised, his eye swollen to the size of an egg.

"Horse threw me," Lee said. "Don't trouble yourself, my son. It's nothing." He coughed into a sodden handkerchief. His chest sounded like a windblown swamp, and the handkerchief, quickly balled into his pocket, looked as though it might have blood on it. Thomas, as if he had not seen, went to his pack and got out a roll of linen and the salve that Libby had put in for him. He smeared some on a strip of cloth and handed it to Lee. "You ought to have that seen to. There's dirt in the wound."

"I don't want any sawbones near me," Lee said. "You do it."

Thomas looked at the water in the bedside pitcher to make sure it was clean, then soaked a piece of linen and washed Lee's eye. "At least my hands are all right," Lee said. "I had my gloves on."

Thomas wanted to ask how it had happened, but sensed that the question would be unwelcome. It was the old man's own business why, sick as he was, he had chosen to be out on horseback in the rain.

"You missed the Dublin boys, Tom," Lee said. "They broke up the bar."

Apparently the Irish recruits had objected to being served uncooked pease and stale bread, while their English counterparts had beef. And although they all had to sleep wherever there was space, on the floor or the landing or in the stables, the Irish had been shoved into a cellar next to the privy. They had refused to pay the eight shillings per week per man which was, by law, due the landlord.

But that was not the immediate cause of the fight. The Irish sergeant had ridden in with news that there had been a skirmish between the King's troops and the Dutch at Wincanton. Under the command of an Irish cavalry officer, the royalists had taken some Dutch prisoners who said that Bristol and Plymouth had freely declared for the Prince. All of the southwest was now said to be under William's thumb.

The English had not believed it. Someone called the man a liar, a dirty bastard bogtrotter looking to spread gloom, and the Irish went berserk, smashing bottles and furniture and heads. It took the arrival of the Provost-Marshal's guard to put an end to the melee. Afterward Lee had gone out to see if he could gather more information. "No luck," he said. "But I found this nailed to the door." He fished a soiled paper from his pocket and handed it to Thomas.

It was a published list of William's sworn allies, put together by the man who had once been Speaker of the House and now was William's Governor in Exeter. There were signatures of lords lieutenant, sheriffs, justices of the peace, former naval and army officers, private gentlemen, clergy: it read like a roster of both Houses of Parliament. Prominent among the noble names, ringed in black to show its importance, was St. Clare's.

Lee coughed. "There are names of good friends — good men — there. As there were on the parliament side during the war." He coughed again and said, "You should have told me about St. Clare."

Thomas set the paper down. "I found out just before we left. Even my wife doesn't know."

He told him about Henry Finch's letter and what had happened on the road from London. Lee drank his tea in silence and then said, with apparent inconsequence, "I killed a good friend at Worcester. My horse had been injured and I was on foot. One of the Roundhead officers charged me and I fired at him point-blank. It blew his helmet off with half his jaw, but I recognized him by his hand. He'd cut himself badly, as a boy, and the scar went right across the palm. With the smoke and those damned soup pot helmets they wore, I had not known him." He paused. "We had been close as brothers, once, at school."

There was nothing that Thomas could think of to say to this. After a moment Lee resumed, "I was reminded of it because I saw his name on that list. Or rather, his son's name. He's a Justice of the Peace. The point is, Tom, there were names of decent men on that paper. Friends of yours and mine. Moderate, law-abiding, God-fearing men."

If possible this made it worse, proving, if proof were needed, how strongly the tide ran against the King. Men such as these did not commit treason on a whim. It was astonishing that such a document had been printed and distributed, apparently without fear of reprisal. Their confidence was disturbing. Thomas began to feel an unwilling sympathy for Feversham, who dared not give orders because he no longer knew whom to trust.

He threw the paper on the grate. The edges glowed red and then turned black before crumbling into ash. St. Clare's name seemed to stand out, bold, livid, until the fire consumed it.

"You call these men law-abiding," he said. "But they have used God to justify their treason."

"No doubt they see themselves as patriots, saving England from Rome."

"The King never intended to force a return to his church. He only wanted to make it possible, under the law, to be a Catholic and still have a citizen's rights. But his enemies have convinced everyone otherwise."

"Not everyone," said Lee. He rubbed his swollen eye. "But I do think there are some — your father-in-law may be among them — who sincerely believe they are saving the country, and would say they intend the king no harm."

"Cromwell said that too."

There was a short silence. Lee covered himself with an old horse blanket, a grey, crusted piece of wool that made him look like Banquo's ghost. From below stairs came a burst of song. The taproom would be filling now, officers and men drinking because there was nothing else to do, even though the Dutch might be around the next bend in the road. Thomas stood.

"Where are you going?"

"To see Feversham and offer our services as scouts."

"I'll come with you."

"I don't know how long it will take. You'd better rest while you have the chance."

Lee, coughing once more and holding his ribs, let this effrontery go by. "Be careful."

Thomas knew he meant "Watch out for the Irish." He smiled a little grimly and picked up his hat.

The rain had stopped, but it had grown so cold out that the mud underfoot had a skin of ice. There was a halo of grey cloud around the moon. The little river channels that ran through the old city of Salisbury were close to flooding their brick embankments, and the rank smell of open ditches and the nearby marshland and water meadows blew on the wind. Tonight the cathedral was lit up like a beacon, and its spire, four hundred feet tall, seemed to pierce the moon.

The King had set up headquarters at the episcopal palace. At least there were sentries at the gate. Thomas produced his papers, crushed and damp from their sojourn in his pocket, and the guards waved him through. Inside the stone walls, the palace was crowded with soldiers, orderlies, staff officers, and couriers. The place seemed to be in a frenzy, more even than the circumstances warranted.

A young aide-de-camp blocked his way. "Sir? Your business here?"

"I need to see General Feversham." Again he brought out his papers. The aide-de-camp looked hard at him and then took off his hat and bowed. Lace, curls, whiff of scent.

"I'll see if the General is at liberty."

There was something wrong about his voice, something wrong too in the overall atmosphere. No happy camaraderie here. Thomas sat down on a bench and waited. He caught a glimpse of General Churchill, grim-faced but calm, talking with the Scottish commander Lord Annandale.

The young aide-de-camp, spurs a-jingle, escorted him to Lord Feversham. The General sat behind a large desk piled high with papers and dispatch bags, in a room thronged with soldiers and blue with tobacco smoke. He looked up at Thomas as if waking from sleep, and rubbed the heel of his hand over his eyes. "My lord. Welcome."

Once more Thomas produced his crumpled papers for inspection, but the Commander-in-Chief barely glanced at them before setting them down again. He was pale, sweating, his fine eyes heavily bloodshot. He looked unfocused, untidy, as if his unshaven chin and creased linen were the outward manifestations of an inner anguish. He was in his shirt sleeves and there were great damp circles under his arms.

"I can only give you five minutes," he said. "There's been trouble."

He added to the fug by filling his own pipe. Then he explained. In the last hour a plot had been uncovered to seize the King at tomorrow's review, and send him to William in chains. Colonel Kirke, at one time commander of a regiment in Tangiers, had been placed under arrest. Charges were pending against other officers. But untangling who was responsible was like pulling a single thread that unravelled an entire garment. Names had led to more names, and so many officers were implicated that it would take all night for General Churchill to interview them. The shock had sent the King to bed with another devastating nosebleed and the review was cancelled, all plans and decisions in abeyance, until his condition improved. Meanwhile there were Dutch patrols only thirty-seven miles away. That much had been confirmed by the skirmish at Wincanton.

They might face the enemy tomorrow or even tonight, and yet the King had been forced to order an inquiry into the conduct of his own troops. Thomas looked into Feversham's eyes and saw real fear there, something not quite under control. Put all the pieces together — Bristol and Plymouth falling, Edward Seymour's list, Kirke's crude plot — and it made a picture of inconceivable corruption. Disloyalty had poisoned every rank and branch of the army. Feversham looked ill; in a less dignified man, his indecision would have been panic. But he still had twenty four thousand men in the field and another six thousand in garrisons. These troops required only a commander capable of giving orders.

"Sir, I can guarantee my men's loyalty. There are thirty

of us, all people I can vouch for. We'll scout the Dutch position, give you the information you need."

Feversham drew on his pipe and said nothing. The silence lengthened. "Sir," Thomas said again. "My friends are loyal. I would stand to that with my life. Send us out."

"I'll reflect on it," said Feversham.

Thomas leaned forward, looking into Feversham's eyes.

"My lord, you need to know what is front of the army. Give me the order."

The same aide-de-camp came up and spoke in Feversham's ear. The general blanched. "Pardon," he said. "The King has sent for me. Pardon. We'll talk again, sir. Where are you quartered?" And he was out of the room without waiting for an answer, his pipe forgotten in his hand, his shirt wringing wet.

There was no point pursuing him. Thomas spoke to one of Churchill's aides and asked to see the General.

"He's interviewing."

"I'll wait."

He sat down again on the bench. Not far away, in a darkened room, the King lay helpless, bleeding into his pillows. But he did not want to think about that. Instead — but this was hardly better — he found himself recollecting the last time he had seen or spoken to James: the council chambers, last June. The King had been in one of his cold rages because the bishops had defied him. He wanted to charge them with treason and send them to the Tower. And, as Milton had said, all hell had broken loose. There was no precedent for putting the Church of England on public trial and it seemed an act of madness to arrest the eighty-year-old Archbishop of Canterbury. But the King had been adamant. Thomas remembered Feversham sitting with his head in his hands, saying nothing. In retrospect, he would have been wise to follow that example. But he had spoken out, telling James bluntly that the arrest would turn the Archbishop into as great a martyr as Thomas à Becket, and kill any hope of religious tolerance. He had pushed the arrest order away without signing it, saying, "I would as soon put my name to your death warrant."

No doubt it was a tactless choice of words, especially to a man whose father had been murdered. And he had forgotten to say "Majesty" or even "Sir." But it was the reference to Becket that had sent James into such an enormous passion. The saint of Canterbury, murdered at the altar because of the ungovernable rage of a mad king — it was an analogy that James found intolerable, especially from a man whom he "had raised from a family of nothings" to be his lord president.

Thomas could have said, with truth, that the de Chastelains had been nobles in Normandy when the Stuarts were fighting to defend a few miserable acres of Scottish bog. But he would not trade insults with his sovereign. Instead he had asked to be relieved of his duties.

"That and all else," snapped the King. "Go."

Had there ever been a swifter fall from grace? For a moment he had not moved. The sun dazzled his eyes and the airless June heat, the smell of men sweating in their lace and powder, had sickened him. Then the King had made a gesture and one of the guards came forward. Thomas thought he might be joining the bishops in the Tower. But a less exalted fate awaited him. Boatmen had rowed him to Richmond and then he had ridden home in the oppressive sultry heat. Halfway there the skies had burst in a thunder storm, and he had arrived wet and chilled to the bone, angry and despairing.

It afforded him no pleasure now that he had been right.

Arresting the bishops had accomplished nothing — all of them had been acquitted — and it had cost James everything, bringing him to this low point now, tonight, where he lay sick in bed while his own army plotted his capture.

A group of officers emerged from a nearby anteroom. Thomas recognized the unfashionable beard and stentorian bellow of black-haired General Douglas. One of the officers walked a little behind the rest, frowning, deep in his own thoughts: a handsome, slightly built man in a faded scarlet uniform, who had a shabby pair of gauntlets shoved under his arm.

He was shorter than General Douglas by nearly a foot and his uniform looked as though he had been sleeping in it. But energy and authority seem to charge the air around him. This was a man brimming with confidence, a commander who would face Schomberg or the Turks or enraged Scots Covenanters with the same unflinching zeal.

"General!" Thomas called, and John Graham, the newly created Viscount Dundee, looked up and smiled.

Dundee was a modest man who had no idea of the impact his forceful personality made on others. But Thomas had seen that personality bedazzle politicians, shopkeepers, bailiffs, royalty, women of all ages, infants, and the General's own troops — cynical, hardbitten veterans, those soldiers, flinty as their native rock. Yet they openly loved this man, counted it an honour to be under his command, would have died at his word. The king loved him as well, loading him with honours: he was Lord Graham of Claverhouse and Viscount Dundee, privy councillor, sheriff, clerk of the council, burgess of Aberdeen, constable and provost of Dundee. Had he chosen, he could have lived in grandeur.

But he preferred simplicity, the hard job of a professional soldier. He kept no state, either in civilian or military life.

There was no crust of gold braid on his sleeve or froth of Brussels lace at his throat or wrist. Instead he wore a flat linen collar over which his dark hair spilled, cavalier-fashion, and he had a plain, knob-hilted sword thrust into his belt. He was unchanged in looks and manner from the lowly captain of horse whom Thomas had met years ago when he had accompanied James, then Duke of York, to temporary exile in Edinburgh.

"General — "

Dundee looked pained. "I've been *John* to you so far. Don't 'General' me now."

"Wasn't it you who said that a General on the battlefield is next to God?"

"Well, we're not on the field yet. Or even near one. What are you doing here?"

"Waiting to see Lord Churchill. But he's occupied."

"He is indeed." Dundee looked around. General Douglas had marched on ahead with the others, his voice carrying as if he were calling players to a football match on the green. "And I tell you, gentlemen, that he lost his head and ran aboot like a fookin' Paddy bastard, and I had him put in irons — "

Dundee's face was expressionless. "Let's find some place to talk for ten minutes. One of the aides can fetch you, when Lord Churchill is free."

The arrival of the sovereign and his staff meant that all the public houses and coaching inns overflowed. But, accompanied by Dundee's orderly and his galloper, they found a seat in the Red Lion in Milford Street. The two officers sat down nearby, within whistling distance but out of earshot.

Dundee, who was as abstemious as the King, took a small glass of *aqua vitae* and set his tobacco pouch and flint beside his pipe. Thomas had seen him do this innumerable times — had seen him scrape the pipe bowl, fill it, polish it, use it as a paperweight or a spoon handle — but had never seen him actually smoke it. Dundee, far more puritan than the Puritans, preferred tea to spirits and reading to card playing, never swore or indulged in seamy gossip, and had no eyes for any woman except his wife. Never had Thomas seen him act with anything but honour and discretion.

But this man, educated and personable, quiet-spoken, was the same one whom the Covenanters called the Devil. They had accused him of every atrocity from torturing infants to drowning women and driving old folk out into the snow to die. In his lust for blood he was supposed to have raped and pillaged like some latter-day Goth descending on Rome. Too proud to defend himself, he would not speak of the homes he had spared, or the prisoners whom he had recommended for mercy or set free. In Covenanting circles, mothers told their children that Bloody Clavers would roast them alive.

It seemed the ultimate irony that he had married into their ranks: Jean, his young wife, came from a Covenanting family so rebellious that one of her uncles had been hanged for treason. But Dundee, having waited until thirty-five to marry, did not allow his personal life to interfere with his duty. He loved his King and his country, the army, and his wife — loved them all deeply, faithfully, honourably, and could see no reason for conflict among them.

He looked tired and fine-drawn, as if even his indestructible energies had been depleted. Thomas recalled that the Scottish troops had been ordered down to England on the first of October, which meant that for the past seven weeks Dundee must have been riding back and forth in attendance on the King.

"I hear you have brought your own troop, Thomas?"

"We're to be regimented into Lord Peterborough's horse."

"Does the King know you are here?"

"I don't know."

"Then you've not seen him? Not spoken to him since June?"

"No."

Thomas had wanted to avoid this rock, and here they had stumbled over it straightaway. He had written Dundee about the bishops' trial, wanting him to hear the truth instead of a garbled version of it from others. But Dundee's respect for the King went so deep that he would never refuse any royal command or disagree with even the most fatuous royal opinion. The King's orders were sacred. No one had any business refusing the sovereign's direct command, even if it meant putting all the bishops in England in prison; there was no justification for disobedience. He had urged Thomas to beg the King's pardon. But Thomas would not apologize for attempting to save the King from his own folly. Nor would he go, hat in hand, to ask for his honours and offices back. Dundee had written, "Your pride would make Lucifer look humble. Have a care, my friend, to what you are doing."

But Dundee said nothing now about the bishops. Instead he talked about General Feversham. "His lordship has told the King the army cannot be relied on. This business of Kirke's… I told him I would use my own regiment to scout the Dutch position."

"I made him the same offer. What did he say?"

"That he would think about it."

Their eyes met. Thomas saw the spark of anger in his friend's, the frustration behind his self-containment, like fire round a door. But Dundee's unshakeable loyalty extended also to Feversham, who was his Commander-in-Chief and the King's appointee. "There is worse to deal with than Kirke," he said. "And this is for your ears only, Thomas. Say nothing to anyone. We had dispatches from the north tonight. York and Nottingham have declared for William, and Carlisle as well."

It was appalling news. Carlisle was only three miles from the Border, which had been left virtually unguarded when the Scottish army had marched to Salisbury. Dundee ticked off the eight cities that now had switched allegiance: Exeter, Bristol, Plymouth, York, Nottingham, Hull, Chester, and Carlisle. Given the weather, the state of the roads, and the disrupted post, this concerted mutiny meant organization, planning, and advance knowledge; it meant a conspiracy far deeper than Kirke's and even more dangerous. William had thrown an iron net over the country.

But it was not a subject for discussion in a crowded room where no one could be trusted. Dundee picked up his empty pipe and after a moment began talking about the bounty the Covenanters had put on his head. There was no money involved; instead, whoever killed him was guaranteed an immediate place among the sanctified. Apparently there were still plenty of his enemies willing to try: in the week before he had left Edinburgh, he had been fired upon twice.

He spoke of it almost as a joke, as if it were the most trifling of problems. He was far more concerned that he had had no recent letter from his wife, who was pregnant with their first child. And he had had his own squabbles at court; for months now the King's Secretary for Scotland, Lord Melfort, had been waging a backhanded war against him, a spiteful campaign of lies and slander and rumour. At one time Melfort had claimed friendship with him and this sudden enmity baffled Dundee. But he trusted they could work together "for the common good of His Majesty's service."

Thomas, who knew the Earl from Court, thought this highly unlikely. Lord Melfort's single passion in life was the welfare of Lord Melfort. All feathers and fribbles, he was nonetheless a dangerous man. He had turned Catholic to please the King, and James, taking his showy conversion at face value, apparently regarded it as a sign of God's handiwork.

It was more likely the Devil's, thought Thomas uneasily. He felt a stir of anxiety for his friend, who, like James, was too straightforward to recognize a liar and too honourable to buy and sell his faith.

"Will you see the King?" Dundee asked.

Thomas said it was more a matter of whether the King would see him. In any case he had no taste for dramatic scenes. He was here, and that ought to be enough.

"And *I* have been called 'high and proud,'" Dundee mused. "Thomas, you will never make lord chief justice."

"Thank God for that."

An aide-de-camp approached their table and Thomas half-rose from his seat, thinking that Churchill was now free to see him. But the message was for Dundee. The King was holding an emergency council of war, and the General was needed at once.

6

"MY FATHER CAN SEE THE MOON."

"Don't be silly, Beatrice," said Piers, without looking up from his book. "Everyone can see the moon."

"I mean he can *see* it. He made a special glass to look at it."

"A telescope," Samuel said gravely. "With two lenses — "

"We know. Even James knows what a telescope is," Piers said. "And James is a halfwit."

"I am not," James said, in a voice thick with cold. "And you'll be sorry you said so, Piers the Pig."

They were in Libby's room, having a picnic on the floor while she corrected Piers' essay on obedience. In the corner Brigid mended Beatrice's petticoat, using the fine, small stitches that Libby had taught her. It had stopped snowing, but rain poured down endlessly from an iron-grey sky and they had been forced to stay inside. There was a deep scowl on Piers' face, and Libby could imagine his rebellious thoughts as clearly as if he had shouted them aloud: he was nine years old, almost ten, and he deserved to be with his father on Salisbury plain, not condemned to the nursery with his brother and cousins. Even Samuel's silent hero-worship was wearing on his patience, and Beatrice had annoyed him by declaring that one day she would marry him and have a new dress for each day of the year.

"It doesn't matter to me what you wear," Piers had said crossly. "I'm not marrying you or anyone. I'm going to live in the woods with my dogs."

The children had tied Thomas' colours to the school

room door, and Samuel had spread out a map on the floor and weighted it down with pebbles — black for the Dutch and white for the King, meticulously placed to show where the infantry and cavalry would be. Larger rocks represented towns. A fleet of paper boats fought in the Channel. Then someone had let Theo into the room and he had crashed through both armies, sending pebbles and paper flying in all directions. "Maybe we ought to make him a General," said Samuel, whose dry observations occasionally made him seem much older than seven.

Libby looked at them all tenderly. If Piers exactly resembled his father, James was like his grandfather — an unregenerate sinner who stole sugar from the kitchen and forgot to say his prayers at bedtime. Samuel — "Socrates" as the others called him — reminded her of a near-sighted little owl. He shared Leopold's fascination with beetles, and Libby suspected that one or two had taken up residence in his shirt. But it was Beatrice, strong-minded and stubborn, who for some reason made Libby's heart ache. This morning she had selected her own wardrobe from what looked like tinkers' cast-offs — a red skirt with the hem unpicked, a green sash, purple plush shawl, and gold earrings. Libby was thankful that Abigail was not here to see it.

"Piers the Pig!" James repeated happily, knowing that he had found a weapon. "Piers the Pig!"

He was deeply flushed and his eyes were bright with fever as well as mischief. His cold had got much worse since he had fallen into the water and Libby was dosing him with liquorice and syrup of violets. He had been allowed out of bed for the afternoon and so far had done nothing except bedevil his brother. Libby put a hand against his burning cheek.

"Do be quiet, James. Piers, you have misspelled *l'amitie*

all the way through this. It's l'-a-m-i-t-i-e. You had better correct it before Master Hammond sees it."

"Halfwit!" James said happily.

Beatrice stood up, clutching her plaid shawl. "I am the Queen," she said, "and you are all my subjects." She picked up a sausage and tapped James on the shoulder. "Sir James. Sir Samuel. I have a ship. You will take it across the ocean and bring me back jewels and spices. And also a camel." She dragged two chairs together. "Here is the ship, and you are the captain, Piers."

"I'll be the captain," James said. "Piers doesn't want to play."

Samuel, ever the peacemaker, brought out some paper. "Piers, will you draw us a map of India?"

Piers, with a great show of reluctance, set aside his book and began to sketch. In a few moments he was absorbed. The four heads bent over the paper. Brigid got to her feet and came to look. "India," she said respectfully. "Now what or who is that?"

"It's a place you find elephants," said Samuel.

Brigid nodded, as if this made sense. Beatrice swung Brigid's hand to make her gilt bracelets jingle. Usually Brigid wore odd bits and pieces of brightly coloured clothing, but today she was swathed in black — black skirt, black scarves, black blouse, and a fringed black shawl. She might have been in mourning, except for her gilt bangles. Half a dozen sparkled on each wrist. A rosary on a chain hung from her skirt pocket and around her neck she wore a cross with a piece of paper that, according to her, contained a powerful charm to keep the Devil away. Her pockets were full of treasures that delighted the children: sweets, beads, hairpins, an elf-stone, dried flowers. In her apron she kept a pair of shredded lace gloves, her only finery. Libby had tried to give her a silk shawl, but she had refused, asking instead for French brandy to soothe her aunt Alys' pain.

Alys, who had found a knot in her breast the size of pebble, was running a fever and could not keep solid food in her stomach. So far Dr. Spencer's prescription of hartshorn and cinnamon had done nothing. Libby, although strictly forbidden to get out of bed, had taken Alys a dish of hot milk spiced with brandy and then had sat with her, holding her hand, while Alys reminisced about her family — in particular her dead sister, Brigid's mother, who had run away with an Irish soldier.

Brigid, born out of wedlock in a mud-walled shanty, had lived in a dozen different places and her faith marked her out in the village as much as her blazing red hair and her tarnished bangles. She was always ready with stories for the village children and she refused to speak harshly of anyone, even the young louts who jeered at her because she was half-Irish. There was an innate dignity about her that triumphed over her strange clothes and her uncertain grammar. She cared for her aunt in the same kindly, practical fashion that she cared for the children, changing the bed linens, emptying the chamber pot, and bringing delicacies to tempt Alys' appetite.

"We shall have you carried upstairs to the room over the herb garden, next to mine," Libby had said. "That way we can look after you much better."

But Alys' small round face had flushed to beetroot at the suggestion. "No, you must never, Madam. You have the children to think on and the new one coming. The doctor will be that angry if he finds you here with me –"

"There is no need to be afraid of Dr. Spencer," Libby said gently. But she knew that Alys was frankly terrified of that learned gentleman and his black bag of instruments and powders. She put more faith in Brigid's peasant remedies than she did in Heneage Spencer's expensive education.

In the matter of her own health Libby usually followed the doctor's instructions, but this time she had rebelled. She discovered that leaving her bed to visit Alys had done her no harm. Rather it was the reverse, and she felt better than she had done in weeks. That same afternoon she had put on her house gown of faded muslin and gone down to the kitchen to ask for bread, thickly buttered, with relish and a collop of beef. She had eaten it all, and drunk a pot of strong tea besides, before summoning the housemaids and the footmen, and ordering a full-scale assault on the house: rugs, floors, windows, beds, linens. The disorder she had seen on her way to the kitchen dismayed her. She wanted every piece of silver polished with chalk and vinegar, all the glassware washed, the woodwork rubbed with beeswax, the floors swept, and the last of the flowers put into vases. She was determined that her husband should not come back to a neglected house, with dust thick on the furniture and the children running wild.

As she toured the rooms she had felt her energies return. This was her domain, and she drew strength from once more being in charge. When she had come here as a bride Thomas had given her a free hand: the Long Gallery, the music room and library, the dining room, the public drawing-room and the small parlour, had been hers to furnish or change as she pleased. But in fact she had changed little. She had her unknown father-in-law to thank for the restorations he had made to the house after Cromwell's time, and the exquisitely coffered ceilings, the new inlaid panelling, and the cream-washed walls somehow harmonized lovingly with the eleventh-century Great Hall and the turreted gatehouse over the moat. She took pleasure in her stewardship of this gracious and beautiful house, enjoying that as she enjoyed all her duties — except, perhaps, that of calling upon the county wives and the Bishop's daughters, listening to their avid gossip while drinking tea and eating crumbling slices of cake.

Perhaps it was fortunate that managing a household of this size left her with few free hours. It was her year-round responsibility to ensure there was enough food, fuel, bed linen, clothing, and medicine for all, that in midwinter they did not run short on candles or salted fish, that the herb and vegetable gardens were turned over, that the servants were cared for when sick and that each attended prayers. She had to stand ready at any moment to welcome one guest or a hundred. And she had had to learn by doing, for her father had not troubled with her domestic education. But she never felt that she had lost by the situation. While Leopold had to spend dull hours closeted with stewards and bailiffs, she had visited the Tower menagerie with her father, drunk chocolate with him in coffee houses, shopped at the newly rebuilt Royal Exchange, listened to open-air concerts on the river, rode on his shoulder through the crowds at Bartholomew Fair. There had been no grandmother or aunt to supervise her, not even a governess until she was twelve, when St. Clare suddenly realized that she was no longer a child. Then, belatedly, she had had to learn how to cook and stitch and supervise a household.

The dogs had pattered behind her as she went from room to room and the children had followed closely, James gripping her skirt with one hand and wiping his nose with the other. Beatrice had run on ahead, wanting to look in every corner and behind each piece of furniture. When they reached Thomas' study, Libby had sent the children ahead and went into the room alone.

He might have left only a few minutes ago. The desk was strewn with papers, and his so-called working vest, a shapeless wool garment knitted years ago by his sister Louisa, hung on the back of the chair. A dish of tea, filmed over with a week's scum, still stood on the desk. A paperweight held down some music sheets and there was an empty tobacco tin on the blotter. A jumble of old letters spilled out of a half-opened drawer. Libby picked up Thomas' vest and held it to her face. It smelled of tobacco and soap and conjured up her husband's comforting presence, his deep abiding warmth, as strongly as if he were in the room. When she put her hands in the pockets she found some change, a small closed knife for mending quills, and numberless scraps of paper with jottings, quotations and reminders: "pay Jno. Somers for window-glazing," "lower meadow drained," and "no tobacco, before God." Pinned to the lining was a quote he had underscored: *non omne licitum honestum.* Not every lawful thing is honourable. His desk drawers were unlocked, and he had left his papers out, for, unlike herself, he had nothing to hide.

But then he was not a woman who had been told, even by her unconventional father, to "keep to her house." She did so, but neither her father nor her husband had plumbed her guilty secret: she corresponded with Aphra Behn, the woman who had scandalized London by staging her plays for money. Aphra had been astonishingly successful and the King had become her patron, but even this was not enough to salvage her personal reputation. A woman was not supposed to aspire to a man's intelligence or be independent enough to make her own living. It was against all nature and undermined the divinely appointed social order. No woman could take on a man's work and still be pure; despite the King's blessing, Aphra was *persona non grata*, Grandmother Eve in modern dress. She was viciously attacked in print, accused of obscenity and sacrilege, but refused to stop writing. In her own fashion she was as much of a bold explorer as Sir Francis Drake or Walter Raleigh. On impulse Libby had written to congratulate her after seeing one of her plays in London, and the correspondence that sprang up between them had continued, off and on, into the present. But Aphra was ill now, some said dying, crippled by an unknown sickness that twisted her limbs and made it difficult to hold a pen. She wrote less and less frequently and there had been nothing at all from her since August. Libby had carefully preserved these letters and in the past few weeks had begun setting down her own thoughts on subjects they had discussed. These musings were innocent enough, being chiefly concerned with women's education, marriage, and health, but some instinct had made her keep them under lock and key, where no eyes but her own could see them. She felt that no one would understand why she felt compelled to write things down or why she wanted some kind of record that would outlast her. A woman's legacy was, of course, her children. But sons and daughters, if they lived, grew up and moved away. The daily cycle of household chores and duties left nothing behind; meals were eaten, beds were made, fires lit, dishes washed, linen mended, and then it all began again as if nothing had occurred — work that was as necessary and invisible as air. In this household it meant she was never idle, and yet it was not enough. It was possible that Grace might understand, but Libby would not confide to her sister-in-law anything that she felt necessary to keep from Thomas. And, as it turned out, Grace had her own secrets.

In Libby's skirt pocket was a letter that had arrived, water-stained and torn, after being delayed ten days upon the road. Grace wrote that she had been on the point of setting out when several of the children at her school had fallen ill. Jacob, who would have been a physician had the law permitted him to continue his studies, at first had suspected smallpox. "I dared not risk bringing it to you," Grace wrote, "and I dared not abandon these children, who have no one to care for them. Thanks be to God, it is not what we feared. But I have found that I am with child myself, and for both our sakes I will not hazard a visit." And she signed herself, for the first time, in Quaker fashion, "thy friend in God."

Libby had sat for a long while with the letter in her lap, as stunned as if Grace had announced her intention of setting up a bawdy house. When she had defended her sister-in-law's choice of suitor she had never imagined anything beyond a decorous courtship, appropriate to Grace's status as a widow. But now Grace was pregnant — at forty-two — and there was no mention of marriage in her letter.

She felt she must bear part of the blame for this ill-considered union. She had encouraged Grace and defended her right to a private life without looking into Jacob's character or background. What did they know of him, after all, except that he was a Quaker who worked in the printing house because he could not study medicine? It was only Henry Hill's charity that had given him employment in the first place. Would they marry and live in Grace's school, or would she move into Jacob's single room over the shop? Would she defy her family and the rest of the world by raising her child alone?

She had been carrying this letter around like a millstone now for several days, unable to think of a suitable reply. This morning while the children picnicked on the floor and drew their map she had been trying to compose a response, but after an hour she had progressed no further than "Dearest sister, I am amazed." She thought with dread of what awaited Grace, who was facing the perils of childbirth at an age when most women were already grandmothers. When girls of fourteen were considered fully marriageable, a woman in her thirties was middle-aged; in her forties she was old; by sixty, dead.

"You've made India too small," said Beatrice to Piers. "It has to be bigger, for the elephants."

"You don't know. You've never been there."

"I want to go there," said Samuel. "In my own ship."

Beatrice jumped up. Her fair hair, which Libby had plaited that morning, had come undone and hung around her small face in feathery, dishevelled wisps. Her eyes, like Leopold's, were round and shiny as blackberries. "I'll come with you. I'll steer your ship."

Samuel looked at her kindly. "By that time you'll have a husband, and you won't be able to go."

"I shall do anything I please," said Beatrice, and she turned a cartwheel, so that her skirts and petticoats fell around her ears. "P'raps I'll have my own ship, a pirate ship, and I'll sink yours."

The boys laughed. "Never mind," said Libby to Beatrice, "perhaps you will."

She remembered that at Beatrice's age she, too, had wanted to be a pirate. She had copied her father's maps, sketching on them an outline of her proposed routes, and St. Clare, not smiling even though she had drawn a nonexistent river straight through Turkey to Africa, had shown her on his globe where her ship would sail. Her father's hand, with its square gold ring on the thumb, had travelled confidently, pointing out the continents, the oceans, and the vast tracts labelled *terra incognita*. He explained that these were lands yet to be mapped, countries which might be full of painted savages or wild beasts, or perhaps were uninhabited, innocent paradises still, like the Garden before the Fall. Persia, Turkey, India, China — she was fascinated by those exotic lands whose very names sounded rich and foreign. Occasionally her father had brought down from its glass case one of his most precious books, Walter Raleigh's *History of the World*, and they would read it together.

In many ways she felt that her father was like Raleigh, personable, extravagant, enmeshed in one drama after another; deeply flawed, and yet somehow splendid even in his faults. Her mother had died when Libby was five and she could scarcely remember her, could not imagine the kind of woman she must have been to live equably with such a man. He was a tender but overbearing father, and she had learned early to stand her ground — a lesson that Leopold had never mastered. Her brother was married with two children and a third on the way, yet he would not speak in his father's presence without permission and he knelt to St. Clare in parting, customs that were dying out even in the most old-fashioned of households. But Libby had never given — or perhaps it was that St. Clare had never exacted from her — such exaggerated signs of deference. She was not the heir to all her father's wealth and honours, and St. Clare had not the same need to mould her to his liking. Rather she had been his comrade, his pet, proof of his modern theory that a classical education benefited everyone. It had been his custom to gather around his table the most important and interesting men from all walks of life, and Libby, as a child, had made an entrance with the sweets, as if she were a sort of confection herself. She would answer one or two questions in Latin or Greek, and then sit in the crook of her father's arm and take a sip of wine from his goblet, or a sweetmeat from his plate, while he recited her list of accomplishments: she had been reading by age three, had written a play, sang most sweetly, played the viol and flute as well as the virginals, took lessons in French, Italian, and mathematics. Inevitably he would unfurl from his pocket the crooked sampler she had stitched, showing it round the table as if it had been the Bayeux tapestry.

She had not paid much attention to his speeches, occupying herself instead with marshalling tart crumbs in a pyramid on the plate or tapping at the goblet with her fork to make the glass ring. The conversation at the table rushed over her head like so much wind and often she had fallen asleep on her father's shoulder, cherished in those protective arms. It had been a happy girlhood, so adventurous and untrammelled that she sometimes forgot what her destiny must be, that one day she must leave her home and link her fate with that of a stranger. But her father had shown himself a man of the new age there as well. She had been allowed to choose.

James had tired of India. He complained that he was thirsty. Libby put her papers away and stood, holding a hand to her back. Grace's letter rustled in her pocket, freighting her with guilt. *Dearest sister, I am amazed.* "Come with me, then, Jamie. Brigid will get you some almond milk and bring it to you in bed. Piers, bring me your composition when you've finished."

"I don't want to go to bed," said James, but he grasped his mother's hand and walked with her down the long panelled corridor to the room he shared with Piers. The ceiling was blue and gold, painted with clouds and cherubs and garlands. James liked to hang upside down from his bed and study the cherubs' pink faces. Brigid said that this was what heaven must be like, although it would be warm in heaven and angels would not have splodges of mildew on their wings.

"When Dr. Spencer comes to see Uncle Leopold, he

shall look at you too," said Libby. She tucked James into bed and then had to sit down for a moment to catch her breath. A silly rhyme jangled in her head.

I know my love by his way of walking
And I know my love by his way of talking
And I know my love by his eyes of blue,
And if my love leaves me, what shall I do?

But she already knew what she would do. She would manage alone, as her mother, grandmother, and generations of women before them had done when war disrupted their lives. During Cromwell's rule her mother had led the household in St. Clare's absence, looking after his property and business interests so well that she managed to conceal a fortune under the stone floor of the family mausoleum. "She was determined," St. Clare had said proudly, "that neither King nor parliament should beggar us." In retrospect it seemed an odd thing to do or say for a family that proclaimed its royalist ties, but there was no doubt that St. Clare owed his fortune's preservation to his wife.

Libby kissed James' hot cheek and began to wonder if she should send for Dr. Spencer sooner rather than later. She regretted Grace's absence and for the first time felt uneasy about disobeying the doctor's instructions. But what else could she do, with a houseful of children and invalids to care for? She resolved to send for one of the village women whom she knew to be kind and sensible, someone who could help with the children. Brigid had her hands full with Alys, and no one was looking after Leopold.

Not that her poor brother was a difficult patient. He lay uncomplaining in bed with his leg splinted and encased in a plaster of flour and egg, and drank ale infused with comfrey to speed the healing. He was supposed to be on an invalid's diet of milk sops and broth, but apparently he, too, had rebelled against medical advice. When Libby looked in on him after leaving James, she saw that he had fallen asleep with the crust of a treacle bun in his hand. There were incriminating crumbs of beef on his nightshirt and he had left a glass of wine on the edge of the nightstand. Libby, moving softly, took the glass away and smoothed the coverlid. Leopold slept on, undisturbed.

In repose he resembled their father. His face had the same look of stern nobility, the same high-nosed grandeur, like that of a Roman emperor. But when he was awake the resemblance vanished. Leopold's dignity was unforced and his kindly nature and sweet temper showed too much in his eyes, those large, dark, beautiful eyes that he had presently covered with a handkerchief in order to sleep. He had removed his wig, which he had set on the knob of his crutch, and his injured leg was propped up on a bolster. The counterpane around him was piled with books and papers. He had been continuing to work while he was in bed, finishing an essay on optics and discoursing with Master Hammond on the variety and nature of beetles. He had tried to help with the children by reading to them and making paper boats — that fleet which had just been scattered over the nursery floor. He was cheerful and patient with his suffering, asking for nothing except books to read. Libby knew that his chief trouble was not pain from his broken leg, but the humiliation of his forced withdrawal from Thomas' company. He blamed himself for the wreck of the baggage train, for the fact that Lee had had to return instead of pressing on to Salisbury. Libby understood that he had wanted to see himself as a man of action, a bold adventurer, and that perhaps it had something to do with

Abigail. Her sister-in-law was a plain, sensible woman, but to Leopold she was all beauty and mystery, Guinevere to his Lancelot. Perhaps he had seen himself carrying her colours into battle, winning glory in her name. Instead he was making paper boats. The irony was that Abigail, had she been given a choice, would have much preferred it this way.

Libby tried to imagine where Thomas might be at this moment, somewhere out on Salisbury plain in the windy cold and the mud. There had been no word yet of a battle or even that the King had arrived to take charge. News crawled with maddening slowness along the winter roads even in peacetime, and for the past two weeks the postal service had broken down and the mails were no longer trustworthy.

She blew out a candle that had been left burning on the dressing table, and closed the door. Out in the hall she met Fulke. It was rare, almost unheard-of, for him to venture upstairs; her meetings with him occurred in the library or the parlour, where they discussed household accounts and she gave him her letters, and he enquired gravely, pink with embarrassment, after her health.

"There are...visitors, my lady. Under the circumstances, I thought it best to inform you myself."

"Visitors! In this weather? Who is it?"

The look on Fulke's face silenced her and she felt the small cold contraction of her skin into gooseflesh. Her heart began to beat painfully. "Who is it?" she repeated.

In Fulke's eyes there was a look she had never seen before, an agony of shame and loathing, and in the instant before he spoke, she knew.

"Madam, Lord St. Clare has brought a troop to garrison the house for Prince William."

7

WELL BEFORE DAWN, the trumpets sounded. Thomas was already boiling the kettle for breakfast. He flung on his greatcoat and went down to the cold, wet inn yard. The street beyond was thronged with a mass of soldiers on horseback and on foot. But this was not the disciplined chaos of moving out. There was something incomprehensible going on. Many of the men were weeping. The road looked as though a baggage train had overturned, with bedrolls, trunks, packs, discarded clothing, and cook-pots littering the ground. No one seemed to be in charge.

A horse and scarlet-jacketed rider thundered into the yard, throwing up clods of mud. The rider flung himself off his steaming mount, and Thomas recognized Captain Creighton, Dundee's orderly. His coat was fastened awry and his face was grey, unshaven, his eyes running with water from the wind.

"What is it?" Thomas demanded. "What's happened?"

"Christ, sir! Have you not heard? General Churchill has deserted. Lord Douglas too, with four hundred cavalry. And Lord Drumlanrig — Lord Annandale — all the Scottish command except Lord Dundee. Kirke's entire division has gone. Even the King's Life Guard has deserted. Lord Dundee sent me to ask you if you would ride with our brigade."

Thomas looked at him as if he were speaking a foreign language. "I swear it's true, sir," Creighton said. "All of them are gone. We have orders to fall back on Reading." He fumbled in his pocket. "Churchill left behind a letter of explanation — he must have written it after the council last night. Here is a copy of it, sir, which my lord bid me bring you — "

But Thomas thrust the paper aside and walked away, leaving Creighton still talking. The shock was so enormous it seemed to stop his blood. John Churchill a traitor! No one had been longer in James' service or deeper in his confidence. The King had given him free access to his most personal papers, his confidential letters and private memoranda, even his diary. There was no information, either public or personal, to which Churchill was not privy. He knew the location, strength, and armament of every royalist troop and garrison, the failings of their commanders, the state of their finances; he was aware of every doubt and concern of Feversham's, every flaw in the battle plan.

His betrayal must have been weeks, even months, in the planning, co-ordinated with those uprisings in the north and southwest, and with Kirke's shameful plot. When Churchill had pretended to investigate that, he had been talking to his fellow-conspirators. His preparations, the councils of war, the furious march out to Salisbury, all had been sham; he had come to the battlefield and then deserted at the most critical moment, ripping the guts out of the army he had been appointed to lead. The results were all around: men cursing, crying, stumbling with their baggage out into the road, looking for their companies and their officers, asking for orders.

Orders. Creighton had said they were to fall back on Reading. Lord Feversham ought to know that being crowded up against the Thames was not a good defensive position. But Feversham was useless, a soft man who had given up all responsibility to Churchill, and now had to pay the price.

The King's feelings at this moment did not bear thinking of. Whatever his sins or errors, he had done nothing to deserve this cruel abandonment in the face of the enemy. He had been betrayed by those who should have been the first to defend him: his friends, his family, his own Life Guard, his Lieutenant-General, and — with the exception of John Graham — his entire Scottish command. Thomas, overwhelmed, forgot that he had come here only from the most dour sense of obligation. He sent Captain Creighton back with the message that he would join Dundee's brigade. Then he went inside to deliver the news to Lee.

As daylight broke they were riding northeast. The road was clogged with soldiers, wagons, dogs, horses, pack mules, and discarded baggage; tents, hastily struck, had been thrown aside with unwanted regimental flags and banners. The retreat was a rout. Hundreds of men had deserted in the first hours of the march. Regiments broke ranks; officers abandoned their men; companies and divisions were hopelessly intermingled. Then it began to rain, and men and beasts reeled along in ice and mud up to their shins. The only point of order in the chaos and the only unit left intact was Dundee's brigade.

Thomas was in the saddle all day, fighting his way through the melee, keeping his troop together as if his life depended on it. Lee, God bless him, showed what he was made of, a man of unimpeachable honour, a man of duty, his calm, solid presence a comfort. But the pallor of his face revealed the cost of his effort. Somewhere along the road he lost his hat, his precious relic of the civil war, and he was soaked through his layers of wool and leather, so chilled that he could not dismount without help.

At nightfall the army halted at Andover. The King, after

dining privately with his son-in-law Prince George and the Duke of Ormond, retired early to bed. The public houses and inns overflowed; those who could not find a bed bivouacked out in the street. Thomas' company spent the night in the cellar of a church. Lee had a bed — Thomas had insisted upon it — and went to sleep, still in his wet clothes, immediately after their cold supper. The rest of them slept on the floor.

The musty stone vault was ice cold and their single lantern did nothing to warm it. There were crates and pieces of lumber stacked against the walls and a jumble of oddments that looked as if they had been culled from the parish workhouse: picks, shovels, broken furniture, a set of dishes. In one corner stood a chipped marble angel that once must have guarded some monument or crypt. The pure, sightless face, missing a nose, looked serenely into the void. Dust covered the folded wings. Mice droppings littered the base. The flicker of lantern-light made it seem, unpleasantly, that one of the marble arms was moving.

Thomas shut his eyes and tried to sleep. But the chilly gloom of the place oppressed him and his mind would not let go of the day's disaster. Churchill would have spent his time today talking to William and Schomberg, laying out for them the exact extent and disposition of the King's defences and whatever strategies Feversham had proposed. And General Douglas would be there as well, letting the Dutch know that the north had been left wide open, sealing with treason that unholy alliance between Scotland and the Dutch Provinces. It was an open secret, after all, that the Covenanters' illegal weapons had come from The Hague. James had not believed it, had said that his "dear nephew" would not serve him so underhanded a turn as to give arms to the people who had helped murder his father... just as he would never have believed, until this morning, that John Churchill was not his most loyal subject and friend. Churchill, the "trusty and well-beloved." Better had he died, Thomas thought. At least then his memory would have been clean, and his friends would be grieving only for his body instead of his soul. Whatever success or glory might come to him in the future, the dirt of this betrayal would stick to him all the rest of his days. And why had he done it? The reasons he had given in his letter — the contents had made the rounds — were as unconvincing as William's own. Personal conscience. Sanctity of the Protestant church. Yet somehow it had not offended Churchill's sensitive conscience to desert his sovereign on the battlefield.

What had William promised him in return? Entitlements and property, the chief command of his armies under General Schomberg? With a new motto: *chacun pour soi*. Each man for himself.

Thomas desperately wanted to stop thinking of it. But his mind drove on, unwillingly yet inescapably, to St. Clare. There was a high likelihood that he was safe from prosecution now that so many others had joined him — now that entire cities stood in opposition to the Crown and the King's army was in full flight. The danger of being bottled up in the Thames valley, with the Dutch to the north and west, seemed so clear that it looked as though the King had deliberately flung himself in front of the enemy's guns. God forgive the thought, but perhaps he was not entirely sane, not well either in mind or body, after what he had endured. And Feversham was not the man to take charge of the wreckage.

The trooper snoring next to him kicked suddenly and his boot made painful contact with Thomas' shin. All around him were furtive rustlings and scratchings. The darkness, gritty and thick, was so palpable that he could smell and taste it. In his mind he saw a map of the country between Exeter, Reading, and London. Oxford was vulnerable now that the royal army was falling back, and Charters was a scant handful of miles to the south, directly in the path of the stumbling troops.

He would send Lee home, with whomsoever wished to leave. The old man would doubtless object. But another few days of rain and cold would either ruin his lungs or kill him outright. And Lee's presence at Charters would mean some protection for Thomas' household.

On that thought he went to sleep.

Not far away, after taking a heavy dose of laudanum, the King also slept. When he rose for breakfast he was greeted with the news that his other son-in-law, Prince George, had ridden off to Exeter with his friend the Duke of Ormond. Sometime during the night the two had stolen away, leaving behind their carriages and dogs and their personal belongings.

Prince George had greeted each fresh disaster with a languid, "*Est-il possible?* " Beyond that he had not shown much interest in his father-in-law's troubles, but had seemed to enjoy the ride to Salisbury as a diversion from his usual stolid routine. James, crumbling a roll between his fingers, said nothing for a few moments after he was informed of George's departure. A single spasm convulsed his face. Then, like an actor, he adjusted his mask. "So," he said. "*Est-il possible?* has gone too. Well, the loss of a good trooper would have been greater." He resumed eating. But the bread seemed to stick in his throat, for he began to cough. His nose streamed blood. Someone thrust a clean handkerchief in his hand. When he rose, he stumbled against his chair.

"Sir –"

"Your Majesty — "

He looked at them, at their frightened faces and their mouths gaping and shutting. Their words were like a senseless roaring in his ears. He mopped his sweating face with his handkerchief. With extreme effort he spoke. It sounded as if his tongue had been hacked off at the root. "Dundee," he said. "AilesburyMelfort...de Chastelain...London."

He let them make what they could of that and left the room. Out in the damp air he felt better. He signalled for his horse and managed to put his foot in the stirrup. An enormous weariness had settled over him, body and soul. There seemed to be a cold dark void behind his eyes. He forgot that he had sent his army to Reading, forgot that Feversham and his staff were in the parlour waiting for his orders. There was only one thought in his mind and that was to go home. He longed for the comfort and company of his wife and son and his poor daughter. Anne would be in need of consolation herself, when she found out what her fool of a husband had done.

He saw Lord Feversham and his staff officers at the door, recognized their appalled bewildered faces and their frantic gestures, but could not make out what they were saying. The roaring in his head resumed. He was thirteen instead of fifty-five, and it was Cromwell and not William who wanted to kill him. It was his duty to escape his jailers.

He kicked his horse to a trot.

Lord Feversham's beribboned aide-de-camp found Thomas in the vicarage parlour with Lee and told him that he was required to follow the King to London. Or at least that was the construction Feversham had chosen to put on the King's unintelligible last speech. A few moments after the aide-de-camp left, Captain Creighton arrived to inform Thomas that Dundee was taking his cavalry to Watford before riding on to London.

The Stand to Horse was trumpeting up and down the high street and Thomas had no time for tact. He told Lee that he wanted him to return to Oxford.

"No. Send the others back, if they'll go. I stay." Lee had to speak in a hoarse whisper because his voice had gone. His eyes were black-rimmed with fatigue and underneath the unfashionable beard his skin was the colour of dirty linen. But he refused to acknowledge either his tiredness or his worsening chest, even when he coughed blood into his dish of tea.

"You're sick. You need a physician. I've sent a note to Dr. Radcliffe."

"Then you have wasted your time." Lee stood, and began drawing on his mud-encrusted gloves.

"Be reasonable. There's a carriage arranged for you — "

"A *carriage*." Had Thomas said "a grave," Lee could not have sounded more astonished. He buckled on his sword belt. Despite his unshaven face and dirty uncombed hair, his dignity was formidable. "Don't presume."

Thomas sat down on the chair that Lee had just vacated, and put his hat on the table. His respect for Lee was such that he would not remind him who was in charge. "You would do me a very great service if you would see to my family," he said. "I told Elizabeth I would be gone ten days or a fortnight, and now that I am for London with Dundee — you know that her health is not good — "

"No," said Lee. "No, by God! That's unfair."

"Unfair or not, it's the truth. I'm for London and you can do me a service by taking the troop back home."

"The King's last order was to fall back on Reading," said Lee. "And that's where I'm going."

Thomas looked at the bristly, sunken face and knew that this was all wrong. But Lee was speaking the truth: the king's order, however impractical, still stood, and he could not be faulted for obeying it. Until given James' personal instructions otherwise, Lee would keep the troop together even though there was no reason for it. Stubborn, Thomas said to himself. Stubborn and prideful. The old man would take on the entire Dutch army by himself if he had the opportunity.

In silence Thomas took off his hat. Crushed, battered, and filthy with mud, it looked more like a bird's nest than a gentleman's hat. But at least it would give some protection from the rain. "You had better take this, then," he said, "since you lost your own yesterday. I have another one, although not quite so fine."

He brushed some dirt from the brim and handed it to Lee as if transferring the Standard. Then he took a small jar out of his pocket and put it on the table. "My wife's physic," he said. "Mix it in a little hot wine at breakfast and supper. And she would tell you to put henbane leaves on your eyes once a day." Then, after a moment he said, as if Lee had asked, "I doubt there will be a battle now. Not with Feversham in command. The King will negotiate. I think that's why he sent for me." Lee frowned and rubbed a hand across his face, leaving streaks of mud from his glove. "You can't negotiate with criminals."

"I thought you said these are God-fearing patriots, thinking to save the country."

"Well," said Lee, "that was before Churchill."

The mention of the name left behind a small cold silence. Thomas knew there was nothing more to be said about Churchill, or any of the others for that matter, including St. Clare.

The Stand to Horse blasted out once again. There was no more time. Thomas scraped back his chair, saying, "When Martin held prayers this morning, I found myself thinking that in Exeter, or wherever they are by now, the Dutch chaplains were likely reading the same chapter and verse. I almost told Martin to save himself the trouble." He could not look at Lee. "I wish you would pray for me."

He had never asked such a thing of anyone before, not even Libby. He could feel Lee looking at him with those black, inflamed eyes, and presently the old man said, as if this were nothing out of the way, "I have always done so."

The vicar's clock chimed the hour. Lee tied his crumpled sash and drank down the rest of his tea. "We survived Oliver Cromwell," he said, "and we shall survive this too. Putting your name on a petition for William is a different matter than offering him the Crown. What's needed is some common sense." He put Libby's tonic in his shirt pocket and patted Thomas on the shoulder. "Be easy about your family," he said. "They are out of harm's way. But someone will ride over to see. It's not far from Reading, after all. If you have a letter ready, give it to me now."

There was a world of kindness in his voice. He fastened his cuirass over his doublet and placed the hat on his white hair, tugging the crushed brim into shape. Thomas could not help smiling, although his spirits were so low. "For God's sake be careful," he said. "Don't put a Dutch bullet through that valuable hat."

"It's the Irish bullets I fear, my son. Those boys are looking for a fight and it doesn't matter to them who they're shooting at — English or Dutch, it's all the same to them."

Thomas had no letter prepared, but he scrawled a note

to Libby and gave it to Lee before letting himself out. Magnus waited for him by the lych-gate, shivering so miserably in the rain that even his ears looked mournful. "Come on, you old fool," said Thomas, scratching the wet draggled fur. "You don't mind a little water."

The high street and surrounding lanes were choked with soldiers, mud-covered, weary, who sat on the cobbles or the verges picking over their belongings or drinking coffee, ignoring the Stand to Horse because there was no one left to enforce it. The King's mad flight had been the final blow to the ailing army and now it was moribund, officerless and flagless. Thomas, pushing his way toward Dundee's billet, knew that if he had a choice he would be going with Lee to stand with whatever remnant of the army made it to Reading. He felt, unreasonably, that he too was a deserter, abandoning his friends to follow an order he was not even sure the king had given. He felt he had not done enough or had not done the right thing. But the entire army faced the same fate: it had been raised and outfitted and brought to Salisbury at enormous cost and effort, and now the king had forsaken it. There was something faintly ludicrous about James sending thousands of men out into the field and marching them straight back again without a single shot being fired — not counting the Irish skirmish, and of course no one ever counted the Irish.

But that was James. His tragedies were on a grand scale and yet there was always an element of farce present. In the three years since his coronation, he had done more to wreck his own reputation than all his enemies combined. And, unlike his brother Charles, he had no personal charm to smooth his way. It was for good reason that his nickname at Court had been "Dismal Jimmy." Few saw beneath the haughty crust to the interior man; fewer still loved him as his brother and father had been loved.

But the King's folly or his lack of social grace did not make him any less rightfully the King. Under the law he possessed something which William did not and would never have while either James or his son lived: the legitimate, God-given entitlement to the throne. James was King by undisputed right of birth and his sovereignty had been consecrated before God and man. No circumstance could alter that fact, even if he went mad and put the Crown on William's head himself.

Lies, treason, broken faith; William would have to climb over a mountain of deceit to reach the throne. And always in the back of his mind would be the knowledge that men who could betray their sovereign once would not scruple to do so again. He would never trust those who had put him in power. Instead he would give his own Dutch friends all the key posts and reward them with the confiscated fortunes of Englishmen who refused him allegiance.

Be easy, Lee had said. Instead Thomas felt a sense of apprehension so acute it was like a fist under his ribs. He remembered how William had turned a blind eye to the murders of Cornelius and Jan de Witt, his tutor and grand pensionary respectively, who years ago had become the scapegoats for Holland's defeat in the French wars. A mob had butchered the de Witt brothers and sold off their bloody eyes and toes as souvenirs. William, far from punishing the ringleaders, had rewarded them with plum Court posts. The de Witts had opposed his control of the army and without them he was undisputed Captain-General, in a much better position to fight the French. Anyone who could stomach that would not scruple to kill an old man and a baby who stood in the way of the English throne.

But William was not in Whitehall yet. And Lee was right. Most Englishmen, lords or commons, would choke on offering him the Crown. It was only fourteen years since England's last war with Holland. A Dutchman was as much of a foreigner here as the Emperor of China, and in that lay the greatest possibility of reversing the flood in James' favour.

Dundee was almost the only officer of field rank left, and his brigade represented all that was left of the Scottish army. Still he carried on with his usual routines, as he would even if he were down to a single man and one horse. Thomas found him in the ale room of the Swan tavern, fastening the clasps of his buff coat with one hand and scrawling a letter with the other, using the seat of a bar stool as a writing table. The trumpets still blared. The soldiers of Dundee's own regiment, the King's Own, were mustering in the courtyard and there was the aroma of fried bread and coffee in the air, along with the usual tavern smells of warm ale and sawdust. Thomas saw Captain Creighton, who offered him a mug of coffee and then left him with the General.

Dundee looked tired and edgy. But, thank God, he wasted no time talking about Prince George or anyone else. He would not speculate or regret or discuss.

"You've had Lord Feversham's instructions?"

"I have."

"Wait a moment."

Dundee finished his letter and shoved it into his breast pocket without waiting for the ink to dry. His expression was so black that the Covenanters' names for him — "Devil" and "Bloody Clavers" — no longer seemed ridiculous. "He and Livingstone are talking about disbanding the army," he said. For a moment his anger surfaced and he struck the chair with his fist. "And I thought *Douglas* was a fool!"

Disband the army that had never fought. Let the men go armed but unpaid, let the Irish loose on the English and the Scots, allow William to ride into London at his leisure... it was beyond belief. On the other hand, Thomas found that nothing had the power to shock him anymore. He rubbed his eyes, feeling the tiredness in them like ground glass. Without thinking he said, "John, you ought to take command." As soon as the words were out, he knew that he was right. It was the only sensible alternative.

But Dundee flushed deeply, as if his most private, shameful thought or hidden vice had been exposed to public view. "No," he said. "My God! No."

"If you relieved Feversham, you could save this army."

"Out of the question."

He sounded angry out of all proportion. Thomas understood then that this was what his friend burned to do, but could not. He would not appoint himself Commander-in-Chief, even to rescue his country from disaster, because he did not have James' warrant to do so. He would do nothing, ever, without the King's writ. He imposed upon himself the same inflexible obedience to the rules that he exacted from his men, and nothing in his life was done out of turn or against regulations.

Thomas wondered why this iron devotion to discipline — an admirable quality which should have commanded his respect — filled him, instead, with something akin to pity.

8

UNRULY CROWDS JAMMED the streets around Whitehall. Princess Anne and her friend, Sarah Churchill, the General's wife, were missing, and the Queen had been accused of throwing them out of the palace. For her own safety, Mary Beatrice could not show her face in public. When she was not seen at dinner or in chapel the day after the King's return, it was reported that he had sent her to France with the Prince of Wales. That brought the mobs out in force. Confirmation of the Queen's departure, details of her escape, were printed up on news sheets that were torn from hand to hand, the ink still wet on the pages. The rumours, like the crowd, grew wilder each hour. Mary Beatrice had murdered both Princess Anne and Sarah Churchill; King Louis was sending over an army; the Pope was coming to take charge.

Then Anne and Sarah were seen in the Dutch camp, safe in the company of the bishop of London. On receipt of this news the King took to his bed, blood gushing from his nose in an unstoppable flood. He ordered the army at Reading to disband and recalled Lord Feversham. The machinery of Court and government ground to a halt so abruptly that some of the privy councillors fled without troubling to pack.

Terror of unpaid and disbanded Irish troops drove the Lord Mayor to allow a parish-by-parish search for Catholics and the confiscation of their weapons. The streets from Shoreditch to Westminster were thronged with drunken, screaming, bloodied crowds who broke down doors and smashed windows to get inside the homes and shops of suspected Catholics. They carried booty plundered from the chapels and houses of the rich, eating and drinking as they roamed from house to house, dressed grotesquely in stolen clothes. Lord Craven, commander of the Household Guard, wheeled out three cannons to protect Whitehall and set up barricades to keep the mobs from storming the King's own chambers. But the Court he sought to protect was a husk. Most prominent Catholics had gone, along with the chief officers of the government and the King's personal household. The great jumble that was Whitehall — streets, houses, gardens, stalls, shops, stables, barracks, the two-thousand-room palace — was like a plague-stricken city from which all the inhabitants had fled. When Thomas landed at the dark river stairs, he could not even find a linkboy with a torch to escort him to the Stone Gallery.

Lord Middleton, the Secretary of State, was acting as groom of the bedchamber and it was he who walked Thomas down the Gallery. Under ordinary circumstances it was open to the public and crowded with petitioners and place-seekers. Now it was deserted, and their footsteps rang in the silence. Lord Middleton, whom Thomas had a great regard for — he was a sensible and humane man, unalterably loyal — lowered his voice although there was not even a dog nearby to overhear. The King, he said, had been in a grievous state after learning of Anne's betrayal. He had received no answer to his request for a meeting with William, and he looked on his nephew's silence as a threat as well as a snub. No one knew what the Prince intended. This week he had published a third Declaration, containing such rants against Catholics that it seemed James' life might be in as much danger as his throne. With only the Declaration to go by, there was no reason to believe that William wanted to negotiate.

"I dread that His Majesty means to follow the Queen to Paris," said Middleton. "I have heard his page say that he has orders to attend the King at one this morning and have a lantern ready. I have talked to His Majesty — Lord Ailesbury has talked to him, and Lord Dundee as well, I believe, but he admits nothing. If there is any possibility he will be candid with you, my lord, then, in the name of God, you must try to dissuade him from so disastrous a course."

Thomas, who had taken off his hat as they approached the King's apartments, rested it against his chest and looked into Middleton's kind and anguished eyes. "Sir, you know the situation I am in. I have not been at Court these six months or more, and have had no word, in public or private, with the King. If he will not confide in you or Lord Ailesbury or his own Major-General, he will certainly say nothing to me."

"Then God have mercy on us all," said Middleton.

He threw open the door to the King's bedchamber. Most of the candles had been doused, plunging the room into deep shadow. A brazier filled with herbs burned in the corner. The drapes were closed. The green velvet bed hangings were open, but it was so dark that at first Thomas could discern nothing. Then he saw the King.

James lay propped against a bolster and his stained linen shirt had rucked up under his chin. He had put off his wig and patches of white scalp showed through the bristles on his close-shaven head. He breathed stertorously, as if through a bubble of blood. A slop basin rested on the sheet beside him. With his right hand he held a wad of soiled linen to his nose and with his left he fingered the beads of his rosary. He might have been seventy instead of fifty-five, and the look in his eyes was dreadful.

Thomas approached the bed and went down on one knee, keeping his eyes on the rug under his boot. The room smelled of blood and slops and boiled milk, like the sickroom of a child. For once he was thankful for the convention that one must not speak until spoken to. He had been prepared for almost anything except this. He flinched from the desolation in those sunken eyes.

A ringed hand extended from the gloomy interior of the bed. Thomas kissed the dry cold skin and waited.

"My lord."

"Sir."

"You rode in with Lord Dundee."

"Yes, sir."

"Why are you not in Exeter with all the rest?"

"Sir," said Thomas, "you sent for me."

James made a noise, something between a snort and a cough. "You have ignored my orders before."

Thomas forced himself to look up. "Sir, believe me when I say that I am Your Majesty's most obedient servant and loyal subject."

For a moment there was renewed vigour in that death's-head face. "Loyal — yes. Obedient — another matter entirely. Don't think that I have forgotten the bishops."

No, James would never forget the bishops. He treasured his grudges as other men cherished gold. On Judgment Day, thought Thomas, he would say, "Don't think that I've forgotten the bishops."

"Yet," said the king after a pause, "you are here."

"Yes, Your Majesty."

There was a raw silence. Thomas could almost see the workings of James' mind. A month ago anyone who opposed him was, *ipso facto*, disloyal. He had his friends and his enemies categorized, and there was no middle ground, no compromise. Now all his cherished certitudes had been destroyed. At the same time that his closest personal friends and his own family had betrayed him, he was mining unexpected sources of loyalty. The world had been turned upside down. James blew his nose, leaving streaks of blood on his chin. His harsh breathing seemed loud enough to be heard out in the corridor. "My daughter has left me," he said. "My son-in-law as well. Most of my generals. And Churchill — " he stopped. Churchill's treason was a wound that went straight to the bone, a betrayal even deeper than Anne's flight into the arms of the enemy. James was a fond parent, but even he could recognize that his daughter was an exceptionally silly woman, besotted with her brandy and her sweets and her domineering friend, Sarah Churchill. Whether she ran to Exeter or stayed in Whitehall with her lapdogs did not matter, except to James as a father. But Churchill mattered. St. Clare mattered. So did General Douglas, and the Bishop of London, and the Governor of Bristol.

The King, without finishing what he had been going to say, asked for water. Thomas got to his feet and poured water from a pitcher into a cup and held it for James to drink.

"I had to send Lord Melfort and Lord Powys away for their own safety," said the King. "Think of it: my Secretary and my Attorney-General were not safe in their own houses. But you've seen that mob out there. Last night, I'm told, they tried to kill the Spanish ambassador."

He paused to blow his nose again on a dirty handkerchief. He sounded tired but perfectly in command of his faculties. Whatever had broken in him at Salisbury, he was neither senile nor insane, as his enemies were claiming. He was silent a moment or two and then said, "Lord Dundee has written to me often on your behalf. Did you know?"

"No, sir, I did not." This was an unexpected humiliation,

since Thomas had refused to excuse himself or ask pardon for doing what he believed was right.

"He told me he would guarantee your loyalty with his life."

"I would sooner guarantee it with my own, sir," Thomas said shortly. James actually laughed, a dry, grim little sound that turned into a cough and set his nose bleeding again. He held his cloth to his face and said, "Some things and some men do not change. Praise God, my lord, you are one of them."

Coming from the King, this was a mighty olive branch. "I saw you at the Great Meeting," James resumed after a moment. "What did you think of Clarendon?"

On his return from Salisbury the king had summoned the temporal and spiritual peers of the realm for a so-called Great Meeting, chaired by the Archbishop of Canterbury, in order to decide what to do. During the course of it, Lord Clarendon, his brother-in-law from his first marriage, had delivered an extraordinary tirade, in effect calling the King a coward and a slave to Rome. Even Wharton had never gone so far. Had Clarendon been mad or drunk, he could not have behaved worse. Yet he had never before shown hostility or disrespect to his brother-in-law: he had the same kind of bred-in-the-bone royalist principles as Lee. It was baffling and disheartening.

"If that is an example of what you can expect from him, sir," Thomas said finally, "I would confine him to Bedlam."

"He blames me for sending the Queen and my son to France. I don't know what else he thought I would do — wait until the crowd tore them to pieces? Give them to the Dutch as hostages? He must know what would happen to them."

So the rumours were fact. The Queen and the Prince had

gone. Thomas remembered what Middleton had said. "Sir, forgive me, but there is talk of your leaving the country too."

James was silent, and Thomas felt his heart begin to race. "Sir, nothing could fit in better with William's plans. You must not think that because some few traitors have gone to Exeter, you are alone — "

"'Some few'? Look around you, my lord."

"Then give command of the army to General Dundee." Reckless now, with nothing to lose, Thomas spoke his mind. "He and Lord Ailesbury and Lord Dumbarton are entirely loyal, sir. If you give them permission to raise troops — "

"I've finally had an answer from my nephew," James interrupted. "He calls himself '*We*' all through it. Orders me to dismiss all Catholics from office...retract my proclamations...give custody of the Tower to the City, even pay his army from public revenues! He behaves as if he is already King."

"Then God forbid you should make it easy for him by going. Whoever advises you to leave is no friend to you, sir, and no friend to England."

But James was not listening. He was running the beads of his rosary through his fingers and looking at the green roof above his head. "I have given Lord Dundee charge of certain matters and a free hand in choosing his allies," he said. "He's named you as one of them. I cannot say more at present. But I charge you to hold yourself ready."

"Sir, if you go out of the country we are undone."

It was like talking to Feversham — the same closed, blank look, the same silence. Thomas wanted to take that sad grey head between his hands and shake it. "In the name of God, sir, stay with us. Lord Ailesbury, Middleton, Dundee — any one of us would safeguard you from him, in our homes or anywhere you choose."

"He means to kill me," said James flatly. "Remember the de Witts."

In the hush that followed, they both heard the mob screaming. "You ought to go now while you still can," said James, so matter-of-factly that he might have been discussing the ferry service to Southwark. "Find Lord Dundee and wait for my orders."

"Sir, I won't leave you. Don't ask me."

"You must." Deep anxiety showed James' eyes, but there was a touch of his old hauteur as James added, "I command it." He blew his nose a third time. "Go. The clerk has some papers for you."

"I want to know when I shall see Your Majesty again."

James' silence was like a door shutting in Thomas' face. Desperation made him plead as he had never thought to do. "You love your faith, sir, and you love England, and your son. Defend them! Fight for them."

"I am fighting."

In the face of this stubborn denial there was nothing Thomas could do except kneel in obedience and once again kiss those cold, thin fingers. James, closing his eyes, said almost dreamily, "I danced with your mother at Hampton Court one Christmas. She had long fair hair like spun silk, and the little jewelled pins fell out when she turned. I gave them back to her with a kiss..." The rosary fell into his lap, and with it the pad of soiled linen. He was asleep.

Thomas straightened the King's rumpled coverlet, refilled his water glass, and backed out the door with his hat in his hand, although, at this point, protocol hardly mattered. Later he could not remember leaving the King's apartments, or what he had said to Lord Middleton. Alone in the Gallery, he found himself staring at a piece of paper that the clerk had thrust into his hand. He had to read it twice before he understood that, like Dundee, he had been rewarded for his loyalty with a new property. But his was Irish, the equivalent of a Trojan horse. He was now custodian of Castle Ballinshea, wherever and whatever that might be — likely some ruin perched on a black bog, with a nearby population of embittered Catholic tenants who passionately loathed the English. Ireland! Only in nightmares would he go there. He crushed the paper into his pocket and went to find Dundee.

At twelve o' clock that night James stole out of his room alone, disguised in a black wig and a plain black suit. He left by the back stairs, saying goodbye to nobody, and took nothing with him except the Great Seal, which he flung into the Thames.

9

ST. CLARE'S COMPANION was Thomas Wharton, a man with the reputation of being drunk more often than he was sober, and whose idea of amusement was setting the dogs' feeding dish before his wife at dinner. His father, Lord Wharton, had fought for Cromwell — somewhat ingloriously, as he was famous for diving into the safety of a sawpit during the battle of Edgehill.

Libby found it hard to breathe. The fact that her father was in such company, wearing orange ribbons at his shoulder, shouted *treason* at her as loudly as if it had been proclaimed from the ramparts. Were they going to quarter troops upon her home? But Wharton was all smiling politeness.

"Garrison the house? Nonsense, madam." He set down the candlestick he had been examining, and ran a gloved finger along the window ledge as if looking for dust or damage. "Your servant is mistaken. There are but twelve of us, friends looking to break their journey for the night. All we need is a hot supper, beds, and some fodder for our horses. Then we will be on our way."

"You cannot stay here."

"Elizabeth," said St. Clare.

She refused to acknowledge him. Beyond that first stunned moment, when she took in three facts — he was dressed in soldier's gear, had not shaved, and smelled of whisky — she had not looked at him or spoken to him. When he tried to embrace her, she had stepped away.

"The horses need rest," said Wharton. "I regret we must inconvenience you for the night, madam." His respect was so exaggerated as to be derisive. Libby, looking up into that rough dark face with its telltale lines of dissolution, could not disguise her anger.

"You are not welcome to stay here, sir."

"*Ca ce voit.*" Wharton took off his plumed hat with a courtier's grace and bowed deeply. "But we shall be gone by daybreak, and will endeavour not to trouble you. We won't even ask for your company at dinner."

"Stop it," said St. Clare. Wharton, like a man taking his ease, unfastened his buff coat, disclosing a set of pistols, and stripped off his gloves. He too was unshaven and his clothes were dirty, as if he had been hours in the saddle on the muddy roads. The look he gave St. Clare showed the fragility of their alliance.

"You are in a damnably ill humour, George. It was your idea to come with me, if you remember."

St. Clare ignored him and spoke instead to Libby. "Daughter, will you see to some food for us?"

"There is a chophouse in the village, sir, where you can buy dinner. Or if you have already spent your thirty pieces of silver, you can rob the poor box in the church — "

Wharton laughed. "By God, she has a fist! I would duck, George, if I were you. Never mind. We'll help ourselves."

Libby turned to Fulke, who was white to the lips. "Take them to the kitchen. I'll be upstairs with the children."

She gathered up her skirts and left the room. When the door had closed behind her she ran down the hall to Thomas' study. Heart pounding, she swept up all the papers on his desk and was unlocking the strongbox when Wharton said behind her, "I love a good tidy housewife. Thank you, sweetheart. I'll take that for you."

She had not thought it possible to be so angry with anyone, to despise any man the way she despised Wharton. He bowed her out of the room, making another ridiculous flourish with his hat, mocking her with his insolent chivalry. There was nothing she could say or do that would not make matters worse. She swept past him, and, knowing that he was watching, took the stairs. But she had to stop at the landing to catch her breath. Brigid met her at the top. A miserable wailing came down the hall. "It's James, my lady," she said. "He's been sick."

Piers emerged from the school room with his composition in his hand, his eyes wide with excitement. "I heard horses. Who's here?"

"No one," said Libby, so sharply that Piers and Brigid both stared. "Go back to your lessons, Piers. Keep Samuel and Beatrice with you." When Piers still stood there, frowning, Libby gave him a small push. "Do as I tell you!"

The reek in James' room made her catch her breath. The sheets had been stripped from the bed and James lay on the feather mattress, his face flushed and sticky.

"He was eating those treacle buns again, my lady," Brigid said. "He and Samuel. But Samuel only had two. James ate all the rest."

Libby sat down wearily and washed James' face with water from the bedside basin. "Well, this is what happens to greedy little boys," she said, but her voice was soft because he looked so wretched. James wiped his nose with the back of his hand and spoke into the washcloth. "I want my papa."

"You know he is not here. You watched him ride through the gates."

Tears blubbered James' cheeks. Theo, who had taken up a post by the bed, licked his ear and snuffled into his hair. James said again, "I want Papa."

"We will have to send him a note. Wait a moment, while I get my pen and paper."

She rose from the bed and said in an undertone to Brigid, "There are soldiers downstairs, Brigid, enemies of my husband's. Go to the stables, as quietly as you can — pray do not let anyone see you — and send John Patrick for Dr. Spencer."

Brigid, with her Irish upbringing, did not need to be told about soldiers. Her face darkened with immediate understanding. "Yes, my lady," she said, and stripped off her bangles and even her shoes so that she might walk silently.

James dictated only half a dozen words before falling into a restless sleep, tossing and turning on his pillow. Libby sat down to wait. In her mind she rode with John Patrick across the sodden fields to the crossroads and the stone bridge, along the muddy track into the village, and up to Heneage Spencer's door. When she heard a step on the stair she went out at once, but instead of Heneage it was Wharton who stood in the hall, holding a red-faced John Patrick by the arm.

"I regret that no one can leave the grounds, madam," he said. "Our presence here is private."

Libby clenched her fists inside her skirt pockets. "Sir, my son is ill."

"So I understand. But I cannot have your groom talking about us."

"Then send one of your own servants for the doctor, someone who won't be known. I can give you directions — "

"Unfortunately that will not be possible. You will have to wait until tomorrow." Wharton let John Patrick go and relapsed into mock deference. "Have you heard from your good husband recently, madam?"

"What has that to do with you?"

"Nothing. Only perhaps you are not aware that the royal army is in retreat from Salisbury?"

"I don't believe you."

"General Churchill has joined the Prince."

"It's a lie!"

"Believe as you like. But I warn you, in confidence of course, that Prince William is en route to Windsor, and he remembers this house quite well from his visit eleven years ago. He has a great liking for this pleasant location, which suits his health better than the fogs of London."

William at Windsor! She refused to believe it. "You wish to threaten us, sir," she said. "A houseful of women and children and servants! Are you as valiant elsewhere? Or do you prefer, like your father during the last war, to hide in a pile of straw until the danger is over?"

If she thought to anger Wharton with this reference to his father's legendary foolishness, she was mistaken. He laughed instead, and was still laughing when St. Clare came up the stairs. Her father was a big man, with the build of a stonemason, and in his cuirass and jackboots he looked even larger than usual. His voice rumbled through the house. "What's this about my grandson being ill, and the doctor not sent for?"

The schoolroom door flew open. Piers and Samuel and Beatrice ran out. "I knew it was you!" cried Piers joyfully. "I looked out the window and recognized your horse. Sir, tell me, have you come with my father?"

In other circumstances the consternation on St. Clare's face would have made Libby laugh. But he hesitated only a moment before he opened his arms. "My dear ones!" he said. "Wait until you see what gifts I brought you."

But Piers, at least, was not to be diverted. "Sir, is my father here?"

There was a brief silence, while Libby looked at St. Clare and St. Clare fingered the diamond in his ear. Piers' tone grew more urgent. "My lord, did you speak with my father? Have you seen the King?"

"You can ask questions later," said St. Clare. "Right now we want our supper, and your mother needs to look after James. What is wrong with the boy, Libby?"

She put a hand on Piers' shoulder, as if restraining or protecting him, and said, "He has a fever, but I am not permitted — "

"To be inconvenienced in any way. So we will find our own dinner," said Wharton. "Run along, boys. And you, too, young mistress." This was addressed to Beatrice, who had ventured close enough to put a finger on the hilt of his sword.

Brigid, still in her stockinged feet, came to fetch the children and return them to the school room. She looked at the men and then at Libby, and put out a hand to pull Beatrice close to her side.

Samuel, looking puzzled, asked his grandfather, "Sir, why are you not wearing the King's colours?"

"Master Hammond is waiting for you," Libby said. "Go."

"Do as you are told, boys," ordered St. Clare.

Piers, clearly dissatisfied, gave both St. Clare and Wharton a long, troubled look before taking Samuel's hand and leading him back to the schoolroom.

"It seems they suspect you," said Wharton. St. Clare turned as if he would rend him in two. "What do you mean by preventing the doctor from seeing my grandson?"

"Why not send heralds to announce our presence?" Wharton countered. "I will not have the entire county upon us only because the child has a fever."

"He is not the only patient who needs attention," Libby said. "Your own son, sir, is in the bedchamber down the hall."

"What the devil is Leopold doing here?"

"He broke his leg trying to get to Salisbury to join the King."

St. Clare flushed and Wharton looked more sardonic than ever. "Christ, George. A family party! You didn't mention that your son had joined the army."

"I didn't know." St. Clare sounded both astounded and outraged. Wharton gave him another cold look. "You ought to know when your dog slips the leash."

Libby could not remember anyone ever speaking or behaving to her father in such a manner, and she was happy to see that he was on the brink of one of his rages. He followed Wharton down the stairs as if he were about to attack him. But they went into the library and she could not hear what was said, or more likely shouted, behind the closed doors.

Suddenly she found that she was trembling. She went back into James' room and sat down by the bed, holding his hand tightly. Soon the children would be eating their supper in the schoolroom, but she would have to stay away; the boys, and even Beatrice, would ask too many questions. Leopold, thankfully, was asleep. She had spooned twice the usual amount of laudanum into his afternoon cordial, hoping that he would stay out of the way until their unwanted visitors had left. In the meantime she struggled to comprehend why her father, after a lifetime spent in honourable service, should have done this shameful thing.

She thought back several months to his departure for the Continent, when he had come by with gifts of fruit and books for the children. He had said something then about The Hague, but she had not attended. He had acquaintances all over and it made no difference to her whom he visited or why. Her only concern at the time had been Thomas' dismissal from Court, which her father had been so displeased to learn about second-hand that he had left in a huff. Libby supposed that he had wanted to reminisce with Thomas about his own troubles. He had retired from Court ostensibly for health reasons, but in fact he had been dismissed after squabbling with the King's Jesuit confessor. Soon afterward he had announced his intention of touring Europe. She imagined her father arriving in state at William's palace in The Hague, with all the exiled English nobles and clergy crowding around him, asking for news — Wharton's father among them, as he had fled to Holland when the King took the throne. No doubt the attention had flattered St. Clare's bruised vanity. Her father was a superb horseman and William had what amounted to a mania for hunting. Perhaps they had struck their bargain then, on the field. Or perhaps the bargain was only in her father's mind, and William, once he had made use of St. Clare's wealth and connections, would have nothing more to do with him.

Long after the candles were lit she remained in James' room, watching over his troubled sleep. Somewhere below, soldiers were eating and drinking and smoking, rifling through the liquor cabinets and plundering the contents of the strongbox. Nothing could excuse her father for bringing them here and she dreaded what Thomas might do when he found out.

She took out her prayer book to read but fell asleep over it. When she awoke she found that someone had brought her a dish of soup and a plate of bread and butter. Alys, looking like a corpse in a winding sheet, had pulled up another chair and was holding James' hand. Her fair hair straggled out from her cap and her eyes were sunk in waxy folds.

"Alys, you should not be up."

"Brigid told me what's going on, madam. I'm feeling well tonight, and I'll sit with master James. He's sleeping better now anyway. You go along to bed, after you've supped. And lock your door."

"Alys — "

"We'll be fine. You rest."

There was such determination in Alys' voice that Libby gave in. There was an ominous ache in her back and she wanted to lie down. "Dear Alys," she said. "Thank you."

She ate a half-slice of buttered bread and kissed both Alys and James on the cheek before going to her own room. She could not wait to get out of her dress and into bed. But when she opened the door she saw her father sitting in the dark, glass in hand.

"You ought to have been asleep hours ago," he said, as if she were a child out late. "I was waiting for you. How is the boy?"

"Asleep. What are you doing here?"

Whatever his answer was, she did not hear it. The pain in her back was suddenly acute. She sat down on the bed. St. Clare began fussing with blankets and quilts and pillows. "Shall I look in on James?"

"Alys is with him," Libby said. She was too tired to be hostile. "You had better rest, since you have so early a start."

Her father set the candle on the dressing table and sat down by the bed. The wine fumes on his breath made her turn her head away. Even in the candlelight his face looked lined and worn, almost elderly. He seemed to have aged ten years in the few months since she had last seen him.

But she fought against feeling any compassion for him. He was clearly unhappy with his new allies, but that was his problem and he would have to solve it.

"Child, I need to talk to you."

"Tomorrow."

"We leave at dawn. You'll be asleep."

"*Tant pis*," she said into the pillow. She heard her father draw in his breath.

"I am here to protect you," he said. "Do you think I care for Wharton's company? I came with him to make sure you did not suffer."

"Next you will expect me to thank you."

"I am no traitor, Libby, and I take it very ill that you should think so."

"Wharton is William's man and so are you."

"I am acting only from concern for my country and my church."

"And it has nothing to do with the fact that you grudge being dismissed from Court three years ago?"

"Of course not," he said. The profundity of rebuke in his voice would have done credit to King Lear. Had he not been a noble, Libby thought, he would have been a natural for the theatre. How the stinkards in the pit would have loved him! That incomparably rich voice, the fine dark eyes, the grand presence — but, like a painted stage set, there was nothing but windblown space behind it. Her father's politicking, his drinking and quarrelling and fits of repentance, even his deep undoubted affection, suddenly seemed overdone and artificial. All these years she had adored him and now she thought him more childish than any of the children. He appeared to think there was nothing that could not be pardoned, that a kiss and a gift would buy peace; he could meddle with treason and flourish, lie to his family and friends, and still be welcomed. But not by her.

"God may forgive you, sir," she said, pulling the blanket up to her nose, "but I doubt that my husband will. Or your son."

"I shall deal with Leopold," said St. Clare. "As for Tom — well, he is in trouble, my dear. I tell you so plainly."

"It is you and your friends who have broken the law, sir."

"Churchill deserted at Salisbury," said St. Clare, as if she had not spoken. "And Prince George with him, and all the Scots except Dundee and Dumbarton. The north is in William's hands and Scotland is undefended. The King has no one left except Feversham, and he's a fool. William is master here, make no mistake."

It brought Libby fully awake. She sat up a little, flinching at the pain. So it was true; Churchill and the rest of them had run like dogs. "Why do you talk as if you regret it? Was this not your purpose?"

St. Clare was silent for so long that Libby thought he was about to tell her politics was not a woman's business, or that he owed her no explanation. But finally he said, "You know that the Bishop of London is a friend of mine. He convinced me that the Prince was coming only to remove those cursed fools from around the King — Melfort and the rest, the Catholics who have been running council and would sell us out to Rome if they could. There was never any intent to hurt the King. The Dutch army and transports were to frighten his little cabal, that was all. The aim was to have the King agree to raise his son in the Church of England. Or so the Bishop thought. But he has not spent the past fortnight, as I have, in the company of Wharton and his friends. It's they who are out for blood. They'll stand for no compromise now, no negotiation or mercy for anyone who is loyal to the King."

A stab of nausea made Libby wish her basin was close at hand. "So you were willing to deal in treason, but you stick at murder. Did it never occur to you that one way or another you would find yourself at war with your own family?"

"There was never going to be a war," said St. Clare. "Churchill wrote to William long ago. He had to bring the army to Salisbury, but he never intended to fight. I think he was waiting for the chance to do the most damage." He rubbed the back of his neck wearily and Libby had to shut her eyes because he looked so ordinary, so familiar, and yet he was saying and doing these incomprehensibly dreadful things.

"You had better talk to Thomas, Libby," he said. "Use your influence. You can't tell me it matters to you whether it's James or William or the Pope himself sitting on the throne."

This was true, but Libby would not say so. She put the palms of her hands over her eyes as if to shut out the sight of the Devil. "Go away," she said. "Let me sleep."

"The King is finished. You need to convince Thomas of that, unless he is to lose everything."

"Go away." She heard the rising edge of hysteria in her voice and clenched her fist against her mouth so that she would say nothing more.

For a time St. Clare was silent. Then he got up from the bed, extinguished the candle between his fingers, and bent to kiss Libby on the forehead. "There, my child," he said. "It's a bad business, but it will work out, if you can only persuade your husband to be sensible."

They were gone by morning, as Wharton had said. Even without going downstairs, Libby knew by the silence of the house that they had left. St. Clare had left a long letter that must have taken him the remainder of the night to write. She put it in her pocket without reading it and went to look in on James, whose health seemed much improved. His fever had broken and now he was hungry.

"No treacle buns," said Libby. She opened the curtains and looked out on another day of rain. Alys was asleep in the chair, her mouth slightly open, snores fluttering the collar of her nightgown. Libby spoke softly, not wishing to disturb her. "Come and find me when she wakes," she said to James. Then, tying her wrapper around her, she awkwardly descended the stairs, reviewing the day's orders in her mind. Send for the doctor. Speak with Leopold. Find someone, anyone, who knew what might have happened at Salisbury.

Fulke met her at the foot of the stairs. His face was peppered with grey stubble and he looked so weary that Libby realized he must have stood watch all night.

"The strongbox is gone, madam."

"I know."

"And they took the new coach and most of the horses. We have only two left, and one is lame. Master James' pony is the only one fit to ride."

"Well, John Patrick will have to take it or walk into the village to fetch Dr. Spencer. I suppose you had better send to the goldsmith for more funds. Is that all?"

"No." Fulke took off his spectacles and rubbed his eyes. "All his lordship's papers are missing, not only the household accounts, but even his personal letters and his essays on the law..."

Libby was silent, remembering some of the rash precepts Thomas had committed to paper. *Torture represented not the power of justice, but its failure...laws that punished theft of a spoon equally with murder were unfit for a civilized society...hanging the poor did not end crime, religious conformity was no guarantee of good citizenship...* Even St. Clare, who liked to think of himself as open-minded, had called him a "damned republican." The irony of it would have made her smile, had she been able.

She thrust the thought away and patted Fulke's hand. "Never mind. You could not have prevented it, and I doubt it will matter."

"They were drinking in the library, madam. Don't go in there."

But naturally that only drove her to see what damage had been done. Thomas' spaniel, Lucy, although not permitted on the furniture, was asleep in the chair by the window seat. The velvet curtains were shut. The fire had gone out, but ashes from the hearth were scattered over the floor. Jackboots had ground dirt into the rug. Books had been pulled from the shelves, drawers and cupboards emptied; a Chinese cabinet was missing, along with a small, gilt-framed painting of the Apostles. Wine had soaked into the sofa cushions and someone had used a dagger to plough furrows in the panelling. Libby sat down by the cold hearth, hands clasped to still their shaking. Perhaps the other rooms were far worse; she would have to take an inventory of each one, but right now it was a task beyond her strength.

Lucy stirred, stretched, and went back to sleep. Libby remained where she was, unable to summon the necessary resolve to move even though she was growing chilled. It seemed that from the first moment of seeing her father in Wharton's company, she had been frozen in a species of waking nightmare. Nothing was as it had been before. The threads of her life had been unpicked as if by some malignant hand. She felt like the princess in the fairy tale that she had read to James yesterday, the captive who had to untangle a hideous ball of spider webs before morning, or die. Her father's words kept ringing in her ears. "The King is finished." She struggled with the knowledge that this was true, and now it was the loyal who would suffer.

That called to mind her father's letter. St. Clare had addressed it to both of his children, but the first page contained specific instructions for Leopold, directing him, astonishingly, to preserve his loyalty to the King — "Do not meddle with the Dutch." But this did not stem from any sense of remorse. It was practicality at its most cynical: if he and Leopold took opposing sides, at least one of them would survive the crisis and be in a position to rescue the other. Until yesterday, Libby would not have believed her father capable of such manoeuvres. She crumpled up the paper and threw it into the cold ashes, thinking that her father, despite his constant meddling in Leopold's life, had no real knowledge of his son. It went without saying that Leo, like Thomas, would never serve the Dutch in any capacity. There was iron underneath the soft ground of that affable nature. And St. Clare, for all his talk of saving the nation, was interested only in saving himself. He would do anything, no matter how degrading, to keep the gains of a lifetime — turn on his new allies as he had on his old friends and then turn again, like a weathercock, without any sense of shame.

Once she had thought her father the equal of Raleigh. But Raleigh, although he died a traitor's death, had never been disloyal. Rather he himself had been infamously betrayed.

She remembered what else her father had said — "Tom is in trouble" — and she shivered a little in the cold.

In the afternoon Dr. Spencer came to attend his patients. Heneage, perpetually grubby and unkempt, with coffee-stains on his shirt and his wig askew, looked nothing like the elegant Dr. Radcliffe. But Libby had entire faith in his intelligence and skill. He radiated a stove-like warmth and reassurance that heartened even the dying. He listened to her description of her pain, put an unselfconscious ear to her belly, and prescribed a mild tonic.

"Absolute rest for you, my lady. There is no need to get up."

"My son — "

"I can find nothing the matter with Master James except a cough, and the discomforts natural after eating four treacle buns and then putting tobacco up his nose with a spoon." Dr. Spencer produced a small lacquered snuff-box, with Leopold's initials on it. "He admits to stealing this from his uncle's room. Fortunately he spilled most of it."

"I see." Libby met his eyes, and Heneage smiled: he had five children of his own, three boys and two small girls as red-headed and freckled as himself. "I gave him a lecture on the evils of tobacco — the foul humours, the mouth ulcers, the cough — I don't imagine he will transgress again."

"And Alys?"

"I have given her laudanum. As for his lordship your brother, I have got him up for the first time to use the close-stool, and there is no reason he cannot be about, with his sticks." He got up from the bed and closed his bag. "Rest," he said again. "And do not trouble yourself with news and rumours. I called upon Lord Burcote this morning — his lady, as you know, is my patient — and he has heard nothing about Salisbury. Nor has the vicar or even the landlord at the change-house. Sure, there is nothing worse than waiting. If I hear anything I will let you know." He smiled upon her kindly. "I am sure the worst is over."

Libby obediently drank her medicine and soon fell asleep. But at some level of awareness she knew that the routines of the household had resumed: the scrubbing, the dusting, the cooking, the children's lessons. In the afternoon

Brigid came to assure her that Master James was reading in bed and that the other children were with Leopold.

Libby slept again and awoke feeling heavy-headed and short of breath, as if she were sickening for a fever. Someone had left a tray of food by the bed and she lifted a corner of the linen napkin. Soup, fresh bread, boiled onions, roast chicken, stewed fruit: she would not be able to eat a quarter of it. But it was her duty to try. She was picking at a crust of bread when Fulke spoke at the door, asking admittance.

If it were rare for him to come upstairs, it was unprecedented for him to appear at her bedroom door. Clearly he had something momentous to report.

"What is it, Fulke? Has my father returned?"

"No. But there's someone else here, madam, in the kitchen...he says he is Sir John Lee's groom."

"Lee?" In her joy Libby threw back the covers and Fulke averted his eyes from the sight of her bare feet. "Sir John is back? Fulke, is he here?"

"His servant says he was riding in this direction from Reading. But he met Wharton's men on the road."

"Merciful God!"

"They've taken him with them, madam. I suppose the servant was no use to them. But Sir John is a King's officer."

"Did they hurt him?"

"His groom says it was he who challenged *them*. They didn't want to be troubled with a prisoner and would have let him go — but Sir John demanded to know their business. And his servant says, madam, that it's true about General Churchill. The Dutch army has reached Windsor. The troops that were supposed to be guarding the bridge at Reading let them through, and stood a drink to William's health."

Libby knew her face must be as pale as Fulke's own, for she could feel the blood run from it.

"But there is some good news too, madam. Sir John's servant brought a letter for you."

From his breast pocket Fulke took a creased and dirty scrap of paper and handed it to Libby. She unfolded it with trembling fingers. When she saw Thomas' writing, her eyes filled with tears.

"If there is anything you need, madam…"

"No, that will be all. Thank you, Fulke."

Some of the message had been torn off. "…desire that Grace will stay. Ask whoever brings this for news. Kiss the boys for me and God bless you my love, my own dear heart."

She refolded the scrap carefully and then looked up, startled, as Leopold thumped in on his sticks after a perfunctory scratch at the door. His face was flushed and creased from sleep, and his eyes were ringed with dark circles. He was more upset than Libby had ever seen him. "The children have just told me that Father was here with soldiers, and I slept all through it. What is going on? Why did you not wake me?"

"Dear Leo, what would you have done? It seemed better to let you sleep."

"It was the laudanum." He pushed his fingers through his cropped hair and looked at her accusingly. "You gave me too much. Why? Did you not stop to think you might have needed me?"

"If you believe Father, he was here to defend me."

She realized that she had unthinkingly dealt her brother a blow. "I'm sorry, Leo," she said. "I didn't want you to see him, and that's the truth." She patted the coverlid and after a moment Leopold sat down, putting his sticks to one side. Underneath his two-days' growth of beard his skin looked sallow. "Father and Wharton!" he said. "How did they come to be together?"

"Does it matter?"

"It does to me."

"Father was not coerced, if that is what you mean." Libby spoke a little wearily, as if they were discussing someone else's misbehaved child. "He has chosen this. He says even General Churchill has deserted, and the Dutch are at Windsor. Wharton's men took Sir John Lee prisoner on the road here, but they let his servant go."

"Churchill has deserted?"

She nodded, remembering that the General had been a guest at her brother's table. Leopold massaged his brow with a knuckle. "And John Lee is taken prisoner?"

"He's not been harmed, his servant said. But they have taken him to Windsor."

Leopold bowed his head as if in church. She reached for his hand and they sat together in silence until Libby pressed his fingers so hard that he looked up.

"I think my waters have just broken," she said, as calmly as she might have said, "the flour barrel is empty." "Call Fulke, if you please, Leo, and tell him to send for Dr. Spencer. If he can't find Dr. Spencer, he must get someone to fetch the midwife."

She was amazed at the firmness in her voice, when her body was trembling and her whole spirit afraid. Leopold, wasting no time, fumbled with his sticks and stood up to give the bell pull a vigorous tug. Before he left he placed a tender hand on Libby's forehead. "God be with you, my dear."

He stumped out. Libby folded her hands on her soaked bedgown and looked out the window. It was growing dark, but she could still make out the shapes of the trees in the park, blowing and tossing in the wind like men-of-war on a violent ocean. Her weariness was so deep that she dozed off, only to jolt herself awake moments later with the realization that Dr. Spencer had gone to Banbury this afternoon to visit his sister and would not be home until late. She should have sent for the midwife straightaway, for she sensed that this labour would not take long.

Brigid came into the room carrying a basket from which she calmly took a series of articles: a knife, a comfort stone, salt, strips of clean linen, a ball of twine, a decanter, a cross, and a bottle of rosewater. As Libby watched in bemusement she sprinkled the rosewater in the air and tied the cross to the bedpost. "Fix on that when the pain comes." Then she picked up the decanter and poured out a generous amount of purple liquid. "It's plum wine, my lady. But we'll not give you so much that it will slow you down." She sprinkled salt on the doorstep — "to keep the Devil away" — and set the linen to warm by the fire. Finally she sat down on a footstool next to the bed and gave her rough, red hand to Libby. "Squeeze as hard as you like."

"Brigid, how old are you?" Libby asked faintly.

"I don't know entirely. I was born the year the plague came to our village."

"And have you assisted at many births?"

"No, my lady. But my mam was a midwife. Did you not know?"

"Indeed I did not," said Libby.

She sipped at her wine, spilling it on her gown when the first contraction struck. When the pain receded, nausea rushed in. Brigid found the slop basin and shoved it into her hands. Up came the plum wine and her crust of bread. As one contraction followed another, she broke into an icy sweat. Her legs shook.

"Scream, my lady. No one will hear."

The plum wine still seemed to be affecting her, for her

voice sounded as if it were coming from someone else. Someone who was drunk, or possibly not quite sound in mind. "I want my mother."

Pain crushed her innards and spine together. She had forgotten what hard work this was and how terrifying, as if her body had been occupied by an invading army and she could do nothing except pray for mercy. It soon became apparent that this child was not going to wait even for the kettle to boil. The contractions came one after another without respite, the crest of one diminishing just as another was building. Then, with a great shudder and a sob, she was freed of her burden and a sick faintness took its place. From somewhere off in the distance, reaching her as if through a churning black whirlpool, she heard Brigid say, "'Tis a girl you have, madam...a fine healthy girl."

In London it was Irish Night.

10

THE HEART OF LONDON was ablaze. Bonfires roared on every corner. From Whitechapel to Westminster and Kentish Town to London Bridge, the streets were jammed with drunken, angry mobs looking for blood. They had pulled down the King's mass-houses, broken into St. James' palace, destroyed the barricades around Whitehall, and smashed the doors of foreign embassies. Goods that were not considered useful — church vestments, paintings, statuary — had been flung into the fires, and a pall of stinking black smoke blanketed the city. Householders stuck oranges on their gateposts or tied orange cloth to their doors in hope that the rioters would pass them by. Word ran from house to house — this was the work of the Irish. The Irish were upon them!

Any known Roman Catholic or member of the Court risked being torn asunder. Thomas, riding out of Blackfriars with his young servant Malachy, had thrown off his lace neckcloth and replaced it with an orange rag. Magnus ran close to his side, whimpering with fear. It was the shortest day of the year and bitterly cold, but the crowds, in holiday mood, drank stolen wine and kept warm around the bonfires. The sky was blood-red, and thick, foul smoke rose up in a solid pillar west of Puddle Dock Hill. Ash fell like snow. Thomas thought in the same instant, "They are firing the king's printing house" and "God help Harry Hill!"

He spurred Pilgrim forward. Malachy's horse, tied to his by a lead rein, plunged and skittered, shying at the noise and the sparks. A drunken crowd surrounded the printing house, which had already been looted. The presses had been carried out and smashed and the books set on fire. In the midst of the chaos a slight young man in shirt and breeks stood with his arms outstretched like an Old Testament prophet, shouting, "No! No! Stop, I beg you!" He plunged toward the blaze and someone stuck out a foot, pitching him forward into the flames. He rolled out, the hem of his shirt on fire, and tried to crawl away from the kicking boots. But the crowd engulfed him.

Thomas uncovered his pistol and fired. Malachy reached for the injured man and flung him crosswise over the horse's rump. "Where is Mr. Hill?" Thomas shouted. The young man gave him a glassy stare. "Fled, with his family," he said. Then he fainted.

Thomas used his sword to drive a path through the rioters, shoving aside the smoke-blackened, drunken faces, the hands that tore at his cloak and boots. Someone in the crowd hurled a broken bottle, missing him by a finger's breadth, and then someone else plucked a brand from the fire and threw it. A burning splinter struck Pilgrim's flank and he reared in panic. People scattered, running away from the danger of those iron-shod hooves. Thomas drove forward, fighting his way out of the crowd with both horses plunging and rearing.

Ahead the sky flared even redder and the air glowed with sparks and flakes of ash. He drew off under the rib of a house on Carter Lane and dismounted, lifting his passenger to the ground. Three minutes at the mercy of the mob had given the young man a broken nose, black eyes, and cracked ribs, but he had been protected from the fire by several books stuffed under his shirt. His head lolled as if he were drunk, but when he opened his eyes, puzzled recognition, and then astonishment amounting almost to awe, awoke in his battered face. "Thomas de Chastelain," he whispered. It sounded as if his throat were crushed. "Surely the Lord has sent thee!"

"I am glad you think so, Mr. Schuyler," said Thomas. With a mix of compassion and distaste he surveyed his sister's lover, whom he had last seen at the dinner table five months ago: Jacob's fair hair, clubbed back like a sailor's, was matted with filth and blood; his bony intelligent face, strong-featured but undistinguished even before his nose had been smashed, was already turning purple, and his eyes were swelling shut.

"The books!"

"I have them there, the ones you had in your shirt. Can you sit up?"

"I can walk. I must get to Clerkenwell."

He might as well have said he would fly. "You'll ride with me," said Thomas shortly. He took a flask from his pack and uncorked it.

"I don't use spirits."

"Drink!"

Jacob choked on the brandy and then began to tremble violently. Thomas took off his coat and threw it over the young man. He was in shirt sleeves now himself and yet was not cold. Sweat ran down his neck and arms. The screams of the mob, the noises of destruction, were louder than before. "We must leave at once. Malachy, give a hand."

"Wait! My glasses," Jacob said. He fumbled around and drew a bent wire frame from his pocket. Amazingly, one of the lenses was still intact. Thomas cleaned it before hooking the frame over Jacob's ears, where it sat at a drunken angle.

"I thank thee, Friend."

Thomas felt a stab of irritation. "Clerkenwell," he said. "Do you have lodgings there?"

"Grace and I live at the school. I must go...she will be anxious for me."

"But Grace is at home with my wife!"

Jacob stared. "No, sir, she is not. She is at the school. Some of the children fell ill, and we had to care for them...."

"Do you tell me that she never left London? That she has been with you all this while?"

Jacob shrank from the incredulous fury in Thomas' voice. "We thought the children had smallpox. She could not risk carrying the infection. I thought thee were aware — " The expression on Jacob's bloodstained face altered suddenly. He propped himself up on one elbow. "Sir, we are together because we have been married. Under the care of the Meeting, with thirty witnesses. I sent thee a letter..."

Thomas, forgetting himself, seized hold of Jacob's shirt. He was stunned, not even so much by the fact of Grace's marriage as by the realization that Libby had been alone since he left for Salisbury. Just in time he restrained himself from shaking Jacob savagely back and forth. He let the young man go and turned to Malachy.

"Get him on your horse. We're taking him to Clerkenwell."

"I can walk, Friend," said Jacob.

Thomas turned to curse him with such bitter fluency that Jacob flinched and turned his face away. In dejected silence he allowed Thomas to heft him into the saddle, where he sat with difficulty, his arms fastened around Malachy and his face dead-white under a palette of ripening bruises. Thomas rode on ahead, his sword drawn and his mind in furious tumult.

Whatever Jacob Schuyler might say, in the eyes of the world the Quaker marriage ceremony did not constitute a valid union. Grace had dishonoured herself. But he considered that less shameful than her failure to care for Libby. He remembered all those letters he had exchanged with Grace, her relentless badgering and pleadings on the subject of Jacob Schuyler, and how, for the sake of peace, he had been patient with her — and this was his reward! Almost he wished that he had let the mob do its worst.

He took Pilgrim down back lanes and alleyways to avoid the crowds, crossing Ludgate Hill, skirting Newgate and St. Bartholomew's. Overhead the sky was lit as if by fireworks, but instead of sparkling wheels and coloured starbursts, there were pillars and columns of fire. The stench of burning houses and goods filled his nose and mouth. He had been in London with his father at the time of the Great Fire, and those days of terror were not easily forgotten. There had been showers of ash and flakes of fire raining down on the streets, which became so hot that the cobbles had felt like burning coals underfoot. The air had been almost solid with grit and smoke and filth, the river crammed with laden tilt-boats and lighters and barges of every description. But then people had been weeping and now they were enjoying a mad kind of holiday, a break from law and order that would bring the city to ruin.

The mob had destroyed the Franciscan mass-house at Clerkenwell and then moved on. A spurious quiet lay over the burned fields. Nothing moved in the charred ruins of the mass-house. Grace's school, a converted almshouse not far away, stood squat and dark under a copse of beech trees. An orange cloth hung from the gatepost and there were oranges skewered on the railing, their skins split and the pips scattered on the ground. It reminded Thomas that he still had the orange rag tied around his neck, and he tore it off and threw it in the dirt. He would not fight this battle under false colours.

As they rode up to the door, a large mastiff rose from somewhere in the dark and rushed toward them. Magnus launched himself into the air before Thomas could prevent him and the ensuing fight rent the silence. Light bloomed in the front window of the house. Moments later Grace appeared on the doorstep, her small person bulky with flannels and shawls and her hands gripping an ancient musket.

"Do not shoot!" Jacob croaked in horror. He stumbled off the horse toward her and she lowered the gun.

"Call off your dog!" Thomas shouted.

Grace stared into the dark. "Thomas? Is that you?"

"Call off the damn dog!"

"Joshua! Down, sir."

The mastiff let go. Thomas grasped Magnus' collar and wrestled him under control. Grace ran to Jacob. "Love! Love, what has happened?"

He ignored her question. Outrage seemed to give him strength and his voice returned in full power. "Grace, put down that weapon!"

But it was Thomas who seized the gun from his sister. It was a rusting matchlock with a four-foot barrel, a weapon so wildly inaccurate that even firing at point-blank range would guarantee nothing. And it was unloaded. He threw it to Malachy, saying, "The printing house was burned. We were nearby and saw the fire. Get him inside, Grace. He's badly hurt."

"I was afraid of this." Grace put her arm through Jacob's to lead him into the house. A few moments before she had been an Amazon prepared for battle, but now she was all sweetness, a woman propitiating an angry spouse. "Jacob, I had neither match or powder for the gun."

"It makes no difference. Our Testimony is clear! 'All bloody practices and principles we do utterly deny'..." Jacob stopped, fighting for breath through his crushed cartilage. He stumbled once more and Grace put her arm around his waist for support. She brought him into the kitchen, sat him down at the scrubbed oak table, and knelt awkwardly to remove his shoes.

The kitchen might have belonged to a prosperous farmer's wife, with dishes in racks and blue pottery displayed on a sideboard. Dried herbs and hams hung from ceiling hooks, and barrels of flour and pickled fish stood on the floor. But in one corner stood a cabinet jammed with costly books no farmer would read: works by Harvey and Vesalius, Culpepper's translation of the *Pharmacopoeia*, Fox's *Epistles*. An array of stoppered bottles and jars stood upon a high shelf and there was a tray of instruments beside it with scissors, lancets, and tongs neatly laid out. Grace roused one of the children to bring food from the cold cellar while she assembled linen bandages and hot water. "Everyone at Mr. Hill's left yesterday," she said, "but Jacob insisted upon staying to protect the books." The note of pride in her voice was unmistakable.

"In which I failed," Jacob said.

"I told thee what would happen." She wrung out a cloth in the wash basin and began, with infinite care, to clean his face. "Look now at thy poor wounds..."

Thomas' scorn overflowed. "Do the Friends pay his room and board here, Grace?"

She flushed. "We are husband and wife, Thomas. Last week Tuesday we were married under the care of the Meeting — "

"So I am told."

He began to tell her what he thought about the care of

the Meeting. But he broke off when a small girl entered the kitchen, bearing a platter with rough slices of bread and cold meat, a dish of fruit, and a jug of thick cream. The child set these down on the table and then disappeared as silently as she had come.

Jacob spat some blood into the wash basin before speaking. "Sir, I have the means to provide for a family. The printing house is gone, but I will find other work until such time as my wife may travel."

"It has come to us from the Lord that we must go where Jacob can train to be a physician and use his skills," Grace said. Thomas wanted to strike that pious smugness from her face. This was how the Quakers spoke, insisting that even their smallest decisions — whether to eat soup or fish, to wear a vest or a coat, sit down or stand up — "came from the Lord." Then he forgot this minor irritation when she went on, "That means we shall not be raising our children in England."

As she spoke she placed a hand over her gown, and for the first time he realized that underneath those concealing layers of wool and flannel, his sister, the week-old bride, was well advanced in pregnancy. She lifted her chin, meeting his eyes without fear. Jacob, like an ox in a windstorm, kept his head down. As well he might, Thomas thought in cold rage. Self-righteous hypocrite, his mouth full of God and his hands roving!

"I suppose that came to you from the Lord as well?"

"Don't be coarse."

"I told thee how it would be, Grace," Jacob said. "I warned thee." He started to blunder to his feet, but Grace pushed him back down and he sunk his battered head in his hands. After a moment she resumed washing his scalp. In the silence they heard one of the children singing.

"I wish you will give us your blessing, Thomas," Grace said finally. Her voice had softened, as if, having made her stand, she now desired peace. "In Pennsylvania Jacob can practice his profession and his faith without trouble. Our families can exchange visits, letters..."

Pennsylvania! Thomas felt a further rush of bewildered anger. The dangers faced by Penn's little colony were legendary: wild beasts, savages, cold, pestilence, starvation, and unending, backbreaking labour. Grace would be deprived of all civilized comforts and subjected to unthinkable risks.

"It's what I want," she said. "I look forward to going."

He recognized the truth of this in her eyes. She was as besotted as a young girl with her first suitor. It seemed possible, even likely given the difference in their ages and her desperation for a child, that it was she who had enticed Jacob, and not the other way around. He looked at her as if there might be snakes crawling in her hair.

"You'll lose your jointure. Have you thought of that?"

Jacob answered for her. "I will provide for her. I have money saved for the passage. Until then I can be an apothecary's assistant, a clerk..."

"The Dutch will not accommodate the Friends as the King did. No one will hire you."

"We will manage," said Grace.

Jacob sat in silence, carefully inserting strips of linen into his bleeding nose. Grace emptied the slop bowl and quietly gathered up the soiled cloths and medicines. Had this been the theatre, Thomas thought, he would have been required to draw his sword and drag his sister from the house after killing her lover. But he could not fight a man who refused to fight back, and Grace was not a young girl in need of protection. She had chosen this for herself and would have to abide by the consequences. He turned to go, ignoring

Jacob's half-gesture of thanks, and shouted for Malachy. Grace followed him to the doorstep.

"Thomas, it's too dangerous to travel. Stay with us."

"I'm expected at Watford, Grace. Then I'm going home." He looked at her and cursed the precariousness of her situation. "I'll leave Malachy with you."

"It's not necessary. No one will harm us here. But you, alone on the road at this hour..."

"I'll be all right. Get inside. It's cold."

She clasped his arm with both her hands. "I wish I could have gone to Libby as I promised," she said. "Tell her so. Kiss the children for me. And wish me well, Thomas. Don't leave like this, hating me."

"I don't hate you."

As if he had not spoken, she said, "I've always wanted a child. Don't begrudge me this happiness."

He looked at the burden she carried with such pride. What dangers would she face, living in the wilderness with a husband whose principles forbad him to defend her? He removed one of his pistols from its holster and held it out to her. "Keep it in a safe place."

Her face paled. "You know I can't do that."

"You might need it to protect your child."

Her eyes showed painful indecision, a struggle between love and honour and practicality. She touched the pistol, then withdrew her hand as if the metal had burned her fingers. "I mustn't," she whispered. "Jacob would be so angry. If he should ever discover it…"

A moment later she seized the gun, thrust it under the folds of her shawl, and fled back into the house.

At Watford Thomas found Dundee and Dundee's friend Colin Lindsay, the Earl of Balcarres, on the point of leaving their lodging in Farthing Lane. "Your news is old, Tom," said Colin. "The King is back."

Thomas sat down, putting his hat on the back of his chair. From tiredness and unbelief he thought he had misheard. "He's already returned from France?"

"Indeed he never left England," said Colin. His face was unshaven and his eyes grainy with fatigue, but he was in good spirits, clearly relishing the adventure. "Some Kentish fishermen took the King prisoner. They thought he was a priest and detained him."

Dundee reached into his breast pocket and handed a paper to Thomas. It was a note from the King, forwarded by Lord Feversham, which read, "I had the misfortune to be stopped at Sheerness by a rabble of seamen who still detain me....Speak to my servants to bring me some linen and clothes...."

"Had you come five minutes later we would have been gone," Dundee said. "But now you can ride with us."

He sounded elated, but Thomas stifled a curse. Now it would be impossible to go home. "Lord Ailesbury and Lord Middleton are on their way as well," Dundee continued, "and Lord Feversham is bringing the Horse Guards."

Once more the King's personal drama seemed edged with farce. To be mistaken for a priest, and kept from leaving the country by a handful of fishermen — had it been written in a play, the audience would have jeered. At the same time, the King was in real danger. At any moment that mob could decide to drown him in the river or turn him over to the Dutch.

"Are you armed?" Dundee asked.

Thomas, without speaking, opened the flap of his coat. Lindsay pushed a bowl of coffee over to him and he drank it in silence and then asked for pen and paper. He scrawled a line for Libby. "Dear heart, I am obliged to stay in London." He hesitated, then added, "I have seen Grace, God pardon her." There was time for nothing else. He folded the paper and gave it to Malachy, then finished his coffee and went out like a man sleepwalking to get back in the saddle. He intended sending Magnus home with Malachy, but the dog whined and howled and he finally allowed him to follow.

The eight bells of St. Mary's church were ringing the Angelus as they galloped out.

11

RESCUED FROM HIS temporary gaolers — washed, fed, anointed with shaving lotion, furnished with clean linen, and royally escorted — the King had arrived in Rochester for the night. It was there that Dundee found him. He had set a killing pace, not caring how many horses foundered underneath him in his haste to reach the King, but James hardly seemed to recognize or appreciate this fact. He welcomed his friends sunnily, as if his flight and return had been entirely ordinary matters of business. His manner was so casual that Dundee was confounded. It made their dramatic dash across the country seem foolish.

But Thomas, kneeling in his turn to kiss James' hand, felt a tremor run through the King's fingers and guessed that exhaustion, not flippancy, was at the root of his odd behaviour. The events of the past few days had taken him to the brink of personal disaster and now that he had been rescued and comforted, he seemed almost dazed by the sudden reversal of his fortunes. And the unexpected sharpness of his first comment to Lord Ailesbury — "You were all kings when I left London" — showed that he was not entirely master of his emotions. He disclosed that he had sent General Feversham to invite William to St. James' palace for a conference, as he had decided to make every possible concession to his nephew. Indeed he had promised to give William all he had asked for, short of the throne itself, which the Prince had never mentioned.

"But that is the only thing he wants, and all the rest is smoke," said Thomas to Dundee later. "He will never negotiate with the King now. It would be too much to his disadvantage." Try as he might, he could not conceal his frustration.

"I told His Majesty as much," Dundee said.

"And what was his answer?"

"He quoted to me the story of the prodigal son."

Dundee looked away as he spoke, but there was a certain irony in his voice that had not been there before. Thomas, having nothing diplomatic to say, decided to keep to himself the observation that at least the prodigal had repented.

Their journey to London turned into a royal progress. In the towns along the way, people were still in a panic, believing that the Irish were about to attack. But at the sight of the King's coach and guards, the townsfolk fell to their knees in thanksgiving for his safety. Five days of anarchy had been enough. James entered London in state, driving from Southwark to Whitehall through wildly cheering crowds. Gentlemen on horseback and citizens on foot joined his escort. Children ran alongside his coach; all the churches in London rang carillons. The same people who had nearly burned the city to ashes four days earlier now lit bonfires to celebrate their sovereign's return. "God save the King!" and "God bless Jemmy!" dinned in James' ears until he wept with emotion.

"How I hate the mob," said Lord Middleton to Thomas. "They burn the King in effigy on Wednesday and cheer him on Sunday."

Thomas thought that James, overwhelmed by this unexpected frenzy, looked ten years younger. He called William his "dear nephew" and mopped his eyes when speaking of their prospective meeting at St. James'. The war, such as it had been, was over. Reunion and reconciliation were in sight. In the meantime the Tower guns crashed in celebration, bells rang, and people cheered and screamed themselves hoarse. The King leaned from his coach, tears of joy running down his chin, to wave at the crowd.

It was his last moment of glory.

Lord Craven, the eighty-year-old commander of the Household Guard, also wept as he greeted the King. But it was not from joy. The old man, a soldier all his life, gave his news the only way he knew, straight from the shoulder: William had answered his uncle's invitation by arresting General Feversham and dispatching three battalions of infantry to march upon Whitehall. The palace was about to be invaded.

The King closed his eyes. A muscle jerked near his mouth. A young girl had given him a pressed flower, and he spun it in his fingers until the fragile petals crumbled. All around him, the crowds were still cheering.

"So my nephew throws off the mask at last," he said. There was a strange note of triumph in his voice, as if this somehow represented victory instead of disaster. Lord Craven begged to muster the household troops and the militia, but the King refused. He wanted no bloodshed on his behalf. No one, not even Dundee, could convince him to defend himself. There was a flushed, congested look to his face, as if he were ill. He put two fingers to the bridge of his nose and then went to his apartments to change his clothes for dinner.

William had sent a deputation of English lords to deliver an ultimatum to the King: to leave Whitehall by nine o'clock the next morning and travel by barge to a house outside the city "for his own protection." But all knew what that meant. James was now his nephew's prisoner. The conquest of Whitehall had been so easy, so effortless, that some of the servants knew nothing about it until the Dutch surrounded the palace. But at James' own order, not a single shot was fired nor a sword drawn in his defence. He ate a wretched dinner and went to bed under Dutch guard.

At midnight Thomas wrote in his journal, "Lord Craven broke his sword rather than surrender it to the Dutch, but he had to give the order for the Household Guard to stand down. Lord Halifax and his friends pushed into the King's bedchamber to insist that he leave under Dutch escort tomorrow. His Majesty is determined to ask for sanctuary in France, and the Prince will allow it, if only to be rid of his uncle with no trouble to himself."

Stone and silence: never had Whitehall been so empty. The cheering crowds had gone; so had most of the King's attendants. The Court, like a clock with a broken spring, had wound down into deathly silence. Blue-coated soldiers patrolled the streets and the palace. Most of the servants had fled, but a weeping pageboy made up the fire in Thomas' room and brought him a decanter of wine and a dish of stew left over from supper. But neither the food nor the wine could warm him. "The Last Supper," Thomas wrote. "God forgive me."

He flung down his pen and put his head in his hands. All his life he had looked for the best rather than the worst, and despair was foreign to his nature. But he saw, as clearly as if looking through Leopold's perspective glass, the consequences of remaining loyal to the King: imprisonment or exile, his family forced from their home, his title and properties given to some friend of William's. Yet the alternative, kissing the hand of that cold, bloody-minded Dutchman, was unthinkable. Even if he stayed retired from public life, he would be obliged to swear loyalty to the new government. And his word had already been given three times over, in public and in private; he would not be an oath-breaker, a liar, and a coward, to save his plot of land. On the other hand, there were Libby and the children to consider. Penury, exile in France or, God forbid, Ireland — did he have the right to condemn them to such a life because he would not say five words to the Prince of Orange?

It was abundantly clear that William was interested only in his own place in the succession, not in English liberty or the Anglican Church. But it was too late now for the men who had committed themselves to his service. They had betrayed their King in order to save their church, and in the end had accomplished nothing except to bind themselves to another master — and that one a Dutch Calvinist instead of an English Catholic.

Thomas remembered how, as a very small child, he had been rousted out of bed one night and taken to the Great Hall, where more than a hundred people, all in rich Court dress, were assembled for dinner. In the roar of conversation the music from the gallery was almost inaudible. In the centre of the candlelit room stood a very tall dark man, the man who had been painted holding the three-foot-long parchment.

"Kneel, child," Thomas' father had said. "This is your sovereign lord."

Three-quarters asleep still, Thomas had responded as he knelt, "Blessed be the name of the Lord," and everyone had laughed, King Charles most heartily of all. Thomas realized that he had erred. Shame made water burst from his eyes and nose. He must have been a filthy sight, choking and sobbing, but Prince James, who was standing nearby, had knelt down and spoken to him kindly. Thomas' father had looked annoyed. "Your Highness should not trouble himself."

Thomas' mother had come forward then to take him by the hand. She spoke to James, who kissed her cheek, while Thomas, forgotten, cleaned his face with his sleeve. Then the Prince had turned aside and walked off arm-in-arm with John de Chastelain, friendly as a brother. Two things had been plain, even to a four-year-old child: James admired Thomas' mother and Thomas' father knew it but did not mind, although he was a proud man who cherished and guarded his family.

It was a strange thing to remember all these years. His mother and father were long dead and James was no longer a young man with a penchant for other men's wives. He was fifty-five and about to become as much of a martyr as his father, King Charles of sacred memory... and all his faithful servants would be swept with him into the void.

Someone banged on the door. Thomas, scraping back his chair, trod on Magnus' tail as he got up. It was Dundee, looking as if he were about to fight a battle. "I've seen St. Clare," he said without preamble. "He rode in with Halifax and his friends. I thought you should know."

"Where is he?" Thomas' voice, infinitely cold, made Magnus' ears twitch.

Dundee sat down on the only other chair in the room and poured himself a half-glass of wine. "I saw him in the Gallery with Shrewsbury. I don't think he remembered me — we have only met once or twice — or else he would have spoken." He drank his wine and then, an unheard-of thing, refilled his glass. Grief and weariness overlaid his features like dust on a portrait. He was still in uniform, although most of his brigade had been sent back to Scotland after the army's disbandment. But he had kept fifty of his own regiment with him, ready to fight at his word, and even with this small number he would have taken a stand against the Dutch, or at least escorted the King to a safe house. But James had refused that too. Having decided that he was going to France, it would take a thunderbolt from God to change his mind.

Undoubtedly Dundee had tried. His voice sounded like gravel, as if he had been talking or shouting for hours. But what could not be changed had to be endured. Already he was planning his next move. He told Thomas that even if the Lowland Scots sided with the English nobles, the Highlanders would never do so. They would fight to the death for James as they had fought for his father under Montrose, and he intended to make capital out of that.

"Montrose," Thomas said. He ought to have known this was coming. Dundee's most famous ancestor was also his inspiration — his boyhood idol, although he would never say anything so fulsome. Dundee had analyzed all of Montrose's campaigns and mapped his every move. It was the stuff of legend how he had escaped Cromwell's net and travelled to the Highlands with only three friends, the kernel of an army that had won astonishing victories for the King.

"Until it was massacred and the Campbells sold the King to Cromwell," said Thomas shortly. Dundee, for all his flint-like practicality, was not immune to dreaming, and surely it was fantasy to think that Montrose's exploits could be recreated forty years later. Yet, according to Dundee, the King had liked the proposal.

"We had thirty thousand men in the field at Salisbury and the King wouldn't fight," said Thomas. "Tonight he let the Dutch walk into his own house. What makes you think he would fight in Scotland?"

Dundee had taken out his pipe, although as usual he would not smoke it. "He said so."

Incredulous, discomfited, Thomas could not say a word. Dundee went on, "I asked him for a warrant to raise troops in Scotland... myself and Colin. I want you with me as well. I know you don't want to leave England. But I think this would be a better alternative than France or Ireland. Unless, of course," he said after a slight pause, "you plan on making friends with the Dutch." His faint smile showed that this was a joke.

"Before the King left Whitehall the first time, I begged him to allow us to raise a loyal troop," Thomas said. "He refused."

"This is different. From France he'll have a free hand. Louis has promised him troops. He intends to land in Ireland first, and after he's established himself in Dublin, he'll bring his army over to us."

Land in Ireland, with French troops...the King was going to ignore his many loyal countrymen in favour of the French, the Irish and the Scots? Or so he said tonight. A month from now he might have changed his mind. It seemed that the King could believe in anything — Louis' friendship, Irish loyalty, a Highland invasion — as long as it was far enough distant in time and space. But he could not deal with the reality of the enemy at the gate. How could Dundee, who was nobody's fool, believe that James would follow through with any of these plans? There was a point at which loyalty had to give way to sense.

"Even if you did put together a Highland army," Thomas said, "it would never succeed against English and Dutch troops. And I won't leave my family here, hostage to William."

Dundee contemplated his pipe bowl. "A Highland army would have won the war for King Charles, had there not been traitors who betrayed it. As for your family, they might be safer with you gone. They would have St. Clare to protect them then."

Thomas started to deny it. Then understanding silenced him. It was outrageous that he should now be more of a danger to his family than St. Clare: *he* was not the one who had thrown himself into a criminal conspiracy. But Dundee was right. Loyalty and treason had exchanged places. Fighting for James after this would mean acting outside the law, with all that entailed — his life, family, titles and estates forfeited if he lost.

"Your sister Louisa's husband, is he not Atholl's kinsman?" asked Dundee.

Thomas could see where this was going. His brother-in-law Douglas Murray was cousin to the Marquis of Atholl, a man whose status in Scotland approached that of royalty. Atholl had his principal seat at Blair Castle, the strategic point of entry to the Highlands; anyone who controlled Blair would control access to the north. But, so far as Thomas knew, Douglas was not a member of Atholl's inner circle. He was a frightened man who locked his strongbox with four keys and had his servants search the house for intruders each night. Touchy, vain, indecisive, he was the last man on earth to ally himself with so wild a venture as Dundee had in mind.

Thomas wanted to tell his friend that too much had changed since Montrose's day — everything except the prejudice felt by both the English and Lowland Scots against their northern neighbours. "Show me a Highlander," ran the old saying, "and I'll show ye a thief." The clans were considered little better than savages, living as they did in that foul climate on an unchristian diet of oats and whisky, occupying themselves with cattle thieving and petty feuds. Even their chieftains often had no better shelter than a dirt-floored hut. Yet in their pride they yielded to no one. They were a poetic, superstitious, bloody-minded race, ferocious as the tribes who had sacked Rome. When they were not attacking their enemies in battle, they fought their friends and relatives for sport.

"You won't get anything from Douglas Murray," Thomas said. "In any case you're going much too fast. Parliament won't consent so easily to a Dutch government, and I believe — " He was interrupted by another knock on the door.

"Speak of the devil," said Dundee, for it was St. Clare, carrying a lighted candle and looking as though he had been in the saddle for days. His clothes were creased and travel-stained, his hair in unwashed strings. He stank of wine. But he still had the diamond in his ear and the gold ring on his thumb. Thomas put a hand to his sword belt, an instinctive gesture, and then remembered that Lord Craven had collected their weapons. St. Clare looked at him and set the candle down. "For God's sake," he said. "I'm not armed."

Dundee rose from his chair, replacing his pipe in his pocket and fastening his scarlet coat as if for inspection. When he chose, his manner could be as cold and royal as the King's. "Sir," he said, "you must have mistaken your lodging."

St. Clare stared at him as if he were a servant who had dropped a plate. "You gentlemen are not acquainted," said Thomas. Even to himself he sounded wild. He fought for control. "General Dundee, I give you Lord St. Clare. Former Lord Lieutenant, former privy councillor, former friend...what out of hell are you doing here, George? Have you come to collect your taxes?"

Rumour had it that St. Clare had been named one of the commissioners responsible for collecting so-called crown revenues from the English, in order to pay off the Dutch army. From Chief Justice to tax-collector: it was work so base that it was astonishing St. Clare had accepted it. But perhaps he had had no choice, once he had kissed William's hand.

Thomas turned his pockets inside out. "As you see, I have nothing to give you."

St. Clare flushed violently. Dundee stood between them. "It's past two of the clock, sir. Why have you come?"

"To warn you. I rode in with Lord Delamere and the rest, and I tell you, they want blood. Yours, if not the King's. You are both at risk if you stay here after he leaves."

"We have been so before, sir, in the King's service," said Dundee.

"General, I tell you that Delamere intends to arrest anyone who opposes him."

"Are you betraying your Dutch allies now?" asked Thomas. "The last I looked, Delamere was the member for Cheshire, not Lord Chief Justice. He has no authority to arrest anyone."

"William is King today in all but name and Lord Delamere is his agent," St. Clare said. "If you have any care for your wife and children, you will listen to me."

If. "God forgive you, sir, what care did you have for them, when you went to Exeter?"

"I saved them," St. Clare roared. "And you as well, damn your eyes! Look here! I went to a deal of trouble to get it." From his vest he pulled a sheet of paper, a safe-conduct signed by old Schomberg himself. When Thomas made no move to take it, St. Clare bridled like a fighting-cock.

"Will you put my daughter and grandchildren on the block with yourself, only so that you might say, 'I kept my word?' Do you think honour will give them a roof over their heads or put food on their table?"

"It will give them a name they don't have to be ashamed of."

"That will console them when they're begging for crusts in some stinking French town. Or were you going to keep them here to become hostages to the Dutch?"

Schomberg's paper had fallen to the floor. Dundee set his boot upon it and, at the same time, held Thomas' arm. For so slight a man, he had a grip of iron. "Thank you for your warning, sir," he said civilly, "but I don't see Lord Delamere as a threat. England's government might be negotiating with the Dutch, but Scotland's is not. Prince William has no power to arrest or even question me, or any whom the King has appointed in Scotland. And as Lord de Chastelain is with my staff — "

"Your 'staff,'" interrupted St. Clare scathingly. "I've seen your staff, General. It consists of Colin Lindsay and Thomas' dogs. As for Scotland's council, if you think the prince would let anything so paltry stand in his way, you are mistaken." He folded his arms, and his eyes, starting forth from his head, looked like a gargoyle's. "But go to, Thomas. Fight for the lost cause if you choose. I'll go before the courts and have my grandsons named my wards. No one would oppose it, when you'll be a criminal on the run. You'll not see them unless and until you stand down."

He was an old man alone, and they were two of them. Thomas picked up the only object to hand, the half-empty wine decanter, and like any mad drunken Irishman he would have hurled it at St. Clare, had Dundee not struck it from his hand. It burst against the tiles and Magnus began to howl.

"Get out," said Dundee. "We've heard what you had to say."

There was nothing civil about him now. Under the crust of the courtier boiled a temper so fierce that even St. Clare could recognize the danger. He took his candlestick and held it to his chest as if protecting himself from a lunatic. His shirt and the tails of his hair were splattered with wine. "There are guards outside. I have only to call and they would arrest you." He backed to the door, his eyes on Thomas. "You're a fool. Who is there to help you now? You should be on your knees to me in thanks."

"Your collar is on fire," said Thomas.

St. Clare had held his candle too close to his chest and his neckcloth had singed. He swatted at the scorched linen, his face turning a dusky plum-colour. He could never bear any sort of ridicule. "By the way," he said to Thomas, "your friend Lee is in prison at Windsor. I thought you would want to know."

With that he opened the door. He had been telling the truth about the guards: an escort of Dutch soldiers waited outside, leaning on their muskets and looking bored. In his own fashion, St. Clare was as much a prisoner as themselves or the King.

But with much less chance of escape.

The Dutch allowed James to have his customary levee. Despite the presence of his gaolers, he had slept well and rose for prayers at his usual hour, afterward taking a vigorous walk along the Mall. Dutch soldiers followed, guarding a throng of courtiers and clergy who had come to take leave of their sovereign.

In this last hour the King seemed to have acquired a deep dignity, amounting almost to grandeur, as his enemies harried him out of his bedchamber and rushed him through breakfast. As with his father, under the worst of circumstances the best of his character showed. In defeat he would show himself more Christian and kingly than he had ever been during his reign. He had decided he would go to Rochester again instead of Ham, as William had ordered — Rochester being nearer the sea, and offering more opportunity for a quick passage to France. William's representatives made no objection.

"It's clear, sir, how much the Prince desires your leaving," said Dundee. "For that reason only, you ought to stay." He still had not given up. But James' face wore that closed, obstinate look with which they were all familiar.

"He intends to do away with me," he said. "You see how I am forced out of my own house." The sun was out, but by the look of the building clouds it would soon rain again, and as they turned to walk back the first drops spattered Thomas' cheek. Brooding on Lee, he had missed the last few moments of conversation. James was charging Dundee and Colin Lindsay to represent him in Scotland.

Thomas saw his friend's tired eyes blaze with a kind of holy fervour. That order — "raise Scotland for me" — would be burned into his heart and brain, sacred as the word of God and even more difficult to keep. But not for Dundee. He would fight with three friends or three thousand, with or without the French or Irish, happily following the glorious path of Montrose. It was no good to think about where and how that path had ended. Had not Montrose himself, poet as well as soldier, written about it fearlessly, the night before he died — "*Let them dispose on every airth a limb...* "?

They knelt on the paving stones to swear their service. A gust of wind nearly tore the hat from Thomas' hand. They might have been onstage with the King's Company of Players, so fantastic did it seem — only the rank oily smell of the river was real, and the scream of the gulls as they fought over scraps of offal. Church bells chimed the hour. The King would not permit them to stay kneeling, but insisted that they all shake hands as friends. Colin Lindsay began to sob like a child. "I shall not forget any of you," James said. His nose and eyes ran as well, though whether from cold or grief, it was impossible to tell. He moved away into the crowd, giving his hand graciously, saying his farewells. People knelt to kiss his hand or touch the hem of his coat — some of them the same people who, days earlier, had been shouting for his head. Already misfortune had begun to sanctify him. "Let him die now, this moment, before he can ruin it" — so ran the thought through Thomas' mind, instantly and fiercely suppressed.

A short time later the King's barge pushed off in the company of a Dutch flotilla. It was raining steadily now and a small, silent crowd had gathered on the riverbank to watch him leave. There were no catcalls from the crowd, no jeers; only a deep, almost fearful silence, as if they were witnessing the King's death instead of his departure.

He had muffled himself for the journey in an old cloak and scarf like some country farmer. But his bearing was regal. He might have been travelling to his coronation instead of sailing into oblivion. Thomas, kneeling on the riverbank, swept off his hat as the barge went by. He was surrounded by Dutch soldiers and the sensible course would have been to keep his head down. But instead he gave a great, hoarse, solitary shout that carried over the water to the barge. "God save the King!"

James lifted his own hat in acknowledgement. Even at a distance it was clear that he was weeping. Thomas remained on his knees in the mud, expecting at any moment to feel a Dutch soldier's hand on his shoulder or the cold barrel of a musket at his ear. But no one spoke or moved. The barge drifted out of sight into the mist, a ghost-ship with a ghost-king, and the rain pattered down from a steel-grey sky.

PART TWO

1

HE SMELLED THE MUSTINESS of the day even before opening his eyes, and knew that he was no longer in his own bed in his own sweet country. He had been dreaming of tulips.

"Snow this morning, Your Highness."

Snow. No riding then. William was accustomed to cold weather and rough living, but he knew it would be folly to risk a chill. He had woken with another asthma attack in the night, and his chest rasped and bubbled when he coughed. Even in the trenches, fighting the French, he had never felt so cold and ill and sick for home.

He dressed swiftly, without ceremony, dispensing with the services of the waiting English nobles. If it disappointed some of them not to hand him his neckband, then so be it. He hated dressing and dining in public and would allow no one except Dr. Radcliffe to see the linseed poultice he was forced to strap over his aching chest. The servant who had reported on the weather brought in the single boiled egg he had ordered.

"Bring tea as well," said William. He kept his hands behind his back to avoid any possibility that the fellow might unexpectedly kiss them. He disliked this English custom, which was as foreign to him as the preference for monstrously large meals. At the banquets he had been forced to attend, he had found that the English ate and drank prodigiously, but without discrimination, loading up their tables with a jumble of roast and boiled meats and casks of indifferent wine. William, abstemious and always a finicky eater, drank weak tea in the morning and at noon picked at a chicken bone or a plate of vegetables. In the evening he took half a glass of Rhenish, brought over from his own cellars.

He pulled back one of the velvet drapes and looked out into the misty grey dawn. He had set up his headquarters in St. James' palace, his wife's childhood home, and slept in the bedchamber where the so-called Prince of Wales had been born six months before. The rooms were richly furnished, but the rain brought down thick particles of coal-smoke that turned everything black. Today's snow would soon be peppered with it. Lately it had been so cold that the canal and the ponds in St. James' park had frozen, and people skated on the ice as they did in The Hague. But there any resemblance to his homeland ended.

He dropped the curtain and sat down at his desk. As he could not ride, it would be one of his writing days. He kept up a broad, disciplined correspondence with people in Holland and throughout his new kingdom. He drove his secretary, Huygens, very hard. But not so hard as he drove himself.

His tea arrived. The servant, as if uncertain whether to kneel or bow, did both. William dismissed him with a brusque gesture, not troubling to see whether he followed etiquette by backing out of the room. Only King Louis cared whether or not someone sat on a footstool or knelt or walked backward through a door. But then Louis, apparently confusing himself with God Almighty, had elevated Court protocol to the status of a religion.

Huygens was eleven minutes late. William discovered that his egg was cold. He drank some of his tea, which tasted of brine, and took up a pen to write to his Grand Pensionary, Michiel Ten Hove. There was enormous work involved in keeping the government of the United Provinces running while he settled England's, and much of it involved ensuring English support for war with France. It would be useful if he could make sweeping *ex cathedra* pronouncements, like Louis. But he had to be careful not to exceed his authority even in his own country, for his status there, although illustrious, was not precisely royal. The prickly States-General of the United Provinces, "their High Mightinesses," would never endorse a monarchy. His titles of Stadholder and Captain-General were not hereditary. Dutch cities were ruled by plainspoken, ordinary men who believed firmly in republicanism. King Louis, who wanted to make all of Europe into his personal fiefdom, had no understanding of this aspect of the Dutch character. It was inconceivable to *Le Grand Monarque* that the citizens of this scrubby, upstart little republic had opened the sluice gates and flooded their own country, just to keep him out.

Nor did the English have any understanding of the Dutch or concern for their peril. Competition for trade and territory was too sharp. William had appealed to his uncle King Charles for help in fighting the French, only to discover that Charles was in Louis' pay. The two kings had agreed to attack the Dutch republic and divide up the spoils.

William had consecrated his life to saving his country from this fate, and years of hard campaigning had left their mark. While Louis travelled in velvet-lined coaches with his mistresses, William was on horseback, camping out with his troops in all weathers. He was troubled with asthma and had grown so thin that his oldest friend, Bentinck, fussed over him like a wet nurse. But as his health eroded his reputation had grown. He had become the hero of the Protestant world, the only prince who dared tweak Louis' big Bourbon nose.

"The saviour of the Protestant faith" was a title he accepted, but not without irony. The English liked to make speeches. Listening to the nobles and churchmen and members of parliament, one would think that they had all said hosannas at his arrival, and had been prevented from joining his army only because of the weather. But he had waited in Exeter for days while these same cowards hid behind their walls. He had more respect for those who, like General Dundee, had refused him outright.

As he dipped his quill into the standish he noticed a film of grit upon his desk. Even his teacup was grimy. It was inexcusable but unsurprising, for in all respects he found the English dirty. They ate and drank like gluttons, seldom bathed, and pissed in public like dogs. Mould grew on their walls and their mildewed furniture was speckled with soot. This would never happen at home, where even the storage closets were scrubbed and dusted, and each bathroom had running hot water. At times William longed for his house at Honselaersdijck the way another man might yearn for a lover. There the spotless rooms were decorated with carefully chosen paintings, fine tapestries, rich but sensible furnishings, and fresh-cut flowers from the elegant pleasure gardens. It was a bright, clean jewel of a house that he would have lived in always, had he been free to choose. But he had been forced to come to the rescue of this contumacious nation and now he was suffering the consequences. The monstrous cold he had caught on his rainy progress from Exeter had never left him and his asthma had grown much worse. He spent his days and nights strapped into his chest poultice, sweating and shivering and coughing up gobbets of green phlegm. The nobles who had signed that letter of invitation to him had not specified that he must be able to withstand the English climate.

Nor had they expressed any appreciation of the sacrifice he was making. They assumed that he desired the Crown for its own sake, that he had actually lusted to come to this miserable fog-bound island and be thrown into the company of men like Churchill and General Douglas, turncoats who were not fit to wipe old Schomberg's nose. Only his closest friends realized what it had cost him to leave Holland. He had traded his beloved country, his health, and possibly his life for England — not for personal glory, but because it was the only way that he could fight Louis and win.

He drank his tea and attacked the sad remnant of his boiled egg. His usually faithful Huygens was now seventeen minutes late and the schedule of the morning would have to be pushed back. As he dug bits of shell out of the yolk he swore an English oath. He would never utter any profanity in his native language, but English, with its coarse "bloodys" and "hells" and "be-damneds," lent itself to cursing.

And English minds were grubby as well. He had no time for a personal life, but he knew what evil was whispered about him, that in bed he preferred men to women and possibly horses to either. He did not understand his new subjects' evident need to traduce him. So far he had been called immoral, homely, unsociable, rude, and — apparently the worst crime of all in this country — ill-dressed. But if he suddenly began holding music parties and arraying himself in cloth-of-gold, he would be charged with extravagance. If he kissed the pallid, freckled women he would be accused of lust. There was no pleasing the bloody English.

He would let his wife please them when she arrived. Then he could get back to work.

2 AT CHARTERS AN INCH of snow had fallen. Beatrice and James rolled in it delightedly, over and over, while Theo tugged at their boots in a rapturous frenzy. Sunlight flashed and glittered on the water, turning it from pewter to diamond. The trees wore a mantle of frost. The children lay side by side on the lawn by the terrace, looking past the snow-dusted turrets and the chimney pots to the blue sky beyond. A crow had perched on the weather vane, and they laughed when a sudden gust of wind spun it around and sent him squawking into flight.

The King's colours and the de Chastelain standard flew from the rooftop. James had dreamed last night about his father, a dream so real that it had been shocking this morning to discover that it was not true. Thomas had not come home during the night, and there was no birthday present hidden in the depths of his coat pocket. Tears started to James' eyes when he thought of it, but he felt he should not cry in front of Beatrice. He was six years old today and had to learn self-control. That was what Master Hammond said.

No one had noticed them leave the house. Mam was still abed after the new baby's birth, and Master Hammond was sick with a streaming head cold that had turned his nose the colour of a ripe cherry. Fulke had locked himself in his office with the account books, and Brigid was tending to Alys. Even the kitchen maids were too busy to pay any attention to the children, for it was baking day.

Recently James had bestowed upon Beatrice his most cherished possession, a silver whistle that (according to

Mam) was loud enough to be heard in Dublin. Beatrice wore it around her neck on a chain. Occasionally she set it to her lips and blew a piercing blast. James wished that it would summon his father back from the city. But Mam said he had to stay in London with the King.

From Abigail's sister they had heard about Irish Night, how wild mobs had torn through London and burned down buildings. By mischance, one of those set alight had been Leopold's house. Sparks from a nearby fire had blown on his roof and the house had been destroyed. Abigail had rescued many of his papers, but everything else had burned to ashes, and she herself was ill. There had been a baby on the way and now there was not. James pressed his own arm, and then his leg, trying to imagine how it was possible to disappear before being born. When he thought of Irish Night he had a picture in his mind of darkly bearded men rushing upon his father with flaming torches. But Uncle Leopold said that it was the Londoners themselves who had burned their city.

In honour of James' birthday Leopold had built another paper flotilla. But he had left it unfinished to rush to London, rattling away in an old-fashioned carriage borrowed from Lord Burcote. As he left he had begged Mam to find or sew mourning clothes for his "poor suffering children." Mam had tried to persuade him that it was not necessary. But in the end she had unpicked one of her own dresses to make a skirt for Beatrice and a suit for Samuel.

James thought Beatrice should not be rolling on the ground in what had once been his mother's second-best silk ball gown. On the other hand, the snow was clean even if the ground underneath were muddy. Soon Beatrice jumped up and brushed off the back of her skirt. Her eyes were pink, as if she had been crying, but her manner was brisk.

She sucked on the little balls of ice that had formed on her woollen gloves and said, "I'll tell you a secret."

A small glow of pleasure warmed James' insides. He was seldom the recipient of any confidences. Beatrice waited a moment and then said, "I saw Master Hammond kiss Brigid. Or try to. She pushed him away and said, 'Oh no, never.'"

James' face fell. He had hoped that Beatrice might have discovered a two-headed hen or a litter of kittens in the barn, but this was of no interest at all. "He says he wants to save her soul," Beatrice said, frowning at his lack of response. "He sent her books."

James was bored. "She can't read," he said. He scooped up a handful of snow and let it fall through his small cold fingers. He had left his gloves inside and was getting chilled, but he would not be the first to admit it.

"I'm teaching her," said Beatrice. "When she puts me to bed, I show her the alphabet and she teaches me her special prayers." To demonstrate, she put her palms together. Her voice took on an Irish twang. "HailMary! Full o'grace! The Lordiswithee entirely, and blessed be the fruit of Thywomb. Jesus!"

"I don't think you should be saying those prayers," James said. He had no idea what the words meant, but he had an idea that his father would not like them.

Beatrice's chin jutted aggressively. "My papa says all prayers are good."

James struggled to think this through. Most people he knew believed that unless prayers were said in a certain manner, generally a Protestant manner, the Devil would find you and pick out your soul like a nut from its shell. Papists were doomed, as were the unbaptized heathen. The thought of Brigid troubled him and he wished that

Leopold were here to explain the matter. But no one, not even Mam, knew when he would return.

Beatrice had confided that she wore her black dress not for the sake of her infant brother, who, after all, had not been a real child, but for Otto, her cat, who had perished in the fire. Otto had been burned along with all of the household treasures — clocks, cook-pots, clothes, furniture, books, the gold-framed painting of St. Francis, Beatrice's canopied bed, her jewel box with the hairpins in it, her straw-haired dolls, and her wooden hobby horse.

She looked up at the flags streaming from the rooftop. "Let's go up to the bell tower," she said abruptly. Work had not resumed on it and canvas still covered the parapet. James thought of that long climb up, and the dizzying height with no wall for protection. "We can't. It's blocked off."

"I know a way."

James hesitated. He was cold and wanted to go inside to warm himself at the fire. But Beatrice was looking at him impatiently. He was too old now to cry and tell her that he was afraid of heights and that his hands were frozen.

"We could play jump-the-candle instead."

Mam had forbidden this ancient game, since the risk of setting themselves on fire was so great, and he thought that this might satisfy Beatrice's odd rebellious hunger. But no.

"I'm going, James. Come along if you want."

"We're not allowed."

"We'll just look at the church and come down." She took his hand and they hurried across the terrace to the rose garden, where in summer Mam liked to read. Snow-sugar powdered the bushes. Blown petals from the last roses were scattered on the ground as if for a wedding. In amongst the rose bushes someone had planted a winter cherry, but the buds had not yet opened. Brigid had said the blossoms were sleeping in their hard brown shells, waiting for the signal to awaken.

Beatrice left the brick pathway and plunged, heedless of thorns, into the midst of the rose bushes. Behind one of the trellises there was a small door, not even child-height, set into the wall of the house. James had spent his short life here without even knowing it existed.

"How did you know this was here?"

"I looked for it," Beatrice said. "Don't you remember Master Hammond told us about priest holes?"

There was a lock on the door, but it was rusty and fell to pieces in Beatrice's hands. They crawled on their hands and knees over the threshold, leaving Theo behind. On the other side there was an opening they could just stand in, and beyond it a steep pitch-dark stairway spiralled down into nothingness. James felt his scalp contract.

"We need a candle."

"I can see. I'll go in front," said Beatrice. "I think this goes to the Lady Chapel."

"It's too dark."

"It's all right. Don't be afraid."

"I'm not," said James. But when something scurried past him in the dark he jumped and nearly lost his footing. Beatrice gripped his hand firmly. "Come on."

The cold air smelled of dirt, wet stone, and age. There was a faint but distinct sound of water dripping. The steps were invisible in the musty dark. The children put one foot out at a time, feeling each stair, and soon Beatrice had to let go of James' hand because there was not enough room to walk abreast. The passageway turned like a screw. It was too dark for James to see ahead. But he heard a faint sound, like a whisper or a sigh, that loosened his belly with fear. The musty, cold smell had become stronger.

"Stop, Beatrice," he whispered. In the silence he strained to listen. The sigh came again, a slight movement of water against stone. The passage was leading down into a pool of water, a flooded cellar or perhaps a cell, where long ago some wretched prisoner might have been shackled to an iron ring in the wall.

"We have to go back," he said. "There's no way through."

Even in the dark James could see that Beatrice's face was bunched into a monumental scowl. She took a step forward. But fear of the water below and what it might conceal made him take charge. He caught her sleeve and said, as masterfully as his father, "We're going back."

Perhaps there was a serpent in that pool, a kelpie, or, worst of all, a waterhorse. According to Brigid, these were monstrous demons that carried children off into the sea and then devoured them, even to their bones and teeth. Only their livers were ever found, washed back on the shore as a gruesome warning to other children. A whimper broke from James' lips. He half-dragged Beatrice up the stairs and when they at last reached the door, he hurled himself through it and cracked his head on the bricks.

The sun was still shining. Beatrice fell to the ground, crushing her dress into the snow. Her hands and her face were smeared with dirt. James, hugging Theo, felt that never again would he fall in with one of his cousin's silly schemes. Likely there was no such thing as a priest hole here at all, and Beatrice had made it up. But as she stood, wiping her palms on her dress, her face was so tragic that his resentment waned.

"Don't worry, Beatrice," he said. "We can ask my father to take us up to the bell tower when it's finished."

"I want to go now," said Beatrice. Suddenly she shouted.

"I want my red shoes. I want my cup with the flowers on it. I want my dolls." She began to cry. James, wholly at a loss, sat mute and dismayed until he remembered the honey cake in his pocket. He had taken it from the kitchen yesterday and forgotten it. He divided the slice in two, offering Beatrice the larger share, and they ate in silence until Beatrice lifted her head and whispered, "Listen."

Someone at St. Mary's was ringing the passing-bell. The muffled, solemn peals tolled one after another without ceasing, the sound piercingly clear in the bright cold air, like the ring of silver on crystal. James felt uneasy. He put the rest of his cake back in his pocket and tried to count the peals to find out the age of the person who was dying.

"Do you think they know about Otto?" Beatrice asked.

It seemed unlikely that the passing bell would be rung for a dead cat, but James was unsure. "Mam will know," he said. "Let's find out."

It was his birthday, after all, and suddenly he longed to be in his mother's arms, clean and warm and comforted, with Brigid making chocolate for them in Mam's little silver pot. He stood, brushing the crumbs from his coat.

"Don't tell anyone about Brigid," said Beatrice, but in any case James had already forgotten what she had told him. Something about Master Hammond and kissing — a matter of no importance at all.

In her chamber, where she was still confined to bed, Libby also heard the church bells. She sent John Patrick to find out who was dying, and when the boy returned his young face was flushed with the drama of his news. He stood in the doorway, the children and dogs crowding around him inquisitively, and pulled off his cap. "No one is dead, my lady. But the vicar says the Dutch have taken London!"

Libby sat up too quickly and had to put a hand to her side. "'Taken'? Was there a battle?"

"No, my lady, they say the Prince just walked into Whitehall with his troops."

"What of the King? Is he prisoner?"

"He's run to France."

The children began talking all at once, waking Kate, who stirred and coughed in her cradle. Under the carved oak canopy nothing was visible of her except a dark head nestled in yards of lace. Libby set the cradle rocking while John Patrick went on excitedly about the Bishop and the vicar. Already the village was taking sides amidst fears that the Dutch might be sending in troops.

"God have mercy," said Libby.

There had been no word since Malachy had come home after Irish Night, bringing Thomas' one-line letter and the extraordinary information that the King had been captured by Kentish fishermen. Somehow since then James had escaped to France, and now William was master of London. Had Thomas, who had gone to wait upon the King, been forced to flee across the Channel as well? Why had there been no message from him?

"What happened to the army?" she asked.

"Disbanded before the King left, my lady. Our men will be coming home. But we won't be seeing Mr. Whitby. The vicar says he's with the Bishop."

So their own chaplain had deserted. Piers put aside the book he had been reading, and came to stand by his mother's bed. "Do you think Father is with the King?"

"I don't know. I think that if he had to leave, he would have sent a message to us somehow."

She reached up to brush Piers' hair from his eyes, but he turned away as if to emphasize that he was now the man of the house and not a baby to be coddled. Libby, folding her hands, felt a small, cold pain around her heart.

"Grandfather is with the Dutch," said Piers suddenly. "He went to Windsor with the soldiers." It was the first time St. Clare's name had been mentioned since the day he had visited. His gifts had been opened and cast aside, forgotten, although James had managed to eat most of his comfits before he lost the box.

"He's a traitor," continued Piers in a hard, unchildlike voice. "But now that William is here, it's Father who will be punished. Maybe he's already in prison, like Sir John Lee."

"We must pray not."

Piers looked scornful, as if prayers were the last resort of women and infants. James suddenly asked in a high, quavering voice, "Does that mean Papa won't be coming home?"

Libby patted his hand. "I don't know, my love."

There was nothing else she could say without a lie. James' thumb stole into his mouth, a habit that had recently reasserted itself. She thought that he looked tired, and he and Beatrice had been very quiet since coming into the room. But then all of the children had been unusually subdued. Leopold's abrupt departure, and the reason for it, had thrown a pall over the entire household. During his convalescence he had entertained the children by telling stories, constructing little machines, and explaining such interesting matters as why all objects fell to the ground at the same rate and how mercury was used in mirrors. To their delight he had demonstrated that the spit in their mouths was full of animalcules that could be seen under a lens. At the same time he described how telescopes brought heaven itself closer, so that sun spots and moon craters and unknown stars became visible. They loved that although he was so knowledgeable, he was almost like a child himself, delighting in games, forgetting to put away his dishes, and allowing the dogs to sleep on his bed. But that letter had changed him upon the instant into an angry and sorrowful stranger. He had said it was only by chance that Abigail had been in London at all, as for safety's sake she had been staying with her sister in Kensington. She had only returned to the house on the day of the fire to fetch some clothes. When he asked, "Is this the will of God?" no one had an answer for him.

Samuel said kindly to James, "The cook made treacle tart for your birthday."

"A gypsy told me it's bad luck to be born on a Friday," Beatrice announced.

All fell silent. Samuel looked uneasy. "Beatrice, you shouldn't talk to gypsies."

"He's right," said Piers. "It's a capital offence."

"Like stealing fish," said James. He started to cross himself and then stopped and wiped his nose with the back of his hand. Libby thought, *I must break him of these dreadful habits before his father comes home.* "What gypsies, Beatrice?" she asked. "Where did you see them?"

"Down in the bottom meadow. There was a family camping. They looked hungry, so I invited them for dinner." Beatrice hopped on one foot and then the other, her brow furrowing as the silence expanded to fill the room. "You don't mind, do you, Aunt Lib? There's only five or six of them. And we always give food to the poor on St. Thomas' day."

"Not to gypsies," said Piers. "We could be arrested."

"Or hanged," Samuel added. His eyes filled.

"Nonsense," Libby said briskly. She could imagine what the Bishop would say about consorting with gypsies. But the Bishop, traitor and coward, was hardly in a position to criticize. "We'll give the people some food. But, Beatrice, you should not have gone down to the meadow alone. Promise me you will never do so again."

"I wanted to hear my fortune, Aunt Lib. The Romany woman said I would marry a foreigner who would be both rich and poor. That's what she said."

"Did you ask her about me? Or Piers?" James looked as though he could scarcely breathe.

"No. But she did say one of you would travel far away and the other would marry a woman who owned sheep."

"You're such a fool, Beatrice," said Piers. Beatrice usually took such insults in stride, but now her eyes began to run and a look from Libby made Piers mumble a graceless apology. "Sorry. Forgot."

James went to the window. The heat of the fire had fogged up the pane and he cleared it with his palm before looking out. "There's someone coming."

"Lord Burcote, I suppose, bringing me the news," said Libby. She had lately suffered a sort of kindly persecution from their neighbour, who had been shocked to hear about Lord Wharton's raid and so rode over three or four times a week to check on the welfare of the household. Dr. Spencer was treating Lady Burcote for the stone and Libby was obliged to listen to detailed accounts of her sufferings. When the baby was born, Burcote had sent over a box filled with out-of-season fruits and flowers from his greenhouse, a case of claret, jars of preserves, and a set of spoons.

"He's in love with you, Libby," said Leopold, and she had laughed at the thought of Lord Burcote, with over sixty years in his dish, acting the gallant.

"No, it's not him," said James. "I see the horse." Suddenly his voice jumped and squeaked. "It's Pilgrim. Pilgrim!" He burst into tears and ran out of the room. All the children followed.

"Wait for me," said Libby. She stood so quickly that vertigo seized her and she reached for the back of a chair to steady herself. "Children, wait!" she called. But the room was empty. Even the dogs had gone pell-mell down the stairs, their nails scrabbling on the wood, their barking a mingled frenzy of anxiety and delight. She reached for her wrapper and pushed her feet into slippers. Her heart beat in hurtful jerks and her legs trembled.

Brigid, who had been coming upstairs with medicine for Alys, rushed into the room.

"Have you heard, my lady?"

"I know. I'm going downstairs."

"You should stay in bed."

"I know."

Brigid, ever practical, held out her arm. "Lean on me, then."

"Bring Kate."

Down the stairs, past the tall window that showed the grey December sky. Down the second flight of stairs. There was cacophony in the hall. James was sobbing harder than ever and Beatrice was shouting. Libby realized that she had forgotten to comb her hair.

But it did not matter. The door stood open, letting in the cold and a skirl of dead leaves, and it was not Thomas who stood there, but John Graham.

The shock after the exertion emptied the blood from her head. The ground rocked and then an arm caught her firmly and guided her to a bench by the door. "Steady," said Dundee.

He expertly brought the chaos to order, sending Brigid for a warm shawl for her mistress, hushing the dogs and calming the children, who had all turned on James in scorn because he had mistaken Dundee's sorrel for Thomas'. James had been screaming hysterically, but something in the General's manner made him stop. He blew his nose and wiped his eyes.

"That's a good fellow," said Dundee. Fulke appeared with a glass of brandy stirred with sugar. Libby took a small sip and then sat with both hands around the glass. "We thought you were Thomas," she said, so quietly that Dundee had to bring his head close to hear. "He has not yet come from London."

The General's brow creased and she saw his sudden understanding of why the mistress of the house would answer the door herself, with a retinue of children and dogs in tow. "Have you had no word from him?"

"Not since Irish Night."

Brigid brought the shawl, and they went into Libby's quiet parlour where a fire had been laid. Sunlight without warmth poured through the windows, showing the dust motes floating up and down. A bowl of dried roses shed brittle petals on the waxed table-top. The walnut-cased clock ticked solemnly on the mantel. Dundee sat with his hat on his knees and Libby took the baby from Brigid and sat down facing him. Kate rested her tender head under Libby's cheek and her small fists bunched together. The other children crowded around the door.

"Come away," said Brigid. "Let them talk. We'll go to the kitchen and see if there's gingerbread."

Piers looked agonized. "Sir," he said to Dundee. "Is my father well?"

"When I last saw him, we had dinner together. He spoke of you...something about your Latin being improved out of all recognition."

"And me, sir?" James clutched at Brigid's skirt. "Did he speak of me? Did he tell you about my birthday?"

Libby closed her eyes. But Dundee paused only half a beat before reaching into his uniform pocket. "Indeed he gave me this in your honour." He closed James' fist around a gold coin. "It belonged to the King, so you must keep it safe until you find something you most particularly want to buy. No tobacco or rum, mind. No cockfights or gin."

"Oh, no, sir. Thank you, sir." James looked as though he would swoon with joy.

"Come away now," said Brigid firmly. The doors closed and Libby smiled at Dundee. Impossible to resist his kindness. "You are more than good, sir. You have just given him what he most wanted...other than his father's homecoming."

She drew the shawl around herself and Kate. Even so she still felt cold. A housemaid brought in a tray and Dundee was silent until the door closed once again. He took his dish of tea with practiced ease. Libby remembered, to her shame, that his good manners had surprised her when they first met. Her father had regarded the Scots as little better than the savages of North America. Yet here was General Dundee, graduated MA from St. Andrews at age thirteen, polished, gracious, his only social stumbling block an ineffable reserve.

He told her how the Dutch had turned the King out of his bed at midnight and forced him from Whitehall the next morning. Thomas, so far as anyone knew, had intended going home after the King departed. They had agreed to meet at Abingdon, where Dundee was quartered.

"I think he must have gone to see Sir John Lee. Wharton took him prisoner — "

"Yes," Libby said. "I know." She jiggled Kate on her knee while Dundee described, in a voice of passionate disgust, how he had waited upon the King at Rochester and found him lacking even servants to make him a fire or cook a meal. He was looked after by his gaolers, as the English garrison had deserted sooner than surrender to the Dutch. But the faithful Lord Ailesbury had stayed, keeping vigil until the last moment when the King had boarded a shallop for France. Meanwhile, that same day, Princess Anne had returned in state to London. Attended by Sarah Churchill and a-flutter with orange ribbons, she had driven to the theatre in her father's coach.

Libby sat in silence, knowing that nothing would bind Thomas to the King more firmly than seeing him in such circumstances — hungry, servantless, betrayed by all but a handful of friends and forced to escape in a rowboat down the Medway, while his daughter entertained herself with his enemies. Her voice hushed.

"What will you do?"

She had asked even though Dundee would not be at liberty to disclose his plans, for the risk was far too great. And there was always St. Clare to consider.

But she had reckoned without his generosity, which manifested itself in the assumption that all his friends were as honourable as himself. "I shall raise the King's Standard in Scotland," he said. "William has not so many friends there as here."

Here at last was a crusade worthy of his zeal. His tone conveyed to her his confidence that she would consent to whatever was required, that she would make any necessary sacrifice, because she too had her duty, which was no less important or noble than theirs. She held the baby to her, rocking back and forth, her eyes on the fire where the logs had burned into ridges of ash. John Graham had spent years at court and in the army, and no man could do that without being exposed to the most sordid aspects of human nature. Somehow he had emerged with his chivalrous ideals intact. His integrity was like a trumpet call back to an earlier age when glory was still possible and honour worth dying for. She could understand why his men loved him.

But then men were free, as women were not, to throw away their lives and homes upon a word. Kate's thistledown hair tickled her nose. If she were able — if she were not a woman, with three children at her skirts and a household dependent on her — would she not long to hazard everything at the side of this man who believed in her courage? She thought of little Jean Graham, alone now since September, and likely to remain so for many more months while her husband tore through Scotland raising an army for the King. Long ago she, too, would have come to terms with the fact that she had married a man who would never do what was safe instead of what was right. The question of whether James were worth it would never cross Dundee's loyal mind — or Thomas', either, although for a different reason. For him it was less a matter of personal loyalty than public justice.

She held the baby so close that Kate began to squirm.

"General, has my husband agreed to join you?"

Dundee was silent a moment. "I think he still hopes for a peaceable solution."

"But you don't believe that is possible?"

"No."

She summoned her courage. "Where do you think he is right now?"

It was as close as she could come to putting into words her fear that Thomas might have been arrested.

"I am sure he is only delayed upon the road. But I can find out. I am at your service — now, or at any time."

She knew that from him this was no mere formula, but a pledge. "If you see Thomas before I do, pray tell him we have a daughter," she said, "and that we call her Katherine Sophia."

She could not quite keep her voice level. Thomas loved her most faithfully, yet sometimes it seemed that even the dogs had more of his company and comfort than she. St. Clare had once told her, "Your only rival is your husband's notion of duty. But you may come to wish a poxed actress upon yourself instead."

She would not admit to anyone except herself that the old reprobate had been right. She could not compete with martyred royalty or Thomas' sense of obligation. *But what of his obligation to us?* she asked in her heart. Must they wreck their home, dispossess their children and live apart, all so that Thomas might keep his word to a man who had sent him away in disgrace? Did it make a pennyworth's of difference to anybody whether James or William slept in the king's bed at Whitehall?

His eyes were upon her, grave and tender, as if he understood her dilemma. Silence fell between them. She recollected suddenly what Thomas had said about the property that Dundee had purchased just prior to his marriage — a noble, four-towered castle overlooking the old town of Dundee on the firth of Tay. He had planted trees there that would take thirty years or more to reach their full maturity. A settled home, children, peace, prosperity; she realized that he prized these as much as any other man, with the difference that he would sooner lose his life than barter faith and loyalty to keep them.

She had been feeling sorry for his wife, but, as he kissed her hand, it occurred to her that perhaps Jean Graham was more to be envied than pitied.

3 CHRISTMAS WAS ONLY DAYS AWAY, and for the children's sake Libby went forward with the usual preparations. From Christmas Eve to Twelfth Night, the house would be dressed with holly, ivy, kissing boughs, and rosemary; the Yule log, kindled with great pomp and ceremony from a fragment of last year's log, would burn night and day for luck; Christmas Day itself meant church and the parish dinner. She had invited Dundee and his men, but he told her that he would not put the household at risk by bringing over his troop. His position was too equivocal. He had written to Whitehall asking what security he might expect if he returned to Scotland without professing loyalty to the new government, and Prince William had replied that if the General chose to "live peaceably and at home," he would be protected. Of course that was the one thing Dundee would never do — live peaceably at home.

There was still no word from Thomas. Dundee had been able to confirm that he had indeed been at Windsor, but nothing more. "I am sure there is no mystery," he told Libby. "After all, it is not above a week since the King left."

A week, ten days or twenty, it was all one; time had slowed for her to the point of standstill. She found herself walking without purpose from room to room. Every corner of the house had been scrubbed. The furniture gleamed with beeswax. Scented candles burned in the sconces. Even the fire irons had been polished in preparation for Thomas' homecoming, although he would not notice or care, any more than he would notice the brocade coverlid on their bed, brought out from storage for the first time this year. She put a hand on the folds of the velvet bed curtains, the deep, rich green that she had chosen because Thomas liked bright colours. The King himself had green velvet upon his bed. But she did not want to think about the King, for then she would think about Scotland. In her mind rose an image of gaunt, storm-ridden fortresses towering over black water and steep cliffs, an icily inhospitable wilderness presided over by angry ministers — descendants of those elders of the kirk who, forty years ago, had abolished Christmas, calling it a dirty, popish custom. Christmas had returned, but hatred of Rome was stronger than ever. Not long ago, the public celebration of mass had set off a near-war in the streets of Edinburgh. There were hundreds of displaced Covenanters in Scotland who hated the King, the King's church, and all the King's servants with an undying passion. Most particularly did they hate Dundee. It was no coincidence that Thomas had nearly been killed in the General's company during what was supposed to have been a peaceful trip to Edinburgh three years ago. But there was no peace in that riven kingdom, or in this one.

She fled from her thoughts to rock Kate in the wooden cradle and sing to her. Dr. Spencer had insisted that she rest, and so she did nothing more strenuous than fold the linens, rearrange the greens, and brew tisanes for Alys, who was still abed. On his last visit Heneage had seemed almost thankful to find an abscess breaking open in her breast, as at least he could prescribe something useful for her relief — verjuice and bran poultices. Alys had endured his attentions in frightened silence and afterward tied Brigid's paper charm around her neck and asked for a hare's foot to put under her pillow.

She fretted about returning to her duties, but it was

taken for granted now that Brigid would stay to help look after the children. Her forthright Irish speech, her beads and bangles, and her wardrobe of patchwork skirts had ceased to seem foreign or odd. Even Fulke had grown fond of her. And John Hammond appeared to be courting her, although he was making uphill work of it. He had given her his precious copy of Foxe's *Book of Martyrs*, which she used as a doorstop as she could not read, and sat with her in church on Sundays to remind her not to cross herself in public. Libby, hearing of this, asked in amazement, "Has he nothing better to say to you?"

"He says that I need to learn to read. And that I should not say 'Mother of God!' when I am angry."

His manners might be tactless, but his convictions were sincere. When Alys' fever suddenly worsened on Christmas Eve, he considered it his Christian duty to join the family to pray for her, even though he was feverish himself from his cold. In his nightcap and furred robe, prayer book in hand, he came to Alys' door and recoiled at the sight of Brigid kneeling before a makeshift altar — a table set with a cross, candles, and a statue of the Virgin. Alys herself was sound asleep, but the children, barefoot and in their night clothes, were all ears. "Hail, Holy Queen, Mother of Mercy — "

John Hammond dropped his prayer book.

"Madam! Can it be that you are allowing Romish prayers to be said for this poor lady?"

His tone brought a flush to Libby's cheek. "Hush, John. Only until the vicar arrives, which I trust will be soon. You may go."

But he seemed so transfixed by Brigid's altar and beads that he did not move. "The Bishop must not hear about this, madam."

"No, indeed."

"If you are betrayed — "

"It will not be by you," said Libby.

John Hammond looked around him as if he expected to see a legion of devils spring from the flowered bed hangings or the painted clothes chest. The little statue of the Virgin seemed to inspire his particular loathing, and with a sudden movement he seized it and threw it violently to the floor. "Popish idolatry! Sacrilege! God forgive you, for you know not what you do!" he roared, and strode out of the room.

Silence fell, deep and ringing as a bell. The children stared at one another in mixed horror and delight. Brigid was crimson, but without a word she picked up the pieces of the statue and thrust them into her skirt pocket. Like singing abruptly hushed, her unfinished prayer seemed to echo in the room.

Piers blew out the altar candles. Beatrice, frowning, stuck her thumb in her mouth, a habit she had lately acquired from James. "Aunt Lib, when the vicar comes, will he hang Brigid?"

Libby pressed her palms to her eyes. "No, sweetheart. Of course not."

"Only witches are hanged," Piers said. "Heretics are burned."

"What's a heretic?"

Libby felt unequal to the task of explanation. "Children, it's late. Bid Alys goodnight and let her sleep."

"Do you think she would like to keep this?" Samuel asked. He held out his hand and Libby flinched at the sight of a centipede on his palm.

"I think not. Put it outside."

She put the children to bed, resolutely refusing to answer any of their questions, and went thankfully her own room. But the big four-poster bed did not invite sleep.

Thomas' half looked emptier and colder than ever. She sat down, leaning her head in her hands. The bedside candle flamed and guttered, throwing shadows from one side of the room to the other. A loose shutter banged back and forth in the wind. Somewhere down the hall, one of the dogs began to howl. It was a sound so desolate that she was filled with grief. Alys, Brigid, John Hammond, even the children — suddenly she was afraid for them all.

She remembered the first time she had seen this gracious house, in high summer when she had come here as a bride, and it seemed to her that she had wandered into the pages of a delightful fable whose ending would always be happy. Youth, health, beauty, a loving marriage, children; all these riches had been poured into her waiting hands and she had nothing more to ask of life except the peace and health to enjoy it. Now all was at risk and she was afraid. She wondered if her judgment or her loyalty was flawed, because, for the first time, she wished that Thomas were less a man of his word. Princes, causes, and politics — what did they matter next to the welfare of his family? Why should his duty to the King be more important than his love for his wife and children?

She knew the answer was not one that she would like. She wiped her face, and got up to fasten the loose shutter.

In the morning John Hammond sent a message requesting an interview. The rest of the household was attending service at St. Mary's, but Libby, as yet unchurched after Kate's birth, had stayed home. She sat in a chair by Alys' bed, winding a skein of bright red wool that was destined to become a cap for James. The fire hissed and crackled and a brazier heaped with coals burned by the bed. It was so warm in the room that presently she closed her eyes. The ball of wool fell from her lap and rolled across the floor. As children she and Leopold had played a game of following a piece of yarn along and around, one room to the next, down the stairs, up the stairs and around the corner, to find some little treasure that their father had tied to the end of it. He had enjoyed such foolery as much as they had, especially at Christmas. How he had delighted in finding the bean in his slice of Twelfth Night cake, which meant that he would be king — rousing his children from bed at midnight to raid the kitchen for sugar-sops and hot ale — hiring musicians to accompany the Yule log to the hearth — putting a nosegay in his buttonhole for church, and nodding benign approval of the sermon until, inevitably, he fell asleep.

A sharp little pain, like a bodkin digging into her side, woke Libby from her half-sleep, and she found that her face was wet. Surely there could be nothing more foolish than to weep over her vainglorious father, who even now was likely sharing his Christmas goose with the Dutch at Whitehall. But at heart he was no more loyal to William than he had been to James. "A plague," Libby said to herself, "on both their houses."

There was a discreet scratching on the door and John Hammond entered. He looked as if he had spent a wakeful night, but he was freshly shaved and his linen gleamed. He had his hat in his hand, metaphorically as well as literally.

"I wanted to speak with you, madam…about yesterday." His voice was so hoarse with cold that he had to pause in mid-sentence to clear his throat.

"Shall I clear the breakables from the room?" Libby asked.

He flushed. "Madam, did you know that Brigid told the children that if his lordship's horses had drunk holy water, they would not have been stolen? That the charm she wears around her neck protects her from thunder, and crossing herself when she shuts a window keeps out the Devil? The other day I found her baptizing a sick kitten. If the Bishop should hear of it, she will hang for a witch."

"There you are, speaking of the Bishop again. His Grace is in London. I think treason a worse crime than poor Brigid's superstitions, and I shall tell him so, if anyone dares inform upon her! Do you understand me?"

"I would never do such a thing, madam. But others might. And I know that His Grace believes ardently in the existence of witches."

Libby recollected that John Hammond's father was a widowed clergyman who had once been the Bishop's curate. John himself, raised in seclusion by gentle, unworldly parents, seemed to have had an enviably peaceful childhood. He spoke so tenderly about his little Sussex village, his father's church and garden, the market square and the green, that he might have been describing fragments of Eden that had migrated to southern England. She looked into his eyes. "John, you cannot possibly think that wearing a necklace turns Brigid into a witch."

"No. But I have seen what happens when the accusation is made." He fixed his eyes on some point above Libby's head. "Once there was an old woman in our parish, a poor creature who confessed to turning herself into a toad so that she might speak with the Devil. She said that she was hungry, and as God had not provided for her, she went to Satan instead. But before she came to trial some of the villagers drowned her in the pond." His voice grew harsh. "I would not want such a thing to happen to Brigid, madam."

Libby's opinion of him rose. Much more warmly, she said, "No, of course not. We must protect her." Curiosity overcame her. "Are you endeavouring to...educate Brigid, John?"

"I am endeavouring to court her, madam." He folded his arms. "But apparently I have failed."

Libby smiled into his cold-reddened, blotchy face. "Don't be discouraged. I suspect she is afraid of prejudicing people against you."

"Do you think so, madam?"

"I do. And perhaps if you were to take back that word, *sacrilege*, you might fare better."

"Her religion is an abomination, madam. Unless I can influence her to change, I could not, in good conscience, remain under the same roof..." His voice faded. Libby, picking up her ball of wool, said, "I think 'good consciences' are responsible for more unhappiness in the world than all else. But you must suit yourself."

John Hammond blew his nose and looked sombre. For the first time Libby noticed the scruffy portmanteau at his feet. "Are you making a journey?"

"Yes, madam. To my father's. That is, of course, with your permission."

"But how will you get there?"

It was Christmas Day. She had no horse to give him and there would be no one travelling the London road; it was more than forty-five miles to the city, and then another thirty into Sussex. Had he arranged to hire a horse and cart in the village? She could not rid herself of an uneasy suspicion that he would take his bag and walk all the way to the vicarage door.

"I will manage, madam. Thank you. And thank you for your goodness."

He started to bow himself out, but she called him back. "Before you leave, make amends to Brigid."

"But how shall I do that? What should I say?"

"Above all do not speak of religion," Libby said. She

smiled a little. "Look around you, John. The children have put kissing boughs all over this house. If you cannot manage to have your talk near one of those, you deserve your fate."

Alys, dosed with laudanum, still slept. Libby put her knitting aside and went to look over the presents of food and money that would be dispensed to the servants and tenants at dinner. Christmas was one of the occasions when the manor fed the village, and tables had been set up in the Great Hall to accommodate all the families in St. Mary's. In the musicians' gallery, the children had set up a tree hung with paper roses and apples. The Hall, like the rest of the house, was redolent of rich good smells.

But Fulke, returning from church, was uneasy. Pranksters or protestors had stuck oranges on the churchyard railing, and in response Reverend Fleming had preached an impassioned sermon on duty. Some parishioners had been uncomfortable with his frank criticism of the Bishop, and Fulke worried that the festivities might turn ugly.

"Everyone knows that my lord is with the King," Libby said reasonably. "William's friends will stay away. And if not, we shall send to General Dundee for reinforcements." She smiled up into his horrified face. "Dear Fulke," she said. "Never mind. They will all be too busy eating and drinking to care."

She tied an apron over her silk dress and went to the kitchen to oversee the tumultuous last-minute preparations. The heat from the great fireplace and the bake-ovens had raised the temperature so much that the doors had been propped open to cool the room. Flushed maidservants in homespun skirts ran back and forth with bowls and platters and dishes, while the small boy who was turning the roast pigeons on the spit sweated furiously as he worked. The cooking had been going on for days now, and the larders and the pantry overflowed with bounty — bowls and pitchers of cream, custard, and frumenty, wheels of cheese, loaves of freshly baked wheaten bread, cold game and mutton pies, roasts with oyster sauce, joints of ham, poached and salted fish; the sweating, dark shelves of the storerooms and the cellars were packed with food enough to withstand a siege — but Libby quickly turned that thought aside. The noise, the heat, and the fiercely pungent smells made her feel suddenly queasy. Obeying some nameless impulse, she threw on her cloak and ran outside.

A winter hush lay over the grounds. The terrace fountains had been turned off and fallen leaves drifted on the quiet surface of the stream that ran through the grounds. It had been so cold that ice encrusted the banks. In the spring, the overhanging willows would trail delicate fronds into the shallows, and clusters of apple and cherry blossoms would silt up like snowdrifts on the grass. All the shutters would be thrown open to let the fragrance air sweeten the house, and the wind would blow some of the pink and cream petals into the rooms. Libby held her cloak shut with one hand and walked along the terrace, remembering, with a small shudder, what Wharton had said about William liking this place.

After ten years of marriage she knew the history of the house as well as Thomas did. The Plantagenets had held Court here; Henry V had used it as a royal residence. The first King James, hunting-mad, had stocked the deer-park himself, and the present King had liked to walk along the river before hearing private mass in the chapel. Six hundred years of living had gone on within these walls. She had come here as a young wife, had borne and buried her children here, had expected to grow old under this roof.

She paused to look up at the sheeted bell tower, and stood

rigid with horror when she recognized a tiny figure standing on the crumbling parapet behind the scaffolding. It was Beatrice. Libby froze for a moment, her hand to her mouth. Then, slowly and deliberately, for she must not startle Beatrice or shout at her unexpectedly, she walked forward to where the child would be able to see her. Presently she stood below the tower. Beatrice waved at her happily, and Libby cupped her hands, calling up to her in what she hoped was an ordinary voice, the voice of a woman summoning her child to supper. "Beatrice, go inside the house."

"I can see the church spire, Aunt Lib!"

"Yes, dear. Go inside." Libby's voice was still calm, but when Beatrice leaned on the parapet she said sharply, "*Now*, Beatrice."

"There are horsemen on the road, Aunt Lib."

"It's likely General Dundee, come for dinner after all. Go inside."

"I don't think so." Beatrice hung over the ruined edge, shading her eyes with her hand as if she were the lookout on a man-of-war, and Libby briefly closed her own eyes. "It doesn't matter who the soldiers are, Beatrice. Go inside at once!"

To her unspeakable relief the small, frizzy head obediently vanished. Libby crossed her arms, clasping her elbows to keep herself from trembling, and went into the house. In the antechamber next to the old chapel she met Beatrice, coming down the stairs and out the door that Thomas had ordered triple-barred with iron. "However did you get up there, Beatrice?"

"I told onc of the grooms you wanted it open," said Beatrice sunnily. Her black skirt was filthy with dust and her hair stood out like blown feathers from her smudged face. Libby put a palm against her cheek and forced herself to speak quietly. "Then, Beatrice, you told a lie and put yourself at great risk. You know the door was barred because the workmen have been repairing the walls. Why would you do such a thing?"

"To see where my house used to be," said Beatrice. Her face changed abruptly and she flung herself at Libby, sobbing into the folds of her rose silk dress. Libby kissed the child's hot, untidy head, knowing that this was not the time for a lesson in logic or geography. Presently Beatrice looked up. "But there *are* men coming, Aunt Lib. And they're not in uniform. It's not the General."

All the rumours Libby had heard about disbanded soldiers flashed into her mind. She tightened her grip on Beatrice's hand. "We will offer them a meal, whoever they are. But you must go back up to Brigid now. Promise me you will stay there and help her look after Kate and Alys. Tell her on no account to come downstairs until I send for her."

Beatrice ran off. Libby fastened her cloak, not only for warmth, but for dignity. She could not meet the enemy, if enemies they were, in a dirty dress. There was no time to summon Fulke. She prepared a speech in her mind as she descended the stairs to the front door: "Gentlemen, on this holy day all are welcome in peace to the hospitality of this house." It sounded well enough — but if they were here to batten upon the household, or, worse, to arrest her husband, there would be scant exchange of compliments.

The dogs, tails wagging, followed her out the front entrance. She took a step or two down from the door and then stood her ground. Her heart was racing, but she would not show any fear. Presently she saw them. They had galloped through the gate and turned the corner of the drive. It was impossible from this distance to see the men's faces or how many of them there were, but the troop was certainly larger than Wharton's. Fifteen — twenty — she could not tell how many, or even if they were Dutch or English. She took another step down, the dogs following in full cry. But suddenly there was a mad note of hysteria in their yelping. Lucy broke away from the pack and shot down the drive as fast as her fat belly would allow, just as the front rider reined in, swept off his hat, and dismounted, all in one move. Behind him, the others drew up at a respectful distance. They were dressed in civilian clothes, but carried themselves like soldiers. One or two wore the King's colours fastened to their plumed hats.

"Libby," said Thomas, "I've invited Colonel Sarsfield's cavalry for dinner. Do you mind?"

4

"WAS THERE A FIGHT?"

"Did you talk to a Dutchman?"

"Where is the King?"

The children had hurled themselves upon him in screaming delight. Piers and James ran for his stirrup cup and a jug of ale, while Beatrice and Samuel clung to his knee. Colonel Sarsfield tactfully took his men off to "wash their boots," and Thomas, sweeping his family into the library, closed the doors and put his arms around them all — wife, children, even the dogs. Magnus, filthy from his journey, nosed his way in, slapping their legs with his tail. Thomas kissed Libby and put an arm around her, but had no time to ask about the baby or her health, for Beatrice was telling him that her family's house had burned down. "We lost everything," she said. "All our furniture and my cat and my button collection."

"It was the house next door that people wanted to burn," said Samuel, anxious to be factual. "They were Catholics. But the sparks landed on our roof."

"Papa is in London with Mam," said Beatrice. "Gypsies ate here, Uncle Thomas. Alys is still in bed and old Burcote comes to visit every other day. Lucy was sick on the rug after she ate some custard, and Master Hammond has a head cold and we haven't had lessons for a week. Oh, and the new baby is a girl."

As if this were a prearranged signal, Brigid entered the room with a small, lace-wrapped bundle.

"This is Kate," Piers informed him. "She doesn't have hair."

"Indeed she has lovely hair," Brigid reproved. She folded back a corner of the shawl and Thomas looked on his daughter's face: a tiny, perfect replica of Libby's, crowned with half a thumb's length of black, spiky hair. It felt like deer velvet under his hand. He took one of the small fists and over the top of the blanket his eyes met Libby's.

"Fourteen days old today," she said, answering his unspoken question. "She was born on Irish Night. At least, that is what I hear it is being called. The night Leopold's house burned. Abigail was there..."

Now all the children were talking at once, telling him the news. He kept his arm around Libby, giving Magnus, who was slobbering all over her gown, a cuff out of the way.

"Did you see Grandfather?" Piers asked suddenly.

"Yes, I saw him."

"I hope you killed him."

Even Beatrice fell silent then, staring. Thomas felt a chill on his skin. "Of course not, my son. Why would you say such a thing?"

"He came here with Wharton's troop," said Piers. "They're both traitors."

Thomas looked at his wife. She knew about St. Clare, then. They all knew. His voice was rough. "Wharton brought soldiers to this house?"

"My father came with him," said Libby. "So as, he said, to protect us."

"They stayed the night and took the horses," said Samuel. "And your strongbox, Uncle Thomas, and all your papers and letters."

A profound silence followed. They were all looking at him, their faces half-expectant, half-fearful, as if they thought he might send off an immediate personal challenge to St. Clare or dispatch the Irish troops to put Wharton under arrest. Even so, they did not understand the enormity of what they had told him.

"Troop, you say." He might have been back in court, interrogating witnesses. "How many men?"

It was Libby who answered. "Only twelve, including my father. They came after supper and left for Windsor at dawn the next morning." She looked into his eyes. "They did take the strongbox and the horses, Thomas. But they left us alone."

"You have two new horses, Uncle Thomas. Fulke bought them," said Samuel.

Beatrice skipped around the room. "One of the soldiers put a silver toothpick case in his pocket. I saw him take it from the cabinet in the dining room."

"Hush, Beatrice," said Libby.

The effrontery of what he was hearing almost refused to register in Thomas' brain. No words could do justice to how he felt at this moment. He looked into Piers' stony face and answered, "We'll buy other horses, my son. As for Lord St. Clare, even as a traitor and a thief he would be safe under this roof, because he is your grandfather. But outside of it — "

Beatrice tugged on his sash. "Sir John was coming to visit us when he met Grandfather, Uncle Thomas. Now he's in prison. Did you know?"

For once he was grateful for her gabble. "Yes, I do know. I saw Sir John in Windsor."

"Is he wounded?" Libby asked.

"I will tell you about it presently. But first I want to meet our daughter."

"Her name is Katherine Sophia," said James. "But we call her Kate."

He took the baby from Brigid and walked with her up and down the room, as much to calm himself as to look at the child. She stared solemnly up at him, with eyes as blue as his own. Her elf-like face was the very spit of both Libby's and Cicely's. Sparrow. Poppet. Madam Gooseberry. "It was only a daughter after all," someone had said to him when Cicely died, "and so not a great loss."

Gently he touched his lips to the wisps of fine, dark hair. He remembered suddenly that Lee had said nothing about St. Clare quartering troops on the house; either he had not known, or he had wanted to spare Thomas from knowing. Nor had St. Clare himself seen fit to mention it that night at Whitehall. Was there possibly a scrap of shame left in the old man? He doubted it.

After his long journey the heat of the fire made him unbearably tired. He sat down on the footstool, still holding Kate, and told them about Lee. "He is at Windsor, though free to leave," he said. "I spent two days trying to persuade him to come home with me." He pulled himself together to explain. "He was discharged. There were no grounds to hold him — he's done nothing wrong. But he won't leave."

"Is he chained to the wall?" asked Samuel.

"By no means. Prince William sent his own physician to attend him, and he has a comfortable bed and meals cooked to order. But instead he sleeps on the floor and lives on crusts."

There was equal love and exasperation in Thomas' voice. Who else but Lee would be mad enough to refuse his freedom? Lord Wharton — of all men! — had offered to pay Lee's bail, along with William Penn's, for that champion of peace was also in prison. But bail meant binding over for trial, and the new government had more to do than harass sick old men. Lee had been discharged upon the condition that he "keep the peace" at home, which he had refused to do. He remained in his cell, giving his food away to other prisoners and sleeping on the floor. "He's sworn an oath that he will not take his freedom from anyone's hands but the King's."

His stubbornness reminded Thomas of the Scottish General, Tom Dalyell, who had protested Charles I's execution by not shaving for thirty-six years — although small good this eccentricity had done either himself or his dead sovereign. Thomas had begged Lee to come with him to Scotland — "No, I am too old" — or go to France — "I spent too many years there already" — or take custody of Thomas' Irish property — "I would sooner hang myself" — or even come to live at Charters — "I am not a charity case." No persuasions had moved him. He would break his vow only at the King's order. In the end Thomas had ridden to Rochester to obtain just that. But James had already sailed for France. The house had been deserted; even the Dutch soldiers had gone. There was nothing left for Thomas to do but turn around and ride back the way he had come. "I have been in the saddle these thirty hours," he said.

"You went into Windsor looking for him and were allowed to leave, just so?" asked Libby. "No one stopped you?"

"I had papers," Thomas said. Dundee had pocketed St. Clare's safe-conduct that evening in Whitehall. The irony of it had made Lee laugh; despite his circumstances he had been in good spirits, as if desiring nothing better than martyrdom at William's hands. On the road Thomas had run into the Irish and Sarsfield had nearly taken him prisoner, until they established that they both fought on the same side.

"Is that what happened to your face?" asked Libby, putting a hand on his cheek. He had not even realized until now that it was bruised. "I don't remember. But I had an escort home after that." Patrick Sarsfield was the Irish officer whose cavalry had engaged William's troops at Wincanton. Now he was on the run, intent on joining James' army in Ireland before William could prevent him.

Talking about it reminded Thomas that Sarsfield was waiting for him, and that his men would be hungry. He gave the baby into Libby's arms and went out to find the Irish soldiers already remounted in the courtyard. Sarsfield said they would take food with them but would not stay, as it would raise the alarm in the village. There was no denying that the presence of a body of Irish soldiers would send people running for their pitchforks, even on Christmas Day. Libby arranged for food to be put into the men's packs, and Sarsfield, courtly and elegant, kissed her hand in thanks and made a graceful speech. Then they were gone, vanishing like highwaymen in a ballad.

Fulke came to inform them that the first guests had arrived. Thomas went to wash off the dirt of his journey and then sat down as he did every year to preside over the tables in the Great Hall. But, God pardon him, he had no wish to be anywhere except in his bed. He was so tired that the voices and faces around him blurred into meaningless confusion and the single glass of wine he had drunk roiled uneasily in his stomach. Libby sat at the other end of their table, smiling at him a little anxiously over the rim of her own glass, a Venetian goblet that looked like a bubble of crushed ice. It had been one of St. Clare's gifts. Thomas suppressed the urge to take it from her and smash it.

Through the haze of his weariness he noticed that she had put off her soiled pink gown and changed into a dress that he especially liked, a rich violet silk whose dusky sheen was like the bloom of a plum. She wore the pearl earrings and the silver locket he had given her on their wedding day. Recent childbed or not, she looked like a desirable young girl, and if he were in the mood to think of such things — if he were in his right mind — he would tell her so. What was the matter with him, that instead of thinking about his beautiful wife, he was ruminating furiously on the crimes of his father-in-law? He could not banish the image of those soldiers intruding on her privacy — drinking, perhaps, from these same wine cups, rifling through the drawers and cabinets, breaking open the strongbox, commandeering beds, food, horses, and only God knew what else besides. With a sudden surge of anger he thrust his plate away and looked over the gathering to see who was there and who was not. He knew already that his own chaplain was missing, and it surprised him how much that desertion rankled. His hastily flung-together troop had never fought together or even assembled for a review, but there had been a spirit of camaraderie among them nonetheless, a solidarity of purpose that he had expected would keep them loyal. Martin's betrayal was particularly galling as his favourite homily had been on the subject of duty: "Let us serve our king as we serve our God." "Lying sanctimonious bastard," said Thomas, then flushed when he realized that he had spoken aloud.

Lord Burcote was missing as well, on the excuse of his lady's illness. There were one or two other families who had not attended. But the rest of St. Mary's had turned out in force, the men awkward in their Sunday starched linen, the women in good black wool, the children scrubbed almost raw and dressed in their best clothing. Usually this day was one of high festival and the mood was jovial. But today people were subdued. The uncertainty of the future and the rift in the parish between the Bishop and the vicar had so sunk their spirits that they ate and drank with timid politeness, instead of the usual roaring good nature.

Thomas knew all of these families by name, and he knew the names and ages of their children, the number and quality of their acres and livestock, the details of their health, their debts, their prospects, and their hopes. What he did would affect all of them profoundly. He hated to bring turmoil upon these people, and yet he could not imagine any one of them saying "God save you" to a Dutch king.

It was in his power to settle at least one of their uncertainties. He stood with his cup of wine and called for silence. "To King James," he said in a strong, firm voice. "God bless and defend him. And anyone who will not say so can take his family and belongings and leave, without penalty or fear, and look to the Bishop for guidance. But know this, all of you. My household, and all associated with it, are loyal subjects of the lawful King."

He did not think much of this speech and the genuine cheers surprised him. When the vicar followed with a prayer for the safety of the royal family, there were heartfelt amens. It seemed to signal a general release. Politics were out of the way and now they could enjoy themselves. The men unloosed their collars and got down to the serious business of drinking. Wives gathered in groups, picking over the bones of the most recent marriage or funeral or baptism. Young girls flirted with their suitors. The children, freed from close supervision, roamed the hall and played with the dogs and hid sweets in their pockets. James went from table to table, finishing off glasses of ale or sack unwisely left alone, until Thomas caught him and carried him off.

As if this had been his purpose in the first place, James leaned his head against his father's shoulder and closed his eyes. His thumb stole into his mouth. Thomas sat down, feeling almost drunk himself with weariness. The steady hum of voices and the clatter of dishes faded into the distance. Someone began to pluck a lute, and the gentle sound washed him far out to sea. He was on the London road, his horse staggering beneath him...he was at Windsor, hearing the crash of an iron door...now he was back in Whitehall, receiving the keys to a ruined house in county Waterford. "But I don't want to go to Ireland," he objected.

"Tom."

He awoke with a jerk. Libby had touched his shoulder. He was alone at the table; servants were carrying off the benches and dousing the torches. Thank God, it was over. The squalid aftermath of the feast surrounded him — spilled food, dirty plates and cups, overturned platters. James had left to sit under the table with the dogs. Thomas pulled him out and carried him upstairs on his shoulders.

The other children followed. Samuel was very quiet and even Beatrice's spirits seemed low. She hopped up the stairs, her hem dragging, and said that no gifts, not even a letter, had come from their parents. That omission seemed so unlikely that Thomas said that he would take the children to London himself, in his own carriage, to ensure that all was well.

"Your carriage was stolen too," said Beatrice. "Papa had to borrow one from old Burcote."

What Thomas wanted to say was unfit for children's ears. He kissed them all goodnight and then, at last, was free to go into his own bedroom. When he sat down to take off his boots, the room seemed to swim around him in a fog. All was exactly the same as when he had left — the dark green bed hangings, the cherry dressing table and brass wall sconces, the lacquered screen. Yet he felt somehow that he had come to a foreign country. He held his boot in his hand and stared at the floor. Presently Libby came in from her dressing room in her silk wrapper.

"Tell me again what happened when the troop came."

"There's nothing more to tell."

She picked up a jar of flower-water from her dressing table, a brush, a pot of cream, and then set these down and came to put her arms around his neck. But her voice was sad rather than cajoling. "Will you not kiss me and try to forget it?"

He was ashamed that she had had to ask. But even as he took her in his arms in silent apology, his mind kept churning through the events of the past day. He did notice how carefully the bed had been made, with lavender-scented linens and the brocade coverlid, their wedding quilt, whose upper corner bore their initials twined together in gold thread. After weeks of sleeping on the ground or in smoky inns, the clean sheets and deep feather pillows were sinfully luxurious, and the shock of Libby's skin against his own was pure heaven. There was nothing sweeter than her presence in his arms. He resolved to say so, to make a speech, for once be the courtier she deserved.

But he was asleep.

Their reunion was short-lived. Parliament had been summoned — a so-called free parliament that was, as Thomas said, about as free as a man locked in a pillory. Lord Middleton had written to tell him that there were six thousand Dutch soldiers stationed in London alone, and John Hammond, returning from Sussex, reported that Dutch troops had been quartered even in his own small village. The country was at the mercy of a foreign prince and an army of occupation. Yet William had said he would do nothing to interfere with parliament's deliberations.

Libby, picking through her sewing basket, asked, "Does this mean he expects to be elected king?" In truth she had been thinking chiefly about Kate's spasms of colic, but she knew where her duty lay. Thomas told her that the Lords would never agree to such a republican arrangement; the question was whether William would be offered, or would accept, the status of regent. So far, like a well-bred maiden considering a marriage proposal, he had said nothing in public to indicate his thoughts.

Libby, simultaneously prying James' sticky hands from the sock she was darning for Piers (he had somehow gone through three pairs only this week) and rocking Kate's cradle with her foot, thought that the real question was how long her husband would stay away. But she would not ask. Nor would she inquire about Scotland, although Dundee, still awaiting his safe-conducts, rode over to confer with Thomas nearly every day. He was already deep into his plans to raise an army, as he had no faith in what might happen at Westminster.

I know my love by his way of walking,
And I know my love by his way of talking
And I know my love by his eyes of blue,
And if my love leaves me, what shall I do?

When the prospect of another separation grew too much to bear, she reminded herself that her own parents had been separated for more than five years by the civil war, and during that time their first child had died. It had been four years more before Leopold was born, and there had been another long separation between his birth and her own. Perhaps she lacked her mother's courage. Or perhaps she was more modern and practical, and saw how senseless were all the wars fought in this century to ensure there would or would not be Prayer Books and bishops in the churches, English instead of Latin, psalms instead of rosaries. Were they to go through it all again, each side accusing the other of blasphemy and heresy? Perhaps her father was right and it was chiefly a matter of money. According to him, the impiety of Rome's doctrine was a secondary issue and one that, in this new age of science and commerce, hardly seemed worth disputing. St. Clare had said that if money and political power were not involved, the King, like the Chinese, might worship his own ancestors if he chose. But she would not recount that particular cynicism to her husband. These days St. Clare's name was not mentioned.

At night when they went to their green-canopied bed she found herself sleepless with dread, twining herself around Thomas' arm or shoulder as if to anchor him beside her. How could he wish to leave them again so soon, when James followed him like a shadow and Piers begged him every day to watch his new proficiency at archery or horsemanship? When Beatrice and Samuel fought for the honour of riding on his saddle-bow, and Kate had certainly smiled at him at breakfast? A dozen matters competed for his attention — the masons were once more at work on the bell tower; pipes for running water were being installed upstairs; there was Kate's christening to arrange, horses and carriages to buy, the home farm to manage. She welcomed each task that diverted his attention from London.

Two days after his homecoming he rode over to Lee's property and found it deserted — the servants gone, the house open to the four winds. He let himself in with the key Lee had given him, and was struck at once by the deep chill of the house, the smell of dust and disuse. The hall clock had stopped; unwashed cook-pots stood on the kitchen table, their insides furred with mould. Thomas set to work, lighting a fire in the drawing-room and sending the children to wash the dishes and pick up the rubbish. On one of the tables he found a book on gardening, open perhaps to the last page that Lee had been reading. Thomas stood looking at it for some moments before carefully marking the page and returning the book to its place. He would not allow himself to think that Lee might never read the rest of it, that he might never again sit in his chair in front of the fire or stroll amongst his beloved rose bushes. But, until his return, someone would need to look after this place. Thomas would have to write to Lee's heir, that cousin or nephew, and inform him that the house was untenanted.

He locked the door behind him and took the children down to the river, showing them how to skip pebbles across it. They sat on the muddy ground and ate a cold lunch of pickled fish and bread. It was a drab January day and the river, cold and sluggish, was the colour of the clouds, a dull grey-black like tarnished silver. The birches and willows were still stripped bare. But for Thomas the day was invested with a kind of summer glamour. He imagined locking his gate and throwing away the key, so that he need never leave home again, nor let the world disrupt his peace. Passionately he wished that he could tell Libby so, but he knew better. Already the new order had intruded on their privacy. Not only had he been summoned to parliament, but he had suffered a visit from the recently appointed sheriff of the county — Lord Burcote, who had decided to accept the post even though, as he assured Thomas, his sympathies were "all with the lawful King."

It was astonishing how easy it had become to reconcile

employment under William with fidelity to James. If men drank the Loyal Toast over a cup of water, meaning it was James in France whom they honoured, then duty was satisfied and they felt free to accept the court pickings that were available. But Thomas could not salve his conscience by passing his wine cup over the water and calling it loyalty. It was no more than a cheat, a childish ruse that allowed men to think they were being honourable when they were not. The fact that so many availed themselves of it only made him the more determined not to join their number. When he told Burcote as much, the old man had been so offended that he took back the box of comfits he had brought for Libby.

"You have lost your beau," Thomas teased her that evening. Libby, with her hand on the dining room window latch, frowned a little into the dark. "Then why is he coming up the drive?"

But it was Leopold, returning with Abigail in Burcote's old coach.

They had meant to come in time for Christmas, but Abigail had not been well. Then the coach had broken down and they had been forced to spend three days at Hampstead waiting for repairs. Abigail, pale as a wraith and wrapped in furs, took to her room as soon as she arrived, with Beatrice and Samuel each clinging to a hand. It was the first time they had seen their mother since the beginning of November, when Leopold had come for what was intended to be a few days' visit.

Thomas was shocked by the change that two months had made in his brother-in-law. Leopold had always been a large man, never fat, but solid and substantial. Now the yoke of his vest seemed too large for his shoulders and his shirt billowed in loose folds around his waist. He wore no ornament, not even a watch or fob, and his clothes, even to his shoe buckles, were black, giving an unavoidable impression of deep mourning. He seemed to have lost not only pounds of flesh, but his irresistible *joie de vivre*. He walked stiffly, using a cane, and propped his bandaged leg on a stool after he had sat down.

A housemaid brought coffee and wine and biscuits. Grating loaf sugar into his cup as if this task wholly absorbed his attention, Leopold was silent at first when Thomas inquired after Abigail. Then he said that she was as well as could be expected. They talked about Salisbury. But when it came to the matter of what happened on Irish Night, Leopold suddenly grew agitated and would not speak of it. He put four spoonfuls of sugar into his coffee and churned up a small maelstrom as he stirred it.

"My father came to see me before we left London," he said abruptly. "He told me to stay out of matters entirely until William is crowned. After that he desires me to take my oath to the new government, but use my friends abroad to correspond 'discreetly' with the court at St. Germain. In other words, lie. Take the oath, but let King James know it was forced from me. Apparently even Churchill has done this."

Thomas did not say that he would believe anything of either Churchill or St. Clare. "There's no guarantee William will be crowned."

"My father seems to think otherwise. And I suppose he ought to know. Did you hear he has been appointed to the privy council?"

"Hot air rises," was all Thomas could think of to say.

Leopold gave his coffee another vigorous stir. "I told him I would not take any oath of loyalty to the Dutch. 'Of course not,' he said, just as if he had not done exactly that, the day before he came to see me — there is no holding to him to anything."

There was bitterness in his voice but also an odd note of reluctant admiration, as if he, Leopold, were the father, and St. Clare the unruly but beloved prodigal son. Thomas realized that to Leopold his father's conduct was a source almost of pride as well as embarrassment: no one was so open in putting self-interest before all else, no one could demonstrate such a splendidly flagrant disregard for duty and honour.

"I don't suppose he mentioned that he threatened to take away my children. He thinks he ought to be their guardian."

Leopold took a biscuit and soaked it in his coffee. "He would never do so. There is Libby to consider, after all."

"How much did he consider her when he brought those soldiers here?"

"That was unconscionable. But he maintains he was protecting her."

"By leaving her without money or horses, and she nine months pregnant? Did you know the doctor was away, and Patrick had to fetch the midwife on James' pony? She never got here in time and it's only by the grace of God that Libby and the child are alive and well. Do you call that a father's protection?"

He had not meant to give way to his anger. None of this, after all, was Leopold's fault. His brother-in-law studied his damp biscuit as if it were something that he had fixed upon a lens. "I don't know what to say to you," he answered finally. "I would ask you to forgive him, but I don't know why you should."

"Let God forgive him," Thomas said shortly. Such a thing as forgiving or not forgiving St. Clare seemed utterly irrelevant. Leopold crumbled the remnant of his biscuit into his coffee. "If nothing else, he did give me an idea," he said. "About corresponding with St. Germain — not in the way that he imagines, of course. I mean ciphering and delivering messages. I have a considerable acquaintance abroad."

"You want to be a sp — "" hastily Thomas abandoned that unkind word to select another. "An agent?"

"Abigail wants to go abroad," said Leopold. "To Italy, perhaps, or Spain. But I think we should stay here and rebuild our house." He carried on with hardly a pause to talk about the house-plans. "I brought some sketches with me. Would you care to look?" He spread a paper over his knee, pointing with the handle of his coffee-spoon to the various rooms. "This is my study. The dining room, music room, library... the children's bedrooms and schoolroom...the nursery..."

His voice trembled. Thomas saw in concern that there were tears in his eyes. But some deep, indefinable barrier of reserve in his brother-in-law's manner made it impossible to offer any comfort. "You must stay here with us while the house is built," Thomas said finally.

"Perhaps we will. I shall have to be in the city a good deal, of course, during the construction. Unless I decide to go abroad after all. Perhaps I should. Perhaps, if I took Abigail to a better climate, she might..." Leopold changed the subject abruptly. "And you, Thomas? What are your plans?"

"I suppose that depends upon what happens in parliament."

"My father asked me to warn you not to attend." Leopold's smile was wintry. "For your own safety, he said."

There could be no civil answer to this and Thomas did not even attempt to reply. They drank their coffee in silence until the children burst into the room, asking Leopold to identify a red spider that James had found in his shoe.

As it was now out of the question for Grace to be Kate's godparent, Libby asked Abigail and Leopold to stand sponsor at the christening. Kate, dressed in her great-grandmother's ivory lace gown, screamed all through the ceremony. It was not much warmer in the interior of St. Mary's than it was outside, and rain poured down steadily from a sky the colour of cinders. As Thomas agreed to renounce the Devil and all his works, the vain pomp and glory of the world, he could feel the cold from the flagstones creeping up through his boot soles. Water streamed down the stained-glass windows, making it seem that the angels, apostles, and holy family were all drowning. It was a private ceremony, but Reverend Fleming still used the occasion to preach strenuously on the subject of obedience. As Kate's screams grew louder he bawled, rather than spoke, the blessing. "Receive this child into the congregation of Christ's flock. Bless the home of this child! *I say the home of this child,* " he shouted, and Beatrice giggled.

When the ceremony came to an end Libby invited him back to the house for wine and cake. It was not even midday, but the coach lanterns were lit. Thomas handed his family into the first carriage and Leopold and Abigail took the vicar with them in the second. Once the door was shut Libby discreetly put Kate to her breast to quell her screaming. Thomas tucked a rug around them while Piers and James squabbled over whom should sit facing front. As the carriages bowled away from the church, the wind gusted so strongly that the window glass shook. "You had better leave early tomorrow," Libby said. "There might be snow."

Piers and James suddenly ceased their bickering. "You're going away again?" James said, sounding aghast.

"Only to London," said Thomas. He had explained the workings of parliament to the children, but it was not a subject that interested them. He doubted that James had understood much beyond the fact that occasionally he wore a long, scarlet robe to Westminster Hall, and sat on a bench with other men in scarlet robes. James looked at his fists, at the bitten nails and the scab on the back of his right hand. "Mam says you're still fighting for the King, even though he ran away."

"Yes, James."

"Why? Because you swore it?"

"That's one reason."

"What if you changed your mind?"

"I won't. Giving your word...it's not something you do without consideration."

"Will you see Grandfather in London?"

Beside him, Libby stiffened. Thomas reached for her hand. "I might."

"Will you fight him?"

He looked into James' anxious face and felt a rush of compassion for the child's bewilderment. "No."

"What if he wants to fight *you*?" Piers asked suddenly. "What will you do?"

The truthful answer would be that he had no idea. But he said, "I'll decide that when — if — it becomes necessary."

James looked fretful. "He gave me a box of sugar roses, and I was sick after I ate them."

"Probably they were poisoned," said Piers darkly. "Probably your face will turn black and you'll die."

James burst into sobs. "Piers!" said Libby, with such anger in her voice that tears rose in Piers' eyes as well. She turned to James and put her free arm around him. "Stop crying. You were sick because you ate the entire box all at once. That's all."

Piers, lip outthrust, looked at his father. "Sir, may I come with you to London?"

"Not this time."

"You've taken me before."

"This is different."

"I am not a baby anymore. I could look after the horses. I could take messages. I don't see why not."

"No."

"It's not fair. What if I came anyway? What if you didn't know?"

"Piers, the subject of today's lesson was obedience. Did you hear a word of it?"

Piers hunched down in his seat, his face scarlet. Thomas could not help thinking back to his own boyhood, when he had had to kneel to his father and say, whether it were true or not, that he was "Your lordship's most obedient, grateful, and devoted" son. Any requests had to be put forward in a letter, and even such a small rebellion as Piers' would have merited a beating. But somehow, looking at his son's miserable face, Thomas could not bring himself to further rebuke him.

In honour of the occasion the children were permitted a slice of cake and a thimbleful of wine. Afterward, when the vicar had gone and Abigail and Leopold had retired to their own room, Thomas sat hand-in-hand with Libby in the Long Gallery. One side of it displayed family and royal portraits against a panelled wall and the other, all windows, looked out upon the park. It had grown colder during the afternoon and a thin mist blotted out most of the landscape. The little stream that encircled the house was filmed with ice.

"Piers wants you to stay home," Libby said, when Thomas spoke of their son's behaviour. "All of us do." She pleated her silk skirt between her fingers and looked up at the portrait of some earlier de Chastelain lady in ruff and farthingale.

"I saw General Dundee's courier again this morning," she said. "Does he have his safe-conducts?"

"Not yet. The note was to let me know he's been summoned to Whitehall a third time."

"Will he go?"

"No. He won't agree to an interview until the Prince gives him his safe-conducts. And William won't give them until John agrees to an interview."

"That sounds dangerous."

"It is. On the other hand, William cannot risk offending the Scots right now."

"When Lord Dundee does receive his papers, will you take the troop and go with him?"

So far they had not discussed this, although Thomas was certain that Libby had been lying awake at night thinking of it as he had, and the subject had grown more burdensome in proportion to their silence. He sought to explain.

"Any fight will be political first. There's no guarantee what will happen. Even if parliament decides in William's favour, it's not binding upon Scotland. As for taking the troop anywhere, officially there is no army and no war. Even John is a civilian these days."

Libby bit her thumb. "My father will be at Westminster."

"Yes."

"The Whartons too."

"No doubt, sweetheart."

"Thomas, don't go."

All their years together she had limited herself to wifely counsel, never instructions or demands. It was as if she could see into his mind and pictured him confronting

St. Clare, drawing his sword, doing something irretrievably rash.

"There is no need for you to be concerned," he said.

She gave him a look such as he had seen her give the boys when they had told some exceptionally brazen lie. "You may be arrested."

"Not while parliament sits. And what would be the charge? I've done nothing against the law."

"I know what will happen when you meet my father and his friends." She paused, and then whispered, "I'm so afraid."

He put his arm around her. "Don't be."

"Then tell me you will not fight them."

The anguish in her eyes was hard to bear. But he could not promise such a thing. He kissed her without answering and she pulled away and went to one of the windows, putting her head and her fists against the glass like a prisoner in a cage. There was nothing Thomas could say. He wished it were in his power to guarantee that no matter what happened, his family would be safe. He felt that it was his fundamental duty to ensure this, at the same time knowing, as anyone knew who had lived long enough, that there was no safety in anything; the only freedom lay in admitting it.

When the family gathered to see Thomas off the next morning, Piers was absent. His bed had not been slept in and he was not in the house. Thomas postponed his departure, sent Pilgrim back to the stables, and took the dogs with him to search the woods. When he returned an hour later there was still no sign of Piers, and the morning had turned much colder. A few snowflakes drifted down from a solid grey sky.

"Do you think he might have gone to the village?" Libby asked.

"No. It's too far to walk, and he has no horse. Wherever he is, it won't be far."

"He didn't take Theo," said Libby.

Leopold, stick in hand, insisted upon joining the search. They worked their way systematically through the brewhouse, the laundry, the poultry-yard, stables, barns, and outbuildings, without success. By now it was past noon and no pretence of work was being done in the house. Libby and Abigail waited together at the dining room table, with the younger children, round-eyed and silent, sitting at their feet. The remains of breakfast still stood on the sideboard. Libby took her sewing-basket out, but she unpicked and stitched up the same threads over and over. Brigid, huddled in the corner with her rosary, kept reproaching herself for not tucking Piers into bed the previous evening. "He said he was too old now for that entirely, and told me to stay away."

"It's not your fault," said Libby for the tenth time. Her eyes went to the clock. "They've been gone for hours," she said. "Do you think they went to the village after all?"

When the men finally returned, flushed with cold and stamping the snow from their boots, there was no need to ask for news. Libby, who had rushed up from her chair, abruptly sat down again. Leopold hobbled to a chair by the hearth and rested his swollen leg on the fender. No one spoke. Thomas, without taking off his coat or his gloves, stood in front of the fire and drank two cups of tea while he considered what to do. It occurred to him that on his search through the house he had not seen the key to the boathouse on its usual hook. He kept that information to himself, however, and taking an apple and a wedge of cheese to put in his pocket, he kissed Libby and struck off through the dense, dripping woods toward the river.

All was forbiddingly still. There were no songbirds at this time of year, and the ground was so thick underfoot with beech and oak mast that his footfalls were silenced. Mist drifted along the ground, as if the earth had exhaled and its breath had condensed into ghostly fronds. The leafless branches scratched at his face and arms. Big snowflakes spiralled down slowly, one by one, in a silence so deep it almost seemed possible to hear them touch the earth. But in only a few weeks, this stretch of wood would burst into new life. Nightingales would sing and the forest floor would be covered with a delicate froth of bluebells. By then where would he be? Somewhere in Scotland with Dundee's army? In prison with Lee? Here at home, writing cowardly letters to Whitehall?

The boathouse doors stood ajar. When he pushed them open, it took a moment for his eyes to adjust to the dark. The interior was cluttered with rope, fishing-tackle, poles, nets, boots, and rags. A strong smell of river water and dust stung his nose. There was no sign of Piers. He had been so sure of finding him here that, for the first time, he felt a genuine spark of fear. He searched under some shelving, opened cupboards at the far end, stirred a pile of rags with his foot. Then he looked inside the boat itself.

Piers was asleep in the stern, his head cradled on his arm.

Relief flooded him. He shook his son awake, squatting down to look him in the eye. "Piers, what in God's name are you doing here? Do you know we've been looking for you all morning?"

"I wanted to see the boat."

"You came down here in the snow for that? Were you planning to go out on the river by yourself?"

Piers said nothing. Thomas, having a good idea of the truth, forbore to press him. He lifted Piers out of the boat and set him on his feet, brushing the dust from his clothes. "We need to go back and see Mam," he said, keeping his voice matter-of-fact. "Give me the key."

He locked the doors and pocketed the key. Piers took his hand. As they walked back through the woods the snowflakes thickened into a sudden flurry. They were enmeshed in a powdery curtain. Piers' fingers were cold and Thomas tucked the boy's hand into his own pocket to warm them. The falling snow, the white silence, somehow united them. When they had almost reached the house Piers suddenly blurted, "What if you die in Scotland?"

It took Thomas utterly aback. He had said nothing about Scotland to any of the children and he knew Libby had not done so either. "I heard you talking to General Dundee," Piers said. "I listened at the door."

Thomas looked down into his son's eyes. "If I go to Scotland, Piers, which is by no means a settled matter, I have no intention of dying. Today, I am only going to London. Is that what's behind this?"

"I heard you tell Lord Dundee that you got a letter from the Dutch. They want you to say that you won't fight for the King anymore. You're supposed to swear that you'll keep the peace." Piers was crying now. "But you won't do it. 'Let them arrest me,' you said."

Thomas put a hand on Piers' shoulder. "No one can harm me while parliament sits. That's the truth. Afterward may be different. But I tell you this: if I am arrested, it will not be for any wrongdoing. Do you understand?"

His voice, so stern and serious, choked off Piers' sobs in mid-flow. The boy nodded. Thomas brushed a snowflake from his son's cold red nose. "Don't tell Mam," he said. "I don't want her to worry."

They resumed walking, emerging from the woods onto the great tract of snow-covered lawn that bordered the terrace. High over the turrets and chimney pots, the flags hung in stiff, icy folds.

"If there's a war," said Piers, "I want to go with you. Do you remember, sir, that my lord Montrose took his son on campaign with him?"

Thomas had seen him reading Wishart's *Deeds of Montrose*. None other than St. Clare had given it to him. It was so long since he had read the book himself that he could not remember the half of it, but one fact he did recall: Montrose's boy had died during that campaign. He gripped Piers' hand tightly.

"He was much older than you," he said, "and Montrose took him only because the King's enemies would have imprisoned him had he stayed. The cases are not the same at all."

5 JUGGLERS, BALLAD-SINGERS, and shopkeepers had turned the grounds around Westminster Hall into a bazaar. Buy a dish of smoked eels or curds, a slice of gingerbread, a pamphlet proving that the Devil was born in Ireland! Buy a canary in a cage, a bottle of ink, a set of pewter dishes, a pair of silk stockings, or a shirt! Look up to see the heads of traitors! It was only lately that the grotesque remains of Oliver Cromwell's skull had blown down from its iron pole atop the Hall.

In the streets nearby, the coffee houses and taverns had good custom, the men packed together like fish in barrels, drinking, smoking, sharing news sheets, and arguing for or against the Dutch, who were an overwhelming presence in the city. Dutch nobles mingled with the English at Whitehall; blue-jacketed soldiers paraded at the Horse Guards. The Dutch stood watch at St. James' palace, stumped through Hyde Park, bought ale and roasted eggs in public houses, and picked over the goods at the Royal Exchange. Dutch voices rang through the streets. There were so many blue coats around Whitehall that Thomas avoided his usual lodgings in King Street and took a room in a coaching inn on the edge of Blackfriars, where he was unknown. Despite the reassurances he had given his family, there was always the possibility of arrest. But so far, with the business of government stalled over Christmas, William had been conciliating toward the English gentry. He had demonstrated his goodwill by releasing Lord Feversham and freeing priests who had been taken prisoner in the post-Salisbury chaos. But Thomas considered that this clemency had cost the Prince nothing. Lord Feversham was already a ruined man, his career finished, and it was in William's best interest to rid the country of Catholic priests. The period of grace was likely to be short.

If only Lee had taken advantage of it! Thomas badly missed his friend's plainspoken kindness, his good counsel and humour. There was no one now to whom he could speak his mind with the same freedom, no one to whom he could admit how detestable he found the Dutch presence and how much he loathed the goings-on at Westminster.

William had congratulated the new parliament on being a fair representation of the nation, but in fact it was a pulled-together assembly whose members in the Commons had been handpicked by the Dutch. The new broom had swept clean. In the Lords, however, there had been a sudden backlash. James had sent a letter to Lord Middleton that spoke of his desire to regain his throne under a free parliament and establish liberty of conscience for all. The circulation of this letter had sent the old-fashioned church-and-king Tories into such agonies of remorse that now they were opposed to William's demands for full kingship.

The rabble swarming around Westminster, however, was unpleasantly pro-Dutch. Anyone who did not sport orange favours was subjected to a fusillade of rubbish and stones. Thomas, running the gauntlet of the mob, was pelted with rotten fruit and spoiled eggs. People buffeted and jostled him, trying to push orange ribbons into his hands. The chant of "William and Mary! William and Mary!" roared around him. In the corner of Old Palace Yard, a straw effigy of James had been locked into a pillory and pounded with rocks and fruit until the head had burst open.

Inside the Hall, the atmosphere was only slightly less

frantic. Here the law courts competed for space with shops and stalls that did a brisk business selling all manner of goods to members of parliament and the general public. Walking from the Exchequer to the Chancery, it was possible not only to hear the most current news, but to buy books, a loaf of sugar, a glass of beer, or even a set of bed linens. But for the first time this homely English commerce was being conducted under the noses of foreign soldiers. So much, thought Thomas, for the sacred rights and liberties of Englishmen.

The Lords met in the White Chamber, a long, narrow room at the southeast end of the palace. On this raw January day it was gloomy as a cave. The air was thick with the smell of sweat, damp stone, burning candles, and dust. A fire had been lit and the walls were dressed with tapestries, but the room was still inhospitably dank and frigid. The stench of the nearby river seemed to blow in with the draughts that stirred the crimson wall hangings. Pigeons flew about in the rafters. The usual order of the House had broken down, members huddling with their friends instead of taking the benches of their rank. The empty throne at the south end of the room seemed to have taken on an almost sinister significance, as no one was even certain by whose authority the Lords had been summoned; the King had fled, the Lord Chancellor was in prison, and half the peers were missing. Despite the cold, the atmosphere fairly sizzled with the hostility and frustration of men hopelessly at cross-purposes with one another.

Thomas took a place next to Lord Middleton, trusting that the company of this eminently civilized man would keep him sane. Already James' enemies in the Commons had declared the throne vacant, arguing that he had forfeited all his rights by breaking the unspoken contract that existed between a sovereign and the people — as if, Thomas thought, the King were an apprentice who had failed his terms of employment. It was unlikely that William would agree to this approach, as it meant that he, too, might be dismissed if his rule were unsatisfactory. The Prince was in the awkward situation of needing to uphold the very thing he was flouting, the principle of hereditary monarchy. No one wanted a republic. Even those who had deserted James at Salisbury wanted to declare him "voluntarily dead" sooner than vote to depose him.

But there were some, Lord Wharton among them, who had made it clear that they wanted James gone upon any terms. At seventy-five, Wharton had not abated one jot of his hostility toward the King. He sat with St. Clare, who was chewing fruit and throwing the skins to the matting, and the sight of these two old men huddled together — ancient enemies, now cronies, and both of them all blow and bluster — infuriated Thomas so much that he could not think. He liked to consider himself a rational being, a man who, given a choice, would use his brain and not his fists to settle disputes. But his anger made a lie of that. All that constrained him was the knowledge that if he were taken into the custody of the Sergeant-at-Arms, it would benefit nobody except St. Clare and Lord Wharton. At the same time he felt that the pleasure of smashing their heads together would be worth the risk of prison.

St. Clare had not vouchsafed him a word, but even his silence was somehow offensive. During the speeches he fidgeted with the jewel in his ear, drank from a flask, raked his fingers through his hair, and scribbled notes to his friends. Now and again he closed his eyes as if fighting sleep, although the atmosphere was anything but peaceful. Lord Halifax, the Speaker, repeatedly had to call the House to order as the debate degenerated into a series of rancorous shouting-matches about whether the King, by fleeing the country, could be said to have deposed himself. Thomas listened in growing anger. When the proposition was made to declare the King "dead," he jumped to his feet. Rage burned up all discretion.

"You have all forgotten one matter," he said. The noise was such that he had to shout. "The Prince of Orange is only *fourth* in the line of Succession. The legitimate heir to the throne is the Prince of Wales, and whether the King dies or abdicates, by right the Crown devolves first upon him. Voting the Prince of Orange the Crown will turn this kingdom into a Commonwealth. The only way to preserve the principle of hereditary monarchy is to raise the Prince of Wales in the Church of England — "

"He's no more the Prince of Wales than you are," said Lord Wharton.

"That's a lie to deceive the ignorant. Do you think this House is so gullible?"

Wharton stood, still wearing his hat, for which Lord Halifax rebuked him. Wharton paid no attention. "Not so gullible that we don't know who our enemies are. You have taken the part of Papists, sir, and foreign spies. You are acting in the interests of Rome."

"No, my lord. You are deceived. But you have a history of hiding from the truth."

The House sniggered. Lord Wharton, never one to respect the rules, started to climb over the benches. St. Clare seized his arm and jerked him back down. The House broke into shouts and jeers of encouragement. Lord Halifax shouted for order. The Sergeant-at-Arms and Gentleman Usher moved purposefully forward. St. Clare stood, his fist crushing Lord Wharton's shoulder.

"The King's so-called son is in France with King Louis, our chiefest enemy," he bellowed at Thomas. "He has no rights and no place in the Succession, and any who say otherwise are traitors." In a gesture straight out of the theatre, he put his hand to his sword hilt. "Traitors!' he repeated, with obvious relish.

Any speech that Thomas might have made went straight out of his head. He drew his own sword. In horror Lord Middleton struck it aside. "In God's name, sir! Remember where you are!"

A shout went up for the Sergeant-at-Arms. Lord Halifax nodded to Lord Middleton, who flung himself on Thomas and dragged him away. Behind them, the House erupted into chaos. St. Clare was still ranting. "Renegades... liars..."

Middleton, appalled, hustled Thomas out the door. But he seemed to find Thomas' behaviour more shocking than St. Clare's. "You came here to defend the King," he said. "Will you give his worst enemies — and your own — the satisfaction of seeing you thrown into the Fleet? Stand down, my lord. I tell you as a friend."

Thomas was too angry to care what he said. "So you think St. Clare is right? That the King's son is a fraud?"

"Of course not. It's your father-in-law who's the fraud. We all know that. Bringing your private quarrel with him into this will not help the King."

Thomas stared at him, baffled and dazed and almost sick with anger. He had not come here to be part of a raree show. He had had something to say — in good faith — but there was no room for such a thing. There would be no true debate, only nonsense about whether it was legal to declare a living king "voluntarily" dead.

He broke away from Middleton and made for the outside

air like a man who was choking. In the yard the smell of bonfires and spilled drink generated a spurious air of carnival, but the drunken crowd was as menacing as any mob howling for blood at a hanging. He pushed his way through the stalls and the line of waiting carriages and hackney coaches, and began to walk without giving much thought to his direction. Presently he found himself in the Strand.

At midday, it was already so dark that it seemed the sun was setting. A light cold rain fell, but the streets were still thronged with people — ordinary people going about ordinary business. The stink of the tanneries and the fish markets, of burning coal and rubbish, combined like musical notes with the stench of unwashed bodies to produce a rich, ripe fugue of London smells.

Head down against the rain, Thomas walked east to Ludgate hill and up to the new St. Paul's, still under construction twenty-two years after the Great Fire. Scaffolding and canvas and a temporary roof hid the church's interior from view, but he had been privileged to see Wren's design and he knew the planned glories of the soaring sky-blue dome, encased in lead, which James had approved and now might never see. From the building site he walked south to London Bridge, and stood for a long while watching the water roar under the great stone arches. The river was a city in itself, a floating work-in-progress forested with masts and jammed with traffic. Among the merchant vessels, wherries, fishing-boats, skiffs, and barges were Dutch ships flying Dutch flags: the enemy nation that once had sailed up the Medway to fire on England's pride now had warships here with England's blessing. Thomas crossed the bridge, looking at the stalls and shops, the tall medieval houses scorched from the Fire but still standing, and walked down Borough high street. Here it seemed that every second building was an alehouse or a tavern or a brothel. Bonfires burned on each corner and noisy drunks, arm in arm, sang "Lillibulero," an old Irish tune that Wharton *fils*, in his cups, had rewritten in honour of the Dutch landing. It had become all the rage, being sung in the streets, the taverns, and even the churches. Wharton had been heard to boast that he had sung the King out of three kingdoms, but in fact the song had not caught on until James had left. Thomas had never hated any music so much as that piece of doggerel.

He visited St. Saviour's church and then stopped at the newly built George Inn to drink and watch the strolling players perform. Their tattered costumes, purplish in the rain, looked like soaked rags. Orange ribbons fluttered from the slats of the wooden balconies that enclosed the courtyard. There was a burst of laughter from the crowd as one of the players started dancing a jig. The joy on the circle of flushed, drunken faces, the raucous cheering and singing, were so disconnected from his own deep sadness that he felt like a mourner who had wandered by mistake to a wedding. His city no longer belonged to him nor he to it, and he was sick with dismay at the rift. Dundee had been right in predicting that nothing would be accomplished in the House. As for his own contribution, what had he achieved except to make a fool of himself?

"But I had to try," he said to his ale cup. He wished now that he had not allowed Middleton to deter him from fighting. What sense did it make to follow the law when no one else did? The rules of civilized conduct no longer obtained. Cowards and liars could accuse others of treason and there was no penalty or redress. To desert the King, to declare him dead and his son illegitimate, had become the new benchmarks of patriotism and piety. Soon parliament was going to legislate treason into law, and the subversion of justice would be complete. The only concern was to find the right formula. But he would not be part of the process.

Drinking to that resolve now seemed the only sensible course of action. He stayed all afternoon at the George, and when the short day had died into an early dusk, he hired a hackney coach to drive him to the Bear Gardens. From there he took a ferry back to the city. There were more bonfires burning in the courtyard of the coaching inn, more drunken voices singing "Lillibulero." Thomas threw them some coins. "For God's sake sing something else," he said. He had been drinking all afternoon but somehow he was completely sober still, cold and tired instead of drunk. Slowly, wearily, holding the rail like an old man with an ague, he took the stairs to his room.

St. Clare was waiting for him.

He was seated at his ease at a small table loaded with dishes. A bottle of wine stood at his elbow and a powerful smell of boiled onions, gravy, and roast pork spiced the room. It was a dingy chamber with a broken shutter hanging loose from the glassless window, and St. Clare in his great plumed hat, frothing silver lace, and cranberry velvet looked as out of place as a duke in a tinker's hut. Thomas stood in the doorway as if transfixed and his father-in-law, without troubling to rise, offered him a glass of wine.

By way of reply Thomas strode to the table and upended it, sending the dishes crashing to the floor. St. Clare jumped as food cascaded into his lap. A dish of chops landed on his boots. Cursing, he seized a cloth to mop his velvet breeks. "What in hell did you do that for? I paid good money for that supper! And you've ruined my suit."

Thomas drew his sword and laid the edge just under St.

Clare's jewelled ear. His hand was steady, but his voice shook. "What are you doing here?"

The old man looked at him stonily. "I came to talk to you. Put that goddamned thing away! You can see I'm not armed."

"You brought soldiers to my *house*, George. You took my horses, a hundred pounds' worth of gold, and my personal papers. You threatened my family — "

"It was Wharton who took your goods. I tried my best to dissuade him, but he was drunk. What would I want with your damned horses? As for Libby and the children, it was fortunate I was there to protect them. Had it not been for me, they might have fared much worse."

He was serious. There was a genuine note of indignation in his voice. "I suppose I should also thank you for accusing me of treason today," Thomas said.

"Rhetoric," St. Clare said. He pushed the sword away with a finger. "You take it much too seriously."

"Do you not think treason serious?"

"Nothing is serious. Except, mark you, the price of this suit. Seventy pounds it cost me! And then there's my dinner. A shilling for each of those chops! God save us, Thomas, all these years I never suspected you of so foul a temper."

As usual St. Clare was performing, but apparently he had decided to turn his hand to farce instead of tragedy. The sheer magnitude of his effrontery was so ridiculous that Thomas, almost against his will, found his anger abating. What use was it to rage at this elderly child who could betray all sides at once without seeing any difficulty in it, who pursued self-preservation with such purist devotion that he made it seem a high and holy calling? No insult or rebuke could pierce that armour.

He lowered his sword. St. Clare, fuming, righted the

table and sought among the smashed dishes for the wine bottle. Somehow it had survived intact. Turning a choleric eye upon his son-in-law, he drank straight from the bottle and said, "Upon my honour, you are become so difficult that I hardly know you."

Thomas could have answered in kind. But there was no point in an exchange of insults. He sat down, laying his sword across his knee, and rubbed his knuckles against his forehead. "You've come here to no purpose, sir. We have nothing to say to one another."

"I came to tell you that there's a warrant drawn up for your arrest," St. Clare said. Reseating himself, he found a chicken bone and began to pick at it.

"Arrest? On what grounds — telling the truth?"

"Is that what you call that farrago about the King's son? Even if the child is legitimate, no one is going to acknowledge it now. The Prince has publicly declared the boy an impostor. Today, in the House, you said that's a lie."

"It is."

St. Clare ignored this. "I've put it out that you are on your way to Greenwich. Thanks to me, you have a few hours' grace to leave the city."

Thomas looked at him with fresh incredulity. Dundee had declared that there was no middle ground between treason and loyalty, but somehow St. Clare seemed to find it.

"What game are you playing, sir? I thought you were appointed to the Prince's privy council."

"I am."

"Then why are you here? Why warn me?"

"Do you think I want my daughter to suffer needlessly?"

"She is already suffering."

"Not because of me," St. Clare flashed. "Let me tell you

that the best service you can do your family is to leave and lie low — France, Ireland, it makes no odds. Just leave! I'll undertake to handle Lord Wharton. He owes me a debt or two."

Thomas did not want to inquire what those obligations might be. It was enough to know that St. Clare was on terms of friendship with a man who had fought on the side of regicides. "No doubt you would find it convenient if I left, so that you can take my children."

"You've taken mine. They think I'm the Devil."

"You have only yourself to thank for that."

Rancour filled St. Clare's voice. "I suppose you think I ought to suffer ruin for the King's holy sake. I did that once, a long time ago, and it's not something I shall do again. At my age, I don't have the time to rebuild as I did after the war. The Prince offered me a good bargain, and I took it." He paused, fishing among the spilled dishes for a spoonful of gravy. "In the last war, I saw my friends shot before my eyes, and watched young children being driven naked onto soldiers' pikes. I saw the King murdered and my house pillaged. But revenge was not on my mind. It was my own plot of ground that I fought for. I knew I would never rest until the last Ironsides were driven from my land, and that's what kept me going. Not any holy zeal for the cause. And you'll come to feel the same, in time. Your own house and your own fortune — those are the only things worth fighting for." He gave a tigerish smile. "Do you think it matters to the Prince what the House decides? Tomorrow he is going to tell Halifax that unless he is acclaimed King in his own right, he will return at once to Holland, and leave us to deal with the French and Irish. You know what that means. One whisper of *Ireland* and the House will vote him anything he wants. The debate is over, my son. Accept it.

There is nothing more for you to do here." He gave another acid smile. "Besides, your friend Dundee finally has his safe-conducts. I sent them myself. I suppose he and his friends will be halfway to Edinburgh by now. You'll have to ride hard to catch them — that is if you still want to throw in your lot with a man who will be hanging from a rope before the next new year."

Thomas passionately wanted to believe that this was all a maze of lies, a ruse to persuade him to get out of the way, but instinct told him that St. Clare was speaking the truth. At the same time it was impossible to gauge the reliability of his information. As if guessing these thoughts, St. Clare said, "I've been meeting with the Scots. That's how I know. One or two of them want English peerages and they're willing to disclose what their friends are planning. And in case you still do not trust my information, I'll tell you — in strictest confidence, of course — that it was a Dutch agent who started those rumours of an Irish invasion back in December. There was never any real danger. But if people panicked then, think what they would do now, when it's public knowledge that James is going to Dublin to raise an army. Believe me, fear of the Irish is far stronger in most minds than any loyalty to the King."

"Yet you have told Leopold to keep in with him," said Thomas, when he could bring himself to speak. "You've written to St. Germain and so has Churchill. Do you not think the Prince knows that as well?"

"Knowing and proving are two different matters," St. Clare said airily. "Besides, all this talk of 'honour' and 'oaths' is nothing but trumpery. The Prince makes use of me, that's all, and I of him. It's a much more sensible arrangement than agonizing over what you might or might not have pledged three or thirty years ago."

He heaved himself to his feet and picked up his belongings in preparation to depart. Swinging his plumed hat in his hand, he looked enigmatically at his son-in-law. "It's not too late to change your mind and come back with me to Whitehall," he said. "A word in the right ear about General Dundee's plans would go a long way to rub out today's indiscretion."

Thomas closed his eyes. "As God is my witness, sir, you turn me sick. I have nothing to say to you."

St. Clare shrugged and drew on his gloves. His voice, hardening, turned spiteful. "You know the proverb. 'As you make your bed, so you must lie upon it.' But don't flatter yourself that you can keep my daughter in it."

He let himself out.

6 FULKE HAD PUT A WATCH ON the house, and the grounds, in the late evening, were inhospitably dark. The verdigris-bitten statue of St. Michael that stood guard in the centre of the courtyard looked like a figure on a tomb. Thomas, priding himself on being a man of reason and education, did not believe in ghosts or witches. But he nearly jumped out of his skin when something moved behind St. Michael and came forward in the dark. To his astonishment it was Piers, shivering in a thin coat thrown over his nightshirt. Thomas caught him up in his arms.

"What is it? What are you doing out here?" Sudden fear seized him. "Your mother — "

"Mam is fine," Piers said. But his face was tragic, blue with cold, and Thomas took off his woollen scarf and wrapped it around him. "It's Theo. He's run away."

"That's all?" In his sharp relief Thomas could have shaken the boy. But some distant memory of his own priorities at nine years old prevented him. "Never mind. He'll come back when he's hungry."

"It's been almost two days," said Piers. "Fulke said we can search the woods tomorrow."

"Very well. But now you must get back to bed."

The shock of warmth and light in the hall made Piers blink and rub his eyes. In his hand he clutched Theo's favourite plaything, a well-gnawed stick wrapped in an old sock.

"My lord!" Fulke came into the hall a little out of breath, a candlestick in his hand and a look of consternation on his face that deepened enormously when he saw Piers. Thomas turned to him with relief.

"Fulke, take the boy upstairs and see that he has something hot to drink. Then come to my office."

It was nearly midnight. He was tired and wanted to go to Libby. But he had to have news of Dundee first, and Fulke would know. He gave his son a small push in Fulke's direction, and the two of them went hand-in-hand toward the stairs. Thomas took one of the hall tapers and went into his study. It was untidy as ever, the desk strewn with notes, jottings, and odd scraps of paper. He turned one of these over and read, "Not every lawful thing is honourable." *Non omne licitum honestum.* In the last few weeks he had come to understand that the reverse was also true.

Fulke returned, still somewhat out of breath from his exertions. "The child has been looking for his dog," he said.

"I know."

There was a little silence, as if neither wanted to be the first to speak. Then Fulke said, "General Dundee was here yesterday. He's received his safe-conducts."

"So Lord St. Clare informed me when I saw him in London. Has the General left, then?"

"He is gathering his men in Christ Church meadow at dawn tomorrow. He said that if you still want to join him, he would meet you on the road. But he has to leave before the Prince changes his mind."

There was a tight coldness in Thomas' chest. Duty had taken him to Salisbury, but this was different. Across the border he would be an Englishman joining with the Scots and Irish against his own country; a traitor in name if not in fact. He took out his watch and saw that "tomorrow" had become "today."

"Does my wife know?"

"It's she who told me."

Again silence fell between them. Thomas went to the window and leaned his hands on the ledge. Nothing was visible in the dark, but in his mind he saw the sweep of the lawns, the ducks paddling serenely under the willows, the wide terrace with its potted shrubs and flowers. He pictured Libby in the garden, smiling as she held a rosebud out to him.

"By this time next month you will all be saying, 'God save good King William.'"

"No, sir."

"But you must."

"Sir — "

"You understand the risk to the household, Fulke, if it becomes known what I'm doing. For safety's sake, you must all be fervent Orangemen. I insist upon it."

"Her ladyship tells me that you intend to call upon your sister and brother-in-law in Edinburgh, sir," Fulke said, at his most stolid. "Not even the Dutch can outlaw family visits."

"Truth has its advantages," Thomas agreed. Once more he sifted through the papers on his desk, picking them up and then setting them down without seeing them. His next words were so difficult to bring out that he could almost taste acid in his mouth. "It may well be that Lord St. Clare is the only one now who can protect the family. Use him if you must, but do not trust him."

There was no need to say more. Fulke was no fool, and he had faced a similar crisis once before, when Thomas' father had been Cromwell's prisoner. He was dependable as daybreak, thought Thomas, faithful as Job. Notebook and keys in hand, he would defend the house and the family with his last breath — though God forbid it should be necessary.

He told Fulke to get some rest and then took the candle to light his way up the stairs. He expected that Libby would be asleep at this hour, but she was sitting cross-legged on the bed, reading *The Laws of Ecclesiastical Polity*. It seemed a formidable choice for bedtime fare, but at least it was not *The Divers Orations*. She looked up and smiled when he came into the room, but her reddened eyes gave her away. Thomas pushed the papers aside, sat down on the edge of the bed, and leaned over, one arm on either side of her, to kiss her.

He had been wondering what he might say to comfort her, and now he knew there was nothing. This moment had been inevitable since the day he had knelt on the riverbank to watch the King's barge pull away in the mist. The peaceful life was not to be theirs just yet. He reminded himself again that his father had been forced to abandon this house to Cromwell. Surely matters stood better now?

The look on Libby's face said otherwise. As he ran his hands through her hair, he felt her tremble. She had drawn the curtains wide open and the moonlight shone into the room, a cold, clear light nearly white as day. The dogs slept by the hearth, twitching in their dreams. Flung over the bedside chair was a tapestry Libby had been stitching, the bright, peacock colours of emerald, sapphire, and ruby glowing in the light. A jumble of cushions lay scattered on the floor.

Thomas had the illusion that here in this great deep bed they were safe. They were roofed in by the green canopy, enfolded in yards of velvet, shut into silence and seclusion where no one could reach or harm them. In the bliss of oblivion they could forget what had happened and what lay ahead. "There is nothing to fear," he told himself, but all the same he held Libby as if she were the one about to do battle.

They did not speak until Libby went to the dressing

table to pour some water into the basin and run a brush through her tangled hair. Then, in the mirror, her eyes met his. "What will it be like?"

He did not pretend to misunderstand. "Hellish, I suppose. When we were out before, in the summer, it snowed."

"Will you be able to let me know where you are?"

"I'll get word to you somehow."

She set down the brush and went to the wardrobe to pull out his clothes. Vests, shirts, neckbands, and waistcoats tumbled to the floor. Thomas got up from the bed and closed his arms around her. "Don't," he said.

She stood with his shirts in her hands, and her eyes overflowing. He kissed her, thinking that if she had married one of his rivals, those fashionable cavaliers who had crowded St. Clare's dinner table, she would now be safe; their wives, unlike his, would have nothing to fear or suffer from the new order.

"This is not what I wanted, Libby."

"Of course not."

"Forgive me."

"It's not your doing."

She gave the shirts into his hands and went to the linen press for a pillowcase. When she returned she was dry-eyed, calm, once more the dutiful wife. She asked those questions that were necessary, speaking about the children, about Leopold, about the money put at the goldsmith's and the bills that were coming due at the quarter. Thomas gave her the name of friends whom she could trust, Lord Ailesbury and Lord Middleton among them, and gave her directions to the city lodging-house where Dundee had maintained a courier. Then he said brusquely, "There's one more thing I want you to do. Write to your father. Let him think you want to reconcile. Even allow him to visit, if you want."

Her face whitened. "You told me you would never allow him in the house again. Why would you change your mind?"

"I haven't. But he can protect you."

"I don't want his protection."

"You may come to need it."

Her eyes, dull and circled with shadows, stared into his. He took her hands and held them against his chest. "We have to preserve what we can now, Libby. Keeping the peace with your father might make the difference."

"So I am to bargain with the enemy?"

"You are safeguarding all that matters. There is more honour in that than in anything I might do."

"Sir John is in prison, and the rest of our friends are in exile. Do I not have a duty here, as much as you?"

"Yes, and you are fulfilling it."

"What about the children? What do I tell them?"

"The truth," he said. "That you are following my instructions. I trust you always, in all things, and so must they."

She looked at him in silence, her face tired and bewildered. "I'll do whatever you ask," she said finally. "Whatever you say."

He put his arms around her, but she turned her face away with a little gesture of distress and went to the water closet. Presently he heard the gush of the new taps running.

He finished packing without paying much attention to what went in the bag. When he took out his Prayer Book, it fell open to the thirty-seventh of the thirty-nine Articles. *It is lawful for Christian men, at the commandment of the Magistrate, to wear weapons, and serve in the wars.* If he had Brigid's superstitious nature he would have said it was a sign. He stood for a moment with the book in his hand, thinking how ironic it was that something intended to bring people together in worship should have sparked off a fifty-year war instead. But the Prayer Book represented all that the Scots loathed — the English church, English bishops, and English interference. The fact that Dundee subscribed to its use was another reason the Covenanters hated him so bitterly.

Only the dogs slept. When it was time to leave, Thomas went to look at Kate, whose cradle stood in the corner of their room. She had fallen asleep on her back, with her fist crammed into her mouth. There was still milk on her chin from her recent feeding and a look of rapture on her face. Thomas stooped to kiss her spiky hair, but she did not stir. Libby threw on a robe and went to waken the boys.

Thomas had been afraid for James, but it was Piers who cried the most. Woken out of a sound sleep to find his father standing by the bed, cloaked, armed, and ready to depart, he gasped and burst into tears. Thomas took him in his arms while James, scrambling to share his father's lap, fell on the floor and screamed. Thomas picked him up.

"Papa, I saved some carrot for Pilgrim."

"I can't take him. He's ridden too far today."

"Then give it to Magnus. He likes carrots."

"He's not coming either. Theo can have it."

Piers buried his face in his father's shoulder. "He's never coming back."

"Of course he is. He'll remember where his food dish is, soon enough."

"Uncle Leopold is building us a model of London bridge," said James. "It's floating in real water. He said he would show us how the tide works. But you won't be there to see it." He began to sob.

Thomas wanted to assure him that this would soon be

over, that their lives would go on as before and all would be well. But even a six-year-old knew better.

"I want to go with you," said Piers.

"I need you to look after your mother and sister."

James bridled. "*I'm* taking care of Kate. Mam says so. I'm teaching her the alphabet. When you come home, she can read to you."

"I intend to be home long before that, my boy."

When he stood to leave, he had to pry James' arms from his neck. The dogs rushed to the door, but he shut it so they would not follow. Their whimpers and the children's sobs seemed to follow him all the way down the stairs.

The window on the landing let in a square of brilliant moonlight, but the hall below was black and silent, cold at this hour without fires or candles. Libby came with him to the foot of the stairs and he put his arms around her, enclosing her in the folds of his greatcoat. He imagined that his own face must mirror the suffering he saw in hers. But he had no comfort to offer, only his love.

If his household survived, it would be as much due to her courage as any efforts of his own.

"Promise me," she whispered. "Promise." She could not articulate what he must promise, but her eyes, imploring, soaked with tears, spoke for her. She kissed his hand. Then suddenly she thrust him away and ran up the stairs.

Fulke was already waiting for him on the doorstep. "You're taking no one with you, my lord?"

"No."

"You ought to have a servant. A groom at least."

Thomas would not say that coming with him was too risky a proposition for anyone. "I am sure the General will loan me a groom."

"One of those Highland caterans?"

Fulke sounded outraged, as if there might be a need for personal service, for pressed linen and polished boots, that was beyond the comprehension or abilities of anyone who did not speak English. "Sir, you really ought to — "

Footsteps sounded behind them and Brigid appeared in the doorway, holding a cloth bundle in her hands. She knelt humbly on the threshold. "For your journey, my lord."

Thomas was half-afraid she had given him saints' relics or a rosary, but when he looked inside the bundle he saw bread, cheese, and a flask of wine. "Thank you, Brigid."

For an instant her face, pale as milk, looked up at him. "I will look after your lady," she whispered. "God and Mary protect you, sir."

Fulke accompanied him out to the courtyard. The moonlight shone full upon him, showing his face grey and tired, the flesh sinking into wrinkled hollows, and Thomas remembered that on his last birthday the old man had turned seventy. They stood together in silence, looking up at the high, white moon and the drifting cloud. "You should have a clear road, with this light," said Fulke. He looked into Thomas' eyes. "I was here when Cromwell's soldiers took your father away. The last he saw of this house, the chapel was on fire, and the Ironsides were bringing their horses into the Hall. But such tyrannies never prosper. Your father came back and rebuilt, just as you will. There will be better times soon. Don't be afraid for them here, while you are gone."

It was the longest speech Thomas had ever heard him make. Fulke took out his watch and wound it, then put it back in his pocket. "I wish I were going with you," he said.

A biting wind had sprung up. The trees bordering the drive shivered. St. Michael stared valiantly into the dark, his greenish, crumbling sword clenched in a half-eaten fist.

Dead leaves spun around him in the wind. Somewhere an owl hooted. Otherwise all was silent. Thomas rode out without looking back to see if anyone waved to him from the window.

He had his sword loosed in its scabbard and his pistol ready, but there was no one else on the road. He cantered over the bridge, through the silent village, past St. Mary's church and the commons. Debris from the wrecked baggage train still littered the road, although anything useful had long ago been stolen. With a mix of derision and pain he remembered his simple faith that the royal army would drive the Dutch out of England in a fortnight.

Presently a bank of cloud moved across the moon. The stars paled. Some night creature skittered in front of him and his horse shied. He pulled it back to order, patting its flank. He had a moment's deep regret for Pilgrim, for his dogs, even for fat, foolish old Lucy. He wondered if Libby and the children were asleep or if the disruption of his leaving had kept them awake. Doubt pooled in his mind like blood from a wound. He should have insisted upon sending his family away to safety. He should have given himself up to arrest. Dundee's ability to make the unreasonable look possible, even practical, was astonishing, but in the frosty dark of a winter's morning, the credibility of his plan broke down. It was faith and not reason that would see them through this, and right now Thomas' faith was a brittle shell.

Dundee's troop had gathered in the broad flat meadow behind Christ Church. They were out of uniform, but no one could mistake them for civilians. As Thomas rode up to meet them the dawn broke, and the first red of sunrise, like a great pennon unfurling, spread across the eastern sky.

PART THREE

1 IF LONDON WERE A CESSPIT, as some maintained, Edinburgh was an ant heap, upended at the base of a fortified rock. Confined by walls and bogland, the town had grown upward instead of out, streeling in a crazy, mile-long jumble between the castle to the west and Holyrood palace to the east. The wynds and closes were so narrow that the jutting rooftops of the houses on either side, nearly meeting, plunged the ground level into perpetual, stinking twilight. Along and around the Royal Mile, people of all conditions lived elbow-to-elbow, nobles and commons jostling uneasily for space in houses that might be six stories tall, with the poorest tenants banished to the out-thrust top floors or the rat-infested cellars and vaults. The castle, a pockmarked fortress perched on a soaring black crag, presided grimly over the squalor. It was the only citadel in Britain that still flew the King's Standard. Its Governor, the Duke of Gordon, had refused to surrender to the authority of the Convention Parliament — the gathering of peers, nobles, and burgesses who were meeting to decide the fate of the Crown. Gordon had been denounced as a traitor for his refusal, but as the Convention had issued the sentence in the name of King James, the exact nature of his offence was unclear. Nor had he been punished. Visitors still came and went through the siege lines around the perimeter of the castle, and Gordon had good-naturedly tossed down money to the government heralds so they might toast the King's health.

But in the congested maze of streets below Castle Rock, it was open war. Each noble attending the Convention had brought his own tail of armed followers with him, clansmen who fought hand-to-hand like rival bands of robbers. At least once a day the ringing of the Common Bell heralded some fresh insurrection, and the streets crackled with musket fire and the din of men fighting with swords, axes, pikes, chains, or even filth from the gutters.

As Thomas sat writing to Libby before the meagre coal fire in his lodging in the Canongate, he found himself searching for safe and newsworthy items to report. He would not tell her, for example, that yesterday, in front of St. Giles kirk, he had been struck by a rock the size of a fist. Nor he would he tell her that Dundee's Loyal Party had almost breathed its last. Many who called themselves James' friends had failed to attend the Convention; others had boldly switched sides. The Duke of Hamilton, who once had been James' advisor, now led William's faction; the King was represented by the elderly Marquis of Atholl, whose heir had declared for William. But Atholl's wits seemed to have foundered under the stress of campaigning against his own son. In a panic he had voted for Hamilton as President of the Convention instead of himself, thereby giving William's friends the majority.

"The weather continues cold," Thomas wrote. "I thank God for the extra shirts you packed." He paused, biting on the end the quill, and listened to the wind howling through the rooftops. "I wish to God I were home," he resumed. That, at least, was perfectly true. What else could he tell her? It seemed the campaign was over before it had even begun; already the Lords of the Convention had voted to offer William the Crown. In Scotland as in England, the Prince had swiftly and effortlessly outmanoeuvred the King.

William had been friendly to the Scots nobles; James, on the other hand, had threatened them with hellfire (and, far worse, confiscation of their fortunes) should they fail him. So angry had the nobles been that the royal cause would have been lost entirely, had Dundee not suddenly announced that he was calling his own convention in Stirling.

"We leave tomorrow at dawn," Thomas wrote. "Atholl says he is with us, and Lord Mar, the Governor of Stirling, has agreed to host the meeting."

He would not add that Dundee had had to bully both men into it. And even Dundee was unclear what the convention might accomplish, except to buy time while James assembled his army in Ireland.

That was another story Thomas deemed unfit to tell his wife. The king was in Dublin, but his Protestant subjects had been so horrified by his arrival that they had barricaded themselves behind the walls of Derry and refused to surrender. James had been forced to lay siege to the town, an undertaking for which he was entirely unprepared, as King Louis had furnished him with everything except troops. He had had to gather an army of Irish peasants, who, by all accounts, had never before held muskets or even worn shoes. The local Irish officials were infamously corrupt, and the poverty of the country was so bitter that apparently there was no horse, cart, or bag of flour available to buy or steal anywhere. Hard-pressed by all this difficulties, the King had no time to spare for Scotland. He kept assuring Dundee by courier that he would send over troops and equipment as soon as the Protestant Irish surrendered Derry — but as the Protestant Irish showed every sign of digging in until Judgment Day, Thomas at least had no faith in these promises.

Again he paused until the ink puddled. His lodging — a stone's throw from the little gabled house where John Knox had composed his sermons — was as cold and comfortless as a crypt. A box-bed took up one corner; a three-legged stool stood in front of the grate; he supped and wrote his letters on a broken side table by the light of a reeking tallow-dip. It seemed to him that the very stones had soaked up Knox's bitterness and his suspicion of anything that resembled fleshly indulgence. A small lump of sea coal was supposed to heat the room, and Thomas' landlady had given him a single tattered blanket for his bed. Morning and night the wind rattled the loose shutter on the gabled window, which projected so far into the street that it seemed to hang suspended over the central gutter. Sodden laundry flapped on a pole thrusting out from a window on the floor below, although it seemed impossible that anything would dry in this raw damp air. An indescribable reek of boiled cabbage, sour milk, tallow grease, and privy rubbish permeated the walls. By mid-afternoon it was dark as midnight. But opening the shutter was inadvisable. The Duke of Hamilton, concerned for his own safety, had hired a rabble of Covenanters for protection — forgetful, or perhaps unconcerned, that only three years ago these same men had sworn to kill Dundee. The so-called "Saints" had packed themselves into cellars and attics around the town, waiting for an opportunity to attack. Dundee's survival in the circumstances seemed almost miraculous, as he scorned caution and continued to walk abroad wearing a showy plumed hat that made him an instantly recognizable target. So far his boldness had protected him and he was unhurt. But he and his men hazarded their lives each time they showed their faces. Thomas thanked God that they were leaving the city, even though this meant that they were on their own. But they would have been so in any case, after James' foolish letter.

Dundee had drafted his own, far more conciliating, document for the King to sign, and he could not understand why James had failed to use it. He insisted that the King could not have been the true author of that threatening letter, and even the abrupt collapse of the Loyal Party had failed to discourage him. He reminded his friends that Montrose had begun his campaign with only two allies and no weapons except stones picked from the fields. He even quoted Cromwell, saying, "A few honest men are better than numbers."

Thomas had asked caustically where these honest men might be hiding. Lord Mar had offered Stirling Castle only after much prodding. Atholl's loyalty was a windblown reed. As he would not force his men to choose between himself and his son, he had left them to their own devices. Few had chosen to follow James. And Thomas' brother-in-law, Douglas Murray, whom Dundee had also hoped to recruit, was the Duke of Hamilton's new secretary and would have nothing to do with the Loyal Party. Before shutting his door in Thomas' face, Douglas had threatened to denounce him as a traitor.

But that was something else he forbore to put in his letter. There seemed to be nothing else he could tell Libby that would be both reassuring and truthful, except that he loved her.

From the depths below stairs there was a piercing shriek from one of the children and then an ominous crash, as if some furniture had been overturned. Thomas had grown accustomed to the strident goings-on in the house — his landlady had five children — but this time the chaos seemed even greater than usual. He shoved his letter into his pack and opened the door. The landing was unlit, but he saw Dundee and Colin Lindsay standing in the murk at the foot of the turnpike stair. The landlady was attempting to untie her dirty apron, show them in, and scream at her children, all at once. One of the boys had knocked over a dressing table full of crockery and his mother had boxed his ears.

But the sight of Dundee produced an instant hush. For the first time since leaving England he had resumed the dress uniform of his regiment: a scarlet coat with blue facings, a cravat of French lace, gold-embroidered gloves, and a fringed silk sash. His silver-spurred boots were polished to a mirror gloss. Had the King himself appeared on their doorstep, the children could not have been more awestruck. He had one hand on his sword hilt and with the other he swept off his plumed hat, a courtly gesture that managed to transform the mother from shrieking harridan into gracious lady of the manor. She curtsied, blushing as she tucked a lank strand of hair back under her cap, and said that she would bring their lordships a whisky posset.

The two men came up the creaking stairs and into Thomas' room. Dundee threw his gloves on the table and paced up and down, while Colin flung himself down on the three-legged stool and put his head in his hands. Thomas, shutting the door, asked what was wrong.

"I have thirty members of my old troop back in uniform," Dundee said, as if this answered the question. "They'll escort us out of Edinburgh at dawn tomorrow." He said that he had sent messengers all over the city, even through the siege lines around the castle, to inform the King's friends of his plans; with luck, he hoped that at least half a dozen lords and their entourages would join them.

The word *luck* seemed to fall like an iron bar. "Not after that damned letter," Colin said.

Dundee rounded on him. "Devil take the letter, and you as well!"

It was the kind of thing he might have said in jest, but

there was no humour in that ragged voice. "I should never have told you."

"Do you not think we all deserve to hear the truth?" Colin asked. He looked at Thomas. "You know that Lord Melfort is now Secretary of War. Well, John asked him, '*as a friend*,' to resign, as no one will accept a government that includes him. His answer was the letter that ruined us."

Thomas understood now the reason for Colin's strange manner and the tension between these friends. "Is that so, John? You thought Melfort would resign because you *asked* him to?"

Dundee's face flamed. "I'll not go behind a man's back. At one time he called himself my friend. I thought, for the good of the King's service, that he would agree. But we'll work around him." He spoke as if Melfort were a natural obstacle, a mountain or a volcano, that could be bypassed, and Colin groaned. "Christ, John! A suckling babe could have told you what would happen."

Dundee's voice took on a different tone. "I will not go behind a man's back," he repeated. "Either Lord Melfort's or the Duke of Hamilton's or, for that matter, your own, Colin. And there's an end to it."

The landlady hurried in with a hot whisky posset. Thomas, dividing it into indifferently clean bowls, found that his hand was unsteady. Asking the Secretary of War to resign — Dundee might as usefully have invited William to return to Holland. It would be almost laughable, were the consequences not so serious. But the thing was done. Dundee, ignoring his drink, resumed his pacing. "The Duke of Gordon has given permission for his men to withdraw if they choose," he said. "He knows that after tomorrow, the siege will become serious. He has less than a hundred soldiers with him now and there is not much food or ammunition.

I've told him to stand fast until we get our reinforcements from Ireland."

Colin muttered something and Dundee, after a brief silence, said quietly that it was treason to doubt the King's word.

"But it's not His Majesty who will be in charge of dispatching troops and supplies to us. It's Melfort." Colin turned to Thomas. "You know that's true. Tell him, for God's sake! The only remedy is to write again and beg Melfort's pardon. We must do it ourselves, if John won't. Pretend that he was mad, drunk — anything. Otherwise, we're finished."

"Send directly to the King," Thomas said. But Colin shook his head. "All correspondence goes through Melfort now."

So James trusted Melfort as unreservedly as he had once trusted Churchill. Would he never learn? James might not have written that indiscreet letter, but he had signed it. He met Dundee's eyes.

"Then Colin is right. Melfort has to be sweetened somehow. Otherwise we'll get nothing from him. I'll write to him."

For a moment he thought Dundee would charge that this, too, was treason. There was another silence, broken only by the rattling of the shutter. "If you wish to correspond privately with Dublin, that's your lookout, Thomas," said Dundee. "But not if you want to ride with me." He still spoke quietly, but he might as well have shouted, "*I am the general of this army!*" Thomas understood that this was less a crude show of rank than an appeal to personal loyalty, but for an instant he was strongly tempted to use this God-sent excuse to wash his hands of the entire business.

"I don't think you can afford to lose me, John. But suit yourself. Write to Dublin on your own."

"I will. And I want you to bide the night with Atholl, Colin, to make sure that he keeps his word." Dundee pushed that out like a battle order. "I'm away now to Lord Mar's." He shoved his gauntlets in his pocket and walked out.

"Wait," said Thomas. He did not want his friend walking alone around the streets in that blazingly conspicuous finery. Dundee, without replying, was already halfway down the stairs. Thomas extinguished the tallow-dip and picked up his hat. "Coming along, Colin?"

"To spend the night with Atholl? Oh God!"

"Put him in fetters if you must," Thomas said unsympathetically. "We might have to do the same with Mar."

But Lord Mar was sick with fever and would not see them. Dundee, frowning, scribbled a note reminding him of tomorrow's rendezvous — although, as Thomas thought rancorously, it hardly seemed possible that the man would forget it was his own castle they were making for. But he held his tongue, parting from Dundee in silence.

Back in his lodging, he prepared for the night by removing his boots and setting his pistol and sword nearby. As he lay in the dark on the broken bed, he thought over what he knew to be true about Lord Melfort: he was the younger brother of Lord Perth, the Chancellor of Scotland, whom William had imprisoned. Both brothers had converted to Rome when James became King, an act which had earned them the undying scorn of their fellow-Scots. Melfort was well-known to be a bribe-taker, back-stabber, political sail-trimmer and inveterate liar, yet he still had the King's ear. He had fled the country well ahead of his sovereign and now he was in Dublin, making a mess of the Irish campaign. What must have been his fury when Dundee, a man of whom he was already almost insanely jealous, had asked him to resign?

Between cold and disquiet Thomas could not sleep. He kindled the fire and tried to read, but sat looking at the pages without making sense of the words. When he closed his eyes he thought of Libby, remembering the day that he had asked for her hand. St. Clare, damn him, although knowing well enough what was in the wind, had not left them alone for a moment and he had finally resorted to writing a note and setting it under Libby's plate at dinner. And then St. Clare, no doubt thinking it high sport, had seated his widowed cousin — sixty if she were a day and deaf as a stone — at Libby's accustomed place. Thomas thanked God that he had written only a half-dozen reasonably innocent words. *Meet me in the privy garden.* How Libby had laughed!

The night crawled by. It seemed like the middle of the night but it was only eleven o' clock. What was Colin Lindsay saying to Atholl? And did they need or want such allies — men who needed to be caged lest they changed their minds?

He dozed on and off, waking when the shutter banged in the wind. An hour before dawn he was up, buckling on his sword and picking up his spurred boots to carry downstairs so that no noise would betray his departure. During the night fog had blown in from the sea, and the deserted streets were curtained in mist. But the dark and the fog were protection and he rode without incident to the rendezvous point on the shore of the North Loch. There was no sign of anyone else on the road. It was so cold that the steaming breath of men and horses condensed into a white cloud. Mist drifted like smoke on the ruffled surface of the bog-water. One of the horses, restive with standing, shook his harness and startled a small flock of birds into flight. The rushing beat of their wings was the only sound in that ghostly stillness.

They waited ten minutes. Fifteen. Thomas brought out his watch and then put it back again without comment. Under the shadow of his broad-brimmed hat Dundee's face showed, if not impatience, a growing tension. Finally a solitary horseman cantered toward them, his neck loosely muffled in a scarf against the cold. It was Colin. When he drew rein, Dundee looked at him and then back along the road. "You're alone? Where are the rest of our friends?"

Colin fiddled with his scarf and his gloves and would not meet his friend's eyes. He said that Atholl, fearing arrest at Stirling, had decided to remain in Edinburgh at least one more day "to divert suspicion." Their other chief ally, the Earl of Mar, was still abed with fever. All the others who had said they would join them had either changed their minds or run for home.

Dundee checked a movement of his sorrel and sat in silence while the full import struck him. His face was a study in containment. "So there is only yourself, then, Colin. But where are your own men?"

A violent flush blotched Colin's face and he said nothing. Dundee repeated his question. "I'm not going with you," Colin said finally, nearly screaming. "I'm going back to town."

In the deep silence that followed, there was a riff of wind, like a sigh, over the bog. The ends of Dundee's sash fluttered, but otherwise he might have been a figure carved on a monument, a stone knight on a stone horse. Colin leaned forward, his expression both anguished and abject. "John, listen to Atholl. Come back with us to Parliament House."

"I can't."

"If you leave, all our plans will go for nothing."

"They are nothing in any case."

"No. Wait the day. If you leave now, you'll give the alarm."

"I've already done so. You must see that."

They were in uniform, carrying the regimental flags. It was too late to bolt back to town and pretend to reconsider. Dundee's fist tightened on the reins. "I have other friends to meet on the road, Colin. I'll wait for you at Stirling — if and when you have a mind to leave Edinburgh."

He drove his spurs into his sorrel's flank, but in desperation Colin seized the bridle. The horse, wildly indignant, snorted and plunged. Colin held on. "In God's name, don't do this alone."

Dundee pushed his hand aside. "I told you I have friends to meet. And if I go to them alone" — for an instant his guard dropped, and his suffering showed — "look to Atholl and Mar and yourself to explain why."

He spurred to a gallop. The troop fell in place behind him. Colin had to pull his own horse aside to let them pass, and as they did so Thomas saw that he was weeping without shame or discretion, the tears running down his chin into his silk scarf. But for all that he made no move to follow. Nor did Dundee look back.

They rode up to the castle and halted on the spur of a hill under the northwest escarpment, the side that was shielded from the eyes of the town. There Dundee dismounted, saying brusquely, "I'll speak with Gordon before we leave." He strode off toward the steep, hundred-foot cliff that buttressed the castle walls, and scrabbled up its face like a goatherd, grasping at tufts of weed and finding invisible footholds in clefts and crevices. His scarlet uniform stood out like a splash of blood against the rock. It took him less than ten minutes to climb to the top. When he reached the ledge that ran underneath the castle wall, the postern gate opened and the Duke of Gordon stepped out with a spy-glass under his arm. The two men held a brief conference. Then Dundee scrambled back down the way he had come, landing dishevelled and dirty but not even winded. It had been an extraordinary performance, but his manner discouraged comment. Instead Thomas asked what Gordon had said.

"He asked me where we intended to go." Dundee wiped his face on his sleeve and stared up at the postern, where the Duke still stood watching them. "I told him wherever the spirit of Montrose shall lead us."

He made it sound almost reasonable, a thing that anyone might say. He replaced his hat, which he had removed for the climb, and swung back into the saddle. Thomas spared a backward look for Gordon, who waved his hat in farewell, a gesture somehow both sad and jaunty.

The thirty-six miles to Stirling were accomplished in fiercest silence. The plague of betrayal had crept in amongst them and all were sickened by it. Thomas knew that eventually Dundee would find some excuse for Colin, for he could not bear that his friends should fall below the standards he himself set; the solidarity of his happy few, the band of brothers, would have to be restored, if only in his imagination. But meanwhile, his certainty that his friends were all of the same heart and mind as he, his belief that nothing could break their faith, had received so ferocious a shock that he looked almost ill.

At Stirling a fresh blow fell. As they approached the town a man in a weathered plaid and feathered bonnet rode out to intercept them. He pulled up and dismounted before Dundee, bonnet in hand. "Sir, you must not stay here. Lord Mar is no longer with you. He's ordered his men to fight. And the other lords have run. There's no one to wait for."

So Dundee would not have his meeting after all. It was Salisbury revisited — betrayal after betrayal, layers of cowardice and shame and lies. "Why have you warned us?" Thomas asked sharply. "Are you not one of Lord Mar's men?"

"No, no, my lord. I've been looking for you on the road. I am Alexander Drummond, with a message from my father-in-law — Sir Ewan Cameron of Lochiel. He said to tell you that he and his clan are most heartily at your service."

Colour rushed into Dundee's haggard face. "Lochiel sent you to find me?"

"Here is his letter."

Dundee seized the paper and read it through twice before thrusting it into his jacket. His eyes were fever-bright. "God be thanked! Do you ride with us, Mr. Drummond?"

"Most willingly, my lord."

"Then let's be off."

Thomas expected at any moment to hear gunfire from the castle ramparts or the backward ringing of church bells sounding the alarm. But no one challenged them. They galloped safely through the sleeping town and out the other side. The quality of the silence was somehow disturbing, as if they had been watched from those walls, if not attacked, and the hairs on the back of Thomas' neck prickled. It seemed that Lord Mar's friends were no more courageous than their English counterparts — all of them were likely hiding behind those bolted doors and shuttered windows, waiting to see which way to jump. They would not fight on either side until it became clear who was winning.

When they stopped at the change-house in Dunblane for a brief meal, Dundee gave Thomas his letter to read. Lochiel, chief of the Camerons, a man of almost princely importance, had invited Dundee to lead a Highland confederacy on the king's behalf — an undreamed-of honour, for no Lowlander but Montrose had ever commanded the clans. And the Camerons were second in influence only to their hated and ancient rivals, the Campbells. With Lochiel's support, Dundee could raise the army he had envisioned. His Loyal Party had been given a deathbed reprieve. He talked about going to his home in Perthshire to gather recruits before setting out to meet Lochiel in his mountain stronghold in Lochaber.

Thomas sought solace in his wine cup and let Dundee talk. He had never been north of the Highland line. But he had heard stories about the tribal hosts who lived there, men whose way of life had not changed in a thousand years and whose creed was written in the blood of their enemies. Lochiel himself was renowned for biting out a man's throat during hand-to-hand battle — an Englishman, as Thomas recollected dryly. What would Louis' finely trained French troops, for whom Dundee had been asking ever since they arrived, make of men who fought like mad dogs?

The taproom was dark, low-ceilinged, smelling of old rushes and dust. Barrels of provisions stood against the smoke-blackened walls. A one-eared dog slept in front of the fire. *Timor mortis conturbat me* …the fear of death disturbs me….. but that was not exactly true. Thomas felt remarkably free of fear for himself; he had known from the beginning the fate that awaited him if this should fail. It was the thought of his family that most troubled him.

Dundee, folding up his letter as he finished his meal, looked confident, at ease, very nearly happy. Thomas wished that he felt the same. But perhaps that was not possible — not here, not now, in this country where he was a stranger. And Dundee was his friend, but his "not if you want to ride with me" still hovered in the air between them, though neither would speak of it. The commander of an army had no need to excuse or explain himself or ask anyone's permission for his actions — but John had no official standing yet and perhaps never would. His army at present consisted of a single troop of cavalry dedicated to a cause that had, at best, only a slight chance of succeeding. And at worst? But that was not something to dwell on.

2 SPRING WAS SO LATE THIS YEAR that the big oak and sycamore trees on the grounds of Dudhope Castle had just begun to leaf. Like a captive princess in a fairy tale, Jean Graham had spent the months of her pregnancy here in lonely grandeur, with only her servants and horses for company. But her husband had promised that he would return before their child was born, and now at last, on this dull, blustery March afternoon, Jean looked out her bower window to see him trotting up the drive at the head of a troop of soldiers. She flung aside her book and rushed as fast as she dared to meet him. She was so big with child by now that she had to grasp the rail with both hands as she descended the stairs.

The day, breaking fair, had turned overcast and the bright regimental uniforms and flags stood out boldly against the grey landscape. Great storm clouds, building up over the firth, had cast deep shadows over the grounds, and a roaring wind shook the trees that bordered the drive. Her husband, spurring ahead of his men, flung off his hat and dismounted into her arms. How thin he was, all bone and muscle, and she — "I am as broad as I am tall," she said, half laughing and half sobbing into his coat. He kissed her again and again, apologizing for turning their home into a barracks. But it would not be for long — soon he would be out campaigning.

Thomas, standing on Dundee's right, saw Jean's face change, turning pale under its dusting of little gold freckles, and he was moved to pity. For a moment she stood silent, her smile fading a little. Her heart-shaped face and cloud of fine, reddish-gold hair, caught up in bright ribbons, made her look almost like a child. But when she put her hand on her great belly the illusion vanished. The gesture was a mother's, protective, instinctive, and her eyes those of a woman who knew what it meant to suffer.

Thirty soldiers had intruded upon her reunion with her husband, and even as they walked in the house arm-in-arm, he was making plans aloud to summon all the Graham kinsmen and tenants to join him before he rode north. Still Jean said nothing. She smiled upon Thomas, giving him her hand and asking after his family and his health like a good hostess at a dinner party. Only the slight tremor of her fingers in his, and the film of unshed tears in her eyes, betrayed her.

To his discomfiture Thomas was given the best guest chamber and a servant to wait upon him, as if he were in truth a visiting friend and not a soldier quartered upon the house. Once more he was in a world of beeswax candles, feather pillows, scented towels, soap, and fine furniture. The massive bed, tented in blue silk, would have slept six across with ease. Behind a gilt leather screen stood a washtub, which the servant presently filled with hot water.

Below the window was a young rowan tree, its branches still bare. Flower beds surrounded a marble fountain whose central figure was a maiden emptying a water jug. Thomas leaned on the sill, watching the grey sky turn black. The storm clouds opened. Rain sluiced down with such force that the fountain threatened to overflow. The downpour shredded the petals from the late snowdrops and flattened the tulips.

He heard a burst of laughter from below stairs. He ought to dress and go down for dinner, make some effort to fit into the company. Three years ago he had ridden and fought with Dundee's troop, and then, as now, he had been a foreigner among them — but now matters had changed. Now the enemy was England. In the service of his King he had become a man without a country.

Jean had thought of everything for his comfort, including sending up a flagon of wine to his room. As he poured a glass he recollected that even on her wedding day Jean had not had her husband to herself — Dundee had been called out on patrol immediately after the ceremony, and Jean had been left to eat the bridal feast and spend her wedding night alone. What was it that drove Dundee to such an extreme of sacrifice, demanding the utmost not only from himself, but from those who loved him?

It was a question that Libby too might have asked. So far Thomas had been sustained by the belief that he was doing what was inevitable and right. But the pain in Jean Graham's eyes challenged that assumption. *I could not love thee, Dear, so much, Lov'd I not honour more* — Libby had always scorned that poem. Perhaps she was right, and no woman alive would want to hear such nonsense.

As if she had been waiting only for the moment of her husband's homecoming, Jean went into labour that night, and in the cold hours of the following morning, she bore her lord a son. Under ordinary circumstances she would have rested in bed, greeting well-wishers and opening gifts, until the official christening party. But these were not ordinary times. Even as Dundee held his child for the first time, the Convention government in Edinburgh proclaimed him outlaw and traitor, with a bounty of a thousand pounds sterling on his head. General Hugh Mackay, a fellow Scot who had served with him in Holland, was despatched to arrest him.

But once again the government had issued its edict in the name of King James, an absurdity that softened the blow. In any case it had been expected. As Jean slept after her ordeal, Dundee took his troop to the summit of Dundee Law, the plateau that overlooked the town. The April day stung with cold. But yesterday's storm had swept away the clouds and rinsed the air clean. The molten blooms of the furze bushes seemed to set the ground on fire. Dundee's cousin, the poet James Philip, raised the crimson-and-gold Lion Rampant of Scotland, and the blue-and-silver Graham banner with its phoenix crest. In full view of the town, with no commissions or warrants or any kind of public backing, the royal army of forty souls officially declared war upon William.

Trumpets sounded. The pipes skirled. The faces of the men around him shone with pride and fervour, but Thomas was thinking about gunpowder. God pity them, did they even have a single barrel?

The scream of the pipes drowned out any speech Dundee might have made. But no words were needed. He stood bareheaded in the cold spring sunshine, his face shining, exalted, as if this were the fulfillment of his deepest wish — to stand on a windblown hill on the roof of Britain, and know he was at war.

To avoid Mackay's soldiers they took refuge in Dundee's boyhood home of Glen Ogilvie, ten miles away. Jean endured the move with fortitude, at first giving orders for the household from the confines of her bed. But by the end of the week she was coming downstairs in her silks and ribbons to preside over the officers' dinner table. She graciously welcomed the Graham kindred who daily arrived to join her husband, ensuring that even in the rough state of the household, there was enough food and enough bed linens to go around. She was newly risen from childbed and before that she had not seen her husband for months; she had been turned out of one home only to have the other used as a barracks; on the very day of his birth, her son had been disinherited when his father had been proclaimed a traitor at the Market Cross in Edinburgh. All this she appeared to accept as part of the burden and honour of being Dundee's wife.

But the morning of the men's departure, she stayed in bed. The troop, now augmented by Graham cousins and Graham friends and tenants, assembled in the grass-grown courtyard at such an early hour that not even the servants were up. Nothing stirred in the chilly silence. Dundee, as if putting himself under some harsh self-imposed discipline, did not turn to look back at his home or give any hint of what it cost him to ride away from it. But he spurred well ahead, making it clear he wanted no man's conversation or company.

Thomas rode with James Philip, who disclosed that he had already begun an epic, in Latin, about the war. He was composing even as they rode. *"Finding himself greatly inferior in numbers, though not in vigour, Dundee moves northward...mid the deep shadows of sombre night, undaunted by the ice-covered rivers — "*

Thomas trusted that the "ice-covered river" was a poetic myth. But in fact it was piercingly cold, more December than April, and the high hills were still deep in snow. It took a day to travel forty miles to the summit of Cairn O' Mount, where they made a rough camp. After a bitter night they ate cold food from their packs and then rode into the valley of Dee to meet Lord Dunfermline, the Duke of Gordon's brother-in-law, at Castle Gordon.

In the Duke's absence Dunfermline was acting as the Gordon chief. Thomas took an immediate liking to this good-humoured man whose sturdy common sense reminded him strongly of Lee. Dunfermline, like so many others of his generation, had got his military experience serving as a soldier of fortune in the Low Countries. He and Dundee had known one another for years, and he made it clear that whatever his friend needed, he should have — whether food, forage, beds for the night, or fighting men. Unlike Atholl and Mar and so many others, he was ready to express his loyalty in a tangible way.

To warm his guests after their ride, Dunfermline had ordered hot spiced ale with roasted apples frothing on the top, and they dined in state in the Great Hall. An enormous fire roared in the hearth, torches burned in iron sconces, and a score of candles stood upon the table, but beyond the light the far reaches of the chamber swam away into a dark cavern that might have been the habitation of bats or owls. Blackened armour and dusty stags' heads hung upon the walls amid portraits of the Gordons. When the plates were cleared, Dundee unfurled a map for their host and used a spoon to sketch their proposed route. He wanted to recruit as many men as possible before going north to Inverness to meet Lochiel's ally, MacDonald of Keppoch, who had undertaken to guide them into Lochaber. If they had enough men, they could split their forces in two and leave behind a troop to garrison Inverness.

"Keppoch," Dunfermline murmured. "I've not met the man. But I've heard of him."

From the expression on his face, it was nothing good. Thomas was about to ask for information when Dunfermline changed the subject. He had had news from Edinburgh: Lord Mar's fever had been genuine after all, for a few days ago he had died; Atholl, making a decision at last, had bolted for England in such haste that he had left half his baggage behind; and Colin Lindsay had been arrested for treason. Upon his return to Edinburgh he had been taken to the Tolbooth, where he was chained to the wall like a beast.

All conversation stopped. Thomas could not look at Dundee's stricken face. He drank his wine, which had suddenly lost its taste, and pretended to study the map, which by now he could have redrawn in his sleep. Colin by his own folly had condemned himself to this fate, but his likely punishment was out of all proportion to anything he might have done. His only true crime, after all, had been a lack of resolve. But a charge of treason meant that if he were not hanged and disembowelled forthwith, he might spend the rest of his life awaiting trial — solitary, fettered, unable to shuffle more than a few steps back and forth in the stinking darkness of his cell. He would be fortunate if death claimed him before he went mad.

Dundee, without speaking, abruptly left the room. After a few moments Dunfermline leaned forward to say that he had been given charge of the little troop of cavalry — did Thomas mind? It was only because he, Dunfermline, was standing in for his chief.

Thomas was astonished. Here was a rare man, someone who humbly offered his life and fortune and who cared more for the common good than for his own advancement — a man to like, but, far more importantly, a man to trust.

Once again he thought of Colin Lindsay, and a sudden sickness flooded him. God spare him such an end! To be chained like that, hand and foot, and left to rot — he would sooner be shovelled alive into a grave.

For a month they pounded the hills for recruits, camping out and riding hard on starvation rations of dried oatmeal and bannock, protecting themselves against the harsh weather by adopting the traditional clothing of the country — thick, coarsely woven lengths of plaid that were worn belted around the waist and slung over the shoulder. As a useful, all-purpose garment — shirt, cloak, and bedsheet combined — Thomas found the plaid unsurpassed in practicality, if not in beauty. But in their rough clothing, and living hand-to-mouth as they did among the bogs and crags of the hill country, they might have been a band of thieves rather than a royal army. Without commissions and warrants they had no legal authority to levy troops or raise funds, making it difficult to establish that they were the King's representatives, legitimately raising troops for their sovereign, instead of mercenaries seeking plunder. And the results had been cruelly disappointing. Even the Gordons had not come out in force; only fifty men had answered the call to arms. Meanwhile General Mackay had garrisoned Dundee town and was on the march with a force of a thousand men. From Cairn O' Mount they caught a glimpse of the enemy, only eight miles off. Thomas, using Leopold's glass, could swear he detected Mackay's red whiskers. But with so few numbers the royalists could not offer a challenge. They headed back north into the hills instead. "*Through the woods, and over the mountains of Cromar*," sang James Philip, economically compressing days of misery into one sentence. They swam, forded, or ferried over turbulent foaming sheets of deep dark water, picked their way at night through steep, snow-filled corries or thick tracts of pine forest, slept out in the rocky fields or in abandoned bothies or sometimes amongst gravestones or the ruins of a church. The summer Thomas had spent with

Dundee's moss-troopers seemed like a gentleman's Grand Tour compared to this wild flight — then at least they had been the representatives of the law, and now they were fugitives. They rode past castles and great houses where once they would have been honoured guests, and sought refuge in places unfit even for cattle; they skirted the little towns with their cobbled streets and smoking chimneys and the ravishing smells of hearth-cooked food, and plunged instead into the desolate countryside where no living things but themselves seemed to breathe or move in the wintry air. Their purpose might be noble, as Dundee steadfastly reminded them, but for Thomas life had shrunk to the practicalities of finding a crust of bread and a dry place to sleep for the night. He wondered how Lord Dunfermline, fifteen years his senior, managed the punishing hours in the saddle and on foot — until he saw his friend furtively anointing himself with goose grease and cutting his boots to accommodate his swollen feet.

With Mackay on their tail they pushed north to meet MacDonald of Keppoch and his men. The little grey town of Inverness beckoned like a torch. After thirty days in the saddle, they would be able to rest in beds and sit to dinner like civilized men.

But when they drew up before the palisades they found the town in a state of siege: Keppoch, having arrived before them, had imprisoned the town's councillors in his tent when they refused to declare for the King, and was holding them to ransom. He and his men had made camp outside the walls, and from the look of it were prepared to stay indefinitely.

Keppoch was dining on the ground outside his tent when the army arrived. Rising unhurriedly, he strolled forward to meet them, picking meat and gristle out of his teeth with the point of his dirk. He was the tallest man Thomas had ever beheld — seven feet perhaps, long-haired and full-bearded, and bristling with weapons. He wore a feathered bonnet crushed over his red hair, a filthy plaid fastened by a brooch the size of a plum, and a velvet cloak that trailed behind him in the dirt. Deerskin leggings tipped with bronze strapped his legs from thigh to ankle, and a monstrous, two-handled broadsword swung from his hip. The fighting men of his clan, most of whom were dressed alike in faded plaids and rough leggings, surrounded him like a Roman phalanx. They all carried targes of bronze-studded leather and enormous swords that looked sharp enough to fell an ox.

The camp was clogged with stolen cattle and jumbled odds and ends of plunder — wine bottles, cups, a mirror, a set of candlesticks, caged poultry, bolts of fabric, cook-pots and more. The men were drinking and some of them, to the hoots and jeers of their comrades, were fighting hand-to-hand. There were women as well, as there would always be in the wake of an army, camp followers who looked as though they could wield an axe or drink a jug with the best of the men.

Dundee gazed over the brawl with a look of growing incredulous rage. Then he dismounted and confronted Keppoch. The MacDonald could have easily seized him with two fingers and hurled him over the palisades. But John Graham was not the man to be intimidated by anyone, no matter how huge or wildly dressed.

"By God, sir, is this how you expect to win allies to the King's cause?" he said. "Do you call yourself a patriot? This is nothing better than robbery!"

Keppoch's face wore a look of such astounded incomprehension it was not clear whether or not he understood

English. He stared down at Dundee, fiery brows knotting, fingers straying to the hilt of his mighty broadsword. Abruptly the noisy chatter of the camp died away. Some of the clansmen picked up their weapons. When Keppoch raised his fist, Thomas drew his sword. But Keppoch had only moved to sweep the bonnet from his head. His hair, released from bondage, spilled to his shoulders like a greasy waterfall.

Astonishingly, he bowed. Then he answered in perfectly good English, offering an explanation, if not an apology, for the disorder. He claimed that the ransom represented a legitimate debt owed to him by the town of Inverness, while the nearby lands were tenanted by the Macintoshes, his clan's hereditary enemies, who by tradition expected and deserved to be plundered. He insisted that he meant no harm to King James, who was, after all, a Highland gentleman like himself. But — this with a mixture of bluster and pride — it was a matter of honour that he collect his ransom.

"Honour!" said Dunfermline. But scorn was wasted upon Keppoch. Dundee's jaw worked. The seven hundred MacDonalds were enough to bolster the army to fighting strength, but it was clear that the price of the alliance was almost more than his ordered brain could stand. "Let me see your hostages," he snapped. Keppoch, with a wave of his bonnet, ushered him into his tent. Thomas, Dunfermline, and David Graham, Dundee's younger brother, followed.

The town councillors had been trussed up like fowl and Keppoch had stolen their shoes. They were in a red-hot rage and every ounce of diplomacy had to be summoned to bring about a ceasefire. When it became clear that the negotiations were failing, Thomas removed his hat and tossed his ready money into it. The others followed suit, bringing the sum up to half the ransom. When Dundee angrily signed a pledge of repayment for the other half, Keppoch brought back the hostages' footwear.

The councillors, plainly thinking they were dealing with a madman, put on their shoes and stalked home. Dundee ordered the MacDonalds to march out. But Keppoch, having got his cattle and his cash, was interested only in taking the plunder back home. With the air of a man making a gracious concession, he left several of his barefooted, tangle-haired gillies to act as scouts. Then he left, driving his stolen cattle before him. The last they saw of him, he had tied a woman's petticoat over his head and was shouting a bawdy drinking song at the top of his voice.

There was no hope now of garrisoning Inverness. Keppoch, having ruined any chance of reaching an agreement with the town, had abandoned his allies after extracting nearly all their ready money; they had no food, no weapons other than their own swords and carbines; and — since Dundee town was garrisoned against them — no refuge except Castle Gordon.

Thomas was ready to sympathize with those who thought the King was cursed. Salisbury, Edinburgh, Stirling and now Inverness — each successive attempt to rally his supporters had failed more wretchedly than the last. But what could be expected when those supporters were men who considered it their God-given right and privilege to rob their neighbours?

Lochiel expected them in six days' time and in the mountain passes it would still be winter. There was no time to spare. But after Keppoch left Dundee turned south instead of north, snatching at the chance to see his wife and child one more time before pushing into Lochaber. He was returning to Glen Ogilvie as he had left, with only his own troop and kinsmen and the Gordons under his banner; unlike Montrose, he had not been able to summon an army out of nothing. Times and men had changed, Thomas told himself, the little phrase repeating like a jig in his tired brain as they rode. But perhaps that was wrong. Perhaps nothing had changed and that was the problem; the Highlanders had always been preoccupied with feuds and cattle raids to the exclusion of all else, and there had always been men like Atholl, whose word counted for nothing.

They had been gone four weeks, and in that time, although they had been too busy to notice it, spring had crept in. The orchard and gardens at Glen Ogilvie had sprung to life. In the grass between the fruit trees and the paths around the house, field daisies and poppies had seeded themselves in glorious disorder. Hawthorn and elderflower bloomed by the front door. The kitchen garden, deep in thistle a month earlier, now sported tidy rows of sprouts. The grass had been newly scythed, the scent redolent of idle afternoons and long summer twilights. After the harshness of the high country, it was almost too much to bear.

Jean came flying down the drive toward her husband, in such haste that she stumbled. When she reached Dundee they flung their arms around one another, and she clutched his dishevelled head to her slight breast as if afraid he might vanish altogether.

A sudden, odd silence fell and for an instant they might have been frozen in a painting. The men in their plaids, the dark fabric lightened here and by the glint of burnished steel or the gleam of a linen collar, stood in the background with the horses; the evening star hung like a jewel in the branches of a fig tree; on an upstairs windowsill a cat slept, framed by the open shutters.

Then, with equal suddenness, the spell was broken.

Dundee took his wife's arm and they went into the house, moving slowly, leaning on one another like people exhausted from illness. The men moved off to bed down their horses and find food. The orchard became a camp. At dinner Lord Dunfermline turned red with pleasure when heard his name mentioned in James Philip's new stanza: "*By the headlong waters of the Spey, Dunfermline meets him, bringing with him some strength of the Gordon clan.*"

Some strength. It was a polite way, Thomas thought, of saying how disappointingly few Gordons had joined them — although, unlike the MacDonalds, at least they had not come only to extort and plunder. The mood of the men was sombre. Dundee clasped Jean's hand and said nothing. Jean, too, was silent, staring at the clock as if time itself had become her enemy. She would have only this one night with her husband before the army had to be on the move again. It was a situation that she was accustomed to as the wife of a soldier, and yet this was different — never before had her husband been marked as a traitor. And never before had they a child's future to consider.

Of all the company, only John and his veterans were career soldiers. A few others, like Dunfermline, had taken service in Holland or Spain. The rest were farmers, scholars, lawyers, poets, and courtiers; men who, even in unruly Scotland, might reasonably have expected to lead a settled life. The campaign so far had achieved nothing, and Thomas wondered if in years to come they would still be plodding around the Scottish hills, growing grey with age and dust and fatigue, while their sons grew into manhood and their daughters became wives and mothers. Would he still be writing to Libby that "all is well"? His standards were crumbling — he was beginning to lie to her outright. The truth was too disheartening. It seemed that Colin Lindsay had been right, for they had heard nothing from Dublin.

The letters that Dundee had been writing, begging the secretary of war for men, money, and supplies, might as well have been hurled into a bog. Even Dundee seemed to think so, although he would not admit it, for he no longer spoke so often about the expected reinforcements from Ireland.

From upstairs came the sound of young James crying lustily. The smell of cook-fires and coffee, of bannock fried in butter, the swish of a broom as one of the servants swept the back step, made the evening seem ordinary, as if the men would sleep and rise to a day no different than any other. But tomorrow they were starting their journey into Lochaber.

This time Jean came out to the courtyard to say her farewells. Her fair hair was loose around her shoulders and her eyes were calm, as if she had reached a point beyond fear and knew the strange peace of renunciation. Those grey eyes seemed to look not at the company but past them, at some kind of vision or revelation she would not share. She held the edges of her cloak together with one hand and gripped her husband's stirrup with the other. Dundee, leaning down from the saddle to cup her chin in his hands, looked into her eyes as if memorizing every detail of her face. For once his usual reticence broke and he spoke with a kind of anguished tenderness, laying bare his love for all to see and hear. "God keep you, my Jeanie, my heart, my only love."

At last she relinquished the stirrup. Dundee touched her hair. Their eyes met and held and she smiled, not cheerfully, but with the stoic acceptance of someone who has nothing left to lose.

Thomas, looking back at her as they rode out, saw that she had sat down on the ground, like a child, and put her head on her knees.

3 TO AVOID ANY POSSIBILITY OF detection they left the main road near Pitlochry and struggled cross-country through the mountains where no one would follow or find them. They crossed Rannoch Moor, the most desolate stretch of earth Thomas had ever seen, a dark valley pitted with bog-pools and strewn with great boulders. Beyond the moor they climbed into a wilderness that seemed to contain every obstacle nature could devise. Steep ravines, dense forest, deep black bogs still covered with treacherous skins of ice, cliffs of crumbling scree, rushing torrents fed by snowmelt, corries adrift with mist — it was a land cursed and forgotten by God. In many places it was too rough to ride and the horses had to be led. Some of the animals foundered in the bogs and had to be shot.

As they climbed, the cold grew intense. Now they were literally following in the footsteps of Montrose, for only he had successfully crossed the mountains in winter. The spring flowers of Glen Ogilvie were forgotten. These mountain passes, with snow beds a hundred feet deep, were held fast in the grip of perpetual winter. Cornices and arches of snow hid the edges of fathomless chasms and the wind on the heights roared unceasingly, cold and bitter, straight from the north Atlantic. When they bivouacked overnight on the shores of Loch Treig, it was so cold that their hair and beards froze and their plaids grew stiff with frost.

Never again would Thomas think of hell as being hot. He had his wool coat and a sheepskin wrapped around him and a plaid thrown over all, but the wind blasted through every fold, turning his blood and marrow to ice. There was no fire, for although it seemed absurd to think there could be any other human soul on this storm-wracked shore, they could not risk betraying their whereabouts to unfriendly eyes. He got up every so often to move around, trying to stamp some warmth into the frozen blocks that had once been his hands and feet, but the cold cut through his thick leather boots and gauntlets as if they had been made of tissue. Ice crystallized on his face.

It was far too cold to sleep. They talked, sang hymns and ballads and alehouse rhymes until one by one their voices cracked into exhausted silence. After that there was nothing but the dark and the cold and the screaming wind.

Thomas had sometimes wondered at the blind devotion Dundee inspired in his veterans. Now he fully understood it. On this monstrous journey he had fuelled them all with his courage as he rode or walked or climbed beside each man in turn, speaking words of encouragement, telling jokes or stories or reciting poems, anything to distract the men from their suffering. In the midst of physical hardships beyond anything any of them had yet experienced, he managed to inspire an atmosphere of adventure and camaraderie.

Just before dawn, the wind finally dropped. As the sun pushed through the mist and cloud, the men raked the ice from their hair and stared in awe at one another's raw, chapped faces and blackened lips. They ate frozen crusts of bannock and then broke camp, their movements as stiff and painful as those of crippled old men. Thomas had lost his horse in the bogs, and, like James Philip, had to carry his saddle on his shoulders. He had to leave behind most of his gear and still found that he was staggering with weariness as they resumed their climb over the mountain. On the other side was sanctuary, the valley of Glen Roy, Lochiel's stronghold. But to reach it they had to negotiate the southern spur of Ben Nevis, the tallest mountain in Britain. Dundee's guide, a MacDonald who admitted that the track across Ben Nevis was "spry" walking, told them they would reach Lochaber by nightfall.

"Hear that, boys?" Dunfermline rubbed his ice-encrusted gloves together and looked as cheerful as his purpled nose and black-rimmed eyes allowed. Thomas realized that, against all odds, the older man was actually enjoying himself. The bite of adversity had brought back the vitality of his youth. Exhaustion, cold, hunger, the presence of the enemy — none of these mattered next to the astonishing fact that they were alive and had acquitted themselves not only honourably, but heroically.

Their route out of the hills took them north by northwest into Glen Spean, where they had to ford a river swollen and roaring with snowmelt. When at last they lurched into Glen Roy, footsore, drenched, and raw-skinned, they had lost horses and gear but not a single man.

The Camerons awaited them.

They were billeted with Lochiel's tenants in "black houses," little earth-packed stone huts that in a single room accommodated both people and livestock . A hole in the roof served as a primitive chimney for the smouldering peat fires. Fish-oil lamps provided light. In the murky interior the humid reek of hide and dung fought with the stink of smoke and fish. As Dunfermline remarked, "black house" was more than a name.

Thomas was housed with a family whose hospitality so far outran their resources that he was reluctant to rob them of even a mouthful of food. But to refuse their offerings would be an insult. The tradition of hospitality here was as sacred as that of blood feud. The young husband insisted that

Thomas occupy the bed, and dine alone at the plank table upon the only cushion while the children of the house, two small boys, watched him solemnly. Knowing that what he took meant less for the children, he ate as sparingly as possible — a pinch of salt fish, a morsel of bannock.

It seemed impossible that families could live, let alone thrive, under such harsh conditions, but the children were healthy and there was no shortage of them — sturdy, fair-haired little boys and girls who ran everywhere without fear, sure of their welcome. They hung on Lochiel's coattails and dug unashamedly into his pockets, looking for sweets or a loose button or a crust of bread, and they were never disappointed, for Lochiel always kept something for them. He was a big, tall man with a mane of thick hair that was still raven-black, and great flowing moustaches whose ends the children liked to tweak. Achnacarry, his grand home located between Loch Lochy and Loch Arkaig, housed as fine a collection of books and furnishings within its walls as any French nobleman's. But the same hardship prevailed in his fir-planked hall as in the clachan; there was not enough food to go around. During the bitterly hard winter even the tough Highland cattle had died of hunger. Yet Lochiel had rejected General Mackay's offer of a thousand pounds sterling to change his allegiance.

When Lochiel had said that he would sooner die than accept so dishonourable a bribe, it was no mere rhetoric — at the time, he and his clan had been subsisting on famine rations of cow's blood mixed with oats. But so ingrained was the Camerons' dedication to their chief, and their chief's to the King, that a thousand pounds, or ten thousand or one hundred thousand, could not buy their loyalty.

"Loyalty is simpler here than in England," Thomas observed, for in this wild, harsh land families depended upon one another and strongly upheld their own, no matter what the circumstances. Grudges and loyalties and blood feuds were as much a part of a man's inheritance as property or gold. The clansmen had no knowledge of politics or law, but they perfectly understood the crime that Prince William had committed when he declared war upon his own chief. If they had needed any more reason to fight, Lochiel's own history would have provided them with plenty of cause; the Camerons had feuded for years with the Campbells, who had crowned years of double-dealing by taking Cromwell's side in the civil war. The Campbell chief of that time had been executed for treason, and three years ago his son had been convicted of the same offence. Lochiel had seized the forfeited Campbell lands and now the new chief, having pledged loyalty to William, wanted his property back. The King's cause had become part of the ongoing fight. Even the youngest Camerons knew that any friend of the Campbells was no friend of theirs. At the same time, Lochiel's mother had been a Campbell, and the Campbell chiefs had fostered him. The spider's web of loyalties and feuds was bewildering to an outsider.

Thomas found everything in this country — men, legends, and landscape — larger than life. Stark mountains, deep gorges, torrential rivers, ice-cold lochs ringed by impassable cliffs; all this was on a scale so much grander and more savage than the English countryside that it might as well have been another world. And the men who inhabited this landscape were equally large and savage. They wielded enormous weapons — basket-hilted swords, old-fashioned claymores, javelins, and Lochaber axes — with the ease of small boys playing with sticks. Each clan chief reigned like a petty king, with one servant designated to announce his presence, another to carry his sword, another to lead his horse, and still another to carry him pick-a-back over water. A chief's piper played for him at daybreak, during meals, and afterward for entertainment; the chief's poet sang stories of his master's battle prowess, which seemed to be all that mattered to these men. "They think nothing of drawing one another's blood," Thomas wrote to Libby. "Yet they will sit down to meat together afterward with great good cheer."

Day by day the clans loyal to James marched or sailed into Lochaber for the Gathering. Dundee, who had fallen seriously ill with fever, ignored his friends' advice and got up grey-faced and sweating from his sickbed to greet each new arrival. The MacDonalds of Glengarry and Clanranald, the MacDonalds of Sleat, the Appin Stewarts, the MacNeils of Barra, the MacLeods, the Frasers, the McNabs, the Macaulays, the McGibbons — one after another they poured into Glen Roy, bringing their hereditary poets and their hereditary pipers, their odd customs, and their fierce quarrelsome pride.

Lochiel had advised that there was no sense attempting to impose traditional military discipline on such men, and Dundee had therefore let them keep their uncouth clothing and weapons and their old style of fighting. His officers abandoned the effort to teach them how to use artillery and instructed them instead how to withstand a cavalry charge, as the clans were accustomed only to hand-to-hand fighting. Again and again Thomas and Dunfermline led their little troop of horse against various clumps of Highlanders, charging them amongst the furze bushes and heather until they were all exhausted. Thomas, sweating in his half-armour in the spring sun, thought how ridiculous they must look. He found the clansmen's patience remarkable. But what they thought of him, an Englishman, remained a mystery. They stared at him as if he were some tribal king from Africa, admiring the silver buttons on his coat sleeves or the pin in his neckband, standing off in humbled awe when he read a book or wrote a letter. They were invariably polite, seeming to hold no grudge that he kept chasing them at sword-point across the haugh. That he was an honoured guest of Lochiel's was enough to ensure their co-operation.

Despite the respect and liking that Thomas felt for Lochiel, and the generosity that met him at every turn, it was not easy to be part of this alien society. The clans who cared for their guests so royally were same men who in battle were seized with an indescribably savage blood lust. Drunkenness, murder, looting, and rape were celebrated in their songs and stories as the perquisites of victory, and not even a man as civilized as Lochiel would think of restraining them. To lead such men, keeping their respect while curbing their violence, was a task that would daunt even the wisest commander. But the clans passionately loved Dundee. His single-handed declaration of war upon the enemy and his march across the mountains had won their hearts. He was a Lowlander and a Protestant who understood no Gaelic; the clans were chiefly Catholics who spoke no English. But his strange bond with them transcended all differences. They called him *Iain Dhub Nan Cath*, Dark John of the Battles, even though he had yet to engage the enemy, and gave him a chieftain's bonnet, with an eagle's feather, to honour his courage.

In the meantime the King was still besieging his Protestant subjects in Ireland and Dundee was still writing letters, asking him to send — or better yet, bring — reinforcements and supplies to Inverlochy, ten miles away. The tone of these letters, brisk and respectful, seemed to take for granted that James would soon arrive in person to lead a combined Irish and Scots army to victory. But Thomas suspected that the King, preoccupied by his troubles in Ireland, had forgotten them entirely. There had been no message from him since the government had captured his courier in March. Dundee, undeterred, sent out letters to all the clan chiefs who had not yet answered his summons — cajoling, chiding, encouraging, directing. Night after night he stayed awake, writing with chilblained hands in the hut that served as his billet, a rush light smouldering next to him and a horse blanket draped over his shoulders. He refused to rest or admit to being ill, even though he shook with fever and could keep nothing in his stomach except water.

Looking at his friend's exhausted face and sunken eyes, Thomas kept silent about his own troubles, which included a cracked bone in his left foot from their climb over Ben Nevis. Such had been the miseries of that journey that he could not even remember when he had injured himself. But when he reached camp he had had to cut his boot to accommodate the swelling, and lately he had taken to stuffing a torn shirt into the opening to ease the pain of walking or riding. He had grown accustomed to it, for there was always discomfort of some kind — chilblains from the cold, seared lungs from peat smoke, feverish gripes from their starvation diet of blood cakes and bran. At night his sleep was shot through with nightmares. Once he dreamed that he was on the summit of Ben Nevis, looking down on a churning, tumultuous ocean. His children played on the shore while Jean Graham walked alone, searching amongst the sand dunes and scrub for her husband. Six-foot breakers crashed against the shingle. "John's with me," shouted Colin Lindsay from the maelstrom. "He's safe." As he spoke he took Dundee by the hair, plunging his head into the cold salt waves, and held him under until his violent struggles ceased.

Jolted awake, Thomas would lie sweating on his pallet in the cow-scented dark, listening to the regular breathing of his sleeping hosts. Sometimes he thought he heard wolves howling in the night. His feeling of displacement was so profound that it was hard for him to believe the same moon shone also upon his own English acres. If he walked out of the hut he would find himself knee-deep in a field of clansmen sleeping in their plaids under a pale mauve sky that at this time of year never quite grew dark — dirty, barefoot men in rags, men without education, money, or even food; an army of barbarians, upon whose valour his own life, and his country's future, might depend. He felt somehow as if he were living in a different span of time and space from his family, that if he ever reached home again he would stumble into a weed-choked ruin empty for a century, while he, like a man cursed in a folk tale, had counted the time in weeks.

He longed for a letter. But while couriers went regularly to and from the Irish coast a hundred and thirty miles away, the mailbags often fell into the wrong hands and it was almost impossible to guarantee the safe arrival of a message. The unfamiliarity of the country and its people, the famine rations, and most of all the silence from Dublin, oppressed him so much that for the first time in his life he could not shake off a deep melancholy. He took what comfort he could from the company and comradeship of a small group of friends: Dundee's brother David, a handful of Graham cousins, Gilbert Ramsay, a young advocate who had left a successful career in Edinburgh to join the company; James Philip; and most of all Dunfermline, whose silent, unflinching endurance and good heart had won the love and respect of them all. Dunfermline was nominal captain of their little troop of cavalry, but no distinctions were made among them. They lived together like a close-knit family of outcasts, sharing their paltry resources and trying, not always with success, to avoid confrontations with their touchy Highland comrades — who once again included the MacDonalds. Keppoch had reappeared with his men as unexpectedly as he had left, greeting Dundee as he might a brother, and offering no excuse or explanation for abandoning the army at Inverness. In an earlier time Dundee would have had him shot as a deserter; but by now he had learned enough about Highland custom to hold his tongue.

Word came that General Mackay had reached Inverness and that his second-in-command, Colonel Ramsay, was marching from Perth to join him. Dundee, needing at all costs to block that rendezvous, gave immediate orders to break camp. The starveling Highland host sprang into a sudden flurry of activity, and by noon of the same day they were marching out of Glen Roy with the warpipes wailing and the drums pounding. The chiefs, ablaze in cloth-of-gold and splendid armour, were on horseback, but their fighting men ran alongside in rawhide brogues, carrying their leather targes on their arms and their weapons on their shoulders. Clarions announced their progress. It was a barbaric and splendid spectacle — "my boys would like to see this," Thomas thought, and then, immediately, "Thank God they are not here."

A ragged group of women, as tough and weathered as their men, followed in the rear, along with a string of shaggy Highland ponies and a pack of dogs. The small troop of cavalry led the way. Beside them the Spey river tumbled and roared on its way to Moray and the ocean. Spring had finally come even to this harsh country; a sparkling sun had burned off the early mist and the encircling mountains shouldered up into a blue sky of blinding clarity. Curlews screamed overhead as if heralding the army's approach.

They marched on Castle Ruthven, a fortress to the northeast where General Mackay was supposed to meet Colonel Ramsay. Ruthven was the only Highland castle garrisoned for William, and its commander had a mere sixty men defending it. But he would neither fight nor surrender. Instead he sent out a messenger under flag of truce to offer his own conditions: if the government troops had not arrived in three days he would give up the castle, but only in return for his men's freedom.

All of the chiefs, including Lochiel, felt they ought to attack at once. Keppoch, indeed, nearly gibbered with rage when Dundee accepted these terms. Had not Montrose's MacDonalds put to the sword an entire band of Campbells, only to prevent them from betraying the whereabouts of the King's army? Why should they not do the same with the sixty men of this traitor clan?

But for once Dundee was unmoved by any reference to Montrose. He would not kill sixty men in cold blood, and there was not enough food or fodder to take them along as prisoners. Nor could he afford to garrison the castle himself. Keppoch, deprived both of his siege and his bloodshed, flung off in disgust to go hunting.

In his friend's place Thomas would have taken the enemy soldiers prisoner, even if it meant marching them in irons across the length and breadth of Scotland. He knew Dundee envisioned an army of officers and gentlemen, but it was hard to see the Highlanders as exponents of high chivalry, especially when Keppoch came back from the hunt so flown with drink that his men had to carry him. It was harder still to know that they were entirely at the mercy of such men. Had the clans been regular soldiers, fed and paid enough to keep them from straggling off in their careless fashion to rob their neighbours, there might have been some kind of discipline. But the lack of money or formal commissions meant there was nothing but goodwill to bind the army together — and goodwill would not put food in men's bellies or gold in their pockets.

Some of the chiefs had gone hunting with Keppoch, but the rest of the men played cards, told stories, or put their bonnets over their faces and slept. They watched the garrison's soldiers hang out their washing on the walls and go out, under flag of truce, to collect food. There was no sign of either Mackay or Ramsay, and at the appointed time the garrison duly surrendered. They were permitted to keep their horses — which they no doubt used, Thomas said to Dunfermline, to ride straight off to General Mackay to report the royalists' whereabouts.

It was a sour start to the campaign. As a consolation of sorts, Keppoch was permitted to fire the empty castle to prevent its future use by the enemy. Then, as the army broke camp, the scouts reported that Mackay was just to the north, at Loch Alvie, with a far smaller force than expected, only six hundred men. And there was still no sign of Ramsay.

It was the opportunity they had been waiting for. Dundee gave the order to pursue. The shame of the failed siege was forgotten as the army set off, the Highlanders covering the ground so fast and tirelessly that they nearly outran the horses. They smashed at a heart-bursting pace through the great dark tracts of pine forest that flanked the river Spey. At the foot of Glen Livet, with the enemy in sight, the Highlanders threw off their plaids and screamed their war calls, a sound so blood-chilling that it was like a weapon in itself. The drums beat a mad tattoo. The pipes shrieked a savage pibroch. Hundreds of Highland voices screamed in an ecstasy of battle-rage. *Come, sons of dogs, and I will give you flesh...*

Thomas had never before heard such a devilish noise. It would have terrified anyone who was not a Highlander. Most of Mackay's troops were green recruits, boys who had never fought a battle, and they turned and ran from the half-naked clansmen as fast as their legs could carry them. The Highland host followed in hot pursuit. At times the two armies were close enough to exchange shouted insults and a smattering of gunfire. But there was no open battle. Mackay pushed and dragged and force-marched his men until they reached the sanctuary of Grant territory. At midnight, near Strathbogie, the Gordons' headquarters, Dundee was forced to call off the chase.

They had not paused to eat or sleep in four days. Dundee was struck down by a violent recurrence of his fever and went sick and shivering to bed, while the clans dispersed to forage for food. But the rich countryside was too much of a temptation for men accustomed to sacking any village they conquered. With no one to constrain them, they roamed from one property to the next, burning and looting and squabbling over the plunder. When the officers rode out to keep some kind of order, the men turned on them as well, furious that anyone should get between them and their sport.

Thomas and Dunfermline, out on patrol, intercepted half a dozen of Keppoch's men running from a burning farmstead, their arms stuffed full of odd pieces of clothing and kitchen goods. The young woman of the house shrieked that her son was trapped in the cow-byre.

The half-destroyed wattle and turf hut was not worth saving, but Dunfermline dismounted and plunged into the smoke to find the child. He fished a small, screaming boy out of the straw and tossed him up to Thomas. The woman, snatching her child, spat on Thomas' boot before running back to her burning house. There was a strong wind blowing and the roof was already engulfed in flames.

"Come back," Thomas shouted. She whirled to give him a look of undiluted hatred, and for the first time he saw that her dress was torn, and that there was blood as well as soot on her face. Her throat was bruised with fingermarks. "My man is bed-rid," she screamed.

"Give us the boy!"

But she only clutched the child closer to her and rushed into the little house which, moments later, seemed to burst asunder, the roof and walls crashing down into blazing ruins.

"Christ have mercy," said Thomas. A gust of wind drove the fire toward them. He found a pail and plunged it into the water-trough before he realized how senseless this was. The house, and anyone still inside, were already beyond human aid. Glowing ash and cinders showered down, scorching his face. The smell was like that of a slaughterhouse.

They had to draw back or be engulfed themselves in the inferno. The horses were nearly mad with terror. Thomas spurred ahead, outdistancing Dunfermline, wanting to reach the camp first.

He saw Keppoch almost at once. He was sitting in the sun, chewing on a bread crust as he examined the spoils of the day: shoes, pots, dishes, jugs and jewellery. There was a child's shirt tied around his neck in lieu of a napkin, and his beard was wet with spilled wine. Thomas rode through the pile of stolen goods, sending them flying in all directions, and raised his sword in both hands as if he would cleave that wild, stringy head in half. Keppoch, springing to his feet in amazement, drew his claymore. His gillies scrambled for their dirks and axes. Then, as Keppoch swung his sword, an icy voice cut through the disorder. "All of you! Put up your weapons!"

Someone had roused Dundee from his sickbed. He had come out in his shirtsleeves, looking as frail as glass, his hair crusted with dried sweat and his face on fire. He looked around the circle of angry men and his voice rose to a surprisingly strong shout. "What the devil is going on?"

"Rape and murder," said Thomas. "Keppoch's men have killed a family."

There was an immediate bellow of outrage from the MacDonalds. "Silence!" Dundee said. "I will hear the charge. My lord — " this to Dunfermline, who had his pistol aimed at Keppoch — "put that down!"

He stood with his hands fisted behind his back and looked at Thomas, who said, "The MacDonalds have burned a farm and the family is dead."

"My men were after the King's enemies," said Keppoch haughtily.

"A child of three and his mother! A sick man who could not defend them! Is that your idea of the enemy?"

"Silence!" Dundee repeated. His burning eyes raked Keppoch from top to bottom, taking in the punched-in hat, the child's shirt, and the unbuttoned breeks. Anger so deep it was almost anguish charged his voice.

"I would sooner serve as a common soldier than command such rubbish as you. Take your men and go."

Even Thomas had not expected this. Keppoch looked as if he had been struck. To be dismissed in disgrace, without fighting — no battle, no glory or plunder — meant being damned forever in the eyes of his clan. A red tide flooded his bearded face. "They were the King's enemies," he said. "They deserved to have their shieling burned."

Dundee turned away without replying. "Wait!" Keppoch barked. He swung his claymore to and fro in his great fist, the anger in his face giving way to a look of drama. "If my men made a mistake, it will not happen again," he said. "You have my word of honour."

When Dundee's silence made it clear this guarantee was insufficient, Keppoch took out his dirk. Shreds of dinner-meat still clung to the blade. "I swear by the head of my father."

Dundee grimaced. "If you stay with us you will do so under guard," he said. "Get out of my sight."

Keppoch thrust his dirk away, his face a deep, flaming crimson. Dundee turned and walked toward his quarters, motioning Thomas and Dunfermline to come with him. Once inside the tent he collapsed, shuddering with chills. His feverish eyes sought Thomas'. "Find Lochiel — ask him to keep a watch on Keppoch and his men. James, you must write a letter for me." He rubbed his face. "Say this: 'To the lords of His Majesty's privy council. May it please your lordships...'"

Thomas, without waiting to hear what Dundee was going to say to Dublin, pushed through the crowd that surrounded the tent to find Lochiel already coming toward him. He delivered Dundee's message. Then, although he knew it was useless, he rode back to the site of the fire. The remains of the house still burned, lighting the sky like a watch-fire. The scorched fields were empty even of crows. A graveyard smell fouled the air.

Dunfermline's hat lay on the ground. Thomas brushed the ash from it and set it on the pommel of his saddle. He let the reins lie slack as he rode slowly back to camp. The blood lust and greed of Keppoch's men had not even the excuse of battle, but their conduct was driven as much by need as by custom — they were unpaid, starving, forgotten by the King for whom they fought. Had James sent the reinforcements that had been promised, Dundee would not be dependent on such men. How often had he urged the King to abandon the unprofitable siege of Derry and transfer his forces to Scotland? The privy council in Dublin had agreed with the good sense of this, but Lord Melfort had not. Solely on his recommendation, the useless battering of the Irish continued and James had stayed in Dublin while his army in Scotland starved and suffered.

Phrases from Dundee's letters burned in Thomas' mind. "*I wonder that you send no gunpowder, were it but four or five barrels, for we have not twenty pounds*" — "*I have told the king that I have neither commission, money, nor ammunition*" — "*I wonder that in three months I never heard from you.*" He had been forced to beg for what should have been given without hesitation, and still had been ignored. And this was the result — more butchery, more horror, and another undeserved black mark against Dundee. The King's army, this uncivil mob of thieves and murderers, would soon be as hated as Cromwell's Ironsides. Slaughter and plunder — that was all the Highlanders knew. Even their legendary battle prowess fell far short of the mark. Of what use were men who fought in short wild bursts and then deserted, staggering home with their spoils? Of what use was a king who would do nothing to help his friends?

The camp was astir when he returned. The tents and flags had been hurriedly struck, men tossing their belongings into packs and saddling their horses. Thomas asked Dunfermline what had happened. "Mackay must have finally met up with Ramsay…the scouts say there are close to a thousand men coming our way," Dunfermline said. He suddenly looked and sounded almost sick with weariness. "There are too many of them and John is too ill to fight. So we are running — but don't say so."

As the word "retreat" was not in the Highland vocabulary, Dundee had given out that they were returning to Lochaber to join up with their own reinforcements. But the chiefs knew better. A miasma of gloom hung over the camp. The men hurriedly scraped up their stolen goods, and many of them, realizing there was no battle and therefore no fresh plunder in the offing, took to their heels — the Keppoch MacDonalds among them.

Dundee was so weak that he had to lash himself to his saddle. The army shuffled westward, covering less than three miles the first day. The enemy was so close behind that it seemed unbelievable they did not clash. Cook-fires were banned, and the men made camp in the roughest possible fashion, throwing plaids over tree branches and sleeping on the ground. Overnight hundreds of clansmen deserted. Lochiel said that this was temporary, that loyal Highlanders habitually drifted home from time to time in order to see to their cattle and crops. But it was hard for anyone else to make sense of this peculiar custom. Even the Gordons under Dunfermline's banner went home, although the Earl himself stayed, stoic as ever in the face of misfortune.

There were no trumpets announcing their return to Lochaber and no stirring martial display. Instead, as they stumbled once more into the refuge of Glen Roy, Dundee called everyone together — troopers, friends, relatives, clansmen, chiefs, gillies — and told them that he was disbanding the army.

He sat tied to his horse like a prisoner, his face a sick, shiny puce, the rims of his eyes blood-red. "Only temporarily," he called out in a harsh, cracked voice. "Only until our reinforcements come from Ireland, I promise you."

With both hands bound to the pommel of the saddle, he could not gesture or dismount. Instead he raised his voice, speaking into a vast shocked silence. "We will never surrender. But we must wait. We must be patient."

He spoke about the five thousand troops that the King had promised to send, and no one challenged his remarks or jeered. The resentment burning in the air was not meant for him, for even the meanest gillie knew how tirelessly he had pleaded their cause with Dublin. He had worked and suffered without complaint until his exhausted body could no longer sustain him, and along the way his word had become almost sacrosanct, his conduct as much above criticism as the King's.

"Our cause is just...."

He was swaying like a drunkard in the saddle and Thomas could not bear to listen. The justice of the cause! What had been accomplished in all the years since Cromwell? It was as if the last civil war had bled seamlessly into this one and the fighting had never ended; Dundee had become Montrose, down to the feather in his bonnet and the plaid around his thin shoulders.

4

AT SIX MONTHS OLD KATE was sitting up, staring around her solemnly while she sucked on a rag. Her favourite pastime was observing the world from her small throne of cushions and blankets. Often James sat with her, naming objects and pointing out various wonders. It was warm enough now for Libby to take her out on the terrace, where they sat by the hour watching the play of the fountain.

When Thomas had left there had been snow on the ground and now it was June. Easter had come and gone, the fruit trees had scattered blossoms delicate as ice crystals on the grass, and the fields were rich with fresh crops. The bell tower had been repaired; spring cleaning had been accomplished. The days had lengthened, so that now the angle of the sun woke Libby where she lay alone in the great bed. Her first thought each morning was the delivery of the post.

She had had only one letter from Thomas, written from Edinburgh, and then silence. There were all kinds of reasons for that silence, and she resolved not to dwell on the worst of them, but to carry on as if nothing were wrong. Her days were always crowded with tasks; it was the nights she dreaded, when the fears that she had successfully kept at bay during daylight hours rushed to overwhelm her.

After hearing the children's prayers she would find chores to keep her busy, postponing as long as possible the moment when she would have to face another night alone. She was working on a cinnamon-coloured curtain for Alys' room, she was letting down a skirt for Beatrice; she had started to read a French romance. She would read or sew or write letters until long past midnight. But eventually weariness would drive her into the bedroom. She would sit at her dressing table in her nightdress, brushing her hair and staring into the mirror, wondering if she were beginning to look old. Loneliness was wearing upon her even though she was seldom alone. She was thankful for the company of her brother's family and the unending needs of the children.

After braiding her hair she would go to bed and lie awake, listening to the sounds of the household at night. The dogs barked. Wind rustled in the trees outside her window. A floorboard creaked as Leopold, working these days on a project whose details he would not divulge, walked softly past her door. She would open her shutters to look at the stars and try to imagine where Thomas might be sleeping and if he were safe. She could not have felt more distant from him had he been on a ship circumnavigating the globe. Jean Graham was often in her thoughts. From her she had the only fresh news since Thomas' letter. Jean had written discreetly about her son's christening and the visit of "friends" to Glen Ogilvie. Of course she could say nothing about the campaign or the current whereabouts of the army — if she even knew.

It was cruel waiting for news. But Libby carried on with her daily round, keeping her mind occupied with mundane duties. She must speak to John Hammond about the children's lessons. Ask Dr. Spencer to call. Mend the bedsheets, make short paste, count spoons — do anything except think about Scotland.

But there was no escaping it. Lord Burcote, recently returned from Court, came to drink a dish of tea with her and tell her the latest rumours flying around London. His speech was peppered with "as I said to the King the other day," "His Majesty told me," and "when I was at Whitehall."

He seemed to have forgotten about his loyalty to the King-over-the-water, as James was beginning to be called. He spoke about the political situation with a gravity that suggested his new responsibilities as sheriff gave him private, privileged access to the inner circles of government.

William had lost no time declaring war on France, but he was outraged — "Outraged!" repeated Burcote, thumping his walking stick — that parliament had refused to vote him sufficient revenues for it, when Louis was openly financing James' expenses in Ireland. There was a continual fear that the Irish and Scots would join forces in the north and overwhelm the English border. On the other hand, Dundee's ragged little army, hardly more than a company of horse, was said to be in a deplorable condition, starving and disorganized. General Mackay was hunting them relentlessly all over the Highlands, and the government had put a price of a thousand pounds sterling on Dundee's head — a monstrous sum that would surely tempt even his staunchest allies.

Libby dared not look into Burcote's wrinkled face as he delivered this news. He went on to tell her, as if taking her interest for granted, that the Coronation in April had been a great success even though there had been fewer attendees than usual at such an event. But Libby's only interest in the Coronation lay in the fact that Aphra Ben had died almost immediately afterward. She had been buried honourably in Westminster Abbey, and now there would be no more witty correspondence or advice from that gallant friend.

It felt like madness that she should be drinking a dish of tea and eating currant cake with Lord Burcote when her husband was somewhere in those high, wild hills of her imagination, hunted by Dutch and English soldiers. He might be wounded or ill, and she had no means of going to him. But surely a battle would have been public news, and Burcote himself would have told her.

"When do you expect your husband to return?" he asked. "Has he not settled his affairs in Edinburgh by now?"

"It will take some time longer, I fear," Libby murmured.

"I suppose he has cautioned you about the prospect of invasion? They say the French and Irish will join Dundee's rebels and put all Protestants to the sword."

"The Irish! Mercy, sir," said Libby, plying her fan briskly. "My lord would never speak about the Irish to me."

Lord Burcote reddened. "Quite right! My wife, too, is terrified of them. But the reward will put a stop to that nonsense. A thousand pounds sterling for Dundee! The man's as good as dead."

Libby snapped her fan shut. "It grows late, sir — your lady will be anxious for you. I would not keep you a moment longer from her side."

She endured his hand-kissing farewells, his gift of strawberries, and then fled to the sanctuary of her garden. An hour or so later, Abigail found her indiscriminately tearing up green new shoots along with the weeds. Taking the mangled plants out of her sister-in-law's trembling hands, Abigail said in her practical fashion, "If the government were confident of capturing General Dundee, there would be no need for such a reward. Remember that so far no one has even been able to *find* him." Their eyes met, and Abigail smiled. "Let's take a walk."

They put on their shawls, collected Brigid and the children, and set off from the terrace. Libby liked the fact that here the flowers were not boxed in formal beds but ran riot like wildflowers, spilling over the brick and stone pathways and growing broadcast on the stream banks and under the large shade trees. She picked a sprig of honeysuckle and twirled it in her hand, closing her eyes to better smell the fragrance. The dogs raced on ahead with the children. But

Lucy stayed behind. She had been so dispirited since Thomas' departure that she had lost interest in her food dish, and had to be coaxed to go outside even when the weather was fine. She spent her days keeping vigil under Thomas' footstool, hers ears twitching when a man's footstep or a man's voice sounded in the hall. But it was never the right footstep or the right voice.

Libby could have said that she felt the same. She picked Lucy up — the once-fat little dog was like a skeleton loose in a fur sack — and carried her in one arm. James, thumb in mouth, clung to the other. Piers ran on ahead with the other dogs. To his joy, the pack once more included Theo; the prodigal had returned, bitten and footsore, a scant hour after Thomas' departure for Scotland. Piers had ridden to find his father at Christ Church meadow that morning and tell him the happy news — but of course by then Dundee's company had already left. Libby was thankful she had known nothing about it until much later. Lately it seemed that Piers, newly turned ten, considered himself above any house rules.

She sat down, setting Lucy free to run, and watched in amusement as Beatrice crowned herself with a circlet of daisies and kicked off her shoes to dance barefoot on the grass like a wood sprite.

"Your feet will get wet," Abigail warned. Beatrice, paying no attention, danced more wildly than ever. The two mothers exchanged looks.

"Can you imagine her as a wife with children, and a husband who might expect dinner on the table before midnight?" asked Abigail. But there was pride as well as exasperation in her voice.

The sun shone. The fountain played. The children chased Brigid and fell upon her in a laughing, screaming heap. Kate, ensconced on Abigail's lap, solemnly patted her own toes, which she had recently discovered. Libby closed her eyes, grateful for the warmth of the sun. But instead of the garden and the laughing children, she saw against her shut eyelids a cold, stark country rife with Dutch soldiers and Covenanters who wanted to kill her husband.

"..and the drawing-room chairs will be striped. What do you think of this blue silk for the walls? Or do you like the Chinese pattern?"

She opened her eyes. Abigail was holding out samples of fabric for her inspection. "Chinese," Libby said, without looking at it. Abigail waited a moment and then tucked the cloth back into her skirt pocket. "Leopold prefers that as well. I would like to visit the Exchange and see some samples for myself, but he says the crowds will be too much for me."

Lately Leopold had shown an autocratic side that had astonished both his wife and sister. He insisted that Abigail wear furs even in this warm weather, prepared medicines for her which she poured into the slop basin when he was not looking, and forbade her any activity except the mildest and dullest of walks. He would not allow her to ride or work in the garden and decreed that she must drink port, which she detested, three times a day. Libby, beginning to drowse in the sun, thought sleepily that women should rise up in rebellion....should refuse to be dictated to, confined, or circumscribed... most of all they should refuse to be left waiting, forever alone, forever standing in silence on the thresholds of empty rooms, while life carried on around them. Time eddied and pooled around her, now deep and still, now rushing in a mad fury that one day would bear everything away, even the earth itself.

"Lord St. Clare, madam," said a voice in her ear. A servant

had come to announce an already evident fact — her father was striding across the lawn toward them, with Leopold, looking deeply unhappy, following a few paces behind.

St. Clare had last visited on Piers' birthday a fortnight ago, and Libby was not pleased or prepared to see him again so soon. But she could hardly deny him when he was already calling the children to him and kissing Abigail on the cheek. Both young women greeted him with marked coolness, but he seemed not to notice.

"I need to speak with you, Libby."

"Take a chair, sir."

"Inside, if you please."

She frowned. James, standing in the circle of her arm just out of St. Clare's reach, asked, "Did you bring more presents?"

"Run along, boy," St. Clare growled. He waved his ringed hands to dismiss the children. But Piers turned to Libby for permission. "Mam? Do you want us to go?"

If she closed her eyes she could almost imagine that it was Thomas speaking. The gravity in Piers' childish voice, the tender concern, was an echo of his father's.

I know my love by his eyes of blue. She smiled a little at her young son. "Yes, Piers. It's all right. Go back to your lessons."

"There are no lessons today, Mam."

She had forgotten that Master Hammond was away. His father had died and John had gone home for the funeral.

Leopold touched her shoulder. "Libby, go inside. We'll stay with the children."

Was it her imagination, or were there tears in his eyes? The skin on her neck and arms chilled and prickled. She followed her father into the house and they sat down in the library, facing each other across a low table. At once she asked, "What is it that you cannot say in front of Leopold?"

"I have already told him."

"Told him what, sir?"

Instead of answering, St. Clare loosened his neckcloth and asked for a dish of spearmint tea. His face was an unhealthy colour, almost livid, and Libby wondered if he were ill. But he ignored her question about his health and asked if she had heard from Thomas.

"He is in Edinburgh with his sister."

St. Clare snorted. "Save that nonsense for the Bishop's daughters. I came to warn you, Libby, that Thomas is known to be with Dundee. Douglas Murray has informed upon him to Lord Hamilton, and Hamilton has informed upon him to the King."

The windows were open. Libby watched the progress of a robin across the lawn — hop — hop — hop, in search of food. Sweat gathered under the bands of her gown. A sudden push of blood in her veins made her ears ring. But she would not give in to terror — not just yet.

"You understand that you and the children are in danger. Their age is no protection. Even the baby might be useful as a hostage."

For several moments it felt as if her heart had ceased to beat. Her vision blurred. Then, with a pain sharp as a stab wound, her pulse bounded again. She took a breath to speak. But St. Clare was not finished.

"You must distance yourself from what Thomas is doing. Write a letter of submission to the government. Give the privy council assurances of your obedience — say that you want to petition the House for a divorce."

She sat frozen, hands clasped in her lap like a well-behaved child's, her eyes fixed on the robin. If she spoke she would scream. Hop, hop — hop. The robin struck the moist green turf and pulled out a writhing worm.

St. Clare leaned forward. "If Thomas were here" — and even in this extremity she noticed that he was once again using Thomas' Christian name, instead of calling him merely "your husband" — "he would be the first to tell you to comply. It's your duty, above all, to safeguard the family."

She would not disclose that Thomas had said almost exactly the same thing. But at this moment he might be dying for the cause she was supposed to betray.

"You must use your influence to help me," she whispered. An odd look flitted over St. Clare's face.

"Why do you think you have been left in peace thus far?" he asked. "I have been telling Whitehall the same faradiddle you have been at pains to feed me, that Thomas has taken no active part in the rebellion. But Douglas Murray has given him up. And I cannot help him any longer. I, too, have enemies. When I was at the Coronation — " he broke off suddenly, breathing hard. His face changed colour from rich plum to grey. Libby, alarmed, tried to give him his dish of tea, but he pushed it aside. He was sweating as if with ague.

"Get me spirits," he said.

"Sir, you are ill. Tea would be better — "

"Spirits, Libby!"

A decanter of brandy stood on the table between them. She seized it and filled a saucer until liquid slopped over the rim. St. Clare drank it off in one swallow. Gradually his colour improved, and he rolled a swollen, fiery eye toward her.

"You might as well know that I have been dismissed from council," he said, "with thanks for my 'faithful service.' Wharton and his friends have plotted against me, and they have the king's ear, if not his liking. Well, I wish them joy, the dogs. They'll not have my carcass to feast on."

He was still breathing as if he had run a foot race. Libby put two fingers on his wrist. "Sir, you should rest."

He gave a humourless bark of laughter. "I will be resting soon enough, Libby. But a drop more of that brandy would not come amiss." She filled the saucer again and he sucked at it thirstily. "Daughter, you must write that letter. I will take it to the council and answer to them for your obedience to the King. It's all that I can do for you now."

"And also for yourself," said Libby tartly. "Otherwise they might know that you deliberately gave them the wrong information, and you would be in danger."

St. Clare shrugged and drummed his fingers on the side of his chair. "Believe it or not as you like, it's the family that concerns me. Leopold is fortunate that his injury kept him from being foolish. He can pay double taxes if he chooses not to acknowledge the King. But Thomas will get no such reprieve. If Dundee is defeated — and he cannot succeed without help from Ireland — every one of his men will face charges of treason. And you know beforehand what the verdict will be. Be sensible, Libby! We have enough heroics."

She longed to cry out that she did not want to be sensible when her husband was not. She, too, longed for the luxury of putting principle before self, of being noble instead of practical. It was unjust that Thomas should have that liberty, while she was held captive by love and fear.

"Think of the children," said St. Clare.

At that moment she almost hated him. Her stomach cramped, threatening to send up her tea and cake. She stared out at the lawn, where the children had come into view. James was standing on one leg, flapping his arms like a bird and howling with laughter while Piers tried to shove him off balance. Leopold was with them, his head turned toward the house, and it seemed — although it was impossible at this distance — that his eyes sought hers and that his compassion gave her the strength to speak. She remembered Thomas telling her, "I trust you in all things, always."

St. Clare poured himself more brandy. His colour had almost returned to normal. "Should Thomas come home a victor in these wars, I will say as many hosannahs as you like," he said. "But in the meanwhile you must be practical. What good will it do your husband to have his property confiscated and his family held hostage? Your own mother, God bless her, would tell you the same. Write the letter. What does it matter how many lies you tell the council, so long as your children are safe?"

Libby chewed her thumb. Not for her the open honourable fight, the frank declaration of war. Women were not expected to have scruples. A dishonest letter to placate her husband's enemies, lies to the servants and the church and the neighbours — these were the puny weapons at her disposal. And not even Thomas would think the worse of her for using them. Had not Margaret Newcastle said that women, denied "all heroic actions and public employments," were like birds in cages, unable to fly free to see the broader landscape? Were she a man, she would stand up as Thomas had done in the House of Lords, and shout that she would sooner die than write such a letter. But a woman was not permitted the privilege.

A small cynical voice in the back of her mind said perhaps it was better so. At least that way, someone survived to mop up after the wars. She could not lay down her life in battle for her family, but she could sacrifice her character. She looked at the children instead of St. Clare when she said, "Tell me what to write."

Her father's face instantly cleared. "Well done, Libby,

well done!" He spoke as if she were a child still, a scholar who had written a brilliant essay or solved a difficult mathematical problem. "We'll write it together. You'll see, it won't be as difficult as you think." He drew back suddenly. "Now, then, my lamb! Don't cry."

"I am not crying."

But of course this was a lie. St. Clare, who lived his life as if onstage before a perennially enraptured audience, had never been able to deal with the reality of tears. Awkwardly, he patted her hand.

5 THOMAS, BILLETED ONCE MORE with his host family in their black house, noticed that the box-bed had a newly woven coverlet. There were butter and eggs on the table now. The children were out playing until the hour, and not the light, marked their bedtime. The dusk seemed to linger until it melted into the dawn and then the sun blazed out upon another day of waiting. They had dug in to await a miracle, but none seemed forthcoming. Dundee, from his sickbed, was still writing letters to win more chiefs to his side. Starvation had finally forced the Duke of Gordon to surrender Edinburgh Castle; the Campbells were arming; there was no word from Dublin. General Mackay was on the march again. James Philip, putting longed-for words in the King's mouth, sang in his poem, "*Madly have I refused in the past help to the Graham, who still me alone follows with all his prayers....*"

Thomas brooded on the only good news — that the government in London was said to be in chaos. The disruption and expense of the war had angered so many that even William's ministers were fighting amongst themselves. It was now clear that the new King had no use for England beyond using its resources to fight the French, and nobody still believed that he had come to save the Protestant church. Nor had Mary been able to make up for her husband's deficiencies. Her excitement at moving into Whitehall, the public pleasure with which she took ownership of her father's treasures, had disgusted even her friends. Thomas thought if the James would only allow his son to be raised as a Protestant, William and Mary would be back in Holland within a fortnight.

But the King would never agree that London was worth a mass. Was he steadfast or foolish? After the weeks he had spent amongst the Episcopalian Camerons and the Catholic MacDonalds, Thomas asked himself if he had turned heretic, as it no longer seemed to matter to him what form worship took; popes, bishops and archbishops, missals or the Book of Common Prayer, candles, altar rails, choirs — or, at the other end, a stark silent church whose only decoration was an hourglass to time the sermon — was it not all shop-wrapping? Religion was mired so deeply in the muck of politics and money that any purity of motive in fighting for the faith had long since gone. There was only one God, but men had devised an infinite number of ways to punish each other for not worshipping Him in the same fashion.

The Quakers' yearning for a new life in a new world no longer seemed so strange. Perhaps he should do the same — sail away, exchange this exhausted society for a fresh one. But even that dream had been spoiled. The Friends who had first ventured to the new world, expecting a welcome from their Puritan brethren, had been hanged instead.

He was thinking of this when Dunfermline burst into the hut, almost screaming. "Tom, the reinforcements have come to Inverlochy at last, and the King himself is with them! *The King*! Can you believe it? God be thanked! God be praised!"

Thomas buckled on his sword and shoved his aching feet into his cracked boots. The camp boiled with activity, the pipes blaring, trumpets blasting, the men-at-arms forming up in rough ranks, the horse-boys running for the chiefs' horses. Dunfermline seized him in a bear's embrace.

"*The King!* " he said again. He was weeping unashamedly, and he was not the only one. Joy had done what hardship and hunger could not and even the roughest gillies sobbed with excitement and relief.

The little army, quickly assembled, marched out of the glen in the sparkling sunshine, with the pipes shrieking in triumph. The Maclean boy who had brought the news, a child of twelve, danced a wild jig alongside the horses. Lochiel, in his best velvet bonnet and a cloth-of-gold cloak, kissed Dundee on both cheeks, like a Frenchman at a party. James Philip rode with the faded blue and silver Standard in his arms and a look of shining happiness on his face. Thomas could only imagine what florid verses he was composing. What could do justice to this moment? They marched down the glen toward Inverlochy Castle at the foot of Ben Nevis, where, forty-four years earlier, Montrose had routed the Campbells in one of his most famous victories.

It had been winter when they struggled over the flank of Ben Nevis into Lochaber. Now even this ice-pure air was soft with the hot, sweet smell of summer, and the thick stands of pine and fir and birch were alive with birdsong. Loch Linnhe shone like a burnished steel blade between the flanks of the hills. Presently the sun grew so warm that Thomas unfastened the clasps of his coat and took off his hat to let the wind cool his face. For the first time since he had left England he was happy, in the sweet, uncomplicated fashion of his youth. The surrounding crags and forests, the rushing waters, and the wind-scoured heights of Ben Nevis no longer seemed so overpoweringly hostile. As an eagle soared overhead he thought of Lee. God willing, this day he might be one step closer to winning his freedom.

They were still a few miles north of Inverlochy Castle when they glimpsed a body of men marching toward them.

Most were on foot, and at a distance it was hard to determine if they were part of the Irish reinforcements or merely a clan detachment answering Dundee's summons. Dundee drew rein, and behind him the pipes crackled into silence as the incomers came into view.

A stocky man in a shabby red velvet coat rode at the head of the line. Behind him trudged a pack of barefoot men, ragged kerns who looked rather like gypsy children following a caravan. They were dressed in cast-off bits and pieces of other men's uniforms, and most were unarmed. There were no outriders or scouts or carts carrying supplies, and the entire force, unrecognizable as King's soldiers, could not have numbered more than three hundred.

Dundee looked as though he were once again in the hot grip of delirium. He looked toward Inverlochy as if willing a French battalion to emerge from the trees. But the countryside, shrilling with birdsong and scented with crushed pine, was empty of anyone except themselves.

"Colonel Alexander Cannon, at your service," said the red-coated officer, sweeping off his hat. He presented his credentials, which Dundee struck aside. "The King," he said. "Where is he?"

"In Dublin, God be praised," said Colonel Cannon, looking baffled and offended.

Not the most berserk Covenanter could have provoked so violent a response from Dundee. "God damn you, Colonel, where are the rest of your men? I was promised *five thousand*, with provisions — arms — "

"These were all that could be spared from Derry," said Colonel Cannon, his chin jutting. "And the English overran our transports off the coast of Mull. You'll have to outfit these men, General, and we'll need some food as well. We've had nothing to eat since yesterday."

For several moments there was no sound except the snorting of the horses and the jingle of harness. The Maclean boy, looking frightened, crammed his fingers into his mouth and whimpered, "I thought he was the King. His red coat..." He began to sob, and his chief, turning on him, gave him a backhanded clout that knocked him flat.

"Leave him alone," said Dundee roughly. "The fault is mine, for wanting to believe such nonsense."

The boy covered his head and rocked back and forth. Lochiel, surveying the Irish rabble, said in a whisper, "Heart of God! We are undone."

Dundee himself said nothing. His stillness spread outward, like ripples in a deep pool, until it reached even the far-most stragglers in the Irish lines. With slow, deliberate movements, like a man sick or sleepwalking, he took off his white-cockaded hat and held it to his chest. A strand of grey hair blew across his face. He opened his mouth. For a moment it looked as if he were on the brink of some welcoming speech. But then his face contorted and he swung his horse around, thrashing it to a gallop as he rode away.

Colonel Cannon's bewilderment gave way to resentment. After all it was not his fault that only three hundred men had been sent instead of five thousand. Nor was he responsible for the capture of the transports. At least he had managed to save thirty-five barrels of gunpowder. He turned to Dunfermline. Where and why had Dundee had fled like that? When would he return? Where would they find some food?

Dunfermline answered him as best he could and introduced the rest of the officers. Thomas, making a slight bow to the Colonel, looked briefly into a pair of angry, pouched, dark eyes. Cannon, a Lowlander himself, showed neither curiosity nor surprise to find an Englishman here amongst these clans. He was intent on one thing only, and that was breakfast.

Slowly the Highlanders began to move, looking at the new recruits with the hostility of dogs whose territory had been invaded. Lochiel led them back up the glen — this time without pipes or drums — and set his gillies to find food and quarters for them.

Among the arrivals was Sir William Wallace, Lord Melfort's brother-in-law, who seemed almost disabled by the shock of finding himself in a dirt-floored hut with only a handful of dried grain and a flask of cold water for his noonday meal. Dunfermline rescued him and took him to Achnacarry, where he could sit at a table like a Christian. But the fare here was equally scanty. Lochiel sat in silence, watching his guests eat up the meagre contents of his larder.

Thomas, driven to get away, struck out from Achnacarry toward Loch Arkaig, walking, despite his sore foot, as if the Devil pursued him. But the Devil was in his own brain. Had the King even seen those useless Irish kerns? Or had he abandoned all decisions to his Secretary of War? Whatever the truth, nothing excused him from responsibility. The shattered look on Dundee's face made it plain that he had finally recognized what James' friendship and promises were worth, and that knowledge had sickened his soul. Cold, hunger, fever, long marches, weary days in the saddle, battle, even death itself — he could face anything with courage, except the indifference of his King.

Thomas sat down against a wall of moss to rest his foot, easing it out of the split boot. He had plunged into the eerie "dark mile" as the Highlanders called it, the narrow path that linked Loch Arkaig with Loch Lochy. It wound underneath beech trees whose interwoven branches created a canopy so thick that even in broad daylight there was no sun on the trail. But he could hear the thunder of water roaring down from the hills and knew he must be near the waterfalls at the foot of Loch Arkaig. He leaned his hands on the pommel of his sword and lowered his forehead onto his hands. His matted hair fell around him. It had been many weeks since he had consulted a mirror, but the appearance of the others told him what he must look like — half-shaven in an attempt to keep some civilized order, but with hair long and coarse as a fishwife's, and clothes so punished by wear and weather that they were shredded into rags. Five months of riding and marching on a mostly empty stomach had stripped so much flesh from his bones that even through his shirt and plaid he could feel the jut of his ribs.

For the first time in days he allowed himself not only to think of his home, but to dwell on it, travelling slowly in his mind from the gates at the entrance of the drive to the solid oak, iron-banded front doors. He walked through the Long Gallery to the music room. He stood in the Justice Chamber and looked out upon the lawns that ran down to the river. He saw the library where the dogs slept, the schoolroom where the children studied their lessons, the little parlour where Libby sewed or read, the green-canopied bed that was their private, blissful sanctuary. He remembered what it was like to be a husband. He seemed to breathe in the fragrance of her hair even as he recollected her whispering into the pillow, "Tom, can the Dutch be so very bad?"

He had fought hard to preserve both his honour and his home, but the King himself had made that impossible. The Stuarts, so cruelly betrayed, apparently had no scruples about betraying others. Charles I had abandoned his friend Strafford to a dreadful death, just as his son had abandoned Montrose. Now James had abandoned Dundee. A dark stain of dishonour wound through the friendships of the Stuart kings; whether they acted deliberately or not, the end was the same.

When Dundee returned he said nothing about where he had been or what decisions he might have made. He looked grim, but his cold, concise orders showed that he had once more put on the armour of command. He took the dispatch bag, which fortunately had escaped enemy hands, and invited Colonel Cannon to dinner with his other officers and the chiefs. For once food was plentiful, as the Camerons had conducted a cattle-raid into Grant territory, and the results, meant for a royal welcome, were now on their plates. The wine and the roast beef should have eased the tension. But Alexander Cannon was bereft of small talk, and Dundee, wanting to hear what was happening in Ireland, interrogated the newly arrived officers almost as if they were prisoners instead of allies.

Lord Melfort had led them to believe that the siege of Derry was about to be lifted, but in fact the citizens had nearly hanged their mayor when he offered to surrender. The King's army, suffering as many hardships as the besieged, remained entrenched before the walls, with no end in sight. Poor food and dirty water had made so many of them ill that even if an all-out assault had been possible, they could not have fought. Meanwhile the costs of the siege were multiplying and Louis' gold was running out. The French had complained to Louis about Melfort, and Melfort had complained to James about the French.

At that point Dundee abruptly stood to indicate that the meal was over. He asked Thomas to come into Lochiel's study, and strode out of the dining hall, his manner so forbidding that Thomas wondered what else had gone wrong or what news there might be that could not be said in front of the others.

Candles burned on Lochiel's big desk and the mailbag lay open, its contents spilling out in a jumble. Dundee flung himself into Lochiel's chair and said, "There was news for you in the dispatches." For an instant Thomas thought this meant a letter from home and his spirits soared, only to crash again when Dundee said, "It concerns your brother-in-law, Douglas Murray. Apparently he's given your name to the government. There's a bill of attainder being prepared against you in England."

After the first jab of disappointment, Thomas wondered why Dundee should be troubled by this. It was only what they had expected. "If we succeed, it won't matter. And if we fail..." he shrugged. "Then it will matter even less."

Dundee hunched over the desk, his arms folded across his belly as if his illness had made a sudden return. "Our commissions have come as well," he said. "Finally." His voice was strange, almost savage. "I have said nothing yet to Lord Dunfermline. But the King has not confirmed his command. He's given it to Wallace instead."

For a full minute Thomas was silent. He vividly recollected the look on Sir William Wallace's face as he had walked into Glen Roy that morning — bewildered, tentative, deeply offended at finding himself in such primitive surroundings. He had admitted frankly that he had no field experience and that he had never before met a Highlander.

"God help me, I don't know what to say to Dunfermline."

"Say nothing. Forget you saw it."

"That's not possible."

"Of course it is. Papers get lost all the time."

"I have my orders."

Orders again. The good of the service. Thomas tried to keep the rage from his voice. "A piece of paper changes nothing. I tell you this: no one is going to take orders from Wallace just because he happens to be Melfort's brother-in-law."

"That's mutiny."

"It's common sense."

Dundee shoved his chair back and paced the room. "There's something else you should know. General Mackay is marching on Blair with four thousand infantry and three troops of cavalry. We have to get there before he does. We leave at first light tomorrow. The clans will follow us, but they may be too late for battle. So it will be our five hundred against Mackay's four thousand. What chance will we have if we are disunited?"

Five hundred against four thousand. What chance, indeed? Either they had to fight a well-fed, well-supplied army that was four times the size of their own, or be trapped in Lochaber between their enemies and let Blair castle fall. But whoever controlled Blair controlled the Highlands. Thomas looked into his friend's harrowed eyes. "John, you can't ask people to die for nothing. Do you think the King knows why you had to disband the army? Why we'll be fighting without food or ammunition, outnumbered ten to one? Tell him. Tell the truth even if no one in Dublin will hear it."

"I have told him. I *have*."

It burst from him like blood from a wound. He struck through the litter of papers on the desk and seized one of them, an unfinished letter to the King. He thrust it at Thomas. "Read it."

He had asked for provisions of cheese, flour, and salt, for guns and powder and cannon, and he had written, "The Earl of Dunfermline stays constantly with me, as do Lord de Chastelain, Lord Dunkeld, Pitcur, and many other gentlemen, who really deserve well, for they suffer great hardships."

Not a word about his own hardships or illness. Thomas set the letter down. "I'll take this to Dublin myself, and get an audience with the King."

"It's too late. We march tomorrow, and I can't spare you. And it wouldn't be of any use anyway. The King says" — Dundee paused — "that he can give us no more than his 'royal thanks.'"

Once more their eyes met. After a moment Thomas asked for his own commission, and when it was in his hand he tore the paper across without troubling to read it. What did it matter if the King had named him captain, colonel, or lord of the world? "That's what you should do with Wallace's," he said. "No one will know."

"*I* would know."

"Are your orders more important than our lives? Let Lord Dunfermline keep his command and explain it later if you must. I think you owe him — and the rest of us — that much."

There was no answer. Dundee had the look of a man who was bleeding to death in silence. Thomas, knowing there was nothing he could say or do that he would not regret later, walked out of the room and out of the house toward the camp. Under the luminous, summer-night sky, the heath was dotted with campfires. The men were eating their fill of roast beef — a luxury all the sweeter because it had been carved from the beasts of the enemy — and drinking their raw rye whisky; MacDonald of Glengarry's piper had struck up a song that seemed to echo the rush of wind and water and the cries of seabirds. But soon the pulse quickened, and he was skirling battle music that had no melody, only a harsh, pounding rhythm that got the men to their feet, whirling and stamping in a mimic of their battle charge.

Tomorrow they would march to Blair to meet the enemy. There would be five hundred of them — eight if those Irish could be counted — against more than four thousand. The numbers kept circling crazily in Thomas' head. Eight hundred. Four thousand. Eight hundred, four thousand. Anger poured acid into his blood. Only a miracle like the one that had parted the sea or crushed the walls of Jericho could give them victory against such odds. As the music reached a crescendo he spoke into the thrumming, sweet-scented, star-filled dark. "Forgive me, Libby."

6 IT WAS NOT THE PARTING of the Red Sea, but overnight the MacDonalds of Sleat and Clanranald marched back into camp, and the first glow of sunrise brought Keppoch swaggering down the glen at the head of seven hundred warriors. So desperate were the circumstances that it did seem almost miraculous that at this last possible moment, the army had been bolstered to nearly eighteen hundred souls. Keppoch, saying nothing about when and how he had left, assumed his usual manner of behaving as if he were Dundee's right-hand man. Dunfermline murmured that their allies were more frightening than their enemies, but even he was relieved to see the MacDonalds. At least now the odds were not so preposterously against them.

They marched out of Lochaber at a double-quick pace, the Highlanders pushing forward on iron legs, seemingly inexhaustible even though they were climbing through granite-gullied mountain passes with nothing in their stomachs. There was no sign yet of Mackay and no one disputed their passage into Atholl territory. Blair Castle, riding the rolling moor like a graceful white galleon, was untouched, still in the hands of Patrick Stewart — which meant that now it was theirs. Once more, in an almost disquieting fashion, they were following Montrose, whose headquarters this had been.

They made camp in the pasture surrounding the castle. Dundee, dining with his chiefs and officers in the banqueting hall, had become his usual self. As if the gruelling march had exorcised all his bitterness, there was no trace about him of his earlier despair. His scouts had located Mackay's army at Pitlochry, only ten miles to the southeast beyond the pass of Killiecrankie, which meant that battle the next morning was a certainty. In the face of that, all other considerations melted away. Even the insult of the Irish kerns had ceased to matter.

But — unpardonably, to Thomas' way of thinking — he had followed the King's orders to turn over command of the cavalry to Sir William Wallace. Dunfermline, informed of this as they left Lochaber, had borne the affront graciously, showing no resentment and saying nothing in Wallace's disfavour. Nor would he attach any blame to Dundee. But he had been deeply wounded in all that mattered to him — pride, honour, duty, personal friendship — and it was plain that he suffered. At dinner he was silent, pushing his flagon back and forth without drinking, and his face, scored and weathered from the hardships of the past months, suddenly looked like an old man's. Partway through the meal he excused himself from the banqueting hall. Thomas followed him out, unable to keep silent in the face of his obvious distress. "James, it's you who will lead us, no matter what piece of paper Wallace has."

But Dunfermline looked shocked. "We will all follow our orders," he said. "I will be no part of a mutiny."

Thomas felt as if he were a schoolboy again, reprimanded for insolence. He found it hard to believe Dunfermline was still bewitched by the fiction that they were knights errant in a holy cause, called upon to rescue a noble and chivalrous lord. The reality was that the King had failed them.

"Wallace was given command only because the King wants to keep Melfort happy, God knows why. Either Melfort has some hold over him, or the King has become feeble-minded. Take your pick."

Dunfermline's face turned grey with horror. "Be silent!"

"Someone has to speak the truth here, James. Do you think it's a coincidence that the transports were intercepted? That instead of the French soldiers we were promised, we have these fools who don't know which end of a gun to load? What about the letters and papers that have been lost? I don't think it's only because Melfort has a grudge against John. I think it's because he's been selling us out to the Dutch from the time we left Edinburgh, if not before, and he wants to ensure our failure. What better way than to send us into battle empty-handed? He's betrayed the King and the King has betrayed us. John will never admit it because the King is God Almighty to him, but if ever a man deserved his fate, it's James Stuart."

"Stop!" said Dunfermline in anguish. He was staring toward the banqueting hall, and Thomas turned around to see Dundee, standing frozen and ashen-faced in the doorway. His face was so taut and drawn with suffering that he might have been a prisoner on the rack. He gave Thomas a single damning look, unforgettable, searing, and then, without a word, turned and went back into the hall. The door closed behind him with the finality of a coffin-lid banging shut on a dead man.

After the evening meal the camp broke into small knots as friends visited back and forth. The men were exhausted from their forced march and faced the prospect of attacking an enemy that overwhelmingly outnumbered them, yet from somewhere deep in their blood rose an unforced cheerfulness. Fighting — with an honourable purpose, to be sure, but still more, with the prospect of profit — was that not why they had pursued Mackay round and round the country for five long months? Now at last there would be a battle, and afterward a royal feast, with the harp and the pipes adding another chapter to the bards' lengthy sagas. What was man's purpose, if not to measure his strength against that of the enemy, and carve out a place in the heroic songs? Peace, ease, the uneventful tending of households and crops — these were things for women, who never ceased wanting their husbands and brothers to lay aside their swords and stay safely by the hearth-fire.

But the desirability of peace had never been a part of the Highlanders' mental furnishings. The idea that a Mackintosh and a MacDonald might sit down to discuss their differences, instead of stealing one another's cattle and firing their homes, was outlandish, almost shameful, and they had no understanding of the Lowlanders who were not as keen for the fight.

A small wind moved through the grasses like mist, and the first stars pricked a sky still flushed with sunset. One of the Cameron pipers began to play, and this time it was not wild war-music, but an exquisite lament whose sorrowing notes fell through the air like a shower of rose petals. It seemed impossible that such a crude instrument could produce that music. There were tears on the faces of the listening men. Then, even as the last note faded, the pipes blared into a raucous reel, and anyone with energy left jumped up to dance. Whisky made the rounds, but not too much, for Dundee would never take a drunken army into battle. And it was battle they craved, more than meat or drink or the arms of their lovers.

Long after the cook-fires had been extinguished, and the men had rolled in their plaids to snatch what rest they could on this short summer night, lights burned in the castle. Thomas lay on his back and watched the stars fade. Still the glow of the house lights remained. He guessed that Dundee was at work on another of those unbearably futile letters, scratching away on endless sheets of paper with the bent and frayed quill that he refused to replace. There would be an unfilled pipe and a glass with one inch of wine in it resting at his shabby elbow. *May it please Your Sacred Majesty. May it please Your Lordship.... May it please the council...*

He wondered why he was still free, why no one had been sent to put him in irons or shoot him out of hand or, with crude Highland simplicity, plunge a dirk into him. After all he was guilty of treason, condemned out of his own mouth. Those things he had said, surfacing like monsters from a peat bog — they were true and yet he should not have said them, not to anyone, and not on the eve of battle. He had crossed an invisible line, exiling himself not only from his friends but from all these loyal ranks ready and willing to die for the cause. That simple and selfless fidelity was impossible for him.

He could leave. He had already torn up his commission. He could take a ship to Dublin, show up in his rags, force the King to recognize that his Secretary of War was a liar and a coward. Or he could go home. He could abandon Dundee and this lunatic rabble and return to the life that God had intended for him. But even as the thought entered his mind, he pushed it away. It was inconceivable that after this he would crawl on his knees to William and swear to obey and defend him. Better to die honourably on a Scottish battlefield. Better to rot in prison.

When, toward dawn, he finally drifted into a fitful sleep, he dreamed of Lee. Indomitable old Lee, faithful to the end. He still wore his old-fashioned padded doublet and his plum-coloured cloak, both torn and mildewed now from his months in prison. His hair and beard, grown halfway to his waist, made him look like a wild man. He stared at Thomas and then began to walk away.

"Don't go," Thomas implored. To his shame he was nearly weeping. "I need to talk to you."

The dream-Lee folded his manacled arms. "I hear Ireland can be very fine at this time of year," he said, "but, frankly, I don't believe it."

Then he turned around, irons clashing. "Don't go," Thomas said again. He reached out for Lee, but his arm went right through the thickly-quilted sleeve of the old man's doublet and out the other side. He could see the bones of his own hand through the fabric. He awoke with a grunt of horror to find one of Lochiel's gillies bending over him, roughly shaking his shoulder.

He had been summoned to Dundee's council of war.

7

HE WAS IN THE BANQUETING HALL, writing letters. A stack of papers sat on the table in front of him. If he had slept at all during the night, it was not apparent. He had not changed his uniform and his eyes were ringed with shadows. But he seemed to have regained the purposeful, almost joyful calm that Thomas remembered so well in times of crisis. Those weary eyes were bright as swords, and he was actually smiling. He set down his inky quill.

"Come in, Tom," he said. "I wanted to speak to you before the others arrived."

There was no anger or even coldness in his voice. Rather there was compassion, the brotherly kindness he might show toward a friend on a sickbed. Thomas advanced into the room, taking off his hat. The hall, not yet readied for morning, had the chill desolate look of a room abandoned after a feast, with the chairs thrust aside in all directions and plates left to congeal on the sideboard. A stale smell of melted tallow, tobacco, and spilled wine still lingered.

Thomas had had the night to think of what he might say, but Dundee gave him no opening. "You could not have meant it. I know that," he began at once, speaking very rapidly, as if to forestall any objection or dispute. "We are all very tired. I have spoken to Lord Dunfermline, and he's agreed that we must forget it. No doubt you thought you were defending both of us, but it's the enemy we must guard against, not our own people."

Amazement and dismay held Thomas silent. Dundee fiddled with his broken quill, getting ink on his fingers. "It's possible you're right about Lord Melfort. I can't say. But the King is entirely innocent. Of course you know that. We must keep together, especially today of all days. There must be no dissent, not even in our own silent prayers, not even when we are as tired as we are now. No. Say nothing " — although Thomas had not spoken — "it's finished and I will not discuss it."

For an instant their eyes met and then Dundee looked away. Underneath the brisk friendliness there was something else, a stark plea for silence and acceptance. Thomas saw that to insist upon an acknowledgement of the truth would break something in his friend utterly. Dundee had once said that anyone who spoke dishonourably of the King must be his enemy, but he could never have imagined that one day this would apply to his own circle of friends. *We happy few, we band of brothers...* even Colin Lindsay had been forgiven, his cowardice somehow transformed into simple bad luck, for in Dundee's mind nothing else was possible. It was unthinkable that anyone should break the vow. He had practised the same alchemy upon Melfort and even the King. Unable at the last to deny the truth of James' betrayal, he had decided instead to ignore it. Now it was Thomas' turn.

Thomas' throat hurt as if a stone had lodged in it. As he stood in silence, the pipers struck up their primitive war music to rouse the camp, and the trumpets blared, giving a blast that seemed to split his head in two. Dundee's face shone. This, at last, was their battle-hour. By now Mackay's army would be moving toward them from Pitlochry — four thousand foot and three troops of horse, all dedicated to destroying them — and Dundee alone bore the weight of command. Now more than ever, he needed an unshaken belief in the sacredness of his purpose and the unity of his friends. Somehow the myth had to be preserved to the end. Except that for Dundee it was no fable; it was God's own truth, straight from the mountain. Thomas, looking into that exhausted and yet radiant face, knew that even if the King were not worth this depth of love and suffering, before him stood a man who was.

"You're right, John," he said at last. For an instant grief overwhelmed him and his voice broke. "I am most damnably tired."

Dundee put an arm around his shoulders. "God willing, we will all rest better after the victory feast."

Scouts came to report that General Mackay had reached the pass of Killiecrankie, five miles away.

8

The hammering on the door brought Libby instantly and fully awake out of a deep sleep. She flung on her wrapper and hurried to the door, thinking that one the children had been taken ill. But it was Fulke who stood outside.

"Madam — more soldiers. Not Lord Wharton this time."

It was three o' clock in the morning. Libby had thought she had reached a stage beyond shock or fear, but now she knew this was not true. Instinctively she drew her wrapper more closely around her as she stared into Fulke's eyes.

"You had better come downstairs, madam."

"I need time to dress."

"I think you should come down right away, madam."

From Fulke this was the equivalent of a screamed order. She went to fetch her shawl and slippers. Then she took Fulke's arm and they descended the stairs together. On the landing she looked out the window as she always did. It was a fine clear night. A brilliant arc of moonlight illuminated the terrace and the fountain.

Fulke's arm trembled slightly. At the last step he relinquished Libby and let her go ahead of him. The candles had been lit and she stepped into a wash of light at the entrance.

The man who stood there, hat tucked under his arm, was well known to her, had in fact been a guest at her father's table. She had danced with him at Court and they had talked about gardens.

"Lord Churchill!" She should of course have said Lord Marlborough. The reward of his treason had been an earldom.

Churchill bowed, his handsome face bearing the constrained look of a well-bred man forced to do something discourteous.

"I apologize for waking you at such an hour, madam. But I am here upon the King's business."

"The King is in Dublin," said Libby.

Churchill continued as if she had not spoken. "His Majesty will be arriving in the morning and desires that you should vacate the house."

For a moment she thought she had misheard, that he had spoken in a strange language she had not understood. It was the middle of the night and William had sent Churchill to throw her out of the house. She could think of nothing to say except, "Why?"

Churchill made a movement that was almost but not quite a shrug. Libby, beginning to feel the room spin around her, took an involuntary step back. Fulke, unobstrusive as ever, held her elbow.

"I sent a letter," she said. "To the privy council. They told me — I was assured — " to her horror her voice failed and she could not finish.

"I know nothing about any letter, madam," said Churchill. "My orders are to clear the house."

"It's three o' clock in the morning, sir. My children — the servants — where are we to go?"

"The servants will stay. But I am directed to escort you from the property."

"Am I under arrest?"

"Of course not, madam. The King does not wage war against women."

"No, he only drives them from their homes in the middle of the night! What if I refuse?"

When he said nothing she went to the big oak door and flung it open. The night was surprisingly mild, as if the air had retained the luminous heat of day, and the stars shone in a milky-blue sky. Mounted soldiers filled the courtyard — there were more than sixty of them. Moonlight glittered on their breastplates and weapons. St. Michael with his mouldering stone sword and stone armour looked shabbier than ever.

She turned back to Churchill. "I wonder you did not bring a full regiment with you. How your new master must despise you, sir, to give you such a task!"

Again he was silent. No doubt he was used to such barbs by now. She recollected what Leopold had said, that before the Coronation, Churchill, like St. Clare, had been in communication with James. Did he know what was going on in Scotland? Of course she could hardly ask. What had made William, who had a war to fight and a country to run, suddenly remember this house? Was it possible that Lord Burcote had at last become suspicious? Perhaps his tiresome questions had not been concern for her at all but something quite different. Perhaps he was demonstrating his new authority as sheriff. Thomas had bitterly offended him by saying that loyalty to the King meant more than passing a wine cup over water. As certain as she was that Churchill knew something, she could not risk any questions. She must carry on to the end with the lie.

"Take what you need for the morning," said Lord Churchill. "The rest of your effects will be sent when you are settled."

But settled where? The Tower? Newgate? She had an instant of deep-rooted panic before she realized that she had answered her own question. Not the Tower, but London. She had money with the goldsmith and Leopold was in the city this week with Abigail and the children. St. Clare was there as well. She would go to her father and demand the help he had promised.

"When do you desire us to leave?"

"I can give you half an hour."

Half an hour to dress, wake the children, speak to the servants, pack the bags, and leave this house where she had lived for more than ten years. She had been haunted by the prospect, had begged God for deliverance from it, had tried to thrust it from her mind — never expecting that it would fall upon her so suddenly, like a mortal illness, in the middle of the night when she was alone and undefended. But she was determined that no one should see how afraid she was. She spoke coolly.

"May I take my own carriage, or shall we be tied to your saddle and dragged?"

"Naturally you may take your own coach and horses."

When she gave an ironic curtsey, Churchill flushed. "Words cannot express how much I regret this necessity, madam."

"Spare me your grief, sir. Do you know how long the Prince of Orange intends to, as you say, occupy the house?"

"No, madam. The King did not say."

Possibly William intended to turn this six-hundred-year-old jewel into a hunting lodge. Possibly he would give it to one of his Dutch friends or even to Lord Wharton, the new Lord Treasurer. Or possibly no one would live here at all, and when Thomas came home — if he came home — he would have to cut his way through a forest of thistle and thorn.

"I must ask you to hurry, madam," said Churchill. Libby looked into his eyes, wondering what secrets were locked into his noble-seeming head, what his true thoughts were.

But he was a finished courtier with years of practice in keeping these to himself.

"May God deal with you, sir, as you have dealt with me and mine," she said.

She was afraid that he might send soldiers with her to watch what she packed. But she was allowed to go upstairs alone. There was no need to give Fulke instructions — he was already on his way to rouse the coachman. Libby went to wake the children, but found them already up and half-dressed. Piers had the stump of a foil in his hand. He must have snatched it from the jumble of odds and ends in his room. Had he intended to come to her defence with his broken toy? James huddled close to Brigid, who held Kate in her arms. There was no time to prepare them for the shock. "Brigid, get the children ready and pack what you can for yourself. You'll have to help Alys dress as well. No, Piers — I can't tell you anything except that we have to leave the house. Go pack."

In the bedroom she flung open the draperies. Moonlight flooded in, bleaching the carpet almost to whiteness and throwing into dazzling relief the dark cherrywood furniture and four-poster bed. There was no time for reminiscing, for sentiment or careful selection. She emptied the contents of her escritoire into a case and went to the wardrobe to pull out a random selection of dresses, petticoats, shoes, whatever came to hand, crushing them into a two-handled wooden chest. She cleared her dressing-table with a sweep of her hand and tossed her jewel-box in with her letters. Then she sought amongst Thomas' belongings to find the vest Louisa had knitted for him, for she must have something of his to keep her sane.

Did this sudden eviction mean that Thomas had been taken prisoner? Had there been a battle? She could not allow herself to think about it, to speculate about what might have happened. They had both known from the beginning what he risked. For her, Thomas' actions could never be merely political. They were instead an expression of his very being and way of life — which now must be altered forever. But all that mattered was that he still lived. Did he?

She must not think. Brigid waited for her in the hall, bags and cases at her feet. But Alys was still in her wrapper and nightcap. "I'll stay here, madam," she said stoically. "I'm too old to travel about. Besides, when the master returns, he'll want to find the beds aired and the silver polished."

Her eyes, sunk in deep wrinkles, looked steadily into Libby's. "I'll be better off here, madam. They won't trouble an old woman. Mr. Fulke will look after me."

A jab of shock, of pure grief, made Libby draw in her breath. She had not thought about leaving Fulke behind. And John Hammond, who was still in Sussex — he would return to find the house tenanted by the Dutch.

The clock struck the quarter. Libby took both Alys' hands and kissed her cheek. It seemed wrong to leave her behind, but equally wrong to take her. There was no telling what awaited them in London.

"Don't forget Dr. Spencer's medicine, Alys. Three times a day, and make sure you have your dish of brandy-water."

"God bless you, madam."

Time had run out. She took her sons by the hand and walked down the stairs in her travelling dress as regally as if she were entering the Banqueting House in a ball gown. Fulke stood at the door. He looked so ill that Libby thought, "This has been too much for him at last." She said, "You must tie orange ribbons to the gate-post, Fulke, and say 'God bless King William' when he arrives."

"Never, madam."

"It's what his lordship would want. You must promise me, Fulke. And do not worry for us. Leopold will help me."

Fulke kissed her hand in silence and she saw that there were tears in his eyes. Anger kept her own sorrow at bay. Burning-eyed, dry-mouthed, she told Churchill, "We're ready to leave."

The courtyard, packed with soldiers, looked like a parade ground. She sent Brigid into the coach first, with the baby. The boys followed with the dogs. But Libby turned away and walked toward the statue of St. Michael. The soldiers, uncertain at first, looking for orders, finally moved to let her through. She would not look at them, would not meet anyone's eyes. She pushed her way through the ranks until she stood in front of St. Michael, close enough to touch his greening arm. The stone face, pitted and crumbling but resolute, stared up into the stars.

Strangely what steadied her at this moment was the thought of her mother. Her memories were few, but she had learned from St. Clare how staunchly her mother had endured her troubles — long separations from her husband during wartime, illness, the death of their first child. But she had been wise enough to hide her jewels and cache of gold so that after the war the family was not penniless. Libby castigated herself for not doing the same. She should have been thinking — planning — she should have been prepared. She should have known that this was a possibility. She should have understood that the letter she had written was not enough to protect her. The fact that William had sent a man of Churchill's rank and distinction to oust her from her home, and yet had not arrested her, was as baffling as his sudden desire to occupy the house.

Would he sleep in the big four-poster bed under the green brocade coverlid? Sit at Thomas' desk in Thomas' chair? Eat and drink from their dishes? Or — even worse — would he rid himself of all the furniture and gut the house, remaking it to his own taste? He might pave over the gardens and knock down the Lady Chapel, fill in the little moat, tear up the footbridge, chop down the trees.

She would not think of it. That had become her new wisdom. Picking up her skirts, she stepped into the coach, and the groom shut the door.

They were delayed on their way by a broken trace. The driver pulled over to make repairs and the cessation of the coach's jolting and shaking was a profound relief. James had been sick, and Kate, who was cutting a tooth, had wailed miserably. Libby leaned back against the squabs, still feeling in her body the lurching roll and sway of the coach. She was so exhausted that none of this seemed real. They were not on the dusty London road at six in the morning of what promised to be another breathlessly hot day; there were no soldiers escorting her; there was nothing to fear. Presently she would open her eyes and find that she was in her own bed with her husband safe beside her. "Why, sweetheart, you've been dreaming," he would say, and he would take her in his arms and comfort her with kisses.

"I'm hungry." James' tearful treble broke her reverie. She rummaged in a basket and brought out an apple. Piers was asleep in the corner, his head lolling against Brigid's shoulder. Brigid too was asleep, her flushed face partially hidden by her hair, which had escaped its pins to tumble in a rough red tide around her shoulders. Kate, quiet at last, lay snugly in the crook of her arm. She had been chewing Brigid's rosary and still clutched the beads in her fist. A little spike of dark hair wisped out from the front of her lace bonnet.

"God in heaven, let them all sleep," thought Libby. There were hours more to go and already the day was stifling. She would not think about the fact that today she was supposed to be giving tea to the vicar's wife, that she had promised to visit a tenant who had been sick, that the cinnamon-coloured curtains were unfinished and the book she had been reading was still on the bedside table. She would not think about the servants who by now would have awakened to find their world changed.

Songs and stories were full of women who in their lords' absence had defended their homes, refusing admittance to the enemy, even firing upon them. They had not tamely surrendered and left their servants and tenants behind. But songs and stories did not reflect the reality of babies, the sick and the old, and the need for prudence in the face of the unknown.

She had tried to put together her fragments of information about Churchill — that while William ate with his Dutch friends, Churchill was forced to stand like a servant; that he wanted chief command of the army, and was angry that Schomberg still held the post; that he had written an abject letter of apology to James, who had forgiven him; that his wife, Sarah, could not abide William and was whispering fresh treason in his ear. Of course all these could be nothing but rumours put about by Churchill's enemies. James, William, Churchill, her father — they seemed to circle in her mind like players in a masque, shifting places, changing costumes, their true selves hidden, their words all lies. The fate of her husband meant nothing to them.

The driver had finished repairing the broken trace. She

ought to tell him to take her to a hostelry where she could wash the children's hands and faces with fresh water and give them something more substantial than apples to eat. But her need to reach London, to see Leopold and her father, was far more urgent. She thrust her head out the window and ordered the coachman to drive on.

9 MACKAY HAD SENT HIS INFANTRY into the gorge first. They were followed by a troop of cavalry and the baggage train, which he protected with a rearguard of infantry and a second regiment of horse. He had stiffened the ranks of his newcomers with three battalions of his own Scots Brigade. But even these veterans had balked when they saw where they were going.

Entering the mouth of the pass was like falling into a lightless tunnel. At their feet, the river Garry, in spate from the recent rains, roared and boiled in a creaming torrent. Above and on either side, jutting escarpments and a dense growth of trees blocked out the sun, plunging the floor of the chasm into a grotesque, green twilight. The ground underfoot was slick with mud, the pathway so narrow that the horses had to be led up single file. But their most difficult task was dragging the three small cannons that constituted their only artillery.

At the head of the column Mackay looked back to see his men flattened out in a thin red line against the side of the gorge. They moved uneasily, with the caution and concentration of men who knew that death might be a single misstep away. The foliage enclosed them like a green winding-sheet.

It was a landscape as cruel as the race that inhabited it. Mackay himself was Sutherland-born and bred, but the poverty of his upbringing had bitten into his soul with such effect that even now, at forty-eight, he hated the very thought of his native land. After so many years away he found the northern wilderness unrelentingly hostile, and its people were as alien to him as a tribe of savages.

It had been a lifetime since he had set foot in the Highlands. As the youngest son of the family, lacking both expectations and resources, he had left home as soon as possible, taking service in the Royal Scots and shipping out to France when the King had loaned the regiment to Louis. At that time Churchill had been serving in France as well, and it was he who had introduced Mackay to John Graham of Claverhouse.

They had been colleagues, if not friends. But their paths quickly diverged. In the course of his service Mackay had fallen in love with the daughter of the Dutchwoman in whose home he was billeted. But as Madame de Bie would not allow her daughter to marry anyone who fought for the hated French, Mackay's suit was declined. It was the turning point of his life. When he looked around him at the de Bie household, admiring its scrubbed and polished tile floors, the shining blue and white plates on the dresser, the bright, braided rugs and the flowers blooming in boxes under the windows, he knew where his allegiance lay. He had never seen so clean a house, so prosperous and pleasant a country. Everything in Holland appealed to him — the fair, flat land, the quiet waterways, the women in their starched linen caps, the scrubbed orderliness of the houses and streets. In Holland there was no tortured landscape of gorges and crags, no barefoot caterans who called themselves Christians and yet sacrificed goats before fishing and threw grass at the new moon. In Holland there was peace, order, civility, and attention to every modern comfort.

He was in love with Holland almost as much as he was in love with Clara de Bie. He quit the French army and joined the Scots Brigade in Holland. For the past fifteen years he had lived pleasantly in his adopted country, not returning to Scotland even when his father and elder brothers died and he inherited the family property of Scourie. He cursed the fate that had dragged him back.

Thus far he had been disgusted with the Convention's handling of Dundee, and had not hesitated to say so. Back in March there had been as many holes in the siege lines around Edinburgh Castle as in a sieve. Not only had Dundee been permitted to escape with his troop, but the men sent to arrest him had deserted, and Colonel Ramsay, Mackay's second-in-command, had run like a rabbit when he thought the Highland army was upon him.

The government army was a disorganized and possibly disloyal shambles. Mackay had demanded money in order to bring his regiments up to fighting strength, ordering a levy of six thousand infantry, twelve troops of horse, and three hundred dragoons. But the Convention had complained of the cost and recruitment had been slow. The core of his army was still the three battalions he had brought from Holland.

He had intended to raise seasoned troops from William's allies and garrison them in strategically located fortresses. But Dundee, taking his small army through the hills with the speed of a brush fire, had not followed the rules; William's friends, even those who had seemed the most reliable, had failed to put their men under arms; and the Convention was continually demanding an account of the army's expenses. For weeks Mackay had been fuming at the delay, the incompetence, the penny-pinching of his allies. To add to his difficulties, he had been ill ever since landing in Torbay; tormented, like William himself, with fever, gripes, and a mysterious pain under his ribs.

His months of marching to and fro had convinced him of the urgent need to bring the clans under control by establishing garrisons in their territory. So long as the

Highlanders were free to roam the hills in their odd manner, stealing cattle and fighting amongst themselves when they were not fighting the English, there could be no peace or orderly government. Civilization stopped at the Highland Line. Mackay envisioned a series of garrisons, joined by decent roads instead of muddy cattle-tracks, that would enclose these feudal tribes like a ring of iron bolted to a prison wall.

As his men approached the crest of the pass, a shot rang out. A cavalryman fell dead. Somewhere behind that dense screen of brush, there was an enemy marksman. The army halted. There was no sound except the roaring river, nothing to see except cliffs and trees. Mackay ordered his reluctant scouts to investigate and they reported sighting a solitary man on horseback. There was no other sign of the enemy's presence. Had it not been for that shot, Dundee's men might have been a hundred miles away.

But that single shot told Mackay what awaited him at the top of this hellish pass.

He shouted an order. The march resumed.

The royal army had assembled on the spur of Craig Eallaich above the river. Dundee was careful to place his men behind the shoulder of a lower ridge that hid them from view. Any stranger coming up from the pass would imagine that this lower ridge was the high ground; General Mackay would think it was his for the taking, until he realized that the entire Highland army was concealed on the hill behind it. When his men cleared the gorge, they would be trapped on the meadow between the hills and the river.

It was well past midday by now, and the air shimmered with heat. There was no talking amongst the men, lest they give away their position. Dundee communicated by means of hand signals and whispers. They waited.

Larks sang overhead, the only sound to break that hot, dreamlike hush. A dusty haze masked the hills. When Thomas closed his eyes against the dazzling sun, he saw fiery circles, one after another, burning against a backdrop of jagged mountains. Under his feet were the first blooms of heather, flowering in scattered patches that looked like rust. Bees droned among the purplish-red blossoms. His eyes felt leaden. It was an afternoon for sleep, for drifting on the river, for lying sweetly in the grass with a lover. In his mind he saw Libby in honey-coloured silk, unpinning her hair. Down and down it fell, a dark, glorious waterfall spiralling around him, pulling him down and down, down —

His head jerked. He had fallen asleep. Dunfermline jigged his elbow and pointed. Below them, on the lip of the lower ridge, there was a glint of armour and the flutter of scarlet cloth: the government troops had arrived. They checked at the sight of the Highlanders settled on the hill above them, and for a moment the creak and jingle and clank of the army hushed. An almost palpable shudder rippled through their scarlet-coated ranks. The clansmen hooted and jeered. Then Mackay, recovering, barked an order and pushed up the steep, brush-covered slope toward the plain between the two ridges. But his men moved with clumsy slowness, as if weighed down with stones. Terror lay before and behind them — the Highlanders on the ridge in front, the wild gorge at their backs. They struggled to form up. The clansmen would have flung off their plaids and charged right then, but Dundee held them back with a sharp word.

Under his enemy's sardonic gaze, Mackay put his troops in battle order, placing them in ranks three-deep instead of the usual six. Dundee in turn lengthened his own line. Of necessity, as his force numbered only half of Mackay's, he moved his ranks well apart. In the centre stood the troop of horse, captained by a pale and sweating Sir William Wallace. James Philip carried the Standard. To the right were the Macleans. Beside them stood the Irish, with the MacDonalds of Glengarry and Clanranald; to the left were the Camerons and the rest of the MacDonalds.

While the two armies drew up their lines, musket-fire peppered the ground between them. Mackay fired his three cannons. They boomed harmlessly away once or twice, the balls falling far short, before the carriages broke and collapsed. The gunners worked to repair the damage while the clansmen on the hill hollered their scorn.

No one but Dundee could have held them in check. He rode up and down the lines, addressing each man in turn even when that man spoke no English, keeping them in good order. Sometime before the start of the march, he had taken the time to put on a fresh shirt. His servant, Tam Johnstone, had polished his armour to a sheen that hurt the eye. Thomas thanked God they were out of musket-range, for no one was more conspicuous than Dundee. Although he had exchanged his scarlet uniform for a buff coat and breastplate, he still wore his distinctive cavalier's hat. With his armour glittering in the blinding glare and his white-plumed profile to the enemy, he rode his big sorrel back and forth unconcernedly along the ridge as if daring Mackay's sharpshooters to do their worst. The clansmen, crouching on the ground to wait, scratched at their sweating necks, slapped the flies away, and called out to him as he passed.

Give the order. Give the order, Iain Dhub. My lord, sir, General, sir — give the order.

But Dundee refused. The sun was still high in its arc, shining full into the faces of his men. And Mackay was not fool enough to attack uphill. There was nothing to do but wait. For two interminable hours, the armies faced each other across the meadow.

The heat was grotesque. Thomas, steamed alive in his cuirass and thick buff coat, almost wished for the cold of Loch Treig. He took off his helmet, and his hair, wringing wet, clung to the back of his neck. Rivulets of sweat ran under his shirt. The air, sultry with the threat of thunder, seemed to press down on his lungs. Black spots danced before his eyes. He blinked, clearing them, and the spots reformed. Clouds of midges had come to torment them.

Dunfermline, who had been riding along the lines with Dundee, looked as if the blood in his head had come to the boiling-point. He mopped his face with a handkerchief and loosed his collar. But, like all the cavalry, he was buckled into a cuirass and wore a steel helmet. There was no reprieve from that.

A half-hour before sunset, the light still burned blood-red along the rim of the hills. The clansmen stripped off their plaids and knotted their saffron shirts between their legs, so they might run unencumbered. Still they had to wait. Dundee gave a short speech. His face in the westering light was purposeful, reverential, aflame with faith and confidence.

"You are come to fight in the best of causes, for it is the battle of your King, your religion, and your country, against the foulest usurpation and rebellion. And if any of us shall fall upon this occasion, we shall have the honour of dying in our duty, as becomes true men of valour and conscience.... In God's name, then, let us go on, and let this be your word: King James and the church of Scotland!"

The sun's edge sank behind the dark shoulder of the hills. Abruptly, the red glare vanished. Dundee drew his sword. "Forward!" he shouted.

Slowly at first, the clansmen began to move. They advanced at a crouching lope, holding their targes to shield their naked upper bodies. The pipes and bugles blared and screamed. The Highlanders shrieked their war-songs. *Come, sons of dogs! Come, and we will give you flesh!* They broke into a run and poured down the hill, roaring and bellowing, spinning their axes and broadswords around their heads.

The fiendish noise boiled in Thomas' ears. His horse fidgeted and pulled under him. He drew his sword. No time to think. Forward. As the Highlanders crashed into Mackay's front lines, the troop of cavalry thundered down the hill. The earth shuddered under the weight of pounding hooves. Once more the cannon were firing. Smoke rolled across the battlefield. Thomas' eyes and chest burned. Something splattered his cheek. The Highlanders, having discharged their muskets, had thrown them down and brought out swords and dirks to cleave the government lines into bloody fragments. Heads and limbs rolled. Pink gobbets of flesh and chunks of bone rained down. *Come, sons of dogs...* Mackay's infantry broke in terror and cast their weapons aside to run pell-mell for the safety of the gorge. The cavalry wheeled and galloped off the field without firing a shot.

At the bottom of the hill, Dundee's troop was engulfed in smoke. Thomas saw Dunfermline check. William Wallace had swerved abruptly to the left, and three-quarters of the troop had followed him. But Dundee had gone to the right, toward the cannon. He stood in his stirrups, signalling Wallace with his white-plumed hat. Then a wall of smoke hid him from view. Shots ploughed into the ground all around them. Wallace seemed paralyzed, going neither forward nor back, his face a staring, white blur. Dunfermline screamed, "Here, to me!" and urged his horse forward. Flashes of cannon-fire sparkled through the smoke. The Highlanders were still screaming, stabbing and hacking at anything, man or beast, that still crawled upon the ground. Thomas tore off his helmet, for sweat was flooding his eyes, and spurred after Dunfermline. He heard a hoarse roaring, a wild, terrible shout, and realized that it was himself, screaming at Wallace to follow them. They bore down upon the cannon. The soldiers who were supposed to be guarding the pieces flung themselves on their faces, arms over their heads. Here the smoke was so dense that it choked the breath. Thomas saw nothing, but he heard high-pitched screaming, the thud of horses crashing to the ground. Bullets sang past his ear. Dirt showered down. James Philip, triumphant with the Standard, stood guard over the cannon and the enemy prisoners.

In the smoke and flames Dunfermline looked like a martyr burning at the stake. He screamed that they had to find Dundee. There was no sign of Wallace. Thomas turned his horse to the right. Unseen guns fired, and he felt a great, jarring blow to his right shoulder. He knew that he was hit and yet he felt nothing, only an enormous vacancy, a blank, blind shock. Dunfermline reached out to hold him, but it was too late. He pitched forward. His sword spun into the air. His horse stumbled, flinging him out of the saddle, and then he was falling — falling slowly, almost dreamily, into a bloody, smoke-filled ocean whose depths went on forever.

In less than half an hour two thousand of General Mackay's men lay dead or dying on the field. The other half of his army had fled in terror to the river. The Highlanders, hallooing after them at a fast run, would have butchered them to the last man had it not been for the baggage horses. These had been left unguarded in the cornfields where the pass debouched, and the lure of easy plunder was too great. The clans, stopping to tear apart the baggage, allowed the government troops to escape to the river. Some of them drowned attempting to cross it.

After the cavalry charge had thundered past, General Mackay found he was virtually alone upon the field. Both his army and Dundee's had vanished into the smoke with such suddenness that they might have been whisked away by sorcery. There was no one, either friend or foe, in the immediate area around him. With great presence of mind he removed his coat and dismounted. Walking slowly, so as not to attract attention, he led his horse down toward the river, picking his way over the pulpy red lumps that had once been his soldiers. The Highlanders, preoccupied with looting the baggage horses, actually parted to let him through.

To his own astonishment he reached the Garry safely. There he collected the wretched remnant of his army, a scant four hundred men, and began to march westward along the riverbank. In his head he was already composing his report to the privy council, letting them know that their pinch-fisted methods of recruitment had given him an army of 'the vilest cowards in nature,' and he washed his hands of them.

10 ALL AROUND, MEN WERE GROANING, but Thomas' ears were so stopped up from the roar of battle that he seemed to be hearing their noises through a thick sheet of ice. He was lashed to a hurdle, helpless, unable to move. He no longer wore a coat. Tremors of cold shook him, but the right side of his body was on fire. There was a bitter taste in his mouth.

Dunfermline's face, grained and seamed with dirt, swam into view. He held a flask in his hand and his eyes were red. He smelled of dust and blood and whisky. "Tom," he said. That was all.

Thomas tried to speak, but his throat was raw and he could only whisper. He must have screamed himself hoarse. He flexed his right hand and the pain stopped his breath.

"You were shot. The ball is still in your shoulder," said Dunfermline. He too had screamed himself out, was speaking in a husky, powder-dry voice. There was a thumbprint of blood on his cheek.

Thomas turned his head. This vast torchlit cavern, stone-pillared and ice-cold, was the Blair vault. That meant they were still in possession of the castle. Slight warmth crept into his chilled flesh.

"The cannon...we took it."

"Yes, we carried the day. Mackay's troops broke. In ten minutes he was routed." But Dunfermline's voice was strangely empty of triumph. "There are six hundred of ours dead so far, and God knows how many of theirs. We've taken five hundred prisoners."

Thomas closed his eyes to think. Again he saw the sun sliding down behind the great bulk of the mountains, and Dundee spurring forward into the blowing smoke. He remembered the clans' screaming war cries and the crash of guns. He fought to remember what happened next. "Was John wounded in the charge?"

Silence. Thomas repeated his question. Still Dunfermline said nothing, but tears began to ooze from the corners of his eyes and track down through the grime on his face. In disbelief and growing horror Thomas willed him not to answer at all, for once the words were spoken they were official, they had substance and meaning; there would be no more hope after that, no more of anything. He did not want to know. But Dunfermline had at last opened his mouth.

"My horse was killed under me. When I was walking back I found John on the field. He was still alive, but in agony from his wound. He must have been shot when he stood up in the saddle. That servant of his, Tam, was looking after him, but there was nothing anyone could do. He asked about the battle. I said it was going well for the King, but that I grieved for him, and he said...I had to put my ear to his mouth to hear him... 'If it is well for the King, it matters the less for me.' That was the last word he spoke. We had to leave his body there and go back to the fight. When we returned for him, we found that someone, those God-cursed Irish maybe, thieves who didn't recognize who he was, had taken his armour and his clothes." Dunfermline began to sob. "The portrait of his wife was gone, the one he always carried with him, and he'd been stripped of his clothes and left with his face in the dirt. Even his boots were stolen."

Thomas turned his own face away. He saw again the wall of smoke, and Dundee raising himself in his stirrups to look for Wallace. A deathly sickness rose in his throat. "Where is he?"

"We brought him here."

"Let me see him."

Dunfermline put the flask in his pocket and whistled up two gillies who lifted the hurdle as if it were a bundle of twigs. Then he seized a torch from a wall-sconce and led the way, clearing a path through the maze of dead and wounded that packed the vault. The bodies lay jumbled together, the living and the dead, lumped under horse-blankets and dirty plaids and blood-drenched shirts that had once been saffron, but now were scarlet. Among the dead Thomas recognized his friends, Dundee's cousin James Haliburton, and the young lawyer, Gilbert Ramsay. Colonel Cannon wandered ineffectually amongst the bleeding piles, his face dazed and haggard and bewildered. With a shock like a physical blow Thomas realized that this man, as ranking officer, was now the army's Commander-in-Chief. "Oh God," he whispered.

The jouncing of the hurdle seemed to shake his bones loose from his flesh. When they reached the wooden bier that stood at the end of the vault, he asked Dunfermline to untie the straps that bound him and prop him up so that he might see Dundee.

The vault was full of noise, but here there was an odd deep pool of silence. The body had been wrapped in plaids and someone had placed coins on the eyes. Torches flared and smoked all around the bier. James Philip, holding the tattered Standard as he might a dead child, stood vigil over the body.

Thomas supposed he ought to pray, but sorrow bled all words from his mind. He saw that someone had brushed Dundee's hair. It stood off a little from his brow, like a child's after a bath. His face was unmarked, serene, almost youthful. But the folded hands were caked with dust and blood and the nails were torn. Thomas inched over to touch him and felt the cruel chill of death, a cold so profound that it was beyond any other cold on earth — deep, unmistakeable, and eternal.

James Philip was sobbing. Thomas wished that he could weep as well. But he had no such relief. His entire being had turned into stone. He sat in silence, holding Dundee's grimy hand.

11

LONG AGO LEOPOLD HAD SPOKEN of the healing properties of green cheese. Thomas could not recollect how or why this was supposed to help, but he asked for some nonetheless, and packed it into his wound. At least it could do no harm. The same could not be said of the filthy knives and dressings used by the surgeon, who in reality was no surgeon at all, but a volunteer armed with butcher's tools. In between patients he wiped his instruments on his shirt-sleeve and tossed them into an overflowing slop-pail. A cloud of bluebottles attended his progress.

There were no medicines available. The only physic in the surgeon's pharmacopoeia was *uisge-beatha*, the Highlanders' fermented barley water that tasted like a combination of peat bog and hellfire. Thomas had drunk enough of this to be sick, but not enough to ease the ordeal of having the ball dug out of his shoulder. The pain had been astounding, as if his arm had been severed at the root. Afterward he had been left, like all the others, to lie in the straw and suffer. The bloody carnage on the field had been less horrifying than that in the vault. The living were sometimes mistaken for the dead, since all were flung together with no care taken to separate them. Occasionally the surgeon hacked off a limb from a man who was already dead. Occasionally someone who was still alive was dragged away for burial. No one had taken charge. Cannon had not visited since the evening of the battle.

Thomas forced himself to sip brackish water and eat his

ration of bannock so that he might grow strong enough to escape this charnel house. There was no word from aboveground, no one seemed to know what was happening. He thought Dunfermline had come to see him, but he had been sunk in a feverish stupor, unable to speak or even think, and he could not remember.

When the Stand to Horse rang out, without any warning, it was as shocking as an explosion. Silence fell in the vault. Then again the trumpets sounded. The gillies who were moving the injured or clearing the dead dropped their burdens and fled without a backward glance. The drums began. Once more the trumpets. The army was marching — the camp was breaking up. But the wounded would be left behind. There was a horrible flurry of activity as those too sick to walk tried to roll or crawl from their pallets and screamed at the others not to leave them.

Thomas glimpsed Dunfermline and called out to him. He needed a crutch, a stick — anything to help him get to his feet.

Dunfermline swayed as if he, too, were wounded, or had been drinking. He looked wrung with weariness. "You don't know, then?"

"What should I know, for God's sake, being cast in here?"

Thomas knew he had been either sleeping or drunk since the battle and had lost count of time. But surely it had not been long since he and Dunfermline had last spoken, not more than four or five days. Surely Dunfermline had come to see him, given him food and water, helped bundle his arm into a sling?

"The clans — they're leaving." Tears stood in Dunfermline's eyes.

"For Edinburgh," Thomas said. Leaving Blair had been

Dundee's plan should the army win. He had wanted to march south at once and seize control of the government.

"No — no. Not Edinburgh."

"Where, then?"

"Home." Dunfermline might have been shouting at a person who was deaf or who did not understand English. "They're going home, Tom. They're leaving us." He broke down. "Christ have mercy! Cannon — he's done for us."

Thomas waited for him to make sense. Dunfermline wiped his eyes with his palms and told him that Cannon, against all advice, had attacked Dunkeld, a cathedral town sixteen miles to the south. The defending Covenanters had hidden in the church with the citizens. But when the Highlanders occupied the town, the Covenanters escaped to barricade and then set fire to the buildings, burning the clansmen alive. In a single day the royal army had been routed, and in a manner so unforgettably horrible that the survivors had mutinied.

Lochiel was so incensed that he had withdrawn his clan. After that, it was every man for himself. The remaining chiefs, hearing that Mackay was once more marching upon Blair, had voted to stand down. The army was disbanding.

Trumpets and bugles pierced the air. "Come with me," said Dunfermline. "I'm for Lochaber and then the Isles. Davie Graham and James Philip are coming, and a few others as well. We shall raise a new regiment and take it to Ireland — "

"A new regiment. Jesus, Mary, and Joseph," said Thomas. He had come to this — cursing like an Irish peasant. "I am not joining your regiment, James. I'm going home."

Dunfermline looked almost stupefied with dismay. "There are government troops everywhere. Mackay is on the road from Perth."

"I know. You told me."

"You'll never get past them on your own. Come with us."

Fight his way back over those forbidding mountains to Lochaber, and then, in weeks or months, escape with whomsoever was mad enough to go? "No," he said. "Not this time. I need to go home."

"You'll be arrested."

"King Charles got out of England disguised as a servant. Surely I can get into it. One of Keppoch's gillies will take me to the border."

Dunfermline looked grim. "What happens when and if you reach home?"

"I don't know."

"Can you mean to submit?"

"I mean to see my family."

"The war is not over," Dunfermline said. "There will be another opportunity."

"Opportunity" was not the word Thomas would have chosen. "No, God help us. It will never be over. The King has a son."

"Yes, and thank God for it!" said Dunfermline. "What are you saying?"

"That I'm going home."

They stood for a few moments in silence. The trumpets were still blaring. Men jostled and shoved each other on their way out of the vault, trampling those who could not walk. The clansmen, utterly fearless in battle, were as craven as any other men once the fight was over. Possibly even more so, since to them captivity was worse than death. Thomas leaned on the stick Dunfermline had brought and, with a certain detached irony, surveyed the screaming, fighting rabble. This, too, was what men were made of. It was the other side of splendid courage and high heroics. "We need to find the surgeon, James, or whatever he calls himself, and organize litters to get the wounded out."

"I'll do that. You go find your gillie," Dunfermline said. "That is, if you think any of them can be trusted."

His tone stopped just short of scorn. Tears were running down his chin and he had not noticed. He searched his pockets, bringing out a few coins and a pebble of bannock. "These will be no use to me in Lochaber," he said. "But you may need them on the road."

"I won't take your money or your food, James."

"There is no 'mine' or 'yours' here. Take them."

It sounded more like a curse than a blessing. They stared at one another. The shouts and screams, the trumpet calls and drums, roared in Thomas' ears. He was suddenly colder than he had been that night on Loch Treig. This then was the end, the wreck of their hopes. But it was also not the end. As he had said, the King had a son. That alone would keep the crusade going, perhaps forever.

Mackay might be two miles away or thirty. But before he left, Thomas had a duty to perform in the little church that stood outside the castle gates. Putting his stick aside, he sat down near the altar and rested from the ordeal of walking. The surrounding yew trees blocked the sun, so that even in the dusty heat of late August the church was cold. The light within the narrow stone walls was dim and green, as if filtered through sea water. There were scratches on some of the flagstones, showing that they had been recently lifted out and then replaced. In the silence he seemed to hear his heart beating. The din and confusion of the fleeing army was far away.

He realized that Jean Graham would not have even the

slight comfort of seeing this, her husband's burial place. Already Dundee's properties had been handed over to the Douglas family, and Jean, penniless, had been forced out of her house. And the baby was ill. David Graham had received a message from her to that effect.

Thomas could not bear to think of her grief. John, like Montrose, had "put it to the touch" and had lost it all. His emblem, the phoenix crest, now seemed horribly ironic, for it looked as if nothing would spring from the ashes of his life. His houses and lands were gone, his family cast out, and already the Covenanters' lies about him were hardening into a legend that would rob him of his last possession, his reputation. He would be remembered now not as the King's saviour, but as Bloody Claverhouse, butcher of the godly. Who would honour the truth of that fiercely loyal spirit? Those who had loved him were defeated and silenced.

But his death had somehow sanctified the royal cause as his life had not. If the Covenanters' lies were growing, so too were the royalists'. John's sacrifices demanded a king worthy of them, and in the clans' songs and stories, James was already becoming unrecognizably heroic. Perhaps it was for the best. Perhaps there were truths it was wise to ignore. Otherwise it would not be possible to carry on. Otherwise none of the clans would have signed that pledge. *We will all die with our swords in our hands before we fail in our duty and sworn allegiance to our sovereign.*

The Highlanders had taken this boldly imprudent vow and now they were going home — back to their cloudy high hills, their shaggy cattle, and their own unending blood feuds. Soon the trampled grounds around Blair Castle would be as deserted as a fairground after a storm. There would be nothing but rubbish and the ashes of the cook-fires to show that a war-host had camped here. The lost cause might spark to renewed life in France, Ireland or God knew where — the clans might gather in Lochaber to redeem their pledge. They might take the field once more. Despite what he had said to Dunfermline, Thomas knew that his duty was not over. He would have to keep on fighting in some fashion, although how, or where, was unknown.

But not with Dundee. Never again with Dundee.

12

LORD ST. CLARE'S HOUSE IN Blackfriars was closed up. The knocker was off the door, the shutters tightly fastened. There was not even a servant in residence. The house had such an air of desolation that Libby wondered if it might have been sold.

Leopold and the family were staying with Abigail's sister her family in Kensington. He had not seen St. Clare during the week and had no idea where his father might be. Nor did he possess a key to the house. "Father and I are not upon those terms," he said. "I haven't spoken to him since he was at Charters."

Indignation at what had happened to his sister flamed in his eyes. For the first time in his life, he was showing that he might have inherited St. Clare's temper. That the Prince of Orange would be so presumptuous as to throw his sister out of her home ignited in his breast a passion of resentment so great that he announced he would go to the privy council at once, bring it to the attention of the Lord Chief Justice, publish it in the broadsheets —

"Leo, you can do none of those things," said Libby. "Remember where Thomas is. We must say and do nothing."

Leopold's flow of speech abruptly halted. Outrage gave way to consternation. After a long silence he pushed away his dish of tea and reached for Libby's hand. "Then you and the children must stay with us, and move into our new house when it's finished."

Libby smiled faintly. "Thank you. But we can't stay here." Their host, Abigail's brother-in-law, was a parish priest who had been recently dispossessed of his living because he would not pledge loyalty to the new government. His purse was threadbare, and his house, already cramped with his own five children, had no more space.

"We would not stay here of course," Leopold said, as if she had spoken these thoughts aloud. "We'd rent a house together. In fact we can open up Father's if we can find who has the keys. I'll make inquiries."

Libby pressed her fingers against her aching forehead. She had gone straight to St. Clare's, not troubling to rest or eat, and it seemed that she was still being jostled and shaken in the coach, that she had never been so tired and frightened and close to her breaking-point. The little room in which they now sat was fiercely hot. The sun showed up thick layers of dust on the furniture. Even the dishes were dusty, and the tea, steeped too long, had been cold and tasteless. Charlotte, Abigail's sister, had been forced to let most of the servants go and the household was at sixes and sevens. Libby rubbed her forehead and voiced a thought that had occurred to her during the interminable hours on the road. "I think I should go to Dublin, Leo. We'd be safe there and I could get word to Thomas. Father can arrange our passages. I'm sure he will know whom to bribe."

"Dublin," Leo repeated, frowning. He sounded doubtful, as if she had said that she wanted to go to Turkey or sail up the Orinoco in search of gold.

"The King will receive me," said Libby. "He could hardly fail to do so, when my husband is fighting for him and we've been turned out of our house."

"You will not care for Dublin, my dear."

"Of course I will not care for it! What does it matter?" Her voice trembled.

Leopold patted her hand and sat thinking for a few

moments. "You don't need to ask Father about your passages. I'll take care of it. In the meantime, stay here with us. It's crowded, I know, but at least you will be safe."

Kate was screaming again. Libby stood, putting a hand to the back of her neck. The small room overlooked a garden, although in the heat the parched vegetables and wilted flowers looked dead. The hedge needed clipping. The front step was crumbling and the air stank of onions and unwashed baby clothes.

She would have to grow accustomed to such living. She was no longer the lady of Charters, dwelling in a gracious home with a hundred servants to do her bidding. She was a woman alone, the wife of a man charged as a traitor, and she was utterly dependent on the charity of others — her brother, her father, and the King. And only one of them was trustworthy.

The heat and the smells, the pounding in her head, Kate's screaming, dismantled her courage. "Leo, what is to become of us? What if Thomas has been taken prisoner or worse? How can I find out what's happened?"

He put his arm around her shoulders. "I'll help you. And no matter what the outcome, you won't be alone. I shall see to it that you and the children are safe."

"But what can you do? You're in the same case."

"I do have a house, even if it's unfinished, and I'm still Father's heir. He hasn't cast me off yet."

"You'll stay here, then? Pay double taxes, and teach Samuel and Beatrice about the King-over-the-water?"

"There are many who think as Thomas does, Libby. And there's much that can be done, even if General Dundee is defeated."

Libby looked at him for a moment and then said slowly, "Why, Leo. I believe you're a conspirator."

"Say rather that I am a loyal man who believes in liberty and honour."

She tried to imagine what role he was playing. It was absurd to think of him meeting spies in some backstreet coffee house, or pushing off at midnight in a small boat to land, secretly, on the French or Irish coast. But with his established correspondence with friends abroad, and his studies for a smokescreen, who knew what he might be doing?

"Does Father know?"

"I have no idea what he knows. But remember he's the one who instructed me to 'keep in' with the King."

Again she put her hand to her head. It was impossible to make sense of St. Clare and his strategies. "Where do you think he is, Leo? Do you suppose he's gone into the country?"

"I'll find out."

He spoke easily. This was Leopold as she had never known him, purposeful and assured, a man no longer troubled by doubt. It seemed, in the last few weeks, that he had even filled out again physically, that he had regained his usual dignified bearing and humour. Whatever his work or mission might be, it had brought him confidence and peace of mind. Gratefully, she kissed his cheek. "Do be careful."

But St. Clare was not so easily found; he seemed to have gone to earth like a fox. He had not been at any of his usual London haunts and he had not gone into the country. Even the housekeeper in London, whom Leopold had spoken to about the keys to the house, had no idea where he had gone. She had been told to lock the house and await instructions, but these had never come.

For Leopold it represented a puzzle that required only

persistence and logic to solve. His father had to be somewhere and someone had to have seen him, spoken to him, cooked him a meal, shod or watered his horses.

"He's likely in Bath, taking the waters," he said. "Or he's decided it would be wise to get out of England for awhile. Perhaps he's travelling under another name. He might be on a pilgrimage."

Libby had to smile at that, which was Leopold's intention. But she could not shake off her feeling of unease. Perhaps St. Clare was too ill to write — perhaps he had been waylaid on the road. It was wholly unlike him to retire in silence, to show discretion or accept a blow without retaliating. He had been removed from council, but she was certain that was not the end of his public career. Even on his deathbed he would fight to have the last word.

In the meantime she had to adjust to this strange new existence. Now the sense of time and circumstance imprisoning her was so strong that she wanted to beat her hands against the walls. Waiting — waiting — for a word from Thomas. A word that — she had to acknowledge it — might never come. Did anyone in Whitehall know, or did anyone care, what was happening in the far north? What Thomas had envisioned as a national uprising seemed to have no more importance for the English than a border cattle raid. He had wanted to remake the world — now it seemed that the world had forgotten him. Scotland, that perpetual thorn in the English hide, was an irritation that the lords of the privy council would remember only when they had finished with France and Ireland. Scotland, a barren, misguided and bitter country harrying England's back — what odds did it make if its poorest and most ignorant citizens declared for the King? It was Ireland that mattered.

Libby left the children in Abigail's care and went reluctantly into London to visit Grace, bringing gifts, but fearing what she might find. Her sister-in-law's child had been due at Eastertide and there had been no word. Libby had written several letters and received no reply. Jacob, of course, would not think to send a letter.

She had never visited the school at Clerkenwell, but Grace had described it so minutely in her correspondence that Libby recognized it at once: a blockish dark building sheltered under a copse of beech trees and enclosed by a broken railing. The wreckage of the mass-house had not been cleared away and a smoky, burned smell still seemed to taint the hot summer air. Grace's property had a desolate look, dusty and weed-filled, as if no one had tended the garden or swept the steps for weeks. The front gate swung askew on cracked hinges. The windows were shuttered. There were no children playing outside and no noise came from the house. The only sound was the whisper and rustle of the wind in the beech trees. Libby paused for a moment to collect herself before lifting the iron knocker.

It crashed against the door with a noise like a pistol shot and she flinched. Twice more she raised the knocker and let it fall. She waited on the step with the sun burning her back and her hands growing slippery from holding her basket.

She was about to turn back to her carriage when she heard a faint noise from inside the house — a scraping, dragging sound, followed after another long silence by the shooting of the bolt.

The door cracked open and a face appeared — flushed, shrunken, pocked with bleeding sores. Libby stared into her sister-in-law's crusted red eyes. Then Grace slammed the door.

"Grace!" Libby called. She rattled the knob.

"Go away," said Grace. "You can see I'm ill. I think it's the plague." She gave a dreadful laugh.

"There's been no plague yet this summer," said Libby, although she had no idea if this were true, and instinctively her flesh quailed at the terrible word. She rapped her knuckles on the door. "Let me in, Grace! I can help you."

"Go away. You'll take the sickness, whatever it is."

"What about the baby? Who is looking after your child?"

There was another long silence and then Grace said, "God." Again she laughed and then began to cry.

Libby, trembling, set down the basket and wiped her hands on her skirt. "Grace, you must let me in. I'll cook you a meal and fetch the doctor. I think you've got measles, not the plague, and I had that as a child. It's safe for me to come in." When there was still no answer she banged the door knocker again. "I'm not leaving you, so you had better open the door. It's hot out here on the step."

She waited. The small breeze died, and the sun turned the porch into a bake-stone. Her dress grew wet with sweat. Her face dripped. She wiped her sleeve across it and shook the doorknob again and called out. Still no reply. Finally her patience failed. She left the basket and turned to go. Then, with a moan, Grace flung open the door.

Heat and odours burst out of the closed-up house. It was like a cave filled with foul smells. All the windows were closed and there was no breath of air and no light. Grace sat on the floor in a dirty nightdress, weeping.

"What if you're wrong? What if it's the plague? Or smallpox?"

"It's not the plague," said Libby. "It's measles and you've scratched at your face until the skin is infected. How long have you been ill?"

"I don't know. A few days — a week. I don't remember."

"I'll make up your bed," said Libby. "Then you can rest. Where's your room?"

"Upstairs. But I'm sleeping next to the kitchen. I'll show you."

Libby helped Grace to her feet and they shuffled a short way down the hall to a small room furnished with a cot and a chair. An empty water pitcher and the stump of a candle stood upon the chair seat. Libby had to put her hand over her mouth as she went in. The slop pails were full and the stench was appalling.

"I used to put the children here when they were sick," said Grace. "So that I could watch them." She moved the water pitcher and sat down on the chair. Libby drew back a soiled and crushed blanket and looked at the grimy bed linen.

"There are clean sheets upstairs in the linen-press," said Grace.

Libby picked up her skirts and hurried out. The heat in the stairwell was crushing. She found the linen-press and removed the clean sheets, which had been expertly folded with sprigs of lavender tucked inside. Looking for a clean nightdress, she opened Grace's wardrobe and found a drawer full of unworn, beautifully finished garments meant for an infant — bonnets, gowns, shirts, sheets, and blankets. Her pulse beat hard. She closed the doors and went back downstairs with the clean sheets and fresh nightgown in her arms.

She took the slop pails out and washed the floors. Then she stripped the bed and remade it, inserting the lavender under the pillows. From Dr. Spencer she had learned the unusual theory that sickrooms were healthier aired instead of sealed up, and so she flung open all the windows. She bathed Grace and dressed her in a clean gown, lit a coal brazier to cleanse the air, and refilled the pitcher with fresh water from the kitchen pump. Grace lay in bed with her hands folded over her slight breast, watching her with feverish eyes.

A search of the pantry turned up a rind of cheese, three spoiled eggs, a pot of preserved quinces, and a furred heel of bread. There had been mice in the cupboards. Libby sent the coachman out to purchase food and washed out the kitchen cupboards while she waited for his return. On a high shelf she found some apothecary's supplies and was able to prepare syrup of roses for Grace's fever. She scrubbed pots and dishes that were speckled with mice-droppings and then went out to investigate what might have survived in the garden. Grace in her earlier letters had spoken lovingly of her fig and pear trees, her strawberry plants and asparagus beds, her rows of vegetables. But whatever had been newly planted this year had already died. Libby found only a few parched lettuces and some wizened beans.

When at last she sat down herself at Grace's bedside she was trembling with weariness. Grace had had two cups of tea, which seemed to refresh her, and her eyes were closed. The house was utterly silent.

Libby mustered her courage. "Grace, where is Jacob?"

"In Pennsylvania, I suppose." Grace's voice was drowsy, almost listless, as if she were speaking of something that had happened long ago to someone else in another country.

"He left without you?"

"There was a girl," Grace said. "At the Meeting House. After our son died..." Her voice ceased abruptly. Libby took her hand.

"Grace, why didn't you tell me? I would have come."

"I wanted to write you. But I was too envious of your good fortune. My little boy — he lived only a day. I closed the school because I couldn't bear seeing the children..."

"How long have you been here alone?"

"I don't remember. I think it was the third week of May when Jacob left."

"I'm so sorry."

"Don't be. I had what I wanted, at least for one day." Grace coughed and spit into a handkerchief. "But I was forty-three last week, Libby. I shall never have my own children now."

They sat together in silence, handfasted. "When I'm well I would like to visit you for awhile, that is if you and Thomas will have me," Grace said presently. "I won't mind when he tells me he was right about Jacob."

Libby found she did not have the strength to say that there was no home to visit, that she had no idea where Thomas was or what their future might be. "Of course," she said. She took out her handkerchief to dry the tears from Grace's swollen eyes. What strange and confining circumstances, what unforeseen sadness, overtook women, and all because of whom they loved or did not love — how helplessly they were borne along in the torrent of other people's lives! She imagined Grace as a child, running barefoot on the grass like Beatrice, picking flowers and singing. And now she was like this, her beauty ravaged and her health and spirit broken, all because she had chosen to love the wrong man.

There was no possibility of moving her right now or leaving her alone. Libby sent out her driver once again with messages for Leopold and the children, and prepared to spend the night on the settle in the kitchen. In the morning she sent for a doctor, who arrived wearing a leather mask and stood at a safe distance upon the threshold, ready to summon guards to board up the house should the disease turn out to be the plague.

A diagnosis that involved not setting foot in the same room as the patient seemed untrustworthy, but nonetheless Libby took heart when the doctor confirmed her judgment that Grace had the measles. It was possible then to hire a village girl to cook and clean. The girl's brother came as well, to clear the property of weeds and mend the railing and the gate. Libby attacked the vegetable garden herself, loosening and turning over the hard soil and replanting the herb pots and flowerbeds. In the evening she distilled medicines, mixing an ointment of fennel and honey, and a wash of milk and alum, to soothe Grace's skin. She brushed her sister-in-law's hair and unpacked the bright dresses, the flowered silks and delicate laces, the petticoats, feathered hats, rosette-trimmed shoes, spangled fans, and fine pale leather gloves that had been stored away in trunks. She did the mending. By working herself to the point of exhaustion it was almost possible to avoid thinking about Thomas and the children. She and Grace, locked together inside the silent house, might have been sequestered on a drifting plague-ship or an island at the edge of the world.

She had meant to stay only a few days, but soon saw how impossible it would be to leave Grace. Leopold sent over a carriage full of delicacies, clothing, books, and flowers, and at the end of the week he called in person, bringing gifts and messages from the children. He said that he would not allow Abigail to accompany him because — this with a beaming smile of ineffable joy — she was once more pregnant. They had not thought it possible, as the doctors had said there would be no more children — but Abigail was doing well. The happiness with which he made this announcement brought Libby her first real pleasure in many days.

"Congratulations, Leo. When will it be?"

"We think the end of February."

While Grace slept they sat in the kitchen, which now was spotless and shining, and Leopold divulged his other news. He had made arrangements to move the family from Kensington to a rented house near St. James' Park, and was pressing his builders to hurry so that his house would be ready by Christmas.

For a few minutes they talked pleasantly about the house and the baby. But Libby sensed that there was another, more urgent reason for Leopold's call. When she asked, he took her hand in both his own and looked into her eyes with such earnestness that her skin crawled. "There's word from Scotland," he said. "But I'm sorry — I don't know what has happened to Thomas. I can tell you only that there has been a battle." He paused. She saw his reluctance, his sorrow and pity, and her body stiffened as if to withstand a physical blow. "My dear, our friends won," said Leopold. "They defeated the government troops. But General Dundee is dead and now the army has broken up. The men are escaping — Thomas has likely made his way to France or Ireland by now."

Libby shrank into her chair. Dundee was dead. And Thomas? Was he food for the ravens as well?

"Lord Dundee — how did he die?"

"He was shot during the battle. But they won, Libby. They won! If Dundee had lived — "

If. The most bitterly useless word in the world. If the wind last October had not blown from the east. If Thomas had not thought it worth his life to keep his word. If William had not liked the country better than the city —

"You must not lose hope," said Leopold.

She would not say that she had lost hope long ago. Her

eyes stung with tears. "Poor Jean," she whispered. So newly a mother, and now a widow — it was as if Jean had compressed a passionate lifetime into five short years. Libby wiped her face with her hands and realized that Leopold was still talking. He had mentioned St. Clare.

"Lord Portland — Bentinck, you know, William's friend — would not admit Father into the King's presence chamber. As a result Father challenged him to a duel." Into Leopold's face crept the expression peculiar to him when he spoke of St. Clare, disgust combined with an odd sort of incredulous admiration. "Portland refused, of course. But William is furious. He must have sent Father away. I'm certain that's why no one has heard from him."

"Perhaps he's in the Tower," said Libby coldly. She felt nothing except a tired wonder that St. Clare was still capable of such theatrics. Challenging William's favourite to a duel — she could not imagine anything more grotesque.

The rapid beating of her heart sickened her. It now seemed imperative that she take the children out of England, and she could think of nowhere to go except Dublin. At least there they would be safely out of William's reach — or, for that matter, St. Clare's. And if Thomas lived, it was Dublin he would make for.

"Dublin!" she imagined herself saying gaily to the children, as if it were a holiday. "We'll dine by the river. We'll see the King."

Leopold was still talking but she had ceased to listen. The herb-scented kitchen, the quiet house, now seemed as alien as a gypsy's tent. Her mind spun. She must ask Leopold to help her with the passages. She must make arrangements for Grace's care. The children must be told. Could she get a message to Fulke? She tried to think of what she should say.

But nothing came to mind except a foolish phrase that repeated itself, over and over, maddening, insistent, like a rhyme from a nursery game. Dundee is dead and Tom is gone. She closed her eyes. But her mind continued to race. Dundee is dead and Tom is gone.

13

IN HER HOUSE AT THE EAST END of the Canongate, the clock in Louisa's parlour quietly ticked away the hours. Her curtains were open, allowing a gleam of light into the opulently furnished room that was crammed like a jewel box with her treasures: a thick Turkey carpet draped, for display, upon a walnut table; wax tapers in embossed silver candleholders; satin-backed chairs scattered with cushions; gold-stamped books behind glass doors; a music stand, sheet music, and a harpsichord with a lid so brightly polished that Louisa could see her face in it — an elegant if rather melancholy face, with a strong nose and heavy-lidded blue eyes. Her dog, a ball of white fluff, followed at her heels. The house was even quieter today than usual because Douglas was in Stirling with the Duke of Hamilton.

Her husband was in high fettle these days, thankful that he had chosen the winning side to support. He had been thrown into a brief, unpleasant panic by the news of General Mackay's defeat, even packing his bags and inquiring about passages to Holland in preparation for flight. But confirmation of Dundee's death and the swift dissolution of the royal army thereafter had relieved him of the necessity. The forces of law had prevailed. Douglas had told Louisa that they would be remaining in Edinburgh after all, and that he would buy her a new dress. He was about to receive a title.

His ambition baffled her, for they had no children, and whatever honours he won would die with him. But his determination to wrest a reward from the government, any government, had paid off. He instructed Louisa to prepare for a trip to London. She had not been there in fifteen years and the prospect was tantalizing.

"'The work goes on bonnily,'" Douglas quoted. That was what the Covenanting ministers had said of the organized slaughter of Montrose's men after their surrender at Philiphaugh. The cruel reference was not lost upon Louisa. But she had learned to stay away from any discussion of politics. The current situation had roused all the malice latent in Douglas' nature and he seemed to enjoy recounting the latest news, gleaned from Hamilton himself, about who had been arrested and tortured in the hunt for Dundee's men. Anyone who had given the General so much as a meal or a bed for the night was considered a traitor.

She rang for tea and disposed herself on one of her blue and silver satin chairs, with her feet on a matching footstool. The dog, Henriette, sprang into her lap and she stroked it fondly, firmly, with a hand that glittered with jewels — her consolation and compensation, she supposed, for her unhappy and childless marriage. She had had two daughters and a son, but they had all died in infancy. Afterward she had suffered one miscarriage after another until, mercifully, age intervened. She suspected that Douglas might be looking elsewhere for his comfort these days. But she kept silent on that matter as well.

She wondered how her husband would manage to surmount the anxiety that would inevitably accompany his new rank. Douglas was inordinately proud of his wealth and position, yet so fearful of losing both that he lived in a constant state of alarm. Lately, like the first King James, he had taken to wearing padded clothing to foil would-be attackers. When Louisa first saw him in his quilted breeks, she had laughed out loud. She would pay for that, of course. Douglas was not the man to overlook an insult.

She spun the rings on her fingers. Even in the dull light of a cloudy afternoon, the jewels coruscated as if on fire. Her mind drifted back twenty-two years to a stiflingly hot summer, the summer of the plague, and the morning of her wedding day, when Grace had found her kneeling on the riverbank, smearing earth over her face and neck.

"Am I hideous? Do I look disgusting?" she had demanded.

"No, only dirty," Grace answered, and Louisa had laughed and then cried. Her wedding gown, an impractical fantasy of gauze and pearls, was daubed all over with mud. "Perhaps, if I'm ugly enough, he won't want to marry me after all," she said. "Or I could be ill. I could say I had the plague." She spoke as if this were a happy thought.

"No one is forcing you to marry," Grace said, coolly unsympathetic. "Call it off."

"It's not that simple. Contracts — debts — are matters you don't understand. Our father and Douglas' were friends, you know. Apparently that justifies everything." Louisa raked her fingers through her hair and then stood to shake the dirt from her dress. "Did you know that Douglas' hands have little black hairs all over the back? And he has a chin like a shovel." She lifted her face up to the burning summer sky. "Was it Ben Jonson who said that marriage is the grave of wit?"

"It was the Duchess of Newcastle," said Grace. "In her new play."

"Well, I would say that marriage is the grave of pleasure, too," Louisa answered. "Here we have a new young King, and all the world is in London. But I am to be dragged off to the bitter ends of the earth — "

"To Edinburgh."

"It's one and the same. You had best watch yourself, Grace. Father must have more than one old friend he's borrowed money from. But never mind! I shall have a fine house and jewels and do exactly as I please. I shall take a lover, too, or a dozen if I want, and drink chocolate all day long."

Only, of course, it had not been so. The jewels and the furnishings had been a backdrop for a life she found so hateful that at one point, even though she was seven months pregnant, she had packed a single bag and left the house — on foot, because the coachman was out. But Douglas had found her and brought her back before she had gone even half a mile. Her father-in-law had said she should be flogged naked through the streets or locked into the pillory. But fortunately Douglas was not resolute — or, to do him justice, cruel enough — to do such a thing. After all she had been carrying his child. Much could be excused on those grounds. They had made it up, after a fashion. But that baby, a son, had died, and year by year after that, their lives had grown bleaker and her loathing of Edinburgh had grown. The narrow, steeply tilted streets with the houses encroaching on either side, the filthy alleyways, the gloomy churches, all seemed to embody the worst of the national character — pinched, stern, mortally afraid of worldly ease or pleasure. The kirk's Covenanting ministers had been outlawed, but their gloomy influence had not abated. Perhaps that explained why Douglas was so keen to amass wealth and yet so agonized lest he enjoy it. Misery, suffering, mortification of the flesh; apparently these were what most pleased the Almighty, and in his prayers Douglas remembered to give thanks even for the three rotting teeth that kept him in pain night and day. Louisa wondered how he was faring with the Duke of Hamilton, who struck her as a man who would have no sympathy with bodily weakness and would not enjoy Douglas' penchant for shovelling mashed daisy roots up his nose to ease the agony in his jaw. Did the duke guess that underneath his fine silk suit, her husband was quilted and padded like the seat of an upholstered chair?

She closed her eyes, half-dozing. The house was so still that when the young parlourmaid arrived with the tea tray, the rattling of the cup against the silver pot startled her as if a shot had been fired. She jumped, and Henriette slid from her lap.

"Madam, there's a tinker to see you out back." The maid's pink little nose wrinkled. "He says he's brought the cloth you ordered."

"I don't recall ordering any cloth. Get rid of him."

"He said to give you this."

She handed over a shred of paper. It contained only a single word, but the handwriting was as familiar to her as her own. Louisa's heart beat hurtfully. She tossed the paper into the fire and wrapped her shawl around her shoulders.

"Don't mention this to anyone," she said. "You know the master doesn't like me buying at the door."

She scooped Henriette into her arms and went through the house to the back, where a shallow set of steps led to the kitchen garden. The day had been warm, even though cloudy, and with the dusk had come a heavy stillness. A dark bank of cloud had rolled in from the east. The sky, the sea, and the encircling hills all looked as black as the dirt under her feet. Thunder rumbled in the distance as she stepped outside.

Her eyesight was poor and at first she did not even see the man who sat in the dirt by the garden gate. Then she took an involuntary step backward.

A tinker, the maidservant had called him. But a dying pauper would have scorned those clothes — a ruined red tunic stiff with dirt and dried blood; tattered sash and torn breeches; a linen shirt that had once been fine but was now in shreds. Orange ribbons spilled from his coat-pocket. His right arm was pinioned in a filthy sling and one of his boots was split down the side. Rags had been stuffed into the gap. A crude birch-branch walking stick lay at his side. He was unshaven and looked deathly ill, flushed and shaky with fever. When she stooped to examine him more closely, she saw something crawling in his matted hair. Her hand went to her mouth and Henriette sprang out of her arms, barking hysterically.

"Louisa, silence that damn dog!"

The voice issuing from the unrecognizable face was reassuringly sane and exasperated. Louisa began to cry. "Tom! My dearest Tom!"

She reached out for him, but he flinched away. "Keep back. I'm filthy with lice. And I smell."

"Do you think that matters? Come in the house. Douglas is in Stirling, and the servants don't need to see you. I'll tend to you myself."

"I know Douglas is in Stirling. Otherwise I would not be here. But I won't come in the house. If you can let me have some food, anything you can spare, and some money, I'll be on my way."

"But you can't go like this, alone and ill..."

"I've come from Blair like this," Thomas said brusquely. "I'm sorry to trouble you, Louisa. But if you can help me — "

"You must take one of our horses."

"How would you explain that to Douglas?"

"I'll say it was stolen."

"Thank you. But it's too much of a risk."

Thunder cracked away to the east. Thomas closed his eyes. "Be a good soul, my dear, and hurry. It's going to rain."

"I can't let you leave like this. Come inside."

She grasped his good arm as if to pull him to his feet. He drew a rasping breath, and thrust her away. "For God's sake, Louisa, do as I tell you!"

She stared at him for a moment and then picked up Henriette and ran as she had not done since childhood, her feet in their thin morocco slippers stumbling over the rough ground. When she reached the house she rushed upstairs. With shaking hands she gathered some of Douglas' clothes from the wardrobe — shirts, a vest, stockings — and pushed them into a sack. The remains of her noonday meal, some quinces and a slice of game pie, still stood on a bedside table. She wrapped the food in a clean towel and put that in the bag as well. Then she hurried to the parlour where she had had her tea, and took a key from the heavy ring in her skirt pocket to unlock a drawer in the china cabinet. From its hidden recesses she drew a small velvet pouch. This was her kist, her secret hoard that Douglas knew nothing about.

She thrust it into the sack and hurried back outside. Thomas looked almost as if he were asleep, but he lifted his head instantly at the sound of her approach and grasped his walking stick to heave himself to his feet. There was something peculiar about his clothes even beyond their ruined condition, and suddenly she realized what that was.

"You're wearing a government uniform!"

"A lieutenant in Mackay's own regiment." He gave the faintest and grimmest of smiles. "It's got me this far safely, and God willing, it will get me home."

"England? Tom, you cannot. The roads are full of government troops — the ports are watched — and your family is not there! Why would you risk it?"

"What do you mean they are not there? What are you talking about, Louisa?"

The first few splashes of rain accompanied another drum roll of thunder. A sudden gust of wind whipped the ends of Thomas' shirt. He stood like Lazarus in his grimy rags and bandages, looking down at Louisa with eyes so full of fear and suffering that she forgot his injunction and put a hand on his sound arm.

"My dear, don't worry. They are perfectly safe. They've gone to Dublin."

"Dublin?"

The look on his face frightened her. She went on, a little breathless in her haste to explain. "Libby wrote to me not more than a fortnight ago. It seems that the King — that is, William — desired your house. She took the children to London and Leopold arranged their passages to Dublin. But have you heard nothing?"

"I've had no letter since I left home."

"That's all I can tell you. She said she and the children are settled in a lodging house and they are safe — Thomas, they are well, and they are waiting for you."

The tears on his face frightened her still more. Reckless now, she put her arm around him and tried to draw him away. "Come in the house and have something to eat. No one will see you."

"No, Louisa, thank you." He was shuddering with fever or cold or perhaps both. The sky had darkened to inky-black and the rain was falling faster now, great cold drops that soon would become a downpour. Louisa hurriedly unclasped the pearls from her neck and stripped the heavy rings from her fingers. "Take these. I'll tell Douglas I lost them."

"I can't take your wedding rings."

"I want you to have them. You'll need money. Use them for the King's war chest."

When he made no move to take the jewels she thrust them into his hand. "Please," she said. "Did you know that General Schomberg has landed in Ireland?"

"No."

"The King tried to bring him to battle, but Schomberg wouldn't fight — his men are too ill from bad water and food. So they've gone into winter quarters in Belfast. If anyone asks, you can say that you are joining them." The clouds emptied. Rain was drumming down hard now and Louisa drew the ends of her shawl over her head in a futile attempt to keep dry. "Thomas — wait — can you tell me what happened? First we heard that you had won, and next that the army had been disbanded."

"General Dundee died. That's what happened. Louisa, don't stand about in the rain. Go back to the house. And be careful. Nothing will spare you, if Douglas finds out what you've done for me."

"I'm not afraid of Douglas."

Lightning hissed and crackled overhead. Louisa touched her brother's cheek with the back of her ringless hand. "Kiss Libby and the children for me."

"God bless you, Louisa."

He stood for a moment looking at her and she thought that he would speak. But another brilliant flash scored the slate-coloured sky and she had to close her eyes against the glare. When she opened them again, he had gone.

She hurried back into the house as the rain pelted down. She was upstairs peeling off her sodden dress and stockings when she heard a step behind her and she whirled around to collide with her husband's chin. He was breathing hard, as if he had been running, and he had tracked mud into the room on his boots. He was still in his travelling cloak and his eyes were bright and steel-hard.

"What, madam? Out walking, were you, in this weather?"

"I was in the garden."

He pushed his cold sweating face up to hers. "Lucy told me you had a visitor."

Lucy. The parlourmaid. Louisa recollected the girl's round, pink face and equally round, pink, plum-like figure, and suddenly she knew how her husband had been spending his evenings. She stood speechless, holding her dripping clothes. Douglas gave what she supposed was intended to be a smile, a dry grinning writhing of his lips away from his blackened teeth.

"To think that if His Grace had not been indisposed, I would have stayed the night at Stirling and so have missed this guest of yours! Where has he gone, madam?"

When she was silent, his hand closed on her wrist hard enough to break it. She said the first thing that came into her head. "The visitor was not mine, husband. It was Lucy's." Fear made her bold. "What, sir, surprised? Did you think you were the only one to share her bed?"

The look on his face told her that this random arrow had found a true mark. The role of wronged wife was not new to her, but this was the first time she had relished it. "She's seventeen. What do you think she finds to love in you besides your wealth? How many gifts have you given her? What jewels?"

How ridiculous he looked, standing there red and uncomfortable in his quilted vest and breeks, stinking of daisy root! She summoned outrage and injury where in truth there was only relief. "She was in this room today, where she has no right to be, and now I find that my rings are missing. Must I ask your trollop for my own jewels back? Or possibly she's already given them to her lover. Go ask her what she's done."

"You will have to ask her yourself, madam. I have business elsewhere."

There was a commotion downstairs, a crash. Henriette barked wildly, a door slammed, the servants were shouting.

Louisa jumped. Instinct stronger than reason made her throw on her wrapper and run barefoot down the stairs ahead of Douglas. In the hallway she stopped abruptly, her fingers to her mouth. Three of her husband's servants, armed with crowbars and wooden staves, were dragging a bundle of blood-soaked rags into the house.

Louisa hardly knew that she was screaming until Douglas rounded on her and told her to stop. His face was flushed with triumph and disdain.

"All your lies could not save him, madam," he said. "I found him not ten feet from the door. I had already sent for the Lord Provost before I spoke to you."

With his boot he rolled Thomas over so that he could look into the bruised and broken face.

"God save the King, brother," he said.

14

JAMES DREAMED THAT HE WAS back in Whitehall, with his family gathered around a dinner table splendidly set with silver flagons and gold plate. In his dream the generations were all together as they could never be in life, for too many of them had died, and the rest were estranged from him. His sisters and brothers, his parents, his first wife, his young children — all dead — sat talking with Mary Beatrice, while his daughters Mary and Anne ate grapes and figs and drank from crystal glasses charged with blood-red wine. Even their traitor husbands were there, William and George, laughing and slapping one another uproariously on the back as would only happen in a dream. Archbishop Laud, dead these forty-four years, said grace; the baby James Francis, remarkably precocious, got up in his christening gown to speak at length about the Catholic church; and then a wooden-handled axe thudded into the table, smashing the dishes, spilling the wine, and his father's elegantly curled head rolled down the cloth and onto the floor, where it burst like a rotten melon.

He woke and lay in the dark with his heart pounding and his eyes streaming. When he was certain that he had not cried aloud, waking his Gentlemen of the Bedchamber, he reached for his nightcap to staunch the flow of blood from his nose. These days he felt as if he were bleeding all the time, whether visibly or not. The August night was stiflingly humid, airless, and the stink of river water filled his bleeding nose.

How he loathed Ireland! When he arrived in Dublin

young girls in white gowns had scattered flowers in his path; he had made dignified speeches about preserving the liberties of both Catholics and Protestants; he had entertained the nobles pleasantly at dinner. No one had spoken of the fact that the quays were jammed with people fighting for places on English ships, or that the cities of Derry and Enniskillen had closed their gates against him in rebellion. No one had warned him that he would not even be able to furnish his army with bullets.

But slowly the truth of Ireland had emerged. It was like unlacing the petticoats of a beautiful young woman only to find a maggot-ridden body underneath. He had been cheated of his joy. He should have known that any nation that had suffered so much at English hands would never recover from its hatred. He should have known that Ireland would kill him.

The curse of Cromwell upon you! There were good reasons why the Irish hated the English and the English feared the Irish. They were mortal enemies locked in a dreadful embrace, wrestling toward a cliff edge. Cromwell had all but drowned Catholic Ireland in its own blood, but before that, the Catholics had risen up and butchered their Protestant neighbours.

Now after years of oppression the Catholics were mad for vengeance and the Protestants were fleeing in droves. Business was at a standstill. The country was starving. So many young men had signed up for the King's service that there was no one left to plant or harvest the crops. The soldiers in the field had no fresh food or clean water or proper weapons. Sickness and starvation, not battle wounds, had killed the besiegers of Derry. Those terrible letters of John Graham's, crying out for help, for even a bag of flour or barrel of powder, had asked of James what he could not give.

Lately he had dreamed about that as well. He knew that he had lost his finest soldier, but more than that, his truest friend, and that he was blamed for John's death as he was blamed for everything. The reeking water, the lack of farm carts, the rampant greed of the local officials and the incompetence of his administrators — it was all laid at his door. Clearly the Lord was dissatisfied, and at night James lay in his bed, sleepless and haunted, casting about in his mind for a way to appease the Almighty. Prayer and fasting, abstinence even from the wholesome exercise of hunting or the amusements of music or cards — nothing seemed to placate God's anger. In an effort to purify himself he had sacrificed nearly all his pleasures. He ate and drank even more sparingly than usual, read nothing but Scripture, fought to keep his thoughts as coldly chaste as his flesh. Since parting from Mary Beatrice he had not so much as touched the tip of his finger to the hair of a woman's head. His knees bled from his hours at prayer. But so far God had refused to relent. Schomberg had used Derry as a bridgehead to march an army into Belfast, and there were rumours that William intended to lead it in person. James felt that a meeting was inevitable, unless he abandoned his campaign and returned to France. But that was impossible. The French already despised him for the loss of his kingdom, and his cousin King Louis, although perfectly courteous and hospitable, was losing patience. He could not spend six months in Dublin and then run back without once taking the field against his nephew.

And as he must not sin by despairing, he tried to keep in mind that other rumours abounded, far more pleasant ones, about how much William was disliked. His pose as Saviour of the Protestant faith had not been any more durable than his alliance with the bishops and nobles who had invited him; he had made it plain that he hated the English, and the English hated him. Their marriage of convenience had failed. On the other hand, in his secret and inmost heart, James admitted that he no longer even knew if he wished to return to England. Life in France under his cousin's protection seemed infinitely more pleasing. But it was not up to him.

"My times are in Thy hand," he uttered. "Deliver me from the hand of mine enemies, and from them that persecute me…let the lying lips be put to silence."

The campaign he had dreamed of — Scots, French, and Irish uniting to smash the Dutch — had not taken shape. He was marooned here on the marshy banks of the Liffey, waiting for deliverance. He would not admit to anyone that he had no idea what to do next. His mind skipped from one possibility to another, round and round, until his nose bled and his head hurt, and still he was not able to make any decisions. The answer to what he ought to do — what he needed to do — seemed to hover somewhere just on the fringe of his awareness, and when he put his mind to think of it, it vanished like the light of a snuffed candle. Then, panicked, he turned to busy work, to writing letters, receiving visitors, riding out to review his troops — anything to look as if he were actually in command.

"Oh God!" He spoke aloud into the darkness of his lonely bed, wishing that for once he would receive a clear, firm directive from heaven — and then be granted the means to do it.

His mind wandered in fretful circles. Why had he chosen to establish his Court here? Beyond the confines of this richly furnished room, much of the castle was a burned-out shell. A great fire four years ago had consumed most of the medieval core, and for safety's sake, even untouched walls and buildings had been torn down. The work of reconstruction was progressing slowly. In his mind's eye James saw black shattered walls, roofless great halls with weeds growing where marble floors used to be, piles of charred and broken stone in place of towers and gates.

He was not a superstitious man and it had not troubled him to stay amongst the scarred rubble. But it reminded him too much of St. Paul's. He did not want to think about his lost cathedrals, his lost palaces, his lost kingdoms. Purified by fire — destroyed by fire — had not God said to Micah, "I am not interested in your burnt offerings or your rivers of stinking oil. I have told you, O mortal, what is good — to do justice, and to love kindness, and to walk humbly with your God."

Do justice. Love kindness. How was he to do that, when his own subjects had forced war upon him? He blew his nose. The bed curtains were open and he could see the shadowy figures of his sleeping gentlemen. Unlike his brother Charles, he did not share his room with a dozen dogs or cram it full of clocks, each set to a different time, so that no one was able to sleep. How had Charles himself tolerated such noise? But Charles had often been absent, sporting in the beds of other men's wives — and not only in their beds. His brother had taken his pleasures easily, lightly, whenever and wherever the mood struck him. In coaches. On garden terraces. In theatre green rooms. Once, when he was young and very drunk, in a laundry tub —

Get thee behind me, Satan! He had to keep his mind pure. Hurriedly he said an Our Father, flinching from the memories that burst like spilled seeds from some uncontrolled corner of his brain. Charles — happy, lustful Charles — was no more. His body was food for worms and his soul had been freed from its prison. If he were able to speak from heaven, he would tell his brother not to fall any deeper into sin.

But it was strange that he could not picture Charles among the angels, eternally praising God. Heaven for Charles would be a banquet attended by spaniels and pretty women, with no ministers or members of parliament in sight. Of course, *they* would all be in hell.

He permitted himself a watery chuckle and then immediately crossed himself to atone for his levity. Spirit is willing — flesh is weak. He sat up and rubbed his hands over his sweating face. The room managed to be both humid and chilly at the same time, and all the comforts of silk and velvet and sable could not compensate for the fact that he was alone. He longed for Mary Beatrice, longed for his child, longed to be back in France with this hideous episode behind him. Somehow he knew, with a terrible certainty, that whatever he did would be wrong; whomever he chose to replace Lord Melfort would be equally hated; his Protestant and Catholic subjects would never put their differences aside for the sake of stability. John Graham's death would be upon his conscience forever, as Montrose's had been upon Charles.' He would never see England or his daughters again.

It was no use, he could not get back to sleep. He flung off the coverlid and asked for a cup of warm wine. His attendants lit candles, brought a tray of fruit, a basin of warm water. He opened his missal and tried to read.

Then, suddenly, as the words jumbled before his eyes, inspiration came to him. He knew what he had to do. In fact it was the only thing he was capable of doing without error or fear, and that was to submit himself utterly, without reservation, to the will of God. If the Almighty in His wisdom chose not to restore him to the throne, he would seek a heavenly crown in place of his earthly one. He would become as the saints. And then not even the French would dare to criticize him.

He pushed aside the wine cup and gave orders for his horse to be brought around. No matter that it was two o'clock in the morning. He would ride until he was exhausted and then he would take an ice-cold bath and plunge deep into dreamless sleep, safe from the ghosts of his father and John Graham and the torment of his memories.

15

THE OLD PART OF THE TOLBOOTH was a grim black pile in the centre of the High Street. At one time the head of Montrose had been displayed on the uppermost gable. Then it had been Argyll's turn. Now again treason and loyalty had been reversed, and had Dundee been captured instead of killed, his skull would have been impaled on that iron spike.

Thomas' cell had a small grating in the door, but no window. There was not even straw to lie upon. Shackled hand and foot to the wall, staring into the dark, he drifted in and out of a twilight sleep. During his lucid moments he realized that he was now in the same case as Colin Lindsay — chained like a beast and left in stinking darkness with just enough water to keep him alive. He could not remember being brought here, but he knew he had a broken rib and smashed nose added to the inventory of his wounds. His face was cruelly painful. The taste of blood and crumbled bone filled his mouth. There was a basin where the bridge of his nose had been. He had to breathe through his mouth.

So far no one had come to question him or speak to him. But it was inevitable that the council would interview him, possibly in that same dark chamber where the Covenanters were said to have been tortured. He tried to shut from his mind images of red-hot hooks, thumbscrews, the rack, and the iron boot.

Blood for blood — men and women burned or hanged or flayed alive in the name of true faith — the unceasing cycle of those persecuted becoming, in turn, the persecutors of others — it seemed that nothing had altered since the beginning of time. In his blundering fashion James had tried to bring about a change, but had been rejected. Men still needed God to justify their brutality toward one another.

The present reality of reeking stone and cold iron, the daily bowl of gruel, the chafing of the shackles against his raw skin, the sicknesses and pains of his body, shivered into nothingness and he dreamed of home. He was rowing on the river with his boys and John Lee. Libby had packed ham and cheese fruit for them, a meal finer than a banquet, and Lee smoked his pipe and talked about Prince Rupert's cavalry. They drifted along the shining water under the willows. A thrush sang. When they tied up at the boatshed, Cicely, his little lost Cicely, ran into his open arms. *See, see where Christ's blood streams in the firmament. One drop would save my soul...*

Tears soaked his face. He had to think. He had to plan. But he had no defence to make. He might as well pray to St. Jude, patron of the despairing. Or make his confession to Almighty God, meekly kneeling upon his knees. That is, if he could move. Maker of all things, judge of all men. Confess my manifold sins....

The clash of the door brought him out of his stupor. He opened his swollen eyes and thought for an instant that the Devil had come in person to taunt him. But it was Douglas Murray, muffled in a cloak that he had partially drawn over his face. His pointed chin and high, round forehead, surmounted by a great two-horned wig, made him look like a malignant imp. He turned his face away from Thomas and stood rubbing the toe of one shoe against the back of his leg, giving instructions to the warder. He issued one order after another and countermanded them, his long, bleak face growing more and more anxious, his voice rising in pitch to a near-gabble. Gradually Thomas understood that, ironically, he had a benefactor of sorts: the Duke of Hamilton wanted him fit for questioning and he was to be moved to a better cell.

"All thanks, brother," said Thomas. It had been so long since he had spoken that his voice cracked with disuse. His broken nose distorted his speech, making it sound as if he had a mouth full of stones.

For the first time Douglas looked directly at him, his face working in passion. "You have got what you deserve. Traitors — criminals — you shall all perish in the fire. The Lord saith, 'They shall go out from one fire and another fire shall devour them' — 'I will judge thee, as women that break wedlock and shed blood are judged.'"

Thomas, thinking of Louisa, kept silent. Douglas' eyes burned with the fervour of a fanatic and the rage that gushed out from him, the bitter malice, was something deeper and far more dangerous than mere political or even personal animosity. If Douglas were a mouthpiece for the new government, it seemed that the cruelties and perversions of the old kirk, its dark desire for blood and vengeance, were about to be resurrected.

But there was nothing he could do to help Louisa — he could not even help himself. Douglas leaned forward and planted a deliberate, well-aimed kick to his face that he could do nothing to deflect. He blacked out from the monstrous pain and when he awoke, he was being dragged out of his cell.

He was taken to a room that had a barred window, narrow as a knife-slit, set into the stone wall. He was given dirty straw for his bed. A doctor came to dress his wounds, probing his crushed nose with ungentle fingers, and a servant shaved him and cut his hair. He was given medicine for his fever. Fetters bound his wrists together, but only his legs were shackled to the wall. His gruel was thickened with shreds of meat.

He had no illusions that this was anything but the ritual fattening of a sacrificial beast. Hamilton was not interested in his welfare. What he desired was information — intelligible information, which a man raving with fever could not give. Thomas considered refusing his water and soup. Starvation would be preferable to what else likely awaited him. It might be months or years before he faced his accusers — if ever. Possibly he would be taken away and hanged without a trial. But in that case, why trouble to keep him alive?

Bolted to the wall like a dog to a gate, he spent his time looking at the rag of grey sky visible between the stanchions of his window, trying to keep sane by planning what he might say at his interview. But his mind, drugged with laudanum, could not hold two thoughts together. *Let them dispose on ev'ry airth a limb...*

Desperately he tried to pull himself out of the fog. He had to concentrate, to consider who might help him. There were loyal men who were still at liberty — William could not arrest the entire nation. The former Lord Advocate of Scotland, Dundee's close friend Sir George MacKenzie, was in Oxford; the Duke of Beaufort, the earls of Ailesbury, Clarendon, Chesterfield and Lichfield, all had remained loyal; there were hundreds of bishops who had refused allegiance to the new government — someone, somewhere, would assist him. Libby would help him. She was in Dublin now and thank God she was safe. But he suffered on her behalf more than on his own. The thought of her living among strangers, grieving for him and not knowing what had become of him, was more hurtful than his wounds.

He could not write, but in his head he composed letters to her, wandering far off in time — first remembering a primrose ball gown she had worn, and then suddenly recollecting the look on her face, exhausted but triumphant, when Piers was born. It was cruel that he had not known she and the children were in Dublin. Had he stayed with Dunfermline, he would have been with his family now.

But it was too late. In his heart he felt that his death was certain; it was only the manner of it that was unknown. Would he be broken on the rack, gutted, torn in pieces, flung to the winds? Or would his enemies grant him the privilege of his rank, and take only his head? He hated the sudden gush of blood through his veins, the way his heart rolled and thumped against his cracked ribs. He sweated to think that either his courage or his body might fail him. What had Raleigh said as he put his head on the block? *So that the heart be right, it is no matter which way the head lies.* But not even the axe could guarantee a clean death. There was a dreadful story about Lord Seymour, the Lord High Admiral, who had staggered up from the block with his head half sawn-off.

He slept. When the key grated in the lock he did not even stir. It would be the warder bringing his usual bowl of soup, made with water that stank of the latrines. Better to starve. Without looking up he asked, "What day is this?"

"St. Michael's."

He was certain that this time he must be either mad or dreaming, because it was St. Clare who had answered. He opened his eyes. His father-in-law stood before him, gorgeously dressed in mulberry velvet, with an ermine cape thrown over his broad shoulders. A heavy chain set with rubies glowed against his breast. He carried a nosegay of hothouse flowers to ward off the prison stink, and his fingers blazed with jewels. But in spite of his splendid clothes, he looked ill. His swollen flesh was tinged a leaden bluish-grey and his face glistened with sweat. On his forehead a vein stood out, livid as a scar. He wore a gold earring in place of his usual diamond.

"My son," he said.

Thomas flinched from the weight of his father-in-law's hand on his injured shoulder. St. Clare bent over, breathing garlic and wine fumes into Thomas' face. "There's not much time, so listen well," he said. "You're to be taken for an interview with Hamilton. I've assured him that you will talk. That's why you were moved." His voice sunk still more. "You must tell him anything you can think of. Where you stayed, the names and strength of the clans, who was for you and who against — "

Thomas felt as if his mind had ceased to function altogether. Here, and not in the miserable flesh of Douglas Murray, was the true Devil. St. Clare pushed his face closer. "It doesn't matter what you tell them. Feed them lies. Drown them in false tales. You'll be gone before they find out the truth."

"I don't understand." He had to try three times to bring out the words.

"I've paid the warder," said St. Clare. "After your interview, you will leave with me. We shall be on our way to Dublin before Hamilton eats his dinner."

"*We* shall be...?" Thomas' exhausted and starved brain refused for an instant to register what he had heard. "Why?"

"I told Libby that I would find you — you or your corpse — and bring you home."

It was the last thing he had expected and to his horror he felt his eyes fill. "I don't believe you."

"Believe this then," said St. Clare. He took out a screw of paper from his pocket and seized a torch so there would be light to read by. Thomas took the paper reluctantly, thinking it had to be a ruse of some kind. But it was Libby's handwriting. "To my own beloved Tom. I live for the hope of seeing you, were it but for an hour, and wherever this finds you, in no matter what trouble or circumstance, I would most joyfully and thankfully share it with you...." His ruined nose watered. He read each word as if it were Holy Writ and then held the paper close to his face, drinking in the sweetness of its rose-water scent.

"How did you come by this?"

"How do you think? She gave it to me. I met her when she arrived in Dublin."

It was impossible to gauge the truth of the man. Thomas pictured his father-in-law being made welcome in Dublin, kissing the King's hand, and anger gave his cracked voice strength.

"Why should you want to help us?"

"I grow tired of watching my daughter weep," said St. Clare. His face, flushed with choler, took on a momentary look of health. "And I'll not stay here to be Hamilton's rat-catcher. Wharton and his friends — they used me and then thought to ruin me — and Portland would not allow me to see the King — but to hell with them all. To hell, I say. Traitors and liars! " He choked and began to cough. After a moment he took a fringed silk cloth from his pocket and daubed his sweating face. "I was King's ambassador to Rome," he said. "Shall I now be the Crown's clerk instead? Hamilton has Douglas Murray to do that job. My God, your father did a poor thing when he married your sister to that rack of misery!"

"Louisa — where is she?"

"I don't know."

"Find out."

St. Clare frowned. "She's nothing to do with us."

"She tried to help me. If you are serious about Dublin, find a way to bring her with us."

"It would complicate matters too much."

"Find a way."

St. Clare looked as if he would refuse. But then some thought sparked a private, cruel smile. He rubbed his earring. "Well. It's true I would not be averse to doing Douglas Murray an injury."

There was no time to waste upon that. "Libby and the children," Thomas said. "They had to leave England."

St. Clare nodded. "Yes. The Dutch took your house. But you'll get it back."

He spoke as if it were a matter of someone returning a borrowed book or shovel. Thomas' head spun. To be offered hope by this man who was neither friend nor enemy, but a hellish mix of both — was it genuine or a taunt? *Men do not care how nobly they live...only how long.* Would that become his truth now, as well as St. Clare's?

"So you are busy in Dublin already," he said. "You come and go as you please, George. What did you find to say to the King?"

"We spoke about many things. His Majesty was graciously pleased to receive me."

"He always trusts the wrong people."

He thought his father-in-law might assume a look of injury or drama, make some protestation. But St. Clare only shrugged. "What's past is done. He can't afford to hold grudges. He's been talking to Churchill as well. Or Marlborough, as he's called now." His lip curled in scorn. "At least he won a title for his treason, but you, Thomas — what reward have you for your loyalty? Look at you."

"And you," Thomas countered. "What's your reward for treason twice over? The King might still be willing to trust you. But I'm not."

"There is no reason why you should," St. Clare said. "On the other hand, my son — what do you have to lose?"

He stood there in his furs and velvets, ablaze with jewels, twirling his nosegay, smiling like Lucifer. Thomas stared at the fiery chain of rubies until he had to shut his dazzled eyes. A nightmare sense of unreality choked him. It was possible that his father-in-law was telling the truth and they would be on their way to Dublin tonight. It was equally possible that this was all a sham, and he was headed straight for the scaffold. But St. Clare was right in one thing at least — he had nothing to lose. Life demanded more courage than death and honour now wore a different aspect.

"Where are you going?" the Duke of Gordon had asked Dundee.

Wherever the spirit of Montrose shall lead us.

John Graham had tried to make their duty a sacred calling, a noble clarion call that would draw men away from their greedy, fruitless preoccupation with themselves. They had been drunk on dreams of kings and honour. But in Thomas' mind it was John himself who deserved the tribute of sacrifice, and it would be for John's sake, not the King's, that he would resist the false ease of despair. And he had Libby and the children to think of. If she were here, she would tell him that only the living could start afresh. Only the living could seek justice.

Was St. Clare's blood money too high a price to pay for life and freedom?

The iron door swung open. He looked up. The warder stood on the threshold, the key ring in his hand.

SELECTED BIBLIOGRAPHY

Civil Blood is a work of fiction, but it could not have been written without the following invaluable resources.

Adam, Frank; Sir Thomas Innes of Learney. *The Clans, Septs, and Regiment of the Scottish Highlands*. 1908. Stirling: Johnston and Bacon, 1984.

Aronson, Theo. *Kings Over the Water*. London: Cassell Ltd., 1979.

Ashley, Maurice. *James II*. London: J. M. Dent & Sons Ltd., 1977.
———*The Glorious Revolution of 1688*. London: Hodder and Stoughton, 1966.

Beddard, Robert. *A Kingdom Without a King*. Oxford: Phaidon Press Ltd., 1988.

Belloc, Hilaire. *James II*. Philadelphia: J.B. Lipincott Co., 1928

Childs, John. *The Army, James II, and the Glorious Revolution*. Manchester University Press, 1980.

Churchill, Winston. *Marlborough: His Life and Times*. Vols. 1-4. 1933. London: Sphere Books Ltd., 1967.

Daviot, Gordon. *Claverhouse*. London: Collins, 1937.

Duffy, Maureen. *The Passionate Shepherdess: the Life of Aphra Ben 1640-1689*. 1977. London: Phoenix Press, 2000.

Fraser, Lady Antonia. *The Weaker Vessel*. London: George Weidenfeld and Nicolson Ltd., 1984.

Higham, F.M.G. *King James II*. London: Hamish Hamilton, 1934.

Hole, Christina. *English Home Life 1500-1800*. London: B.T. Batsford Ltd., 1947.

Jones, Clyve, and David Lewis Jones, eds. *Peers, Politics and Power: the House of Lords 1603-1911*. London: Hambledon Press, 1986.

Jones, J.R. *The Revolution of 1688 in England*. New York: W.W. Norton and Co., 1972.

Kenyon, J. P. *The Stuart Constitution*. Cambridge University Press, L966.

Kirkwood, Rev. James; Edward Lhuyd; John Lorne Campbell. *A Collection of Highland Rites and Customs*. Bodleian Library. D.S. Brewer, Rowan and Littlefield for the Folklore Society, 1975.

Linklater, Magnus, and Christian Hesketh. *For King and Conscience*. London: George Weidenfeld and Nicolson Ltd., 1989.

Mendelson, Sara Heller. *The Mental World of Stuart Women.* University of Massachusetts Press, 1987.

Mackie, R. L. *Scotland.* London, George G. Harrap and Co., 1916.

Ogg, David. *England in the Reigns of James II and William III.* Oxford: Clarendon Press, 1957

Philip, James of Almerieclose. *The Grameid.* Trans. Rev. Alexander D. Murdoch. Edinburgh: T. and A. Constable for the Scottish Historical Society, 1888.

Scott, Andrew Murray. *Bonnie Dundee.* Edinburgh: John Donald Publishers Ltd., 1989.

Speck, W. A. *Reluctant Revolutionaries: Englishmen and the Revolution of 1688.* Oxford University Press, 1989.

Stone, Lawrence. *The Causes of the English Revolution 1529-1642.* London: Routledge and Kegan Paul, 1972.

The Memoirs of James II. Trans. A. Lytton Sells. London: Chatto and Windus, 1962.

Traill, H.D. *William the Third.* London: MacMillan and Co. Ltd., 1906.

Thompson, Flora. *Lark Rise to Candleford.* 1945. London: Penguin Books, 1973.

Trevor, Meriol. *The Shadow of a Crown: The Life Story of James II of England and VII of Scotland*. London: Constable and Co. Ltd., 1988

Turner, F. C. *James II*. London: Eyre and Spottiswoode, 1948.

Turner, Edward Raymond. *The Privy Council of England in the 17th and 18th Centuries*. Baltimore: Johns Hopkins Press, 1928. Rpt. by University Microfilms, Ann Arbor, Michigan, 1967.

Van der Zee, Henri A. *William and Mary*. London: MacMillan and Co. Ltd., *1973*

ACKNOWLEDGMENTS

This book, like the child of the proverb, has been raised over many years by a village of thoughtful people. I wish to thank Antanas Sileika, Director of the Humber School For Writers, for his assistance and encouragement; John Pearce of Westwood Creative Artists for his diligence, patience, and support; and Dr. Warren Elofson, Head of the Department of History at the University of Calgary, for his kindness in reviewing the manuscript. Any existing errors of fact or interpretation are, of course, my responsibility. Thank you to my husband, John, to whom this book is dedicated, for a lifetime of steadfast love and inspiration; and thank you as well to our children, Rob, Matt, and Anne-Marie, and to our extended family and friends, who have all lived patiently with me and King James and cheered us on. Thank you to Tessa, who years ago typed the earliest draft of this story; and thank you to my father, Roy McEwan, who always believed it would happen.